Praise for Donna Andrews:

"This quirky, long-running cozy series shows no signs of losing steam." —*Publishers Weekly*

"If you long for more fun mysteries, a la Janet Evanovich, you'll love Donna Andrews's Meg Langslow series." —*Charlotte Observer*

"A long-running series that gets better all the time. A fine blend of academic satire, screwball comedy, and murder." —*Booklist*

"Meg grows more endearing with each book." —*Richmond Times-Dispatch*

"Fans will find all the beloved hallmarks of this award-winning series: fresh characters, an engaging puzzle, and delightful humor." —*Library Journal*

ALSO BY DONNA ANDREWS

Owl Be Home for Christmas
Terns of Endearment
Lark! The Herald Angels Sing
Toucan Keep a Secret
How the Finch Stole Christmas!
Gone Gull
Die Like an Eagle
The Lord of the Wings
The Nightingale Before Christmas
The Good, the Bad, and the Emus
Duck the Halls
Hen of the Baskervilles
Some Like It Hawk
The Real Macaw
Stork Raving Mad
Swan for the Money
Six Geese A'Slaying
Cockatiels at Seven
The Penguin Who Knew Too Much
No Nest for the Wicket
Owls Well That Ends Well
We'll Always Have Parrots
Crouching Buzzard, Leaping Loon
Revenge of the Wrought-Iron Flamingos
Murder with Puffins
Murder with Peacocks

The Falcon Always Wings Twice

A Meg Langslow Mystery

Donna Andrews

St. Martin's Paperbacks

This is a work of fiction. All of the characters, organizations, and events portrayed in this novel are either products of the author's imagination or are used fictitiously.

Published in the United States by St. Martin's Paperbacks, an imprint of St. Martin's Publishing Group.

THE FALCON ALWAYS WINGS TWICE

For information, address St. Martin's Publishing Group, 120 Broadway, New York, NY 10271.

www.stmartins.com

ISBN: 978-1-250-79750-6

Our books may be purchased in bulk for promotional, educational, or business use. Please contact your local bookseller or the Macmillan Corporate and Premium Sales Department at 1-800-221-7945, ext. 5442, or by email at MacmillanSpecialMarkets@macmillan.com.

Printed in the United States of America

Minotaur Books hardcover edition published 2020
St. Martin's Paperbacks edition published 2021

10 9 8 7 6 5 4 3 2 1

The Falcon
Always
Wings Twice

Chapter 1

"I think they're plotting to bump off Terence today," Michael said.

"Bump him off?" I echoed. "Not for real, I assume."

"Don't get your hopes up. Bump off his character. In the Game."

"I could live with them bumping him off for real," I said. "Just as long as they pick a time when we both have alibis."

Michael chuckled. No doubt he thought I was kidding. Of the two dozen actors, musicians, and acrobats my husband had recruited to perform at the Riverton Renaissance Faire, Terence was my least favorite by a mile. He was rude, selfish, greedy, lecherous, and just plain obnoxious. Unfortunately, he was also an integral part of what we'd come to call "the Game"—the ongoing semi-improvisational entertainment that had become so popular with visitors to the Faire.

"Most Renaissance fairs just replay the story of Henry the Eighth and one or another of his wives," Michael had said when he'd explained the idea to my grandmother Cordelia, the Riverton Faire's owner and organizer. "Or Queen Elizabeth beheading Essex. What I have in mind is something much more exciting. We have this fictitious kingdom, and all the actors belong to one or another of the factions fighting to control it, and they plot and scheme and duel and seduce and betray each other. And they do it loudly and publicly at regular intervals all day long, in period costume and elegant Shakespearean prose."

"Sounds like a cross between an old-fashioned soap opera and that *Game of Thrones* TV show," Cordelia had said. "I like it."

And thus was born the troubled kingdom of Albion.

The Renaissance Faire was Cordelia's latest entrepreneurial project. She'd started the Biscuit Mountain Craft Center a few years ago in a converted art pottery factory and it had grown from a summer-only venue to a year-round institution offering classes in a wide variety of arts and crafts. This summer, she'd decided to limit the classes to Monday through Thursday, and organize the Renaissance Faire Friday through Sunday.

Of course, her venture relied heavily on the talents of various family members—especially Michael, who took charge of the entertainment, and me, in the role of her second in command. I didn't know whether to hope the Faire succeeded or secretly root for a failure that would let us return to spending long, lazy, relaxing summers back at home in Caerphilly.

I glanced across the room to where Michael—aka Michael, Duke of Waterston—was preening in the mirror. Okay, maybe preening was a bit harsh. After all, he was getting ready to go onstage. He appeared to be performing minute adjustments to the billowing sleeves of his white linen shirt and the fit of his red-and-black leather doublet.

I could have used the mirror myself, just for a minute, to see if running a comb through my mane had tamed it sufficiently for me to go out in public or if I should just pull it back into a rough French braid. Probably wiser to opt for the braid in either case. I'd be doing blacksmithing demonstrations at 11:00, 3:00, and 6:00, and in between I'd be running around like crazy, taking care of the thousand and one problems that would crop up during the day.

Odds were at least a few of the problems would include Terence. Would be caused by Terence. Would bring me totally into sympathy with any reasonably nonviolent plot to get rid of Terence.

"What happens if they kill off Sir Terence in the Game?" I asked aloud. "Can Cordelia fire him? Or will you have to bring him back as a different character?" Much as I disliked Terence, I had to admit that he was good at whatever you called what Michael and his troupe were doing. He was among the best at improvising faux Elizabethan dialogue, threw himself with relish into his role as Albion's archvillain, and was sufficiently skilled at stage combat that he was permitted to draw his sword occasionally—though only in scenes with others of similar skill. Most of the actors—and for that matter, most of the costumed staff—were under strict orders not to draw their swords under any circumstances, for fear that they'd skewer themselves, each other, or the innocent paying bystanders.

"Dunno." Michael shook his head slowly. "The show would be a lot less lively without him."

"Yes, but everyone here would be a lot happier," I pointed out. "And—"

Someone knocked on our door.

"Who's there?" Michael called.

"Are you two coming to breakfast?" My grandmother Cordelia.

"Are we late?" Michael glanced at the wrist where his watch would be if he weren't in costume.

"No, breakfast isn't over for another half an hour," I told him after checking my bedside alarm clock. Then I raised my voice to call out. "Come in!"

Cordelia opened the door with a little more force than necessary and strode in.

"Good. There you are." Her tone seemed to suggest that she'd been searching for us long enough that the effort had made her cranky. Which was pretty silly—neither Michael nor I were early risers. What were the odds that we'd be anywhere but in our bedroom before breakfast? She, on the other hand, was a total lark, so I wasn't surprised to see her already decked out in the red-and-black brocade gown she wore for her role in the Game, as Good Queen Cordelia of Albion. Maybe that was part of the problem. I'd have been cranky too if I'd had to get up this early on an already warm July day and put on a corset—not to mention a farthingale, the Tudor version of a hooped skirt.

"Good morning to you, too," I said aloud. "Something wrong?"

"Can you come down to the Great Room and deal with your grandfather?"

"Grandfather?" I was surprised. "What's he doing here? I assume you weren't expecting him."

"Of course I wasn't expecting him. And yet there he is, filling up the Great Room with all his anachronistic gear and demanding that I find a quiet place where he can put his birds." She was toying with the slender jeweled stiletto in her wrist sheath—was she only doing it for effect? Or had her annoyance with Grandfather already reached a level that had her subconsciously reaching for weapons?

"Birds?" Michael echoed.

"What's he bringing birds for?" I asked

"I have no idea. He hasn't deigned to explain them to me."

More likely she hadn't stayed around to hear his explanation. Not for the first time I wondered how she and Grandfather had managed to put up with each other long enough to produce Dad. And I mused that it was probably a good thing the teenage Cordelia's letters telling Grandfather she was pregnant had all gone astray. If they'd ever actually gotten married, one of them would undoubtedly have killed the other long ago. On their good days they managed an uneasy truce that allowed both of them to enjoy the company of their descendants. Evidently this wasn't a good day.

"He showed up with a cage full of wrens." She pursed her lips. "Well, only three wrens as far as I could see, but they're in a very small cage, and besides, I fail to see why he thinks we need any of his wretched birds."

"I'll talk to him."

"Remind him that we've got falcons hunting here," she added, as she turned to go. "So he should keep his charges in their cage if he doesn't want them becoming hors d'oeuvres. Of course, maybe he'd like that. You know his irrational fondness for predators."

"I'll talk to him," I repeated. "In the Great Room, you said?"

"Last I saw. While you're at it, explain to him that we don't have a spare room for him, and even if we did, I'm not sure I'd let him have it."

"No room at the inn. Check."

"Thank you." Her face relaxed a bit, and she gave me a rueful smile, as if to reassure me that she wasn't blaming me for Grandfather's shortcomings. "Sorry. Not fair to take it out on you."

With that she sailed out.

I sat down on the bed.

"I thought we were going down to deal with your grandfather," Michael said.

"And to have breakfast." I closed my eyes and took a deep breath. "I just want one more moment of peace and quiet before starting the day."

I opened my eyes again and looked around the room. It was a very nice room, simple and serene, furnished with vintage country oak furniture and decorated with some of the crafts produced by Biscuit Mountain students and instructors. A white-on-white quilted bedcover. Fresh peonies in a hand-thrown vase. An old-fashioned rag rug. Several watercolors of Appalachian wildflowers.

And one of the most comfortable beds I'd ever slept in. Or did it only seem that way because I wanted so badly to crawl back into it and sleep till noon?

"Okay." I stood and grabbed the authentic medieval-style brown linen foraging bag I used to hold all the things I need to haul around with me—my baggage usually exceeded what I could stow in a belt pouch. I patted the bag to make sure it held my notebook-that-tells-me-when-to-breathe, as I called my giant to-do list, now housed—at least on Ren Faire weekends—in a leather binder hand-tooled with dragons and unicorns. I made sure I had a couple of the fake quill pens I used to write in it.

Armed with my trusty notebook, I could feel my good mood returning.

"All ready," I said. "I suppose we should go deal with Grandfather before he spoils Cordelia's whole day."

Chapter 2

We exited our room and made sure it was locked, because we'd long ago figured out that no power on Earth could keep the tourists from sneaking into the main building and exploring anyplace unlocked. Cordelia didn't mind having them in the craft studios—she made sure the six on the ground floor each had an appropriately costumed crafter on duty at all times to give demonstrations and keep equipment and finished products from disappearing. A gratifying number of people got excited enough to sign up for future classes. But having random tourists snoop in our bedrooms was another story.

We hurried downstairs to the Great Hall, a huge double-height room that had once served as one of the Biscuit Mountain Art Pottery Factory's main work rooms. Cordelia hadn't completely redecorated in Renaissance style, but the existing Mission or Arts-and-Crafts furniture wasn't jarringly anachronistic, and the few decorative touches she'd added—faux tapestries, a suit of armor in one corner, a pair of crossed broadswords over the mantel—made the room a satisfactory Renaissance Faire setting for any but the most persnickety purists.

Especially when the room was thronged with costumed Faire workers—a smattering of Riverton residents eager for the weekend jobs, quite a few of my fellow craftspeople, and a horde of eager college students. And Michael's actors, of course, already hamming it up.

Out on the terrace, the three acrobats were somersaulting, cartwheeling, performing handstands and backflips—their warming up exercises. I wished, not for the first time, that they wouldn't do them quite so close to the railing that separated them from the twenty-foot drop onto the wooded hillside below. The juggler was rehearsing tricks at the far end of the Great Hall—not using Cordelia's best teacups this time, so I left him to it.

But Grandfather was nowhere to be seen.

"Probably in the Dining Hall by now." Cordelia had appeared at my elbow and seemed to be reading my thoughts. "Making his second or third trip through the buffet line."

She led the way and pointed to where Grandfather was sitting with Dad and my cousin Rose Noire. Dad was in the long black robe that he insisted a Renaissance-era doctor would wear. The wide-brimmed black physician's hat and the bird-like plague doctor's mask were on the table beside his plate, so he was ready to go on duty. His first aid tent was right beside the large booth where Rose Noire would be selling her organic herbs and teas, potpourris, hand-dyed wool, and dried-flower headpieces, which worked out nicely—he could roam the Faire as much as he liked, knowing that if anyone showed up in need of his medical services she could summon him in minutes.

Rose Noire's own outfit wasn't quite as rigorously authentic—in fact, it looked as if she was planning to audition for the role of Ophelia in some New Age–themed production of *Hamlet*. But it would pass muster under Cordelia's relatively relaxed scrutiny. Grandfather, on the other hand—

"And he's not in costume." Cordelia's scowl grew, if possible, even fiercer.

I'd have said Grandfather *was* in costume. He usually was by my standards—just not Renaissance costume. His entire outfit was calculated to telegraph "Bold scientific adventurer! Man of brains and action! Twenty-first-century pioneer!" As usual, he was wearing shades of brown, green, and khaki: a faded green Blake Foundation t-shirt, dark khaki cargo pants, and a sort of fisherman's vest in a lighter shade of khaki—or maybe the same shade but slightly more faded. His sturdy brown hiking boots were spackled with half a dozen colors and textures of dirt or mud.

And the numberless pockets covering both pants and vest were bulging with potentially useful items. At count-less moments over the years I'd seen him patting half a dozen of the pockets before pulling out items as various as fishing line, duct tape, a tourniquet, an EpiPen, waterproof matches, a compass, a metal tinderbox, water purification tablets, Dramamine, Imodium, sunscreen, Band-Aids, a slide rule, Benadryl, tweezers, antibiotic ointment, eclipse-watching glasses, a pocket-sized flashlight, safety pins, waterproof pens, pencil stubs, a first aid kit, and random coins from six continents and countless countries.

Very picturesque. But yes, a walking anachronism. I suddenly had to suppress the urge to giggle, and put on my most solemn face.

"I'll talk to him," I said. "Cheer up. Michael and I will take care of it. Go back to enjoying the Faire."

She frowned at me for a moment. Then her face re-laxed. She nodded and strode off, looking a little more cheerful.

I strolled over to Grandfather's table. He and Dad ap-peared to be discussing the relative merits of sausage and bacon, having heaped their plates high with an ample test supply of both—no doubt to Rose Noire's great dismay, since she was a committed vegetarian.

"Meg! Look who's here!" Dad sounded a little anxious. Perhaps he'd seen what Grandfather's arrival had done to Cordelia's mood. Rose Noire gave a little wave and dashed off.

"I need to set up my booth," she called over her shoulder.

Yes and she probably also wanted to get out of the way if my grandparents were going to have it out.

"So what are you doing here?" I asked Grandfather.

"Not very welcoming, are you?" Grandfather seemed to be enjoying himself, watching the various costumed staff members dashing about.

"Not entirely awake," I said. "And not all that happy to be playing referee between you and Cordelia before breakfast. Sorry if I sounded unwelcoming—let's try again."

I stood up straighter, arranged my features into the bright if slightly artificial smile I used for dealing with particularly annoying tourists, and pretended to spot him for the first time.

"Grandfather!" I exclaimed. "How nice to see you! I had no idea you were coming. And what are your plans for this beautiful day?"

"I think I liked you better surly," he said. "I thought maybe I'd see if your grandmother would like the benefit of some real expertise."

Real expertise? I'd be the first to admit that Grandfather was a man of many talents—biologist, environmentalist, even television personality, thanks to all his wildlife documentaries. But if he had any expertise in history it was news to me. Dad also looked puzzled but said nothing.

"And I brought the birds," he said, waving his hand vaguely at a small cage that sat on the floor near the end of the table. "*Troglodytes aedon* and *Thryothorus ludovicianus.*"

"Wrens," I said, remembering what Cordelia had told me.

"Oh, very good!" He sounded surprised—even impressed. "Yes, two house wrens and a Carolina wren. Finally getting serious about your bird identification, I see."

"I just don't get what you plan to do with them."

He fixed me with what was obviously intended to be a look of withering scorn. Long exposure had made me largely immune to his tricks.

"I thought perhaps you'd like some actual wrens at your Wren Festival," he said finally.

I couldn't help it—I burst out laughing as it dawned on me: he thought we were saying Wren Fest, and assumed we were talking about an ornithological event, similar to Owl Fest, the ornithological conference he'd held in Caerphilly over the holiday season.

"Ren Fest is short for Renaissance Festival," I explained. "More commonly called a Renaissance Faire. An historical reenactment. No birds involved."

Chapter 3

"No birds involved?" Grandfather blinked in surprise. He looked around at the costumed actors as if seeing them for the first time. Then he leveled his glance at Dad and frowned slightly.

"Why didn't you tell me?" he asked.

"I didn't know you didn't know." Dad looked stricken at the thought that he had failed in his filial duty.

"You didn't see the big sign over the front gate welcoming you to the Riverton Renaissance Faire?" I asked.

"I was busy with my binoculars, looking for the warblers." Grandfather's tone implied that mere human signage was beneath his notice. "Your father told me he'd spotted some cerulean warblers along the road up here. Have you seen them? Magnificent blue plumage."

"The vast numbers of people in costume didn't tip you off?" I refused to be distracted by warblers, however decorative.

"I thought maybe it was one of your grandmother's peculiar notions." His disapproving tone implied that Cordelia had been guilty of any number of notions that were not only peculiar but downright questionable, like shooting Nerf guns at whooping cranes' nests or organizing a Morris dancing performance in the middle of one of his bird-watching expeditions.

"Well, now that you know what's really going on, are you planning to stick around? We can find you a costume."

"Are costumes required? You make all your visitors wear

costumes?" Grandfather gripped the front of his fisherman's vest as if afraid we'd confiscate it.

"No," Dad said. "Although a lot of them come in costume or rent one when they get here."

"It's turning into a big moneymaker, costume rental," I said. "We ran out early the first two weekends, so Cordelia recruited Mother to help ramp up production."

"Your mother is sewing costumes?" Grandfather sounded as if he thought that would be interesting to see.

"Mother? What could possibly give you that idea? I said. "She supervises. And designs some of the fancier costumes. And charms the tourists into spending more on costumes than they originally planned. I can probably get you a family discount on yours."

"I'm sure your mother will let him have one for free," Dad said.

I wasn't so sure, but if it would keep the peace, I'd pay for his costume.

"And the costumes make it more fun," Dad added.

Grandfather frowned as he watched a couple of Michael's performers stroll by. They were costumed as minstrels, in brightly colored tights and short doublets. Not Grandfather's idea of fun.

"Maybe I should just go home." His voice sounded flat, as if by revealing to him the real nature of the Faire we'd destroyed all his joy in life. I felt a pang of completely unwarranted guilt.

Dad sighed and wilted slightly. I deduced that he had brought Grandfather with him. You'd think he'd have found some time, on the hour-long drive up from Caerphilly, to explain where they were really going. And if he had to take Grandfather back, he'd miss the first few hours of the day's Faire. Probably the whole day if he ended up having to amuse Grandfather at home. Which, quite apart from disappointing Dad, would leave us short-staffed in the first aid tent. My cousin Horace—who in addition to being a Caerphilly deputy and a veteran crime scene technician was also a trained EMT—was here as part of the Faire's official security, but having Dad around increased my peace of mind. And Cordelia's.

"Well, now that you're here, you might as well stick around and enjoy the experience," I suggested.

Grandfather scowled.

"I hear there's good owling here," I added. The prospect of birdwatching might reconcile Grandfather to sticking around. Especially if it involved owls. Grandfather was fond of predators of any kind.

"Oh, yes!" Dad brightened. "Last weekend I heard calls from several barn owls and a great horned owl. And possibly an Eastern screech owl—it was a little too far to tell. I've been so busy the last few weeks that I've hardly done any nature hikes, and I've only managed to set out two of those little motion-sensitive nature cameras you gave me. But we should make a point of getting in an owling expedition this weekend."

"We're already too late for owling today." Grandfather sounded as if Dad had arranged this on purpose.

"We can go tomorrow morning," Dad said.

"And in the meantime, you can spend some time with the falcons." I could have kicked myself for not mentioning them in the first place. As predators went, falcons were near the top of Grandfather's favorites list.

"Falcons? What kind?"

"A peregrine falcon and, I think, a red-tailed hawk," I said. "Or is the other one a Harris's hawk? Well, you'll know when you see them. Have some breakfast first, and then once we round you up a costume, Dad can take you over to Falconer's Grove."

"Fine." Grandfather turned and began striding toward the buffet. "Just remember that I'm not wearing tights," he called over his shoulder.

"I doubt if Mother would let you," I said.

"I'm sure they can find you a nice nobleman's robe," Dad called out. He looked torn between trotting after Grandfather and staying to placate Cordelia, who was still hovering. "Something elegant and distinguished."

"Maybe that alchemist's outfit we used for your brother's guest appearance last week," Michael suggested. "It should fit nicely—he and Rob are about the same height."

"And just where is he going to stay?" Cordelia asked.

"That's no problem," Dad said. "We brought his big tent—in fact, all his camping gear; everything he takes on his expeditions."

"He'll be fine, then," I said. While Grandfather was perfectly capable of roughing it if he had to, he saw no reason to inflict needless suffering on himself or his companions. His camping gear was all state of the art, and his tent was considerably more comfortable than most five-star hotels.

"Not a stick of it in period," Cordelia said. "Make sure he sets it up inside the woods, where the tourists can't spot him."

I was relieved that she sounded more matter-of-fact than annoyed. Progress.

"No problem," Michael said. "Plenty of room in Camp Anachronism." Most of the Faire participants were camping out, and very few of them wanted to do so in period, so we'd set up a large fenced-in campground in the woods, out of sight of the tourists. "And I'm sure the boys will want to move into the fancy tent, so Dad and Grandfather can keep an eye on them."

"And vice versa," I suggested.

"Then I suppose he can stay." Under the circumstances, that almost counted as gracious hospitality. Cordelia turned to go, then hesitated and came back, evidently with something else on her mind.

"You ever figure out what was up with Nigel last weekend?" she asked.

I glanced at Michael, who looked puzzled.

"The disappearing act," I reminded him. "You were going to ask him."

"Not that I want to micromanage what the actors are doing," Cordelia said. "But from what I heard, he flat out vanished around noon and only reappeared a little before closing time. Not a big problem—I was just wondering. You all seem to have worked around him in the Game, and I didn't see any signs that he was . . . well, you know."

Yes, we knew. We were all keeping an eye on Nigel Howe, nervous that his relatively newfound sobriety might not last. He and Michael had met many years ago on the set of a soap opera. Michael, fresh out of college, was the new kid on the block, and Nigel, only a few years older, had seemed poised on the brink of stardom, with his pick of several movie roles waiting as soon as he served out the last few months of his contract. I had never quite figured out whether alcohol had wrecked Nigel's career or whether he'd started drinking heavily after a series of disastrous career choices, like turning down parts in smash hits for parts in real stinkers. Maybe a little of both.

But he'd cleaned up his act in the last couple of years, thanks to tough love from a few friends like Michael and regular attendance at twelve-step meetings. He was hoping to use his summer job at the Ren Faire—and the glowing recommendations he was determined to earn from Cordelia and Michael—to help convince directors and casting agents that he was employable again. We were all rooting for him—but if he'd fallen off the wagon . . .

"Migraine, from what he told me," Michael said. "He seemed perfectly sober when I talked to him that evening. He was fine all day Sunday."

"And worked tirelessly all week," I added—for Michael's benefit, since he'd spent most of the past week down in Caerphilly supervising the installation of a new septic field at our house.

"We started him off on kitchen duty," Cordelia said. "Until he thought to mention that he sews well enough to help out on the costume crew. He's been doing a great job there."

A few of the actors and Faire workers only came Friday through Sunday for the Renaissance Faire, but most of the non-locals took advantage of the opportunity to stay through the whole week while the craft classes were in session, working a second job in return for room, board, and minimum wage. The work was far from grueling, the food excellent, and the surroundings beautiful, so Cordelia had no trouble filling up the kitchen crew, the grounds crew, the housekeeping staff, and the costume shop that had been working so diligently to make more rental costumes.

"I'll keep my eyes open for a chance to talk to him about it," Michael said. "Ask how things are going. If there's any kind of support he needs."

"If he really does have migraines, I might be able to help." Dad sounded eager. "I've been doing a lot of research. And it's come in handy, hasn't it?" He beamed at Cordelia, who nodded.

"I don't have a lot of migraines these days," she said.

"You see! I'll talk to him sometime today." With that, Dad trotted off toward the buffet.

"I didn't know you suffered from migraines," I said to Cordelia.

"I don't," she said. "Never did. Just an average number of perfectly ordinary headaches. But I used to say I had migraines to get myself out of doing things I really didn't want to do, like chairing church committees or attending my next-door neighbor's vegan potluck dinners."

"Sounds useful," I said. "And Dad took away all your excuses."

"Oh, no." She chuckled. "Now I just say that I'm following my doctor's orders and avoiding trigger situations.

Works just as well, without all the bother of pretending to be sick. I throw around words like prodrome and vasodilation and you'd be surprised how eager they are to let me off the hook. But getting back to your father—he really does know a lot about migraine, so he might be able to help."

"Just don't bring up the subject in front of Rose Noire," I said. "Because if she hears about it she'll want to concoct an herbal tea to supplement whatever Dad recommends, and if it tastes like most of her medicinal teas I'd just as soon keep the migraine."

"Duly noted." She was scanning the room with what Michael and I called her problem-finding X-ray vision. The tension in her face gradually eased—no doubt because she was seeing nothing but costumed staff bolting their breakfasts and dashing out to get ready for the Faire's 10:00 A.M. opening. Then she frowned again. "And now I have to get up long before dawn to take the old fool owling."

"Says who?" I asked.

"If you think I'm going to let your grandfather wander around my property unsupervised, you have another think coming. Someone has to make sure he doesn't fall off the mountain."

"Someone has to," I agreed. "No reason it has to be you. Let Dad do it. He'd probably enjoy it."

"No offense, but James has never been all that good at managing his father. I won't rest easy unless I'm there myself."

With that she strode off. Michael and I headed for the buffet line.

"Bother," I said. "You know what this means, don't you?"

"That someone needs to go along to keep the peace between your grandparents." He was piling his plate with bacon and eggs. "Because that's another thing your dad isn't very good at. What time do we need to get up?"

"You don't have to go," I said. "You've got a long day tomorrow."

"And you don't?" He had moved on to the fruit section of the buffet and was loading up on fresh berries. "We'll go to bed really early. It'll be a lovely family expedition."

Michael was a big believer in the idea that if you worked on adopting a positive attitude you could often achieve it. And much of the time it actually worked.

"So are you sorry yet that you turned down Laertes?" I was holding the tongs, trying to decide between sausage and bacon.

"Turned down Laertes? Are you kidding?"

Chapter 4

We turned to see that Jacquelynn Morris—Jacks for short—another of Michael's actors, was in line behind us.

"In *Hamlet,* I assume," Jacks went on. "Unless some other playwright has had the nerve to steal the name. So what production are you scoffing at?"

"The one Neil O'Malley is directing at the Arena Stage," I said, as I helped myself to both sausage and bacon.

Jacks's eyes widened at the name of the famous—or would it be infamous?—director.

"Ooh," she said. "O'Malley may be crazy as a bedbug, but he's also brilliant. I can't believe you turned down a part in one of his shows."

"I didn't exactly turn down a part," Michael said. "Someone claiming to be one of his assistants called to invite me to an audition. I thanked her and said I already had a gig."

"No offense," Jacks said. "But there's no way I'd choose the Ren Faire over a production at the Arena. If they offered me—well, Ophelia's probably not in the cards anymore." Jacks was a buxom redhead about my own age. She glanced down ruefully at her figure—which was quite striking, especially in her corseted costume, but very far from the waif-like ingénues the bad-boy director tended to cast in his shows. "But Gertrude's a good meaty role. And being in one of O'Malley's shows could make your career."

"Or wreck your life," Michael said. "I was in one of his shows—a couple of decades ago."

"Oh, my God!" Jacks was clearly impressed. "Was it fabulous?"

"It was a train wreck." Michael shuddered at the memory. "O'Malley was quite possibly the most self-indulgent, egotistical jackass I'd ever met. Working with him was one of the last straws that convinced me to go back to school, finish my degree, and see if I couldn't get a job teaching drama."

"Still—maybe he remembers you." Jacks didn't give up easily. "Maybe that's why he wants you to audition."

"If he remembers me, it would be as a brash young actor, almost as cocky and self-centered as he was," Michael said. "And I'm more than half convinced the call was a practical joke."

"Still." She shook her head again and glanced discontentedly at the buffet. She was holding the tongs now and looking regretfully at the bacon. "Well, we all have to lead our own lives. What the hell." She shrugged and helped herself to three slices of bacon. "I'll burn it off today." She waved and went over to a table where several other actors were already eating.

"If you were doing Laertes, you wouldn't be getting up at sunrise to go owling," I pointed out.

"No, I'd probably be staying up till sunrise listening to O'Malley brag about all the famous people he knows. Owling's probably more fun." He paused for a few moments, then asked, "What time is sunrise, anyway?"

"Let's not look it up just yet," I said. "I think I'll be happier not knowing for the time being. But it occurs to me that if I could get Faulk to do tomorrow's eleven a.m. blacksmithing demonstration, I might be able to sneak in a nap after the owling expedition." I finished filling my plate—actually I'd chosen a large bowl, as usual, so I could take my breakfast with me—snagged a fork and turned to go. "I'll ask him now."

"Good idea," Michael said. "Tell him hi for me."

"Will do." As I wound my way through the Dining Hall, nibbling bits of fruit and bacon and returning greetings from people I passed, I found myself chuckling as I thought about how far we'd come. The first time Michael had met Faulk, my blacksmithing mentor—how long ago was it? Pre-twins and then some—he'd been insanely jealous. Faulk was only a little shorter than Michael's six foot four, with thick blond hair, arrestingly blue eyes, handsome features, and the kind of lean, muscular physique that you get from a decade of blacksmithing. Michael and I had only just started dating, and maybe he felt a little threatened by the sudden arrival of someone with whom I shared both a long history of friendship and a beloved profession.

I'm not sure how long it would have taken him to get past the jealousy if he hadn't found out that Faulk was gay, and thus in no way a rival for my affections. And by now, Faulk and his husband, Tad, were old and valued friends.

In the Great Hall I ran into Dad and Grandfather. Evidently the alchemist's robe had met with Grandfather's approval. It was made of black velvet and heavily decked with faux rubies and small silver charms in the shape of various alchemical symbols. And it was ankle length, even on his tall frame, so it almost completely hid his slightly anachronistic hiking boots. He also wore a floppy black velvet hat with a sweeping white plume—which meant I didn't have to worry quite so much about sunstroke— and carried a six-foot staff topped with a black raven. He looked very impressive, and his facial expression and body language showed that he knew it.

"This will do," he said, nodding down at his costume. "What's wrong with your mother, anyway? Normally she'd have been hovering around to adjust my costume, but she just sits there in her chair grimacing. And every time I tried to ask her what's wrong, the costume ladies shushed me." Was he really worried about Mother, or did he just miss being fussed over?

"She broke several bones in her right foot, and it's in a walking boot," I said. "Not that she's walking yet—we're still pushing her around in a wheelchair. If you're curious, I'm sure Dad would love to explain exactly which bones she broke and how well they're likely to heal, but for heaven's sake don't let him do it in front of her. She's deathly afraid she'll never be able to wear heels again, and if that happens, she might give in to temptation and strangle the klutzy actor who tripped her." Yet another black mark on Terence's record.

"Hmph," Grandfather began. "At her age—"

"There you are!" Dad raced in. "Can you take your grandfather over to where the falcons are? I have to run over to Camp Anachronism. Possible sprained ankle." With that he headed for the door.

"Who's the latest patient?" I called after him. Since we were still two or three minutes short of our ten o'clock opening time, the patient couldn't possibly be a tourist—which meant it might be someone for whom I had to figure out a replacement. Like the proverbial show, the Faire must go on.

"Madame Destiny," he called back.

I breathed a sigh of relief. While a sprained ankle would certainly be very uncomfortable for the Faire's official fortune-teller, it wouldn't be a disaster for the Faire. Madame Destiny spent most of the day sitting in her tent anyway, muttering deliberately enigmatic predictions over palms and tarot layouts. And if she wasn't ready to open her tent as soon as the Faire opened, we'd survive. I'd noticed that it took most people till afternoon to work up enough nerve to have their fortunes told. Or maybe to consume enough beer or mead.

And delivering Grandfather to his destination wouldn't

take me out of my way—the blacksmith's shop Faulk and I shared was just outside the entrance to Falconer's Grove.

"Come on," I said to Grandfather through a mouthful of toast. "I'll take you over to the mews and introduce you to the falcons and their keepers."

"Lead on." He didn't seem the least bit impressed that I knew "mews" to be the proper name for the place where you kept a falcon.

As we stepped out onto the front portico, the bells rang, signaling the opening of the gates. Here and there costumed participants sprinted in one direction or another, to make sure they were at their assigned posts when the first tourists came in.

I stopped to savor the moment. The last hour before the Faire opened was always a little tense as we worked through whatever problems and complications threatened the success of the day. But once the opening bell rang, my spirits always rose—and from what I could see, everyone else felt the same. The day had begun! The Game was afoot!

Just inside the gates on either side of the lane were the costume rental shops—men on the left, women on the right. The staff who ran them would bear the first brunt of the entering crowd. I could see them taking deep breaths and bracing themselves for the initial onslaught of costume-seekers.

Until my eleven o'clock blacksmithing demo, I had nothing specific to do. Cordelia and I generally spent the first hour strolling about making sure everything was going well, and I could do that just as easily while leading Grandfather. Well, trying to lead him and not having much success. He stopped every few feet to stare at something—impressed in spite of himself, I suspected.

And there was a lot to stare at. The costumed wenches who wandered about selling candied apples, hot pretzels, flowered headpieces, and other food and souvenirs had been gathered in a cluster, giggling at something, but now they broke apart and began loudly calling their wares. Two photographers were already at work—high school camera enthusiasts to whom Cordelia gave free admission in return for being allowed to use the best of their shots on the Faire's website. The strolling musicians were in a huddle near the main stage, doing a bit of last minute lute and cittern tuning. The Muddy Beggar was settling down in his favorite puddle and daubing a few last bits of pictur- esque grime on his face and the brown and beige tatters that made up his costume. The savory smell of chickens roasting and sausages and onions being grilled wafted over from the largest and most central refreshment tent. The three acrobats were walking around on stilts.

"Looks like a good crowd already," one of them called down.

I spotted Michael and George Sims, another of the actors—aka Sir George of Simsdale, Michael's arch rival in the contest to inherit the kingdom from Good Queen Cordelia. They were standing outside Dragon's Claw tav- ern holding tankards filled with the diluted, lightly sweet- ened tea we used to simulate beer and mead. Even from a distance, I could tell Michael was giving a pep talk to George, whose default mood seemed to be morose. If we ever staged *Winnie the Pooh* he'd have made a perfect Eeyore. He and Michael were preparing to launch one of their verbal jousts as soon as a critical mass of tourists ar- rived. Grandfather stopped to watch them.

"Michael's got an impressive outfit." For some reason he was frowning in disapproval.

"He's Michael, Duke of Waterston," I said. "Leader of one of the factions vying to rule the Kingdom of Albion after Queen Cordelia goes to that great throne room in the sky. George, the guy in green and gold standing be- side him, is his arch rival."

"Then if Michael's a duke, how come you're dressed up

as a peasant?" he asked. "No offense intended—it's a flattering peasant getup, but shouldn't a duchess be wearing velvet, too?"

"Yes, a duchess would be wearing velvet, and floating about giving orders to the servants instead of working in the smithy," I said. "So within the Game, I'm not Michael's wife—I'm the beautiful, virtuous, but low-born maid the duke loves but cannot marry."

"Virtuous? Then how do you account for the twins?"

"In Albion, they're Michael's nephews."

"Ah. I suppose your grandmother needs to have you blacksmithing for the tourists. Still—you're getting short-changed, aren't you?"

"If you call wearing homespun instead of velvet in ninety-degree weather getting shortchanged, then yeah. I'm getting shortchanged. Works for me."

"Well, if you're happy. Sometimes a little suffering is good for the character." He gazed down at his own impressive black velvet robe with a look of childlike satisfaction. We'd see how interested he was in continuing to suffer as the day got warmer. "Let's go find those falcons."

We continued making our slow way toward Falconer's Grove. We inspected the leatherworker's wares. We bought drinks at the tavern—mead for Grandfather and lemonade for me. We watched the jugglers perform their act, sending everything from maces to tankards to flaming torches flying through the air. We listened to a duet of "Pastime with Good Company," by the minstrel and Nigel—who looked fine. No sign of headache or hangover. Good. His part in the Game had become a fairly central one. Sir Nigel was a nobleman whose sole child, Lady Dianne, was not only a wealthy heiress but a beautiful one. With the exception of Michael, all the unmarried noblemen were vying for her hand. The vying got a lot more interesting with Terence around to play the eager suitors against each other.

I was beginning to think I'd have to abandon Grandfather to his own devices before we reached Falconer's Grove. We were almost at the entrance when we encountered a large throng of tourists laughing loudly at something.

"More actors?" Grandfather found a thin spot in the crowd where he could slip forward to the front, and I followed. In the center of the group Terence, my bête noire, was conversing with Lady Jacquelynn and Lady Dianne. Jacks, in green and purple, seemed to be enjoying the encounter, guffawing at Terence's double entendres and then topping them. Dianne—Nigel's in-Game daughter, a slender, beautiful blond woman of twenty or so in pale blue velvet that matched her eyes—was outwardly smiling, but I could tell she wasn't having a good time. Hell, even the tourists could probably tell.

Terence didn't seem to notice. Or maybe he didn't care. As he stood—no, posed—in his glittering outfit—purple velvet, green satin, and more cloth of gold than seemed quite necessary—he echoed any number of Renaissance paintings of kings and grandees. Holbein's portrait of Henry VIII, for example. As if in deliberate imitation of Bluff King Hal, Terence's feet were planted wide apart, his shoulders were squared back, one beringed hand fingered the hilt of his dagger, and the other grasped a six-foot oak staff topped by a metal ornament in the shape of a creepy coiled serpent. He was a handsome man, handsomely dressed, and clearly he knew it.

Yet even the tourists never seemed to think of him as a possible rival to Michael and George in the battle for the throne of Albion. Curious, that.

I focused on what he was saying.

"And then he called to his good wife, 'Come, and see how fond your daughter is of the nightingale. She has caught it, and has it fast in her hand!'"

Terence smirked. I recognized the ending of a tale

from Boccaccio's *Decameron*—one of the naughtier bits, as they would say on *Monty Python*. Jacks—and most of the audience—laughed loudly. Dianne could only manage a pained smile. Or maybe she was just doing a good job of staying in character—after all, in the Game she was not only beautiful but virtuous and a bit naïve.

"Well, God ye good morrow, Sir Terence," Jacks said when the laughter had died down. "I must away to attend the queen."

"And I as well." Dianne sounded relieved.

"Will you desert me, sweetings!" Terence put the back of his hand to his forehead and pretended to be on the verge of swooning. "Shall I be so bereft?"

"Needs must, good sir." Jacks held out her hand to be kissed.

"Till we meet again, good lady." Terence bowed low and delivered a loud, wet, sloppy smack to the back of her hand. The tourists found it hilarious. Jacks frowned a rebuke at him, although I could tell she was actually amused.

Dianne was clearly planning to leave with her hand un-molested, but Terence straightened up, took a few steps toward her, and grabbed her hand.

"And must you depart, my fairest one? Alas!" He bent over her hand. Dianne forced a smile and resigned herself to endure Terence's slobbering.

The smile disappeared when, instead of kissing her hand, he jerked on her arm and twirled her into his arms, like a dancer dipping his partner.

"Aha!" he exclaimed, and bent as if to kiss her. Dianne turned her head and pushed at him with both hands. I didn't think she was acting.

"You are too bold, Sir Terence." Jacks smacked Terence with her fan and glanced over at me as if seeking help.

But before I could step in to interfere, Grandfather strode forward, waving his staff.

"Unhand that damsel, ye poxy varlet!" he shouted.

Chapter 5

To my astonishment, Terence actually stopped pawing at Dianne and turned to stare at Grandfather. For that matter, Dianne, after managing to use the interruption to escape from Terence's grip, was staring, too. They were probably trying to figure out who the devil Grandfather was. His costume and grasp of Renaissance idiom were better than what most tourists ever managed, and yet they knew he wasn't one of their troupe.

"This is Magister Blake, Queen Cordelia's new court alchemist," I explained.

Dianne got it.

"Well met, Magister." She dropped a low curtsey. "Your knowledge and wisdom are well known to all in Albion."

Grandfather preened and bowed back. Terence frowned and looked puzzled.

"Not well known to me," he muttered.

"Meg's grandfather, stupid," Dianne hissed.

Terence continued to scowl at Grandfather. And Grandfather scowled back. If they were planning a scowling competition, Grandfather would win it, no question, thanks to a combination of a natural talent and decades more practice.

Then Grandfather turned to me.

"Shall I turn him into a toad?" he asked rather loudly, "I could do it like that." He snapped his fingers. "Easiest thing in the world."

The tourists roared with merriment.

"Why bother?" I said. "Hardly anyone would notice the difference."

The tourists loved that, too, and Jacks threw her head back and howled with laughter. Even Dianne tittered. Terence looked disconcerted for a moment, then strolled off with an air of nonchalance—although the sharp way he dug into the ground with the tip of his snake-headed staff did rather give him away.

The watching tourists applauded as if we'd just acted out a brilliant scene.

And from the way Grandfather ate up the applause, I realized I'd probably just created a monster.

"Falcons are this way," I said, tugging on his sleeve.

He let me steer him away from the crowd, though he continued to beam graciously on them as we passed, and wave his raven-headed staff in a manner vaguely reminiscent of a bishop blessing his flock with a crozier.

I spotted Cordelia nearby, staring at him with a strange expression on her face. I left Grandfather trading insults with the Muddy Beggar long enough to go over to her.

"Something wrong?" I asked.

"Nothing." She shook her head vigorously. "It's just that every once in a long while I find myself remembering, just for a moment, what I saw in him. Only for a moment," she added hastily. "But while it lasts, it's a curiously unsettling experience."

I reclaimed Grandfather and hustled him along. We went by the blacksmith's shop on our way into Falconer's Grove. Faulk was inside the forge area, perched on a tall wooden stool, answering questions from some of the tourists. And I was pleased to see that Josh and Jamie, my twin sons, were there in the shop area, keeping their eyes on the merchandise and ready to ring up any sales. Seeing them standing a little self-importantly in the entrance, I was struck again by how mature they looked. And it wasn't just that they were surprisingly tall for twelve-year-olds.

Well, maybe that wasn't so surprising, since I was five ten and Michael six four. All too soon they'd be eye-to-eye with me.

"Stop it," I muttered to myself.

"What's that you say?" I'd forgotten Grandfather was within earshot.

"Nothing."

I strolled over to the fence, took the two remaining slices of bacon from my plate, and waved them at the boys. Josh dashed over.

"Spike's already had his breakfast," he said. "We don't want to upset his stomach with too much bacon."

"Good thinking," I said. "Just keep these on hand in case you need them."

"In case he does something good and needs a treat." Jamie beamed at the idea.

"Or in case another stupid tourist steps into the pen and you need a distraction to help pry Spike off his ankle," I said. Spike—aka the Small Evil One, our eight-and-a-half-pound fur ball—was spending his days in a nice, shady pen just outside the forge's back door. Any would-be thieves clueless enough to be fooled by his deceptively cute and fluffy appearance were taking their life in their hands if they tried to sneak into the shop by the back door.

I waved at the boys—and at Faulk, who probably wondered where I was going—and hurried to deliver Grandfather. I still had time before my 11:00 A.M. demonstration.

To the north and east, the beginning of the woods marked the end of the fairgrounds—the woods, plus a line of deer mesh fence we'd strung up from tree to tree about six feet into the woods. The black mesh was almost invisible until you got close to it, but it did a good job of stopping anyone who ignored the warning signs—signs with slogans like BEWARE! HERE BE MONSTERS or DRAGON BREEDING GROUNDS—DO NOT ENTER or simply ABANDON HOPE ALL YE WHO ENTER HERE. In that direction, once you passed the campgrounds and left Cordelia's land, there was nothing for miles but thousands of acres of woods, mostly belonging to various state or national parks, so we wanted to make it harder for the tourists to wander off and get themselves lost.

We'd located Falconer's Grove in a place where a clearing jutted out into the woods, and helped cut it off from the main part of the Faire a little more by situating the Blacksmith's Shop on the left of its entrance and the Herb Shop and first aid tent on the right. The falconers liked the location because it somewhat shielded the birds from the noise and distractions of the main part of the Faire. Cordelia liked it because it reduced her anxiety that the falcons would pounce on some utterly inappropriate prey—like a chicken roasting in one of the open-air kitchens, or a particularly plump infant. The falconers assured her that their birds would never do any such thing, but Cordelia was never one for taking chances.

At the far end of the grove a rough-hewn rail fence surrounded the falcon's enclosure, which contained the actual mews—a small wooden shed with a sturdy roof and well-ventilated sides, where the falcons could sleep or take refuge from the crowds, with an attached chicken wire enclosure in which they could take the air. In front of the mews, but still a safe distance from the fence—and each other—were three wooden perches, two of them occupied.

And even though we were now about as far from the front gate as you could get and still be within the fairgrounds, already a small crowd of tourists were clustered along the fence. Greg, the senior member of our two-person falcon team—aka Sir Gregory Dorance, the Queen's Own Falconer—was standing just inside the fence in a doublet whose black, brown, and gold colors echoed the birds' plumage. He was answering questions from the tourists while keeping an eye on the two birds seated on their perches on either side of him.

"She's a peregrine falcon," he was saying, indicating the bird to his right.

"*Falco peregrinus*," Grandfather muttered, nodding. "Handsome specimen."

Greg flashed him a quick smile at the compliment.

"Her name's Gracie," he went on. "She's pretty big for a peregrine. Of course, female falcons are usually larger than the males."

"Marked sexual dimorphism, yes." Grandfather was studying Gracie with keen eyes, nodding slightly as if approving what he saw. She was nearly two feet tall with glossy plumage, bluish-black on the back and wing tips and mottled white and tan on the breast and belly. A brown leather hood decorated with purple tassels covered her head, but she seemed to be following everything that happened around her, turning with a quick, sharp motion when she detected a sound coming from a new direction. Several tiny bells attached to the hood with strips of leather jingled when she moved.

"They don't mind wearing the hoods," Greg was saying. "It calms them."

"Yes, without the hood they can become hypervigilant," Grandfather said. "Constantly looking around for prey and getting frustrated when they can't go after it and worse, being startled by anything they perceive as a threat. But they're so visually oriented that they pay no attention to anything they can't see."

"Exactly." Greg seemed to be taking the interruptions to his talk quite calmly. "With her hood on, Gracie's interested in everything, but nothing bothers her. Harry is different."

He indicated the other bird. Harry was slightly smaller than Gracie, only a foot and a half tall, and his plumage ranged from medium brown on the back and head to tan and white on the underside. Even though he wasn't hooded, he was paying no attention to Greg or the crowd, and seemed quite absorbed in rubbing his bill vigorously against his perch.

"He's a red-tailed hawk," Greg noted.

"*Buteo jamaicensis,*" Grandfather added. "A bit small."

"Yes." Greg frowned at Harry. "As a species, they run larger than peregrines, but Harry's a male and a relatively small one to boot." I caught a faintly negative tone in his voice—disapproval or disappointment, maybe. Was he merely unhappy about Harry's lack of size? Or was the hawk unsatisfactory in some other way?

"I see he's feaking," Grandfather said. "Good sign."

"Feaking means that he's rubbing his beak against the perch to clean it and shape it," Greg said for the benefit of the rest of us. "The falcon equivalent of using an emery board on your nails. Generally a sign that the bird is calm and contented. Which is pretty much Harry's normal state. Even without his hood, he's so calm you could set off firecrackers here in the grove and he'd just look around for a few seconds before going back to feaking. Or preening," he added. "That's what he's doing now."

Harry had stopped rubbing his beak against the perch and was now running it through his feathers, grooming and fluffing them.

"Important to keep the feathers in good condition," Grandfather announced. "The uropygial gland at the base of the tail produces preen oil, which the bird spreads throughout its plumage using the beak. The jury's out on whether it has any real antiparasitic effect."

"But it does keep their feathers nice and shiny," Greg said.

"Mind if I leave you here?" I said to Grandfather. "I have to go give a blacksmithing demonstration."

"Don't worry about us," he said. "We'll be fine."

Either he'd adopted the royal "we" in imitation of Queen Cordelia or he'd already declared himself part of the falcons' entourage. I caught Greg's eye and nodded at Grandfather.

"If you need me, I'll be at the smithy," I said.

Greg nodded back as if he'd picked up on my message—although I wasn't sure myself if the message was a request to look after Grandfather or an apology for inflicting him on Greg. Maybe a little of both.

"Would you like to see one of them hunt? " Greg asked, turning to the tourists pressed against the fence.

"Of course!" Grandfather exclaimed.

The tourists were also eager. I wouldn't have minded myself, but I had a blacksmithing demonstration starting in about one minute. I hurried back toward the mouth of the grove.

As I approached the smithy I spotted Jamie peering anxiously in my direction. Relief flooded his face when he spotted me, and I saw him call something over his shoulder.

"We thought you weren't going to make it," he said as I entered the smithy.

"I was only next door with the falcons," I said.

"And Great," Jamie said, using the boys' usual nickname for Grandfather. "He can be kind of distracting."

"Poor Great," I said. "Even you guys have got his number. Let me throw on my gear and I'll start the demo."

"I'll tell Josh to get everything ready!"

Chapter 6

Nice that I could rely on the boys to prep the forge for my demo. They'd recently decided that blacksmithing was at least moderately cool and had begun learning the rudiments in whatever time was not already taken up by homework, baseball, music lessons, acting in college and community plays, and play-testing any new video games their Uncle Rob's company was developing. And Faulk was there to supervise.

So I slipped into the back room to change. Spike peered through the chicken-wire fencing that kept him from entering the forge. When he realized it was only me and not his beloved Josh or Jamie, he growled—but softly, since I was his main source of food and treats whenever the twins weren't around.

I changed into the outfit I'd devised for blacksmithing. Vaguely period trousers of heavy brown fabric, because wearing skirts near an open fire was an invitation to being flambéed at the slightest breeze. Of course, women blacksmiths in less enlightened times had worn skirts, but I didn't think absolute authenticity was worth dying over. An authentic knee-length leather apron, which would keep sparks from igniting my cotton blouse or, worse, landing on the bare skin above it. And a pair of highly anachronistic steampunk-style goggles, because I also valued my eyesight more than authenticity. I pulled on a pair of deerskin work gloves—heavy enough to protect against sparks and provide some cushioning against all the iron and tools I'd be handling, while flexible enough that they didn't limit my dexterity.

And all the while I found myself wondering what the big deal was. If I was late, Faulk could start the demo, couldn't he?

Or could he? As I moved into the forge, he slipped into the shop to help with sales while Josh joined me for the demonstration. I almost did a double take at how . . . unwell Faulk looked. He was only a few years older than me, and regular blacksmithing had kept him lean and fit. But today he looked tired and dispirited. And paler than usual—his face was closer to the off-white of his billowing shirtsleeves than the light brown of his doublet.

I shoved the thought out of my mind. I could fret over that later.

"Welcome to the Riverton blacksmith's shop," I said to begin my spiel. "And yes, I'm one of the two blacksmiths. I don't know how things are in the outlandish parts most of ye seem to hail from"—here I swept my gaze over the motley crowd of tourists with a well-practiced bemusement that never failed to get a laugh—"but here in Albion, women can, indeed, become blacksmiths, thank you very much. Some of us were married to blacksmiths and took up the trade when widowed. Some of us had blacksmiths for fathers and no brothers to inherit the business. And some, like me, took a liking to the craft and became apprentices in our own right. Are we clear on that? Because I don't want any of you to wait until the middle of my demonstration to tell me a woman can't possibly be a blacksmith. Or worse, ask why I'm doing the work instead of my lazy lug of a partner over there."

The crowd laughed, and no one stepped forward to argue that it was a complete anachronism to have a woman blacksmith at a Renaissance Faire. I was prepared to debate the question if need be—I could cite the fact that

London's Worshipful Company of Blacksmiths listed women in its 1434 charter—granted the list contained sixty-five brethren and only two "sistern," but still, we were there. I could whip out copies of medieval woodcuts showing women working at forges. This wasn't the first time I'd done a reenactment, so I was well prepared to deal with naysayers and chauvinists. But it was a relief that at least this time around, I didn't have to.

In a pinch, I could almost do my demonstration on autopilot, and at the start, with my mind still filled with worry over Faulk, I wasn't as into it as I usually was. I hoped the tourists didn't notice. While Josh worked the bellows that fanned the flame in my forge, I explained the process—that the forge could get up to 2,000 degrees centigrade, more than hot enough to soften iron or steel so they could be worked with a hammer.

As I liked to do, I pulled my iron bar out early—before it had reached the dramatic red-hot phase—and demonstrated that even though it was still apparently unchanged, it was already hot enough to turn a bit of paper into ash.

"So if I drop this and it starts rolling toward your feet, don't grab for it—run away!"

While they were laughing at this, I finished heating the bar, then removed it from the forge and displayed it to the crowd, who gave a satisfying "oooh" when they saw the red-hot end.

"Now comes the hardest part," I said. "Hitting the bar."

Laughter.

"No, I'm serious—this is an eight-pound hammer." I held it up. "It's not all that easy to lift. Hitting exactly the right spot on the bar with it time after time—that's tough. Watch."

I laid the bar on my anvil, then proceeded to do a little fancy hammering, working rapidly and methodically up and down the red part of the bar until the last foot of it was partly flattened.

While the bar was heating again, I allowed some of the audience members to lift the hammer and marvel over its heaviness. Then, when I took the bar out again, I gestured to Josh, who grinned with delight. He picked up a slightly smaller hammer, donned his own goggles, and took his position on the other side of the anvil.

"Of course, if you have an apprentice, you can work twice as fast, though you have to be careful not to smash each other's fingers."

With that, Josh and I began a well-rehearsed routine, alternating blows on the iron bar, each of us going almost as fast as I'd done when hammering alone. After a few seconds of this, the tourists began applauding. It suddenly occurred to me that it might be rather amusing if we got the musicians to show up during our demonstration to play—or even sing—a few bars of Verdi's "The Anvil Chorus." Or would enough of the audience get it? I shoved the thought out of my mind for later consideration. I needed to concentrate to keep from hammering Josh, or getting hammered myself.

By the time I called a halt, the business end of the bar was as flat as it needed to be for the next phase.

"Anyone want to guess what this is going to be?" I asked. After fielding a couple of wild guesses—a sword? A horseshoe? A butter knife for giants?—I held up an example of what I was planning—a fireplace poker with a flat-sided business end and a handle shaped like a curving vine.

"If you want to see the next phase of the poker, drop by at one," I said. "And if you're impatient to see more blacksmithing even sooner, my colleague, the distinguished blacksmith—and swordsmith—Faulkner Cates, will be doing his first demo at noon."

I gestured toward Faulk, who doffed his feather-trimmed hat and made a partial bow. The tourists applauded with enthusiasm, and half a dozen of them gathered around me to ask questions. At least that many went into the shop beside the forge. Josh followed them, ready to help with what I hoped would be a surge in sales.

Eventually the questions tapered off, and I was free to leave. Actually, under other circumstances I'd have stayed to help with sales while Faulk did his noon demonstration, but today I had other plans. While Faulk was safely occupied with his demo, I was going to talk to his husband, Tad, to see if I could find out what was going on.

"You think you and Josh can handle sales for a while?" I asked Jamie. "I have a couple of things to take care of."

"We'll be fine." Actually, I could tell from his expression that he thought he and his brother could handle the practical side of ironwork sales much better than either Faulk or me.

He just might be right.

"Faulk, I'm leaving the boys to hold up my side of things," I called. "Hey, is Tad here already or is he coming tomorrow?"

"He should be up at the house," Faulk said. "Working. Or maybe just basking in the presence of electrical outlets and a Wi-Fi signal." Understandable. Tad was a brilliant programmer, never happier than when multitasking on two or three monitors and keyboards. Luckily he was also a complete ham, and enjoyed dressing up in costume when Faulk attended Renaissance fairs or other historical reenactments. Absent costumes and the chance to ham it up in them, camping out probably met Tad's personal definition of cruel and unusual punishment.

"Great," I said. "I have a tech question to ask him."

"Mom, if your laptop's acting up again—" Josh began.

"My laptop's fine," I said. "And I'd be smart enough to ask you two if it wasn't. This is one of those abstruse, which-way-is-the-computer-industry-going questions."

"Abstruse?" Jamie echoed.

"She probably wants him to check to see if we're up to

something online that she and Dad wouldn't approve of," Josh said.

Actually, I relied on their cyber-savvy grown cousin Kevin to do that, but I decided it would be easier if I let them—and Faulk—assume that I did want Tad to snoop behind them.

"Later," I said. "And call me if you need me."

On my way out, I stepped a little way into the grove to check on Grandfather and the falcons. Grandfather was now wearing a leather falconer's gauntlet with Harry perched on it. He appeared to be giving a large and appreciative crowd a lecture on the anatomy of a falcon's wing. He pulled out Harry's wing to illustrate some point, then released the wing and began flapping his own free arm. Harry took it all in stride. He only showed the slightest interest when Grandfather pulled open his robe to reveal the fisherman's vest beneath and began patting the pockets in search of something. After inspecting and discarding a pack of chewing gum, a Swiss Army knife, and a tiny can of WD-40, Grandfather smiled triumphantly. He held up something silver and glittering. Harry lost interest, but Greg moved closer to inspect whatever it was. Probably one of the new generation of super-tiny tracking devices Grandfather was currently testing.

"Mistress Meg!"

I turned to find Cordelia had entered the grove, flanked by Jacks and Dianne as ladies-in-waiting.

"Good morrow, Your Majesty." I sank into a suitably deep curtsey. Cordelia smiled and beckoned for me to rise and approach.

She frowned in Grandfather's general direction. Then she realized that tourists were clustered around us, expecting a scene, and gathered her wits to provide one.

"What business does our court alchemist have with our falconer?" Somehow she'd learned to project her voice as well as the professional actors—tourists in the back of the crowd had no trouble hearing her. And it was curious how naturally she'd taken to using the royal "we." "We like it not that he meddles with our birds."

"I do not know that he has any business here," I said. "He's here for his own pleasure, so if Your Majesty has need of him elsewhere in the kingdom—"

"We were not aware that we had need of an alchemist anywhere in Albion," she said. "So we would be well pleased if he were to stay in Falconer's Grove where we need not see him."

"I will convey Your Majesty's pleasure to Magister Blake." I made another low curtsey. "But Your Majesty—may I make a suggestion?"

Cordelia nodded graciously.

"Methinks Magister Blake would be a great deal more likely to stay in the grove if he thought you didn't want him there."

The crowd laughed at that. Cordelia didn't bother to disguise her annoyance at this bit of truth, and her reaction provoked more laughter.

"Well spoken," she said, when the laughter had died down. "Convey to Magister Blake whatever you think will encourage him to avoid our sight."

"Yes, Your Majesty."

Cordelia turned to go, then turned back for a parting shot.

"And we hear he has threatened to turn several of our subjects into toads."

"Only the annoying ones, Your Majesty." I thought it was time for another particularly obsequious curtsey.

"We have sufficient toads in the kingdom already. Tell him that if he makes any more toads, we may decide to make him shorter—by a head."

With that she turned and sailed off, followed by laughter and applause. And I realized the crowd was now looking at me to continue the entertainment.

To my relief, Michael stepped out of the crowd.

"Her Majesty has given you a difficult commission," he said.

"She has," I said. "And they always say 'meddle not in the affairs of wizards, for they are subtle, and quick to anger.'" Thank heavens for the boys' recent obsession with rewatching all three *Lord of the Rings* movies—in the extended director's cuts. Bits of Tolkien were almost as useful in the Game as bits of Shakespeare. "An alchemist's a kind of wizard, isn't he?"

"Aye, that he is. So let me convey Her Majesty's pleasure to Magister Blake. He will not be so quick to work his magic on a peer of the realm."

He strode off toward Grandfather, taking nearly all of the crowd with him. I made good my escape and headed toward the house.

Chapter 7

As soon as both Michael and Cordelia were out of sight—along with the crowds trailing them—I took a deep breath and relished the feeling of being, at least for the moment, offstage. My outfit—a long brown skirt and a dark-red laced bodice over a white blouse—wasn't all that different from what the tourists could rent if they decided to go for the budget end of the costume shop's offerings. I might pass unnoticed in the crowd—just another commoner. For a few minutes, at least, I could forget that I was on duty.

In fact, I decided to make my stroll to the house a leisurely one, and pretend, just for twenty minutes or so, that I was a tourist, seeing the Faire for the first time.

I watched as the jugglers strolled by, throwing around a collection of real coconuts and fake cannonballs. I stopped by the ring-toss booth to watch a little boy—so short he had to stand on a stool to play—win a tiny bright-blue stuffed bear.

"The prizes are pretty chintzy," I overheard a teenage kid behind me say.

"Yeah, but that's 'cause the games aren't rigged," another kid replied.

I turned down one of the food lanes and found my mouth watering. Breakfast wasn't that long ago—was I really hungry, or was I just giving way to the delicious smells? Fish and chips and roasted turkey leg smells wafted from the left while the odors of pork pockets, steak-on-a-stake, and shepherd's pie assailed me from the right. Farther on I could choose between crepes, fried cheese, fried pickles, corn on the cob, hot pretzels, cinnamon rolls, and several flavors of Italian ice. I usually waited until the Faire was over to indulge in the mead, but there were coffee, tea, lemonade, limeade, fruit slushies, root beer floats—

I hurried out of the food lane.

"A little mud, milady?" I was passing the Muddy Beggar. "It'd look a treat on that pretty skirt of yours." He held up a handful of particularly viscous mud with the solicitous look of someone eager to repair a conspicuous defect in my costume.

"Not today, but thank you, good sir beggar," I replied. And then I hurried on, in case he felt like creating more street theater than usual. His best gag was to pick particularly neat and tidy tourists out of the crowd, greet them as long-lost friends or cousins, and amuse the crowd by tottering toward them while exclaiming "Let me embrace you!" He was strictly forbidden to actually muddy tourists but he might consider cast members fair targets. And while I wasn't technically a cast member, I got sucked into the Game often enough that few people remembered that.

Though I stayed long enough to see him return to his usual stock in trade—hurling colorful, wildly improbable, yet largely PG-rated insults at the crowd.

"Thou impious cur!" he roared at a passing tourist who laughed at him. "Bootless fustilarian! Thou poxy pusillanimous puttock!"

I made a mental note to look up "fustilarian" and "puttock," in case the beggar was sailing a little close to R-rated invective, and strolled on.

I waved or nodded as I passed the booths of friends from the craft community, and rejoiced to see the crowds of tourists lining up to buy leather belts, glass witch balls, crystal jewelry, hand-loomed napkins in a rainbow of colors, pewter dragon statuettes, plush stuffed unicorns, wooden serving spoons, blank books bound in leather or velvet, stained-glass suncatchers, feather-trimmed masks, fake skeletons, authentic kilts, and hundreds—no, thousands—of other goods.

Suddenly I snapped back into my role as Cordelia's assistant—and enforcer—when I saw Terence and Nigel talking together in a quiet spot behind the Dragon's Claw—the sort of spot they'd have chosen if they wanted to keep their conversation offstage. They looked earnest, intent, and not very happy with each other.

I eased into a strategic spot by the side of the puppet-maker's stall, where a rack of marionettes would make it hard for them to see me. I angled myself so if they did spot me they'd assume I was watching the Punch-and-Judy show in progress. But I kept my eyes on Terence and Nigel, trying to figure out what they were up to.

What Terence was up to. I was pretty sure the main thing on Nigel's mind was getting through the day with his sobriety intact, a goal that would be made substantially easier if he could limit his exposure to Terence.

The shrieks from Punch—and the crowd's laughter—kept me from eavesdropping, but it was pretty clear from the body language that Terence was trying to talk Nigel into something. Something Nigel didn't want to do. Something Nigel thought was a pretty terrible idea. Terence seemed to alternate between coaxing and blustering. And I suspected he was winning Nigel over. Not with the coaxing, I suspected. With the blustering. Maybe you could even call it threatening. I was positive Nigel was reluctantly agreeing to something he really didn't like.

But what? Something in the Game, most likely, since in real life, they had no particular connection that I knew of. But Terence had developed a fondness for taking the Game in strange and unpredictable directions. Admittedly, by this fourth weekend of the Faire we'd started falling into patterns, reusing plot devices that had worked out well. For example, the overall plan the cast had informally agreed to work with today was for Terence to sow discord between Michael and George, the arch-rivals, culminating in a brief duel late in the day. This plot had a number of advantages. It gave everyone a few scenes in which to shine. It was an easy theme to improvise on. It gave Michael and George, the two actors most qualified to do so, the excuse to fight a duel—a duel that had been carefully choreographed in advance and rehearsed ad nauseam to avoid any chance of bloodshed. And most important of all, the crowd ate up the rivalry plot, noisily rooting for one contender or the other—well, mostly rooting for Michael. George was a fine actor, but he didn't have Michael's looks, charm, or panache. So there were multiple reasons for sticking to the agreed-upon plan. Most of the cast were happy at the prospect of being able to hone their performances, especially polishing and reusing successful bon mots.

Terence, on the other hand, was always trying to start really peculiar plot threads that limped along if they didn't fall flat. The most glaring example was his attempt to kick off an alien-abduction scenario during the second weekend. The tourists, primed for jousts and jesters, couldn't figure out what to make of Terence's prattling about "wee gray beasties with peculiar eyes" descending from the sky. Michael had saved the day then, announcing that Terence had lost his mind and having Cordelia sentence him to sit in the stocks for the entire afternoon so he couldn't interfere with the saner plotline the rest of the company was spinning out. Terence had seemed to behave a little better after that. But still—I distrusted anything Terence might come up with. He cared less about amusing the tourists than amusing himself.

Eventually Nigel broke off their conference. I'd never learned to read lips well—an omission I vowed, not for the first time, to remedy when time permitted. But with a little help from his facial expression and body language, I picked up the gist of what he was saying, even if I missed a few words.

"Okay, okay. I'll do it. Now leave me alone."

He hurried off in the direction of the grove, shoulders hunched, face pinched with anxiety. When he'd put enough distance between him and Terence, he paused, plucked a lace-trimmed handkerchief out of his left sleeve, and used it to dab the sweat from his face and his high, balding forehead. Then he started off again with a more dignified gait, nodding graciously to tourists who greeted him from either side.

Terence watched him go with the satisfied smile of a cat who knows his latest mouse has no hope of escape. And then he swaggered off in the opposite direction.

What was he up to?

We'd find out soon enough. And by now, most of the cast was sufficiently wary of his wayward behavior that it wouldn't take me or Michael to head him off at the pass if he tried anything truly outrageous. Nearly everyone in the Game would help. Jacks, in particular, would positively jump at the chance to squash him like a bug.

Nigel would be the weak link—Nigel and George. I made a mental note to see what I could do to change that. Nigel hated conflict, which meant he usually gave in to whatever Terence suggested to avoid a scene. Would it work if I gave him blanket permission to say "Queen Cordelia has expressly forbidden that!" whenever Terence suggested something? Maybe. But George actually seemed to find Terence's antics amusing. Not much I could do about that. So I shoved the whole thing out of my mind, at least for the moment.

I was approaching the house—in Game parlance, Queen Cordelia's summer palace. Three of the minstrels in their blue-and-gold tunics were serenading the crowd from the white-columned front veranda—a good thing, since having the musicians in front of the front door tended to reduce the number of tourists who wandered inside. I slipped behind them and into the Great Hall.

Inside I ran into poor George. Normally he looked quite dashing and elegant, as befitted Michael's chief rival in the contest to inherit Albion—especially when wearing his main costume, made of emerald-green velvet and cloth of gold, with matching shoes and hat. His tunic was cut rather longer than usual, which helped to minimize the fact that his legs, clad in black woolen hose, were on the scrawny side. He was no male model, but most of the time he managed to make the best of what nature had given him.

At the moment, though, he was a sopping-wet mess. His tunic clung to his body in the most unfortunate way, revealing how much padding and puffing contributed to his usual dashing look. His chest wasn't actually concave, but it rather looked that way atop his small pot belly. His woolen hose bagged and drooped unflatteringly. Even the damp, bedraggled plume on his hat seemed to be wilting morosely.

"What happened to you?" I asked. "Did you fall into the lake?"

"We have a lake?" he said. "I wish I'd known. I could have told Terence to jump into it."

"Not another prank. Do you want me to speak to Terence?"

"No need. It was all part of the Game. Went over well with the audience." His smile was a little wry, but on the whole he seemed to be taking the prank rather calmly. As usual. Terence played more pranks on him than on anyone else in the cast, and so far I hadn't seen any of them shake George's enviable equilibrium. I was surprised Terence hadn't given up—surely for a prankster like him, half the fun was in seeing the victim's reaction. Maybe he was determined to keep playing pranks on George until he got a reaction. I suspected he was in for a long campaign.

Or maybe he played more pranks on George because it was safe. George wasn't going to punch Terence in the nose, as Greg Dorance had over a prank Greg felt had put the falcons in danger. Or throw a glass of mead at him as Jacks had the first—and last—time he'd goosed her. Or threaten to fire him, as I had after he played a mean-spirited prank on Nigel. George had even told stories about particularly outrageous pranks Terence had played—on him as well as on others—during past productions they'd been in together. Maybe he actually bought into Terence's assertion that lively and imaginative tomfoolery—on- or offstage—was a hallowed tradition of the theater.

"Incidentally," George went on, "I'm supposed to be convinced that it was Michael who arranged for me to be hit by the water-filled goatskin while leaving the Dragon's Claw. In the Game, that is. We'll be having a nice, juicy confrontation over that later."

At least that fit in, more or less, with the agreed-upon plot du jour.

"Did Terence waste a real goatskin on a stupid prank like that?" I asked aloud.

"No, it was a water-balloon tricked out to look like a goatskin." George smiled. "Even Terence has his limits, though I suspect they have more to do with stinginess than good taste. Anyway, I plan to don my spare outfit and then see if the costume crew can clean and dry this one. I need to look my best if I'm going to be appearing alongside Michael this afternoon."

"I'm sure the costume crew can work wonders," I said. "If they balk—"

"I'll throw myself on your mother's mercy." He chuckled. "I don't suppose we could arrange for me to have three costumes? Not that I'm greedy, mind you, but these quick cleanup operations are hard on the costume crew."

Yes, and the costume crew already had enough to do. Cordelia had arranged to provide costumes for all the players and participants on salary—and had made sure everyone had a spare costume, on the theory that if we wore the same costume three days in a row in the heat of a Virginia summer, the tourists would start avoiding us by Saturday morning and fleeing the Faire altogether by Saturday afternoon. We'd converted two of the three big rooms on the lower level of the studio wing into the laundry center. One room held big tubs for the garments that had to be handwashed—a very small number, limited to the major players in the Game—a flock of ironing boards, and yards and yards of clothesline. The other held rows of industrial washers and dryers for the more durable shirts, shifts, skirts, and breeches rented to the public or issued to the rank-and-file employees.

"Just explain to Mother that it's all Terence's fault and I'm sure she'll take care of it," I said. "Although maybe I'll also speak to Terence about not pulling any pranks that mess up his colleagues' costumes."

"Or at least saving those for Sunday afternoon, when the costumers have all week to clean up after him," George said. "By the way, is it true that Michael turned down a chance to play Laertes in Neil O'Malley's production of *Hamlet* to do this Ren Faire?"

Blast. Jacks must have been gossiping. And if I found that annoying, I could only imagine how Michael felt.

Chapter 8

"Yes, strange as everyone seems to find it, Michael turned down the chance to audition for O'Malley." I hoped George would drop the subject.

"Wow." He shook his head in disbelief. "No offense to your grandmother—"

"But Riverton isn't the Arena Stage. I know." I was already getting tired of defending what I thought was a supremely wise decision. "Michael's agent—ex-agent, technically—passed along a query about whether Michael would like to join the hordes auditioning for His O'Malleyship. So all Michael turned down was the chance to appear alongside the thousand or so other actors invited to read for the role. Besides, even if he wanted to work with O'Malley again, it would have interfered with more than just the Faire. Michael has grown very fond of his whole other life in academia." I didn't need to add that Michael was now a tenured professor in Caerphilly College's Drama Department, with every chance of becoming the department chair in due course, and therefore liberated from the need to jump through hoops for dictatorial directors. Why rub it in? "O'Malley's production's not until late spring," I went on. "Which means, from what I've heard about him, he'll rehearse his cast all winter, and I get the feeling those rehearsals are both eccentric and grueling."

"Well, yeah," George admitted. "His methods are a little weird sometimes. But he's a genius."

"So he keeps reminding everyone." I'd read enough

articles in which O'Malley showed no reluctance to blow his own horn.

"And did you hear he's signed Zachary Glass to play Hamlet. Zach Glass!"

"Zach Glass? Seriously?" Even at the height of Glass's considerable fame I'd been immune to his particular brand of vapid, toothy charm, and time hadn't been kind to the former teen heartthrob. Was he playing Hamlet because he'd belatedly discovered an interest in serious drama? Or because no one in Hollywood was hiring him anymore? "Sorry, but can you actually see Zach Glass playing Hamlet?"

"Well, no," George admitted. "But evidently O'Malley can. And he's the genius. Imagine the possibilities!"

Unfortunately I could.

"I'm sure it will be very interesting." Growing up, I'd absorbed Mother's teaching that if I couldn't find anything nice to say about something, I could always call it interesting.

"Wait," George added. "Did you say 'even if Michael wanted to work with O'Malley again'? They've worked together before?"

"A long time ago in a galaxy far, far away." The boys had also been rewatching all the *Star Wars* movies. "If you're planning to audition for O'Malley, you'll have to ask Michael if a recommendation from him would help or harm your chances."

"Roger. Well, I've probably dripped on Her Majesty's nice oak floor long enough. See you later." He headed toward the door that led to the workshop wing, where the costume shop was located.

I looked around for someone who might know where Tad was and spotted two of the strolling food merchants just leaving the kitchen, where they'd doubtless gone to restock their wares—a young woman carrying a tray of rock candy clusters and a young man pushing a hot-pretzel cart.

"Have you seen Tad?" I asked.

They both looked puzzled and shook their heads.

"Just who is Tad?" the young man asked. "It is a who, right? Not a what."

It occurred to me that they might never have heard Tad's real name—they'd probably only met him in the role he played in the Game.

"Sir Tadjik, the Moorish ambassador," I elaborated. "Thirty-something African-American guy in a turban and a green, red, and yellow robe—"

"Oh, Tadjik. Yeah." The young man smiled—Tad was popular with nearly everyone. "He's here somewhere."

"He's hiding out with his anachronisms in the jewelry-making studio," the young woman said.

A little odd—why didn't he just use Cordelia's office? She'd told him to make himself at home there. But maybe he felt he was intruding. And the jewelry studio, like Cordelia's office, was not only on the lower level of the studio wing—the level we'd locked up to keep out the tourists—but also on the side of the building away from the Faire, so it was probably quiet, if that was what he wanted.

I thanked them and headed for the studio in question. As I passed by the costume shop I peeked in and saw Mother, seated in her throne-like chair, frowning slightly as she watched two seamstresses fitting George into his new outfit. Her costume included almost as much sky-blue velvet as Dianne's—not surprising, since their eyes were nearly the same shade of blue.

Downstairs I passed by the empty racks where most of the staff would deposit their Renaissance clothes at the end of the day, a smaller rack full of t-shirts and blue jeans shed by people who came down to the shop to don their costumes for the day, and a bank of small lockers where those same people could store any valuables they didn't want to carry around in their costumes. I heard the subdued rumble of a washing machine—probably sheets or towels for the limited number of bedrooms in the main house. The massive costume laundering wouldn't begin till tomorrow. Thank goodness Cordelia had been farsighted enough to invest in excellent soundproofing for all the studios—the kind of soundproofing that could let you have a carpentry or metalworking class in one studio without disrupting the serenity of the yoga class next door. Still, this corridor was more peaceful now than it would be tomorrow.

When I opened the door of the jewelry studio a strange sight greeted me. Tad wasn't wearing his costume, although I could see it thrown over a chair in the corner in a heap of vivid red, green, gold, and black. He was dressed with surprising restraint in a pale blue shirt and khakis. He'd pushed back all the furniture in the room against the walls, leaving a central open space in which he was sitting at a small table, talking on his cell phone, with his laptop open in front of him. Okay, that last part wasn't the least bit strange; Faulk sometimes complained that Tad seemed to have a pair of umbilical cords connecting him to his mobile and his computer. What was strange was the backdrop behind him—a huge seamless bright-green screen eight feet tall and ten feet wide that completely blocked his view of the huge floor-to-ceiling windows behind him, to say nothing of the Blue Ridge Mountains outside—a view many people paid a premium to see from their rooms. A matching green cloth covered the table.

I paused in the doorway, surprised. When he looked up and saw me, he stuck his left hand up to the side of his laptop screen, palm outward, in a stop sign. I deduced he wanted to finish his phone conversation without interruption. His thin brown face was clenched with anxiety.

"Hang on—can I call you back? I just got the call waiting beep and it could be them. Yeah, I'll keep you posted. Right."

He pressed a button on his phone. Then he lowered the lid of his laptop and took a deep breath.

"Sorry," he said. "On the phone with my beastly boss."

"I didn't mean to interrupt you."

"Actually, I'm glad you did," he said. "It can be like pulling teeth getting him off the phone."

"Happy to be of service, then." I stepped further inside the room, and then Tad and I both winced as I stepped on a board that squeaked so loudly that during this week's jewelry class we'd rearranged the tables to make sure no one stepped on it. Maybe it was time to get Cordelia's handyman to take a look at it.

Later. I gestured to the enormous green background. "What the dickens is that?"

"That," he said, "is the technological marvel that allows me to be here today instead of up in Northern Virginia in my cubicle. It's a green screen."

"So I noticed. The color's not growing on me—rather a bilious shade of green, if you ask me."

"Also known as a chroma-key background. Here—I'll show you." He lifted up the laptop screen again, made a few swift keystrokes, and then grabbed a freestanding computer monitor that was perched on the far end of his table and turned it so the screen was facing my way. On the monitor I could see Tad, seated at his table, looking into the laptop's camera. The green screen behind him was so bright it almost glowed.

"Not really your best color," I said. "Makes your skin look sallow. And what's wrong with Cordelia's décor, may I ask?"

"Much prettier, but it's not the background my boss wants to see me in. He'd rather see this."

Tad's fingers flew over the keyboard and suddenly the green background disappeared and Tad appeared to be sitting in an office cubicle made of bland gray fabric panels.

"It's the same way they do special effects for the movies," he said. "I have a program that makes anything green become transparent."

"And instead of the green background you see a picture of your office." I nodded my comprehension. "Are the pictures actually realistic enough to fool him?"

"I built in a certain amount of picture degradation to make it more plausible," Tad said. And it's not just pictures—it's video."

As I watched, someone went past the entrance to the cubicle, calling out "Hey, Tad." The printer against the far wall of the cube erupted into life and spat out several documents. A phone rang in the distance.

"Very impressive," I said. "But what's it for?"

"My wretched boss doesn't believe in telecommuting." He rolled his eyes in exasperation.

"How twentieth century." I kept my face deadpan.

"I know—can you believe it? He doesn't think you're doing your job unless you're sitting there in your cubicle tapping on your keyboard. He'd have a cow if he knew I was down here, a couple of hours' drive away."

"You can't just call him on your phone and lie to him about where you are?"

"That used to work, until he discovered webcams and FaceTime and Skype. Now he doesn't just want to hear from me, he wants to see me and look over my shoulder."

"But what if he decides to walk down to your cubicle to talk to you in person?"

Tad's fingers flew. The scene changed from his cubicle to a table at what was obviously a Starbucks.

"If I switch over to my phone, I've got even more scope." Tad typed a few more commands, then picked up his cell phone, stood up, and moved away from the table and laptop. The scene changed from Tad standing in Starbucks to Tad standing beside an industrial-sized copier

machine. Then Tad standing in line at a deli. Tad in an
office corridor with several business suit–clad people
having a conversation behind him. Tad standing by a row
of sinks in what I deduced was the office men's room.
The illusion was broken when a man in khaki pants and
a white dress shirt came through the door into the bathroom, walked right through where Tad appeared to be
standing, and positioned himself in front of a urinal. Tad
hastily killed the video feed and the bright green screen
reappeared.

"Sorry," he said. "I already told my on-site coconspirator
to take that one down. Not what I had in mind when I told
him to put the cameras anyplace I was likely to be if I
wasn't at my desk."

"So this is a team effort," I said.

"Yeah. They all hate my boss's guts as much as I do."

"But why are you putting up with him at all?" I asked.
"You're Thaddeus Freakin' Jackson, programmer extraor-
dinaire. There are plenty of places that would kill to hire
you."

"Yeah, but most of them want to hire me as a consul-
tant these days," he said. "The gig economy is big in IT.
And the problem with that is you have to pay your own
benefits. Which isn't such a big deal when you're so young
you have trouble even imagining you might need health
insurance someday. But Faulk and I are neither of us kids
anymore. One of us has to get a job where we can get coverage."

I wasn't sure I wanted to hear this. Faulk was only a
couple of years older than me, and Tad was at least five
years younger—they were both very far from over the hill.

But he was right—none of us were kids anymore. And
I knew very well how lucky I was that Michael's post on
the faculty of Caerphilly College included an excellent
health plan, among other benefits. If he'd still been
working as an actor instead of a drama professor, maybe

I'd be thinking seriously about doing exactly what Tad was doing: getting a job—any job, however miserable—for the benefits.

"Okay, it's a pretty cool tactic." I waved at the green screen. "And I bet it's a lot of fun to put one over on your beastly boss, as you call him. But if he really would be that upset to find you away from the office—"

"He'd go ballistic." Tad shuddered slightly. "He'd can me on the spot."

"Then why not play it safe? Clock in at the office the way he wants you to. Why risk everything this way?"

"I want to be here for Faulk. He needs me."

"Is there something wrong with Faulk?" Ironic that the conversation had finally come around to the very question that had inspired me to hunt down Tad in the first place.

"He's not himself, in case you hadn't noticed."

"I'd noticed. What's wrong?"

Tad shrugged and avoided my eyes.

"Is he depressed? Because that's what it looks like to me."

Tad sighed, closed his eyes, and nodded ever so slightly.

"Is he seeing someone? Like a therapist? Because if he's depressed, it isn't something to take lightly."

Tad's face had relaxed a little. Maybe hearing me say it out loud took some of the weight off him. He took a deep breath.

"I know that," he said. "But until I got this job, we didn't have health insurance. Even now that we do, it's not exactly the greatest plan I've ever seen—takes forever to work through all the red tape, and you wouldn't believe the time I've spent on the phone arguing with them. But any day now we should be getting the referral we've been waiting for."

"Damn." I wasn't sure what else to say. It wasn't a very satisfactory answer. If Faulk really was suffering from depression—

"Talk to Dad." I could see Tad frown at the suggestion,

so I added, "He might be able to help—and keep it off the record, if he knows the situation. You don't want Faulk giving way to despair or anything this close to getting help. I know it's probably a little hard to believe, but Dad's actually not bad at crisis counseling."

"I'll think about it."

"One more thing."

"Yes?"

I had intended to ask how long Faulk had been depressed, but seeing how Tad braced himself—almost flinched, in fact—I decided to drop the issue. For now.

"I always thought you used blue screens for that kind of special-effects stuff."

His face relaxed.

"Well, yeah. Blue screens used to be more common. And they're still around—you'd have to use them for some things, like if you were trying to film Robin Hood and his merry men with the Lincoln-green outfits. But green screen's the gold standard these days—it works better with digital cameras. And Robin Hood and Peter Pan aside, people are less likely to be wearing green than blue. I have a blue screen and a program to use it, just in case. But so far the green's done the trick."

"Useful to know," I said.

"And now I'd better actually get some work done before the beastly boss calls again."

"Well hinted," I said. "I'll leave you to it."

I shut the door and headed back upstairs.

Chapter 9

I paused when I reached the main floor landing. Why hadn't Faulk said anything? And why hadn't I noticed? Okay, I'd noticed that Faulk was not quite his usual energetic, good-natured self, but I'd put it down to his being worn down after months of the kind of grueling travel schedule you had to keep to make a living as a blacksmith on the craft fair circuit. But apparently it was more than that.

I'd talk to Dad. Ask him to keep an eye on Faulk. Tad probably wouldn't want me to—but he hadn't actually forbidden it.

I made my way back to the main floor, being careful to lock the door to the lower level behind me.

In four of the six classroom studios tourists were watching demonstrations, buying craft items, and, with any luck, signing up for future classes in basket weaving, watercolor painting, gourd crafts, spinning, weaving, leatherworking, carpentry, sculpture, jewelry making, and—of course—blacksmithing. The other two studios contained the custom costume shop, where visitors who'd been bitten by the Ren Faire bug could order the costume of their dreams for wearing at future festivals. George was standing at attention in front of Mother, who was holding up half a dozen swatches of blue or green velvet in front of him, evidently trying to decide which was the most flattering shade for his new costume. I nodded approvingly and hurried on. Not a bad idea for me to get back to the booth. Do what I could to keep Faulk in a good frame of mind. I could stop by the first aid tent on the way and put Dad wise.

Out in the Great Hall I found Grandfather studying the decoration over the fireplace, which consisted of two swords crossed in front of a shield that bore the fake crest of the Kingdom of Albion—a large ginger cat holding a tiny black-and-gold dragon by the scruff of its neck.

"There you are," Grandfather said. "Can I have one of those swords?"

"No," I said.

"Not to keep—just for today."

"No."

"Why not? It's not as if—"

"Those two swords are welded to the shield," I said. "To keep the tourists from grabbing one of them and doing stupid things with it. If you want to carry around the whole thing, be my guest, but I should warn you, it weighs somewhere north of fifty pounds."

Grandfather studied the swords with a peeved expression on his face. I headed for the door. As I went out onto the veranda, he fell into step beside me.

"Well, then, where can I get a sword?"

"The first question is, why you think you need a sword? Can't you do enough damage with that?" I pointed to his staff, with the elegantly carved raven on the top.

"Everyone else has a sword."

I paused, put my hands on my hips, and gave him a look I normally saved for the boys.

"Well, not everyone," he said. "But there are an awful lot of weapons here. Even some of the tourists are wearing them."

"We try to talk the tourists out of weapons when they enter," I said. "And if we can't, any that aren't fake are supposed to be peace bonded." As I set out again, I fished into my pocket and held up one of the fluorescent plastic zip ties we used for that purpose. "Which means as soon as they enter the grounds we make them wrap one of these things around their weapons to keep them from being drawn."

"And if they object to this peace-bonding thing?" he said. "Because it kind of spoils the look of the costume."

"That's deliberate," I said. "We'd rather not have weapons at all."

"Or if they pretend to cooperate and then rebel later? Wouldn't take more than a quick slice with a pocket knife to liberate their weapons."

"If you see anyone who's done that, you just report them to one of the palace guards." I pointed to the one who happened to be passing, resplendent in a black-and-red uniform that echoed Cordelia's favorite garb. "You can spot them at a distance by their bardiches."

"Their whats?"

"Bardiches. It's a type of pole arm."

"You mean that long staff with the wicked curved double-headed ax on the end of it?"

"Yes," I said. "Those were fun to make."

I admired my handiwork for a few moments, and felt a brief twinge of regret that safety concerns had prevented me from putting an authentic razor-sharp edge on their crescent-shaped blades.

"One of those would do nicely," Grandfather said. "You have any spares?"

"They're reserved for the palace guard," I said. "You want to be a palace guard? It's a lot of work, and I'm not sure you'd pass the physical. Stick to the staff."

"Wait." Grandfather pointed to the figure carrying the bardiche. "Isn't that palace guard your cousin Horace?"

"It is," I said. "Both of the guards are off-duty law enforcement officers—Horace, and one of Chief Heedles's officers from here in Riverton. And the chief deputized Horace, so he'll have powers of arrest if needed. So I'm serious—you see anyone waving real weapons or doing anything else illegal, you find a palace guard."

"Simpler just to turn them into toads."

"If you can manage that, go right ahead."

"*Rhinella marina* would be best," he mused. "The cane toad. One of the most poisonous toads there is. Although *Phyllobates terribilis*—the golden poison arrow frog—would be a lot more decorative. Fascinating as cane toads are, there's no getting around the fact that most people call them ugly."

"You do realize it's all pretend, right?"

"Well, I know that." He gave me an irritated look. "That's no reason not to enjoy ourselves. I was just thinking. We've got an exhibit of the *Phyllobates terribilis* back at the zoo. I could bring a few of them along next time. Have conversations with them. Threaten to add to their number if people don't toe the line. Make the malefactors nervous."

Next time? Had I done too good a job of amusing him? What would Cordelia think if Grandfather decided to become a Ren Faire regular?

"Let's see how it goes this weekend," I said aloud. "For now, just sic one of the palace guards on anyone who's misbehaving."

"You're no fun," he grumbled. "Where do I get one of those?"

He was pointing at a tiny little girl eating a roasted turkey leg not much smaller than she was. I wondered if her parents had noticed that when not gnawing on it, she sometimes grew tired of holding it up and let it drag on the ground behind her.

"I assume you mean the turkey leg," I began.

"Yes, it looks much tastier than the toddler."

"Do you see the lute maker's shop?" I pointed down one of the curving lanes of tents and booths, at the end of which you could spot the shop in question, mainly because of all the lutes, guitars, citterns, violins, lyres, dulcimers, and harps dangling from its roof.

"They sell food there, too?" Grandfather asked.

"No, but if you walk down to the lute maker's shop, you

should be able to spot the turkey leg stall. Or take a deep breath and you'll smell it."

"Not really in period, you know," Grandfather pointed out. "*Meleagris gallopavo,* in either the wild or domestic variety, is native to the New World, not the old."

"But the Spanish started pillaging the New World in 1492," I said. "And turkeys were one of the things they brought back. William Strickland, a navigator who sailed with one of the Cabots, is supposed to have introduced them to England. In 1550 they gave him a coat of arms with a turkey on it."

"You just happened to know that?" He sounded almost impressed.

"No, I got tired of people saying the turkeys were anachronisms, so I did a little research on the subject. Of course, in England, it's unlikely that the common people would be eating turkey—they were a luxury item up until about the twentieth century. That's why it was such a big deal in *A Christmas Carol* when Scrooge brought the Cratchit family the prize turkey. But here in Albion, Good Queen Cordelia has helped encourage the turkey industry."

"Good for her." He didn't sound all that sincere. "I think I'll go sample one. See if they were worth encouraging."

He strode off, flourishing his raven-headed stick.

I wondered what time it was. One of these days, I'd pick up some kind of pendant watch that wouldn't scream "anachronism" if I pulled it out of my pocket in public. For the time being, I ducked behind something and sneaked a peek at my phone. One thirty.

If I set out now, and wasn't interrupted by too many people with crises along the way, I could pick up lunch, eat it somewhere quiet, and still get back to the forge in time for my two o'clock demonstration.

"Meg! There you are!"

Chapter 10

I turned to see the Italian ice cart bearing down on me, propelled by a very angry young serving wench.

"You've got to do something about that man!"

Well, I could always send one of the boys out to bring back lunch.

I wasn't surprised when "that man" turned out to be Terence. To my relief, he hadn't dropped anything down her low-cut blouse, pinched her rear, or committed any of the other kinds of sexual harassment we'd had to call him on during the first weekend. And I had to marvel at his ability to invent new ways to be obnoxious.

"He bought a lemon ice—actually bought it this time, and with real, modern money. But then he took one bite out of it and pretended to be poisoned."

"Good grief," I muttered. "Not again." He'd torpedoed mead sales the previous weekend by doing something similar in one of the taverns.

"So then he acts out this slow agonizing death, complete with multiple rounds of totally unrealistic convulsions, and at least three melodramatic deathbed statements. Oh, the tourists all laughed, of course, but do you think I've sold a single ice since then?"

"I'll talk to him."

Predictably, Terence managed to avoid me for the next half hour. Never mind. It wasn't as if he were a puppy, who had to be corrected immediately to have any chance of realizing what he'd done wrong. If anything, the fact that Terence was doing such a skillful job of avoiding me meant he knew he was in for a tongue-lashing. So maybe the longer he suffered the better.

My two o'clock demonstration went well—and it was particularly well attended because Cordelia came to watch, followed by a large crowd of tourists. Toward the end of the demonstration she took a hand in it.

"Prithee, Mistress Meg," she called out. "Dost thou see this blade?" She reached over to the sheath on her left wrist, pulled out the tiny jeweled stiletto, and held it up in a shaft of sun to make sure the glittering red stones embedded in the hilt caught the light. The tourists oohed and ahhed. I wondered if any of them could tell—or even suspected—that the stones were real garnets instead of the cubic zirconias, Swarovski crystals, or rhinestones most costumes sported.

"Ah." I pretended to examine the blade. "A fine weapon." I didn't know if she wanted the tourists to know it was my handiwork, so I didn't add "if I say so myself."

"Couldst thou make us another dagger to match? We'll make it worth thy while."

"Aye," I said. "Happy to serve Your Majesty." I handed the dagger back and she tucked it back in the wrist sheath—carefully, because unlike most of the weapons used in the Game, the stiletto had razor-sharp edges.

"Here's gold to seal the deal." She poured four or five shiny gold-colored disks into my gloved hand and closed my fingers around them before I could tell for sure whether she was handing out some of the fake pirate coins we used when money changed hands in the Game or whether she'd just given me enough real doubloons or sovereigns or whatever to fund the boys' college education.

I'd peek later. For now I sank into a deep curtsey.

"Thank you, Your Majesty."

She nodded and sailed off, followed by many—though

not all—of the tourists who'd followed her here. A satisfying number stayed for the wrap-up of my demo, or headed directly into the shop.

"Wonder why your grandmother suddenly needs a new dagger," Faulk said, sotto voce, as we were handling the flood of sales that followed.

"Maybe she's feeling more bloodthirsty than usual," Jamie suggested.

"Of course she is," I said. "She's got Terence *and* Grandfather on her hands. She needs to be prepared in case she has to deal with them both at once."

Faulk and the boys found that hilarious. I continued to wonder. Did she really want a new dagger? So she could have matching ones on both wrists, maybe? Was she starting some kind of storyline in the Game? Or did she just want a chance to show off a toy she was very fond of?

I'd ask her later.

The afternoon wore on. The boys insisted on surprising me with lunch, but fortunately they knew my likes and dislikes, so I happily munched on sausage on a stick, corn on the cob, a loaded baked potato, and a cherry limeade slushy.

"I hope this is an authentic Renaissance cherry limeade slushy," I said, frowning at it. "Not some modern fake version."

"We helped stomp the cherries and limes," Jamie said, deadpan. "By hand."

"Actually, by foot," Josh added. "Were you planning to eat that last bit of sausage or can I give it to Spike?"

Faulk did his 3:00 P.M. demonstration, which was nine parts talking to every part blacksmithing. Ordinarily I'd have given him a hard time about how lazy he was being, but after talking to Tad I held my tongue. And hoped he didn't hear the teenage tourist who said, "Maybe we should come back and see the lady blacksmith again. She actually does blacksmithing."

George, looking almost back to normal in his blue-and-white velvet substitute costume, was found to have a sign taped to the back of his doublet that read "Prithee, smite me with thy foot in the nether regions."

"I was wondering why Terence clapped me on the back and congratulated me," he said, when I called him over to the forge and removed the sign. He chuckled as he tucked the paper inside his doublet. If anyone else did that I'd wonder if he was planning to retaliate in kind. George was probably just going to take it home and put it in his scrapbook. "Fond memories of my summer at the Faire."

"I could tell him to lay off," I said aloud, stifling the uncharitable thought that George needed to grow a backbone.

"He wouldn't pay any attention," he said. "And it doesn't matter. Amused a few tourists, I expect. Ah, look—it's winging again!" He pointed upward.

Winging? I glanced up to see Gracie hovering in the sky above the grove. Well, I suppose "winging" covered it. I'd have just said it was flying. Evidently Greg was doing some kind of demonstration.

"I love watching the eagles fly," George mused.

"Eagles?" Jamie hurried out. "Where?"

George pointed up at Gracie.

"That's a peregrine falcon," I said. "Not an eagle. No eagles there that I've seen."

"Ah. Good to know." He didn't sound as if he thought the difference all that important. He watched placidly as Gracie descended out of sight. "I still like watching him."

"Her, actually," I pointed out.

"Was it Gracie?" Josh stuck his head out of the forge and peered upward. "Too bad I missed her."

"Don't worry." George was still gazing upward. "He—er, she'll be back. The falcon always wings twice. See! There she is again!"

"He," I said. "That's Harry. Different bird. In fact, different species—he's a red-tailed hawk."

"Really?" George shaded his eyes and peered upward as Harry flew in graceful, leisurely circles. "They all look the same to me. I just like watching them. So free. I could watch them forever, except I think I should be going soon." He reached inside his doublet and pulled out a pendant watch so precisely the kind I wanted that I couldn't decide whether to ask him where he'd bought it or keep my mouth shut and pick his pocket.

"Yes, time for me to run along," he said. "They're expecting me at the Dragon's Claw."

With that he hurried off. Well, for him it was hurrying. In any of the other actors it would have been sauntering.

"He's kind of dim, isn't he?" Josh said. "Mistaking Gracie for an eagle."

"Not everyone has ornithologists in their family," I said.

"And he's such a wimp," Josh added.

"Josh, you know better," I warned.

"Okay, I shouldn't call him names," Josh said. "But why does he let Sir Terence pick on him so much?"

"And act like it doesn't even bother him?" Jamie added.

"Maybe it doesn't bother him," I said. "Maybe he thinks Sir Terence's pranks are funny. Or maybe he's figured out that it really annoys Sir Terence when you don't even react to the pranks."

The boys looked thoughtful at that last idea.

"Maybe he's not so dim," Jamie said.

"Maybe," Josh said. "He still needs to get a clue about birds."

Behind the shop, Spike erupted into frantic barking. But we heard no cursing and no yelps of pain, so we weren't surprised when Michael came in through the back of the shop.

"How goes it?" he asked.

"See what I made?" Jamie held up the wrought iron leaf that had been his part of my latest demonstration.

"Oh, really practical," Josh said. "Faulk showed me how to make this." He held up a utilitarian and highly functional pothook.

"All in all, it's going well," I said. "In fact—bother. Can you guys watch the shop? I just spotted Terence, and I need to talk to him." I pulled off my leather apron, threw it onto the hook, and ran in the direction I'd seen Terence going.

"What's he done now?" Michael had come after me, and his longer legs made it easy for him to catch up with me.

"Pretended to be poisoned again. And now he's going to pretend not to understand why I'm mad at him—but if he doesn't have a guilty conscience, why has he been avoiding me all afternoon? And damn! He's given me the slip again."

Michael, who had half a foot of height on me, was craning his neck.

"I see him." He pointed to the right. "Over by the Dragon's Claw."

By the time we drew near, Terence was obviously in the process of gathering a crowd so he could stage a scene. But scenes normally required more than one actor, and so far no one had stepped up to join him.

That didn't seem to discourage Terence.

"Harken, my good friends!" Terence bellowed. "I have glad tidings!"

The tourists were crowding around with looks of eager anticipation. Yes, for all his faults, Terence was a crowd pleaser. A few fellow players of the Game began drifting nearer and joining the crowd but their expressions were less joyful. They ranged the gamut from mild annoyance on Michael's face through resigned tolerance on George's to something unnervingly close to panic and dread on Dianne's. I made a mental note to take her aside and find out if anything was wrong.

Michael had taken up a place at the edge of the crowd, but behind a lot of fairly short people, so he had a good view while being less likely to be drawn into whatever was about to happen. I joined him, and we watched as Terence paced up and down, preening, joking, and waiting for his audience to reach its peak. He flourished his snake-headed cane with such expertise that I wondered if he'd ever taken lessons in baton twirling.

"What's he up to?" I kept my voice low enough that only the nearest tourists could have heard, even if they weren't all focused on Terence.

"No idea," Michael said. "Last time I heard, the plan for the day was still for him to sow ill will between me and George by reporting insulting things we'd supposedly said about each other."

"Leading to the dramatic scene when someone reveals his nefarious plot just in time to stop the sword fight between you and George. Yes, that's what I thought we were doing."

"But if that's what he's up to, he should be talking to George. Or me. Not the crowd." Michael frowned at Terence—and made no effort to hide it. After all, Duke Michael and Sir Terence were bitter enemies in the Game. And not all that chummy out of it these days.

Grandfather strode up to stand beside us.

"What's that jackass up to now?" he asked, his voice almost soft enough to make the question discreet.

I shrugged. Michael was focused on Terence, poised to jump into the Game if needed. Jacks and Dianne appeared to be lurking nearby, no doubt for the same reason.

Nobody trusted Terence.

Chapter 11

Just then Nigel came strolling along. He paused when he saw Terence, seeming surprised and just a little uneasy.

"Ah, methinks I see the good Sir Nigel!" Terence exclaimed. "Well met, reverend sir."

Nigel looked anxious—or was it annoyed? The "reverend sir" was a bit much. Terence was only a few years younger than Nigel, although he didn't look his age, while Nigel looked every minute of his and then some.

"Good morrow." Nigel's voice suggested that it really wasn't, though that could be remedied if only he could escape Terence's clutches. Then again, maybe I was reading my own emotions into his brusque, guarded tone. Still, he stepped forward so he was in the open space near Terence, ready to play his part in the Game.

"With your permission, good sir, I will share the joyous tidings." Terence beamed at Nigel, who sighed and visibly braced himself. "The gracious Sir Nigel has at last harkened to my pleadings. He has agreed to grant me the hand of his only child, the beautiful Lady Dianne! Wish me joy, my friends!"

The tourists all clapped, and a few of them shouted "huzzah" in the approved Ren Faire fashion.

"Bloody hell," Michael murmured.

After turning in a circle so all the assembled tourists could see his beaming face, Terence turned his gaze on Dianne. Who shrank behind Nigel.

"Now, now, my sweet!" Terence exclaimed. "No need

to hide our love any longer. Your father has blessed our match. Is't not so Sir Nigel?"

"Er . . ." Nigel looked briefly thrown. Then he rallied. "He hath, my lords, wrung from me my slow leave by laboursome petition, and at last upon his will I seal'd my hard consent."

The words sounded familiar—a quote from some play Nigel had been in, I assumed—dredged out of memory to keep from being left speechless.

"*Hamlet,*" Michael muttered, as if reading my mind. "Polonius."

Terence reacted as if Nigel's words had been a ringing endorsement.

"There you have it!" he exclaimed. "So come, my pretty—let's have a kiss to seal the bargain."

Terence had only taken a step or two toward Dianne when she turned and fled, shoving aside any tourist unlucky enough to be in her way. The audience erupted in laughter. Terence pretended to be crestfallen.

"Alas!" he soliloquized. "My lady love flees me. Have I mistaken courtesy for love? But no! She is merely shy. It will be quite different when we are free from prying eyes."

He leered so obviously that the audience began laughing again.

Michael and I exchanged a glance, and I could see that he had the same worries I did. Being betrothed to Dianne in the Game would give Terence much more opportunity to interact with her. More excuses to put his arm around her shoulders or waist. To beg her for a kiss.

To harass her. So far his behavior toward Dianne hadn't crossed the line—at least not that I'd seen or heard about. But what he was apt to get up to in the Game under cover of being Dianne's betrothed—or, worse, her husband—

"We need to break this up," I muttered to Michael.

He nodded. So, for that matter, did Grandfather.

"But for now—Father!" Terence trilled. "May I anticipate the happy event and call you by that blessed name?"

"As your lordship pleases." No mistaking the hostility in Nigel's voice.

"Let us seal the bargain, then!" Terence turned and took a few steps into the audience, who parted as if by magic. He reached one of the small tables belonging to the nearby Dragon's Claw, picked up a waiting pair of ornate pewter goblets, and hurried back to Nigel's side.

"A toast!" Terence said, handing Nigel one of the goblets. "To the coming union of our families!"

Nigel rolled his eyes slightly and lifted the goblet. Then his eyes widened.

"This is mead!" He held the goblet at arm's length as if it contained a deadly poison—which was exactly what it was from his point of view.

"Yes—a draught of honey wine, to celebrate the coming honeymoon. But what is this—you scorn my draught? Is't thus you treat your son-to-be?"

Terence put on the hurt expression of a small child who has just been told his dog died. The tourists were frowning at Nigel, and a murmur of discontent began rising from the crowd.

"Really rude," I heard one woman say.

"Come on, toast with him," someone else called.

"We have to do something," I whispered to Michael. He nodded and frowned, no doubt plotting how best to intervene.

"What's the big deal?" Grandfather muttered.

"Recovering alcoholic," I muttered back. "One drink could cause a relapse. Michael, let's—"

"Beware!" Grandfather shouted as he shoved through the crowd.

Michael had taken a few steps forward to enter the scene, but Grandfather beat him to it. He strode toward Terence and Nigel, holding his raven staff up before him, his black robe billowing behind and casting sparkles around the clearing as the sunlight bounced off the various faux jewels and silver-colored cabalistic devices sewn onto it.

He grabbed Nigel's goblet and sniffed at its contents. He waved one hand over the mouth of the goblet and made some strange and complicated finger movements.

"*Danaus plexippus,*" he intoned. "*Quercus stellata. Microstegium vimineum!*"

The last bit of Latin seemed to do the trick. He jerked back as if he spotted something dangerous in the goblet. Then he nodded, his expression grim.

"You didn't drink any of this did you?" he demanded, turning to Nigel.

Nigel shook his head.

"A lucky escape," Grandfather said. "It would have been the death of you. There's deadly poison in this goblet! And you, sir—" He whirled to scowl at Terence. "What is the meaning of this? Were you trying to poison Sir Nigel?"

"Not I, sir." Terence pretended shock. "I handed him one of the two goblets at random. Why, I could just as easily have drunk from it myself! And I left them there on the table—someone else could have tampered with it."

"With it?" Grandfather asked. "Or with them? Let me see yours." He gave Nigel's goblet to Michael, who was at his elbow now. Then Grandfather held out his hand, and Terence obediently handed over his goblet. Grandfather sniffed it, and looked thoughtful.

"Curious. Not poison, this. But still—it has the stink of magic about it. I must take these back to my laboratory and study them."

"I'll fetch more mead for our toast," Terence said.

"No!" We all whirled to see Rose Noire standing at the edge of the circle with her arms thrust skyward, holding a crystal ball in one hand and a flowering branch in the other. "You must not toast this union today. The stars are completely unfavorable. If you value their lives—and your own—you must shun the company of your fiancée and her father until the danger is past!"

Normally Rose Noire looked about as menacing as a week-old kitten. But clearly she'd gotten into her part as the sorceress uttering dire prophecies and was channeling Circe, Medea, and Macbeth's three weird sisters. Her hair was twice as frizzy as usual and surrounded her face like a truncated halo. And her eyes glowed with a fierce passion normally only seen when people pooh-poohed the medicinal effectiveness of essential oils.

Terence was momentarily taken aback. Then he recovered and gave a laugh that wasn't quite convincing.

"Nonsense," he said. "I do not fear the stars! If—"

"Sir Terence."

Cordelia had arrived, and her tone of quiet command had stilled Terence. In fact, it had stilled the entire crowd. Michael hastily made an elaborate, low bow. I made the deepest possible curtsey. The entire crowd followed our example, actors and tourists alike. Terence's bow was especially protracted, as if he welcomed the chance to avoid her eyes.

"Will someone tell us what is afoot in our kingdom now?" Cordelia asked.

Nigel's jaw set and he favored Terence with a dark look. Terence assumed a look of innocent curiosity.

Michael stepped forward.

"Your Majesty, Sir Terence just announced the news of his betrothal to Lady Dianne—news I assume you already know, since it is customary for you to be consulted on any such proposed alliance between your nobles."

I wanted to call out "Well improvised!" But now was not the time, so I merely put my hand over my mouth to hide my sudden grin.

Cordelia didn't even try to hide her smile, though she did manage to make it seem rather menacing.

"Indeed." She turned her eyes on Terence and studied him for a few moments with much the same expression you'd expect to see if she'd found a slug in her salad.

"His Grace the Duke of Waterston makes an excellent point," she said. "We always take the keenest interest in the matrimonial plans of our nobles. And we do not recall being consulted on this *proposed* alliance."

Terence winced slightly at her emphasis on "proposed."

"Your Majesty," he began.

"We will let you know our pleasure in the matter once we have had ample opportunity to consider it." Cordelia stared at him and he dropped into another obsequiously deep bow. "Sir Nigel, you will send your daughter to us, that we may know her mind."

"Yes, Your Majesty," Nigel said.

"Your—" Terence began.

"You have our leave to go." She stared at him until he got the message and bowed, murmuring apologies. Cordelia watched Terence slink away, then turned on her heel and stalked away in her most imperious manner.

I noticed that Grandfather was looking discontented—no doubt he felt Cordelia had stolen his thunder.

"Well done, Magister Blake," I called out. "If not for your quick action, Sir Nigel might be dead by now."

"Yes, well done!" Michael echoed. We led a round of applause for Grandfather, and then one for Rose Noire, who dropped a curtsey and hurried back to her booth.

"And I will inform Her Majesty what I learn from studying the contents of these goblets," Grandfather announced. "Come! To my laboratory!"

Chapter 12

While the tourists applauded—a few even cheered—Grandfather came over and handed Terence's goblet to Michael.

"Just where is my laboratory, anyway?" he asked, sotto voce.

"How about Dad's first aid tent?" I suggested.

"As good as anyplace. At least I think I know where that is. Bring the mead." He strode off—luckily in the right direction—and Michael and I trailed along.

Dad had never been entirely happy with the somewhat anachronistic banner flying above his tent, which bore a red cross on a white field and the words Ye First Aide Pavilion.

"You do realize that the Red Cross symbol wasn't even invented until 1864, don't you?" he'd protested.

But after resigning himself to Cordelia's ruling—"we have to give people some clue where to go for medical emergencies"—he'd consoled himself by hanging an articulated skeleton to the left of the entrance and a flea-bitten stuffed badger to the right. And at least the banner made it easy to spot the first aid tent from afar.

When we reached it, I lifted the tent flap and peered inside before we entered, in case Dad had an actual patient. But the only person there was Rose Noire, who seemed to be filling him in on the recent contretemps.

"And I have no idea what he was about to do when—Here they are!" Rose Noire turned and beamed at us.

"I hear you and Rose Noire saved the day," Dad said to Grandfather.

"Couldn't just stand by and do nothing." Grandfather preened slightly at the praise.

"Just how did you know to show up?" I asked Rose Noire.

"Dianne ran in and asked if she could hide in my tent," she said. "And when I heard what was happening, I sent Josh to fetch your grandmother and went to see if I could help."

"Is she still in your tent?" Michael asked.

Rose Noire nodded.

"Let's let her stay there for a while," I said. "I'll let Cordelia know where she is."

"Just what were those Latin incantations you made over the goblets?" Michael asked Grandfather, before he could start feeling neglected.

"*Danaus plexippus. Quercus stellata. Microstegium vimineum!*" he repeated. "The scientific names for the monarch butterfly, the post oak, and Japanese stilt grass."

"Ingenious!" Dad exclaimed. "Using your knowledge of Linnaean taxonomy to play your part as the alchemist."

"It seemed to do the trick. Cheers." Grandfather had reclaimed one of the goblets Michael had been carrying. He lifted the goblet and took a healthy sip of mead. "Ah! Good stuff."

"But not something Nigel should be consuming," Dad said. "Even if it's done under duress, breaking a long, successful period of sobriety could have serious physical and psychological effects."

"You're preaching to the choir," I said. "Michael and I saw what happened with Nigel a year or so ago, when someone talked him into joining a champagne toast. But if you want to go and try getting Terence to understand what a heinous thing he was doing, be my guest."

"I'm going to put him on probation," Michael said. "I'll

go and clear it with Cordelia, to make sure she's okay with it—"

"I can't imagine that she wouldn't be," I said. "But good to present a united front when he complains."

"And if he does anything else to threaten Nigel's well-being, he's out on his ear," Michael went on.

"Or if he bothers Dianne again," Rose Noire put in. "From what she told me, he hasn't exactly done anything that crossed the line into something reportable, but . . ."

"But I bet he's always hanging out just on the safe side of that line," I put in. "So the accumulated effect is that she feels harassed."

Rose Noire nodded.

"Staying away from Dianne should be part of his probation," I said.

"I'll go find Cordelia." Michael strode out.

"Can I go back to Dianne?" Rose Noire asked. "She's upset. I don't want to leave her alone for long."

"Of course," I said. "Fill her in on what's happening. And reassure her that the Game can limp along just fine without her until we settle Terence's hash."

Jacks burst into the tent, her normally cheerful, ruddy face looking stormy.

"Where is she?"

"If you mean Dianne, she's hiding next door in my tent," Rose Noire said. "I'll go check on her." She slipped out through the side entrance that led to her tent.

"I should never have left her alone," Jacks said.

"Has Terence's behavior been so bad that she needed that kind of protection?" I asked. "Because if that's the case, we need to hear about it. Michael and Cordelia and I, that is—so we can deal with it." For that matter, if it had gotten that bad, why hadn't we heard about it already?

"Well. If you ask me—" Jacks frowned and thought for a moment before continuing. "By my standards, nothing I've seen was that bad—but I'm a tough old bird. I came up in times when nobody even paid lip service to a woman's right not to be harassed. Terence's behavior seems to have come as a shock to her. I don't know what he might have gotten up to when I wasn't around. Even if all he's done is what I've seen, I expect the cumulative effect has been pretty awful."

Michael appeared in the tent's entrance.

"Her Majesty," he announced, then stepped aside and bowed. Cordelia strode in. We all bowed or curtseyed for the benefit of the large crowd of tourists who were trailing along behind Cordelia—well, all except Grandfather, but even he waved his raven-headed staff in what could be interpreted as a salute. Then Michael dropped the tent flap closed and we all returned to the twenty-first century.

"Michael says he wants to put Terence on probation," she said. "Is there any reason we can't just fire him?"

"Hell, no," Grandfather said. "I say can him immediately. Escort him off the mountain and tell him he'll be arrested for trespassing if he so much as sets foot here again."

He took a generous swig of mead and sat back, arms folded, satisfied that he'd given his opinion, and it was up to us lesser mortals to execute his idea.

Cordelia looked puzzled, as if unsure whether to resent his presumption or marvel at finding herself, however briefly, in harmony with his point of view.

"We can probably fire him," Michael said. "But if we did it immediately, without giving him a chance to clean up his act—or even tell his side of the story—I'd be afraid he'd come back and try to sue us for wrongful termination."

"I don't think he'd win," Cordelia said.

"No, he probably wouldn't," Michael agreed. "But even losing, he could cost us a lot of time and money. So let's put him on probation. Maybe he'll shape up. In case he doesn't, let's talk to a lawyer as soon as possible about exactly what we need to do to fire him without causing ourselves problems."

"Pretty sure we have at least one lawyer in the family who specializes in employment law." I pulled out my phone. "Let me see if Mother can round one up who can call you for a quick consultation."

"I like that idea." Cordelia's fierce smile was back. I began typing a text to Mother. "Though Michael seems to have a rather good idea how we should proceed."

"Unfortunately, being part of the Drama Department's management team has given me a lot of experience with employment law," Michael said. "It would have been nice if we'd formally reprimanded him for a few of his past offenses—"

"Reprimanding Terence has become one of my main summer pastimes," Cordelia said. "Of course, I did it privately, so as not to cause him undue embarrassment."

"Did you happen to document any of those reprimands?" Michael sounded guardedly optimistic. "In writing, I mean."

"Yes, with a memo to his personnel file," she said. "And gave him a copy of each of the memos. At least five of them, if memory serves—one on refraining from inappropriate conduct with or in the presence of tourists, two on things he did to Dianne, and two on stuff he did to poor George. I know George always says it's all fine and he doesn't want to make waves, but there's a limit."

"Excellent," Michael said. "Then we can do a formal probation memo and cite however many previous reprimands you have on file."

"God, I hate bureaucracy." Grandfather sounded slightly hollow, since he still had his nose in the mead goblet.

"And part of Terence's probation is that he doesn't go anywhere near Dianne or Nigel," Michael said. "We can work around it in the Game."

"Yes," I said. "He needs to behave as if both of them have a restraining order against him. Odds are life has already acquainted him with how those work, but if it hasn't, Horace can explain it to him."

"Hell, I'll ask Chief Heedles to come up and explain it to him," Cordelia said. "I've seen her put the fear of God into a trio of intoxicated biker dudes. Remind me, where's he sleeping?"

"Down in Camp Anachronism," Jacks said. "Most of us players are down there—including Dianne."

"Camp Anachronism?" Grandfather echoed.

"The regular camping grounds," I explained. "Where you can let your hair down and revel in the modern amenities you've been doing without all day."

"Where we set up your tent," Dad added.

"Ah." Grandfather nodded. "Are there other camping grounds? Ones where you stay in character and do everything authentically?"

"Yes, but they're full up," I said quickly. Clearly Grandfather was getting way too enthusiastic about Ren Faire living.

"In fact, there's a waiting list for them," Cordelia added. "Maybe we should move Terence up here to the house."

"Wouldn't that be rewarding him for his misbehavior?" Jacks asked. "Why not move Dianne up here?"

"Because the only free room we have is a storage room that housed a scullery maid in less enlightened times," Cordelia said. "I could see stuffing Terence into it, but I wouldn't inflict it on Dianne. It's dank, windowless, badly ventilated, and smaller than most modern prison cells."

"And infested with camel crickets," I reminded her. "Hundreds of them."

"I withdraw the suggestion." Jacks shuddered.

"We could have another go at cleaning out the crickets," Cordelia said. "If anyone feels like bothering."

"We could," I said. "I seem to remember that it usually

takes a day or two before they come back in any real numbers. And if I'm wrong about that—well, he won't be lonely."

"May I just say 'ick'?" Jacks shuddered.

"We'll consider that an option, depending on what he has to say for himself." Cordelia reached into one of her hidden—and probably anachronistic—pockets and pulled out her gold pocket watch. "First I'll talk to Dianne. And I'd like to deal with Terence before I preside over the jousting at four. Can someone find him and drag him up to my office?"

"I'm on it," Michael said.

"Me too," I said. "And I'll enlist the palace guard."

"If I see him and can restrain the urge to throttle him, I'll deliver him," Jacks said.

"I'll go out and look for him." Grandfather drained his goblet and stood. "If he refuses to come with me, I'll threaten to turn him into a toad."

"You have your missions," Cordelia said. "Make it so!"

Chapter 13

We fanned out through the fairgrounds, enlisting other actors and staff as we encountered them, so within a quarter of an hour, nearly everyone who wasn't a tourist was looking for Terence. To my surprise, it was Grandfather who succeeded in rounding him up—while making a sweep past the porta-potties, I ran into Terence marching along at the point of Grandfather's staff. Terence laughed and waved his own staff when he saw me.

"Seems I've been taken captive by this rather intimidating character." Terence sounded amused.

"Keep walking." Grandfather tapped him in the back with the staff, not all that gently.

"Good," I said. "Cordelia is eager to see you."

"Cordelia?" Suddenly Terence looked a lot less cheerful, and glanced around as if thinking of bolting.

"Yes. Cordelia." I took his arm in what I hoped was a casual manner. But escaping from a blacksmith's grip isn't that easy, and if he thought Grandfather was a helpless old dodderer—or that he would be afraid to use the staff—he was badly mistaken.

And besides, Terence had an image to maintain. He recovered his composure and continued nodding and smiling at the tourists until we were safely inside the house.

Someone must have called ahead to warn Cordelia. She was waiting for us in the Great Hall.

"Mr. Cox." She sounded cool and calm. I knew that was a sign of how very angry she was. "We have a few things to discuss. In my office, please."

She turned on her heel and marched off. Assuming he'd follow? Or maybe trusting that Grandfather and I could deliver him. Probably the latter. We followed them downstairs and along the hall. Grandfather kept the staff pressed into the small of Terence's back until he was on the threshold of Cordelia's office. I tagged along at the end of the procession and watched as the door shut behind the two of them—though not before Cordelia glanced at me in what I knew was a wordless request to stick around in case she needed me.

"Well, that's taken care of." Grandfather nodded in satisfaction. "I think we should celebrate his capture. Do they sell that excellent mead at all of the taverns?"

"They do," I said. "But I'll take a rain check. I'm going to wait here to see if Cordelia has anything that needs doing after she talks to Terence."

"Like escorting him off the mountain." He nodded. "Call me if you need backup."

He stumped off, whacking his staff against the floor with every other step.

Peace and quiet descended over the corridor. I could hear the music coming from the Faire—something with bagpipes—but very faintly. Down the hall, from the half-open door of the jewelry studio, I could hear the clicking of Tad's computer keys and the occasional squeak as he got up and walked over that loose floorboard. I scribbled an item in my notebook to ask Cordelia's handyman if there was anything he could do to fix it. The laundry rooms were silent—had the crew finished for the day or were they just taking a meal break?

Either way it was blissfully peaceful. From behind the door to Cordelia's office I heard a low hum of voices. Mostly her voice. Of course. She wouldn't yell at him. She'd just make it absolutely clear that he had to shape up or ship out. I couldn't make out the words, but I could imagine them. I didn't ever want her that angry at me.

I sat down on the lowest step of the stairs that led up to the main floor, far enough away that it wouldn't look as if I were trying to eavesdrop if they came out and saw me. My brain was teeming with a million things I could be doing if I wasn't here waiting to help deal with Terence. But this was important, too. I focused on taking the sort of calming yoga breaths Rose Noire would probably be nagging me to do if she were here, and watched the dust motes dance over a patch of sunlight that made a patch of gold on the oak floor of the hallway.

After about fifteen minutes, Terence stepped out into the hall again. He was holding a sheet of paper and wore a dazed expression.

Cordelia followed him out of her office, closing and locking the door behind her. Then she glanced up and saw me.

"Mr. Cox has been notified that any further infractions on his part will result in the termination of his employment." Her tone was crisp and businesslike. "If you become aware that he has caused any more problems, please take appropriate action on my behalf."

With that she strode down the hall and climbed briskly up the stairs. Terence's gaze followed her, and if looks could kill, she'd never have made it to the main floor. The naked anger on his face shook me—did he not realize I was there, or just not care if I saw his expression? When she was out of sight he stood in the middle of the hallway for a few moments, glancing down at the piece of paper in his hand.

I pulled my phone out of my pocket and checked the time.

"Joust starts in fifteen minutes," I said. "If you're going." The joust drew the biggest crowds of any event at the Faire, and we usually managed to set at least one scene in the Game there—today, presumably, a public clash between Michael and George. Terence would normally be a major player in that.

"Yeah." He nodded, not looking at me. "Give me a minute."

I nodded. As far as I was concerned, he could have an hour. In fact, if he decided to go and sulk in his tent for the rest of the day, I was fine with it. Michael and George could manage their confrontation without him. I turned and began climbing the stairs.

About halfway up, I heard something downstairs—a shout? Several shouts. I headed back downstairs again, a lot more briskly than I'd gone up.

The shouting came from the jewelry studio.

"This is fabulous!" Terence was exclaiming. "You've got your whole little video studio set up here!"

"Get out!" Tad shouted.

I started running.

When I burst into the room, I saw Terence preening in front of the green screen and admiring himself on the side monitor. Tad's laptop screen was filled with the frowning face of a pudgy middle-aged man in a white shirt and red tie.

"Tad?" came a voice from the computer. "Who is this person? What's he doing in your office? And why he is wearing those weird clothes?"

Tad didn't answer. He was sitting on the floor with his head in his hands.

"Wow!" Terence said. "Tad, if I didn't know better, I'd think we were in your office! Where is he—is he down the hall in another studio?" He pointed at the laptop.

"What the hell is going on," said the face on the laptop screen. The face that was looming closer to the camera in his own laptop, presumably with the misguided idea that if he got close enough he could see more of what was going on at the other end. "Tad? Where are you?"

"You're going to be amazed," Terence said. "You thought Tad was back in his office, right? He's not. He's down here at the Riverton Renaissance Festival, and—"

I'd started across the studio when I realized what was going on, and that was when I got close enough to hit the laptop's power button and slam down the lid.

"Why'd you do that?" Terence asked. "We were just having a little fun. I bet—"

"Get out!" I pointed to the door.

Tad's phone was ringing. He was looking at it.

"My boss," he said.

"Out!" I shouted again, right in Terence's face.

"Aw, come on," Terence said. "I want to see—"

I grabbed his arm, dragged him out of the studio, and slammed the door. Terence collapsed against the opposite wall, laughing. No, make that giggling.

I pulled out my phone and called Horace.

"What's up, Meg? Aren't you coming to the joust?"

"I need you and your partner at Cordelia's office ASAP."

"Roger."

He hung up. I put my phone away, crossed my arms, and stared at Terence.

He went on laughing for a while. At first I assumed his over-the-top hilarity was a reaction to the stress of getting chewed out by Cordelia. But after a while I decided he was deliberately prolonging his laughter to avoid talking to me. It had begun to seem less natural. And he was sneaking in glances at me.

Eventually his laughter trailed off. He wiped his eyes.

"Sorry," he said. "But I couldn't help it. The look in his eyes when I stepped in front of his green screen and blew his cover."

I just kept staring. His smile gradually faded.

"You think maybe I should go in and um . . . see if he's okay?"

I said nothing.

"Maybe I should apologize?" Terence ventured.

Just then I heard running steps on the stairs. Horace and Lenny, the Riverton deputy, came down the steps two at a time. Which wasn't all that safe, since they were still carrying their bardiches. I'd take them to task about it later. Terence would probably be amused if I said anything like "haven't I told you a million times not to run with bardiches?" And amusing Terence was not on the list of things I wanted to do right now.

"Meg, what's wrong?" Horace asked.

"Seize that wretch and put him in the stocks." I pointed to Terence.

They hesitated, standing with their jaws open.

"Oh, very funny," Terence said.

"Queen Cordelia's orders." I ignored him and focused on Horace and the other officer.

"Nonsense," Terence scoffed. "She's not even here."

"No." I turned back to him. "But before she left, she told me that if you caused any more problems, I should do whatever I thought we needed to do to handle the situation. What you just did to Tad is definitely a problem."

"But I was only kidding!" Terence protested. "I offered to apologize."

"You're always kidding," I said. "And you always apologize when we call you on it. That doesn't make it okay."

"This is ridiculous," Terence said. "I was only pranking him. I thought his whole setup was pretty ingenious. How was I supposed to know his boss has no sense of humor? And he was lying to his boss, right? So it's not as if he's innocent. You're not going to put me in the stocks for that." A sudden thought hit him. "And you've got no authority to lock me up."

"No." My voice had gone very quiet, and realized I sounded a lot like Cordelia. "But we have the power to kick you off the premises. It's either the stocks or the highway. You've been repeatedly harassing Dianne and deliberately causing as much trouble as you can for everyone else. I heard Cordelia tell you she wanted you on your best behavior, and what you did to Tad just now makes me wonder if you have any idea what that means. So you have a choice. You can sit in the stocks—you know perfectly well we don't actually lock them, but we will have a guard to see that you stay put so we don't have to worry about you causing any more problems today. Or you can pack up your stuff, collect your last paycheck, and leave right now."

"But—" He stopped, looking stricken, glanced at the palace guards, then blurted out, "But where am I supposed to go?"

I suddenly remembered what Michael had said about Terence after the first weekend of the Faire, when I'd asked him why he'd hired someone who was such a jerk.

"He needs a break," Michael had said. "His girlfriend just kicked him out of the apartment they've been sharing, and I'm sure she had good reason, but he can't afford a new place at the moment because he just lost a lucrative commercial gig that's been keeping him afloat the last couple of years. So yeah, he's a bit of a jerk, but he's in a jam, and he's good at this kind of performing, and the fact that we're rescuing him from sleeping in the streets might make him tone it down a bit."

Okay, the part about toning it down hadn't worked out. But from the look of desperation on Terence's face, I gathered Michael hadn't exaggerated the rest of it.

"For now, you go to the stocks." I kept my tone gentle, but firm. "You'll still be in the Game—still earning your pay. And anyone who wants to interact with you can drop by there."

"And after that?"

"That's ultimately up to Cordelia. We can't very well thrash this out with hundreds of tourists eavesdropping. Behave yourself for the rest of the day, and after the Faire closes we'll see what we can work out."

He nodded glumly.

I gestured to Horace and the other palace guard. They stepped forward and arranged themselves on either side of him. Terence took a breath, then raised his chin and began to march toward the stairway. Anyone who saw him would think he was perfectly fine, unless they noticed how tightly he was clutching his snake-headed staff—so tightly that his knuckles were white.

I actually felt a little sorry for him, but I kept my face stern. It would be just like Terence to look around to see if I was softening.

When he and the guards had disappeared up the stairs, I slumped against the wall and let out a breath in relief.

Behind me I heard slow clapping. I turned to see Tad.

Chapter 14

"Good riddance," Tad said. "If you ask me, you should lock him in the stocks and throw away the key."

"Is your boss still furious?"

"He's now officially my ex-boss, and since he just now blocked my number, yeah, pretty sure he is." He laughed humorlessly. "Blocking me. The swine! He wouldn't even know how to do that if I hadn't taught him."

"Give him the weekend to calm down."

"He won't." Tad was pressing the heel of his hand to his forehead as if feeling the onset of a headache. "He already had Human Resources call me with orders to drive up there right now to turn in my ID card and collect my stuff."

"Right now?" I pulled out my phone and checked the time. "That'd take two hours without traffic, and it's almost four o'clock, which means it's already rush hour. They'd be closed by the time you got there—or do they plan to stay there until you arrive?"

"He ordered them to, but I told them don't bother. He's not my boss anymore, so he doesn't get to tell me what to do with my weekend. Monday will be soon enough." He closed his eyes, took a deep breath, then opened them again. "I should go tell Faulk."

He straightened up and went back into the studio. I followed him and watched as he donned his red, green, and gold velvet robe, his white turban, and the jeweled belt that supported his scimitar—although since Tad wasn't a qualified swordsman, it was actually only a fancy crescent-shaped leather scabbard with a fake scimitar hilt at the top.

I wasn't sure whether his outfit was all utterly authentic or whether Mother, who'd designed it, had allowed herself to be influenced by Tad 's vision of what the well-dressed Moorish ambassador to the court of Albion would wear. All I knew was that Tad looked quite striking in it, and normally he was one of the few players in the Game who could rival Michael in swashbuckling and drama. Today he seemed completely dispirited.

"I've seen corpses livelier than you are right now," I said aloud.

"I blew it." He fiddled with the sleeves of his robe in a pale echo of the preening he normally did when he put on his dramatic—and flattering—costume. "And I didn't just blow it for me—I blew it for Faulk."

"You had some help from Terence," I said. "Look—talk to Dad. See what he recommends."

If all Faulk needed was a therapist, I was sure we could solve this. Dad might know someone willing to do a little pro bono work. For that matter we probably had a few therapists in the family—I'd see if Mother could find one willing to give Faulk a steep family-friend discount. Not that I was going to say that to Tad until we had something lined up. And not that help from a family shrink could replace having health insurance in the long term. But I could reassure him a little.

It didn't seem to be working. He shook his head almost imperceptibly.

"Look, the problem's not insoluble," I said. "You've been trying to do it alone—well, just you and Faulk. Time you let your friends in on what's happening. See what we can do to help."

"Thanks." He smiled, ever so slightly. It was a grateful smile, but it didn't look like a hopeful one.

"I should go," I said. "Put in at least a token appearance at the joust."

"Yeah." He visibly straightened his spine. "I'll go break

the news to Faulk. You'll probably see me hanging around your booth a lot—assuming he doesn't tell me to go to hell."

He trudged out, shoulders drooping.

I stayed behind long enough to turn off his equipment—at least the parts of it whose off buttons I could locate—and lock up the studio so everything would still be there when he returned.

The jousting was over by the time I reached the edge of the large, open field where we held it, and I could see from afar that Cordelia was handing out large red and black rosettes to the winners. I found Grandfather ambling away from the field with a discontented look on his face.

"Well, that was a disappointment," he said. "Not real jousting at all."

"What do you mean, not real jousting?" I choked back a sudden surge of irritation—a little of it at him, but most of it at Terence, so it wasn't fair to let fly at Grandfather.

"They don't actually aim at each other," he grumbled. "They go one at a time and aim at this little ring dangling on a string."

"Do you have any idea how hard that is?" I couldn't help it—my voice got louder. "How hard it is to ride so steadily and aim so exactly that you can spear something the size of an embroidery hoop—or maybe even a curtain ring—dangling on a string, when you're going thirty miles per hour? Do you know how long it takes to train the horse to do that? To learn to do it yourself? But I suppose nothing will suit you unless there's a chance you'll see blood. Human predators, that's all you want."

He cocked his head to one side.

"What's got you so upset?" he asked. "I know I annoy you sometimes, but I don't think you can blame the mood you're in right now on me. Haven't seen you for an hour or so."

"Long story," I said. "I'll fill you in later."

He harrumphed and stalked off in the direction of the falcons. I was heading in the opposite direction, toward the area just inside the entrance that we'd defined as the town square—that was where we'd put the stocks. I was almost there when my phone rang. Vibrated, actually, since none of the sounds I could program it to make sounded like anything that would normally emanate from the wardrobe of a woman of the sixteenth century. The Muddy Beggar's phone produced a variety of belches, farts, and raspberries, but I had no desire to emulate him.

I ducked into a sheltered area behind Madame Destiny's tent before pulling out my anachronism. It was Cordelia calling.

"Where's Terence?"

"In the stocks." I explained what he'd done to Tad.

"Damn. Keeping him on is looking less and less doable. We'll see if Mo Heedles can get through to him. She's on her way. I'll tell her where to find the stocks."

"Roger." I hung up and went around to the front of the tent, where the fortuneteller's mother habitually sat knitting as she kept her eye on the cash box, the contents of the tent, and the immediate world. Granny Destiny—not her real name, but the only one she'd given anyone—wore a shapeless brown garment whose hood concealed the earbuds she used to listen to opera all day. She sat in an apparently random pile of brightly colored pillows and scarves that actually concealed a superbly comfortable chair, and fended off the occasional chatty tourist by uttering nothing but demented cackles and vaguely menacing prophecies.

Across the square, Terence was hamming it up as Horace and Lenny made a show of pretending to lock him into the stocks. The seated stocks—after all, he'd be there a couple of hours. And the tourists seemed to like the standing stocks better for photo opportunities.

"There goes the neighborhood." Granny Destiny's normal voice always sounded incongruous emerging from her shapeless costume. "What's he done now?"

"What hasn't he done? He's under orders to stay there till closing."

"Damn—does that mean you're not firing him?"

"No, it just means we're not firing him before the end of the day. After that, all bets are off."

"Shall I let you know if he doesn't stay put?"

"Yes—me and the town watch."

"Uh-huh." She nodded, and a contemptuous frown crossed her wrinkled brown face. "You should can him," she added. "Good riddance to bad rubbish." She pulled the hood back over her earbud-clad ears and settled back to keep watch.

On the far side of the stocks I could see the Muddy Beggar wallowing in his puddle, eyeing the crowd for someone to taunt, now that the crowds leaving the jousting were headed this way. I caught his eye, nodded in Terence's direction, and got a nod in return.

And bless their hearts, the tourists began surrounding the stocks, trading jests with Terence. Well, better that than pelting him with rotten fruit, I supposed. Although Terence didn't seem to regard them with the delight he usually displayed when a crowd was focused on him. Horace had tucked his snake-headed stick within reach, and Terence glanced at it a time or two. Maybe he was expecting the rotten fruit.

Then Mo Heedles strolled up to the stocks. At times I thought she was wasted as Chief of Police in relatively sedate Riverton. She'd have made an excellent undercover officer. Or a spy. Her face, though perfectly normal and arguably rather attractive, was curiously hard to remember when you were no longer in her presence, and she had an almost uncanny ability to go unnoticed until she deliberately called attention to herself.

But once she did . . . Well, Terence probably wasn't going to enjoy their conversation.

Satisfied that Terence couldn't spit without multiple

witnesses, I headed back to the forge for my last Friday demonstration.

The day barreled to its close. During the queen's address to her loyal subjects (aka the closing ceremonies) Michael and George managed to bring off their duel without Terence, although it was obvious to me that if we fired Terence we'd need to find another arch-villain to stir things up throughout the day. George seemed to take defeat at Michael's hands philosophically, but I made a mental note to ask Michael if they'd also rehearsed a scene in which he let George win. Surely even someone as self-effacing as George would enjoy having that happen every once in a while.

And Cordelia announced, to great applause, that the betrothal between Sir Terence and Lady Dianne was off.

"Whoa," I overheard one tourist say as he and his friend were slowly making their way to the front gate. "Her Majesty was seriously ticked off at that Terence dude. Do they hang people here in Albion?"

"I think they behead them," the friend said.

"Maybe we should come back tomorrow and see how they pull that off."

"I'm game," the friend said. "I never did get back to the place with the turkey legs."

They strolled out of earshot, making their plans for a repeat visit.

"Excellent," Cordelia said when I repeated their conversation to her. "We do seem to be getting a gratifying number of repeat customers. And attendance was up eleven percent over last Friday. At least something's going right."

She'd had another talk with Terence. I was almost surprised that she didn't fire him over what he'd done to Tad.

"I'd like to," she said. "I know you and Michael feel sorry for him because his girlfriend kicked him out, but he probably did something to deserve it, and I see no sign that he's too broke to find someplace else to stay. But technically he hasn't violated any of my ultimatums."

"Not yet," I said. "And I'm feeling less sorry for him by the hour."

"He's on notice," she said. "Assuming Michael can line up a replacement for next weekend . . ."

"So does that mean he's definitely out after this weekend?" I tried not to sound pleased and failed utterly.

"If he doesn't commit any offenses that would justify firing him, we'll have one more actor in the Game," she said. "The way things are going, we can afford it. But what do you think the chances are of him keeping his nose clean?"

"Slim to none."

She nodded in agreement.

We deliberately didn't broadcast the news of how very much hot water Terence was in. But his term in the stocks hadn't escaped general notice. Or the fact that Cordelia had had his tent moved to the far end of Camp Anachronism, with Horace's and Lenny's tents as a buffer between him and the rest of the campers.

"And what are we supposed to do if we catch him doing something nefarious?" Horace's round, normally calm face looked slightly annoyed. "Behead him with our bardiches?"

"They're not sharp enough for beheading," I pointed out. "The most you could manage with the bardiches would be clubbing him to death."

"Yeah, I've been meaning to complain about how dull they are." He was trying to keep a poker face, but I could tell he was joking. "Seriously—what do you want us to do?"

"Just keep your eyes open," I said. "If you catch him doing anything illegal, arrest him, and if you catch him breaking any Faire rules or doing anything Cordelia warned him not to do, make him pack his bags and escort him to his car."

"He doesn't have a car, remember?" Horace said. "He's always cadging rides and trying to borrow people's cars."

"That's right." I felt a little of my sympathy for Terence returning. Not only did he not have a car, he'd brought with him all his worldly possessions, to the great annoyance of whoever had driven him down here—one of the jugglers, if memory served. The dozen or so large, heavy boxes were locked up in Cordelia's storage room for safekeeping, and I had the sinking feeling that whether we kicked him out now or let him stay till the end of the season, Cordelia would end up arranging to get them back to Terence when he finally found a place where he could take them.

"I could drive him down to the bus station and see that he leaves town," Horace suggested.

"Yeah, that would work," I agreed. Cordelia would probably consider the cost of shipping his boxes a cheap price to pay for his departure. "But not tonight."

"Just as well," Horace said. "I'd better go. Lenny and I are taking your mother back to Cordelia's house in town."

The three-story Victorian house in which Cordelia had grown up wasn't actually in town by my definition—it was several miles beyond the edge of Riverton proper—although it was still technically within the town limits. For that matter, so was the craft center itself, thanks to a bit of creative gerrymandering a century ago by one of our ancestors who didn't trust the surrounding county. Now that Cordelia spent most of her time up at the craft center, she had set up the house as a bed and breakfast, with a widowed cousin as hostess. And she'd reserved one of the nicer rooms for Mother for the whole summer—the air-conditioning was more reliable there, and we quickly realized that Mother wasn't all that keen on the rather boisterous and largely outdoors social life that occupied the staff after hours.

"I think your mother will find the whole experience much more pleasant if she can wake up at her own speed and enjoy a nice, quiet cup of tea before she has to deal with all our costumed crazies," Cordelia had said. I agreed—and the broken foot made it doubly important for her to have a place to get away.

Dinner, and the usual after-dinner festivities, were merrier than usual, in no small part because we'd banished

Terence to his tent. I didn't quite share in the general merriment, having noticed that Tad and Faulk were also absent. In fact, I was actually relieved to have the owling trip as an excuse to leave the gathering early.

Several people who'd had a tankard or two of wine or mead became excited at the thought of going owling with us, but their excitement faded when they learned it would mean setting out an hour before sunrise.

"Did we ever look up what time sunrise will be?" Michael asked while we were getting ready for bed.

I pulled out my phone and opened the weather program. "Ick—five fifty-nine."

"So the owling party will take off at four fifty-nine."

"I am not taking off at four anything. Let's round that off to five o'clock. That's bad enough."

"Agreed. How much time will you need to get dressed?"

I pondered briefly.

"About one minute." I stood up and walked over to the closet. "Because I'm going to put on my hiking clothes right now and go to sleep in them. All I'll need to do is pull on my shoes. Well, shoes and jeans." It would still be warm overnight.

"A good idea." Michael began pulling back on the t-shirt he'd just shed.

We both made sure our jeans, hiking shoes, and phones were easy to find, and turned in. I tried to think of anything else we'd need and came up blank.

"I've set the alarm clock," I said. "And the alarm on my phone."

"My phone's set, too. And I've texted your dad to ask him to make sure we don't miss the expedition. He said 'okay.'"

"I'll unlock the door so he can come in and shake us awake if needed."

It wouldn't be the most comfortable night I'd ever spent at Biscuit Mountain, but at least sleeping almost fully dressed would make the morning less painful.

Chapter 15

Saturday

Getting up to go owling was every bit as painful as I'd expected it to be. In fact, more painful. I hadn't been keen on the notion of setting out an hour before sunrise. But I'd misheard. The expedition wasn't setting out an hour before sunrise but an hour before first light, which was defined as a full thirty minutes before sunrise. So Michael and I were still fast asleep when Grandfather barged into our room, hauled the covers back, and began shaking my shoulder and shouting at us to rise and shine.

At least that's what Dad told us Grandfather had been shouting. All I remembered was being rudely awakened from a vaguely threatening dream by someone grabbing me. I threw a punch at what I thought was an attacker and accidentally gave Grandfather a black eye.

"You have to admit, he's a tough old bird," Michael murmured as we watched Dad check Grandfather out to make sure I hadn't given him a broken nose or a concussion.

I nodded. I was relieved that Grandfather seemed to take the black eye in stride—had, in fact, seemed strangely proud of my self-defense abilities. "Damn good right hook," he said. "Chip off the old block."

After all that we managed to take off only ten minutes later than planned. Grandfather led the way, striding ahead with the vigor of a man half his age and at a speed that was hard for the rest of us to match—mainly because the rest of us had enough common sense to at least try looking where we were going so we wouldn't stumble over too many roots and stones. Rose Noire trotted along right behind Grandfather, trying to light both his way and her own with her LED flashlight, which she kept pointed down at the trail to minimize its effect on nearby wildlife. Luckily Grandfather seemed to have a charmed life and hardly tripped at all. Michael and I trailed along behind Rose Noire, followed by Cordelia, with Dad bringing up the rear, where he could spot anyone who lagged or stumbled, all the while murmuring calming things to his mother when Grandfather got on her nerves.

I wasn't sure why Cordelia had insisted on coming along. She could go owling here at Biscuit Mountain anytime—why do it at the start of what was already going to be a long and trying day? Maybe she was determined to show that she was just as invulnerable as Grandfather. And some of her remarks to Dad seemed to suggest that she resented the proprietary air with which Grandfather treated the local owls.

"Thinks he knows more about my owls than I do," she muttered at one point. "Hmph."

We stumbled as quietly as we could manage along the periphery of the Royal Encampment, the clearing just inside the woods where the several dozen tourists willing to pay for the privilege were camping out in brightly colored replicas of the sort of tents you'd have found at a Renaissance-era tournament. Cordelia only provided the tents themselves and a pair of modern porta-potties camouflaged with thatched roofs to make them look ever-so-slightly like authentic period privies. You'd have had to pay me to occupy one of those tents, but there was actually a waiting list for them, and more than one party showed up complete with what I assumed were replica cots and stools and cooked their meals in cast-iron pots over the fire pit. Clearly Cordelia had tapped into something.

And who knew? If Dad was right about the wide variety of Strigiform species living in the nearby woods, perhaps predawn owling expeditions could be another tourist offering at Biscuit Mountain. Maybe that was the reason Cordelia had come along—to scope out a new business opportunity.

Past the Royal Encampment and into the woods. Grandfather shushed us—quite unnecessarily, since the avid birders in the party already knew we needed to keep quiet and listen for owl calls, and Michael and I weren't really awake enough to talk.

The sun still hadn't risen, but even here in the woods the blackness slowly gave way to gray as we hiked, so we could see when Grandfather stopped, held his hand up dramatically, as if signaling us all not to move a muscle, and then nodded in satisfaction when a hooting noise rang out in the distance.

"*Strix varia*," he said.

"Hoot owl," Cordelia translated.

"Also known as a barred owl," Grandfather added. "Their other vocalizations—"

"Are something they could hear for themselves if you weren't talking," Cordelia snapped.

Grandfather looked annoyed, but saw the wisdom in what she'd said and contented himself with pointing in the direction the hooting was coming from. Rose Noire flicked off her flashlight, either to avoid startling the owls or to make it easier for us to concentrate on the distant hoots. Then we heard another sound at closer range, although it sounded more like a cross between an owl's hoot and a horse's whinny.

"Screech owl!" Cordelia and Dad whispered in near unison.

"*Megascops asio*," Grandfather added.

We stood listening to the two owls for a while. Dad, Rose Noire, Cordelia, and Grandfather seemed totally absorbed, and at least momentarily in complete harmony. Michael did his best to stifle an enormous yawn. I leaned against a tree and wondered if it was possible to nap standing up. If we stayed here much longer I was going to have a try. It was peaceful here with everyone just standing around listening to the owls. And while it was still far from light, the dark was gradually growing less intense. My eyes adjusted, and I could at least make out everyone's silhouette.

"Was this where you heard the Great Horned Owl?" Grandfather whispered to Dad after a while.

"No, it was deeper into the woods. A quarter mile in that direction." He pointed off to our right.

Grandfather nodded and, after another minute or two of listening, he headed off in the direction Dad had indicated.

"Be careful of—*damn!*"

The silhouette of his head disappeared, and we heard an assortment of crashing, rustling, and thudding noises that seemed to suggest he was rolling downhill through some shrubbery.

"Dad!" Dad called, as he went bounding to the rescue, producing still more crashing and thudding noises. "Are you all right?"

"Fine," he said. "Barked my shins a bit."

Michael and I followed Dad down the shrub-covered hill and got to Grandfather about the same time he did. Dad dropped to his knees to inspect his father's shins. Michael turned back to help Rose Noire and Cordelia down the slope. So I got the first good look not just at Grandfather—who seemed fine, except for a spot of blood on one pants leg—but at what he was waving.

"Who left this here, anyway?" Grandfather complained.

'What is it?" Michael asked, from halfway up the slope

"A walking stick," Grandfather replied.

Yes, and it looked familiar. I took a few steps closer to get a better look.

"Terence's walking stick," I said.

"The one with the snake?" Michael asked.

"Yes," I said. "What in the world is it doing out here?"

"I was fine until my shin hit that blasted metal snake ornament on the end," Grandfather complained. "I should give him a piece of my mind, leaving dangerous objects like that lying around where anyone could trip over them."

"I have a bad premonition about this," Rose Noire intoned as she turned on her flashlight again. I wanted to point out that to count as a premonition, you needed to have it sometime before ominous things had begun to occur. But she was making herself useful with the flashlight, so I refrained. After waving the beam around until she found Grandfather with it, she was now holding the light steadily on him, which would make Dad's first aid easier.

"That's Terence's stick all right," Michael said.

But while Rose Noire had been waving her flashlight beam around I'd spotted something.

"Move the light to the right a little," I said. "Slowly."

"I need it to see what I'm doing," Dad complained.

"Humor me for a sec," I said.

Rose Noire followed my instructions. The beam left Grandfather and traveled slowly over the underbrush until it landed on—

"There!" I said.

"Oh, my goodness!" Rose Noire exclaimed.

Terence was sitting on the ground with his back against a tree and his legs stretched out in front of him. At first I thought he was staring at us, but after a couple of seconds I realized that the glassy immobility of his eyes wasn't a stare.

Dad left Grandfather and hurried over to Terence's side.

"What in blazes is *he* doing here?" Grandfather asked.

"Everyone stay back," Cordelia said. "I expect this will be a crime scene, so let's mess it up as little as possible."

"You want me to call 911?" Michael asked.

"Already on it." I had pulled out my phone as soon as I saw Terence's blank stare. "You call Horace and tell him to bring Lenny, the Riverton deputy. They're both down in Camp Anachronism."

"Maybe I should just go fetch them," Michael suggested. "Not sure how else they'll find their way here."

Just then the dispatcher answered. I put my phone on speaker.

"This is 911—what's your emergency?"

"This is Meg Langslow up at the Biscuit Mountain Craft Center." I was pleased at how calm and efficient I sounded. "Some of us were on a pre-dawn owling expedition in the woods surrounding the center and we found—" I hesitated and glanced over at Dad, who had donned gloves and was checking Terence for signs of life. He looked up and shook his head. "Found a dead body," I finished.

"Oh, my!" the dispatcher exclaimed. "Can you give me a precise location? And do you have an ID on the deceased?"

"We're about a quarter of a mile northeast of the main building," Cordelia said. "Tell the chief to take the old logging road."

I relayed that to the dispatcher.

"And the deceased is Mr. Terence Cox," I added. "One of the actors performing at the Renaissance Faire."

"Goodness," the dispatcher said. "Was that Ms. Cordelia's voice I heard in the background? Is she okay?"

"I'm fine, Ashley," Cordelia called out.

"I'm sending the nearest patrol car up to secure the scene," Ashley said. "And I'll call Chief Heedles right away."

"When you talk to the chief, remind her that one of

her deputies is here. We'll fetch him now." I glanced at Michael.

"On it," Michael said. He strode off into the woods, giving every impression of knowing exactly where he was going.

"And my cousin Horace is here," I said. "So if she decides she needs any forensic work done, I'm sure he can help."

"Does it look like she'll need forensics?" Ashley sounded uncertain. "I mean, if it's just a sad accident."

Dad trudged uphill and held out his hand for me to give him the phone—which I did.

"This is Dr. James Langslow." His voice had a confident, almost self-important tone that you only heard from him in medical emergencies or at crime scenes. "I don't want to disturb the body too much before your local medical examiner gets here, but I'm pretty sure she'll find the cause of death to be a knife wound. And since the knife's stuck in his back, I expect we'll find the manner of death to be homicide."

"Oh, my." Ashley seemed taken aback for a moment. "Are you all in a safe place there?"

Dad returned my phone.

"We should be okay," I said. "We'll keep a close eye out in case whoever did this comes back."

"I'd appreciate it if you'd stay on the line for the time being," she said. "In case the chief has questions. Or if you see anything you need to report."

"Will do," I said. "I assume you're contacting the medical examiner?"

"Already done."

"Might be a good idea for one of us to go back to the center," Cordelia said. "So we can show the police the way when they get here. Rose Noire, do you think you can find your way there?"

"Of course." She offered her flashlight to Cordelia, who shook her head and pulled out her own from a pocket.

"Maybe you and Dr. Blake could both go back," Cordelia said. "You could see to getting his injury patched up and then lead the officers here."

"Can do."

Rose Noire and Dad both tried to help Grandfather up, but he brushed off their efforts and scrambled to his feet with encouraging ease. He rummaged through the pockets of his fisherman's vest and, after examining and discarding a jeweler's loupe, a tube of Super Glue, and a miniature sewing kit, he produced a pocket flashlight and waved it triumphantly before trudging off with a limp that I hoped was mostly for dramatic effect. Rose Noire nodded to us and hiked off after him. I wasn't sure they were going in the right direction, but I trusted that Rose Noire's instincts would get her out of the woods eventually, and in the meantime, at least we'd have peace and quiet here at the crime scene.

Chapter 16

Cordelia also seemed to relax after Grandfather was gone.

"How long do you think we'll have to wait here?" I asked. "I know we're pretty far from town."

"Could be five minutes, could be half an hour." She shrugged. "Depends where the nearest officer was when the call came in."

Sooner would be better than later. The more time went by, the more people would wake up—both camping tourists and Faire staff. The last thing we needed was a horde of people traipsing through the woods, obliterating clues. In fact—

"Ashley," I said. "Can you suggest that whoever's coming to the scene might want to arrive without the sirens? If the officers can manage not to wake up all the campers it'll reduce the chance of interference with the crime scene."

"Good idea."

I glanced over to see what Dad was up to. He was rummaging in the battered black-leather messenger bag that served as a portable medical kit when he went hiking or bird-watching. If Terence had been merely injured, I was sure Dad, armed with the contents of the bag, would have managed to save him.

As I watched he pulled out a tiny portable camping lantern, which he turned on and hung from a nearby tree branch. Despite its small size, the lantern's LED bulbs gave a surprising amount of light.

"There," he said. "That should make our medical and forensic exams easier."

It didn't make sitting here with Terence's body easier.

"Should also help Chief Heedles and her officers find us," Cordelia remarked.

I watched as Dad gently touched Terence's eyelids and felt various places on his neck and jaw.

"Rigor mortis starting to set in," he said.

"I assume that means he wasn't stabbed just before we got here." I racked my brain for some of the medical lore Dad was always dispensing. "About two to six hours ago, right?"

"Yes." Dad was peering at Terence's face. "Given the warm air temperature, probably closer to the two-hour end of that range."

"So whoever did this isn't likely to be still lurking in the bushes," Cordelia said. "A pity. Not much chance of catching him."

I had to smile. Most people would have been glad to learn the killer was long gone. Cordelia's first thought was disappointment that we wouldn't get the chance to lay hands on the culprit.

"And of course it has to be him." She nodded in Terence's direction. "I know it's a horrible thing to say when the poor man's not even cold, but I'm not surprised. That man could inspire homicidal thoughts in a saint."

I nodded. I hoped Chief Heedles found the killer quickly. Because otherwise—

I hit the mute button on my phone.

"You think the chief will let us have the Faire today?" I asked.

"I'm busy marshaling my arguments in case she tries to close us down." Cordelia looked determined.

"Could be it will scare people off," I suggested. "Having a murder here at the Faire."

"In the woods near the Faire," she corrected. "And obviously you have a much rosier view of human nature than I do. I only hope we aren't overrun with bloodthirsty ghouls looking to gawk at a crime scene."

"Good point. Let's bring that up with the chief."

I unmuted my phone.

"Do you have an ETA on Chief Heedles?" I asked Ashley.

"About ten minutes."

Dad was still absorbed in examining Terence's body. Only visually—evidently he'd decided he'd done as much as he should before the M.E.'s arrival. But in addition to the lantern, he had turned on his cell phone's flashlight and was methodically running it up and down the body. Cordelia was watching with apparent fascination.

I turned to face in the opposite direction—the direction I assumed the chief would be coming from. I struggled to stifle my yawns. I speculated about what Rose Noire and Grandfather were doing back at the house, and whether Michael was heading back from Camp Anachronism with Horace and Lenny in tow. And I tried not to resent the fact that Grandfather had hustled us out into the woods before dawn without benefit of caffeine.

"Maybe we should have exiled him to the maid's closet after all," Cordelia said. "Maybe he'd have stayed put in the house and would still be alive."

"He could have come here from the house almost as easily as from Camp Anachronism," I said. "And if he was staying up at the house, maybe he'd have been killed there."

"Good point." Cordelia gave a faint shudder. "Okay, I'm glad we left him down at Camp Anachronism. A pity you had to waste your time cleaning out the maids' closet."

"I didn't," I said.

"Then who did?" Cordelia asked. "Someone did—they even sprayed the place with that organic bug spray—the whole kitchen still reeked of citronella when I got my coffee this morning."

"Maybe the kitchen staff did it." Not that I cared who'd done it, but it beat talking about Terence's dead body. "Maybe the camel crickets were spreading."

"Could be."

Having run that topic into the ground we lapsed into silence. I searched my mind for something else to distract myself—and Cordelia—from Terence, with his blank, staring eyes. I peered up the path to see if I could spot any sign of the chief.

Evidently my sense of direction wasn't as good as I thought it was.

"Good morning."

I started and turned to see Chief Heedles hiking toward us through the woods—from almost the opposite direction from the one in which I'd been staring. Normally my sense of direction was rather good, but perhaps it, like most of my brain, hadn't had yet awakened.

"Chief's here," I said into the phone. "Signing off now."

"Thank goodness you're here," Cordelia said. "There he is."

She indicated Terence's body with the same grand gesture she normally used to present the winners of the jousts and other competitions to the cheering crowds.

I decided to chime in on the practical side.

"Terence Cox, age forty-six," I said. "Actor. Lives in Northern Virginia as far as I know—at least the address we have on file for him is in Loudoun County, but I think that's actually the address of the ex-girlfriend who kicked him out a few months ago. He's been mostly couch surfing lately. Michael might know more—Michael hired him to be one of his performers here at the Faire, and like most of the participants who want to stay here full time he works two or three days a week around the center doing . . . what has he been doing anyway?"

"As little as possible," Cordelia said. "I don't like to speak ill of the dead, but he was a moocher. Theoretically, he was part of the wait staff, but I think the rest of the dining room crew were just as happy when he didn't show up."

"Not the most popular member of our happy little family here at Biscuit Mountain," I said. "In fact, I hope it won't complicate your investigation too much, but I expect quite a few people have been heard to exclaim variants on 'I could strangle that man!' over the past few weeks—me among them."

"Doesn't appear that he was strangled, though," the chief observed. "Dr. Langslow, didn't Ashley tell me that you said he was stabbed?"

"In the back," Dad said. "With a knife. Not one of yours, I'm pretty sure," he added to me in a reassuring tone. "Looks like a cheap reproduction with a few too many fake jewels in the hilt. Rhinestones." He wrinkled his nose as if the tackiness of the murder weapon offended him.

I was just glad to hear it wasn't one of mine. And probably not Faulk's work, either, if Dad was right about the rhinestones. Faulk only just barely approved of the small number of real garnets I'd used on Cordelia's stiletto.

"I took a picture of it." Dad held up his phone. "Not a great picture—we can get better once your medical examiner has pronounced and Horace has worked the scene. But—"

"I'd like to see it anyway." The chief pulled out her own phone. "Do you have my—"

But yes, Dad had her number, and had already texted the photo to her. And, for good measure, to me.

"Does it look familiar?" the chief asked when we'd both studied our phone screens for a minute or so.

"Unfortunately, yes," I said.

"Unfortunately?" she echoed. "It belongs to someone you know?"

"I don't mean that I recognize that specific knife," I said. "But from looking at the handle, I'm pretty sure I've seen plenty like it. Cheap import. Available online from any number of websites, plus there's a booth called the Bonny Blade that sells them here at the Faire. I wouldn't be surprised if they unload a dozen or so every weekend, many of them to people who drool over the ones Faulk and I sell but blanch at the price. And a few of the more economical-minded performers might be sporting blades like that."

"So finding it here at—well, near—the Faire is not surprising?"

"The only surprising thing is that its owner succeeded in stabbing someone with it without having the blade snap in two," I said. "If it's the kind of knife I think it is, you'll probably find it's made of cheap, brittle metal. And the ones the Bonny Blade sells aren't all that sharp—if that one turns out to have a decent edge on it, I'd suspect premeditation more than sudden impulse."

"And if it's still dull," the chief went on. "I expect using it to stab someone would require greater strength than you'd need with a well-sharpened blade."

I nodded my agreement.

"So Mr. Cox was generally unpopular with his fellow residents here." The chief had pulled out her pocket notebook to make notes during our discussion of the dagger. Now she was holding her pen poised over a page. "Anyone in particular who might have it in for him?"

"You're going to need a bigger notebook," Cordelia said. "Look—unless you're going to tell me I need to shut down the Faire over this, I have a few things to do this morning. And for that matter, if you tell me I have to shut the Faire down, I'll have even more things to do."

"And shutting down the Faire would be a big mess," I said. "There are probably hundreds of people already on their way here—"

"Thousands," Cordelia corrected. "And—"

"We're a good half mile from the actual fairgrounds," the chief said. "And I'd rather avoid the publicity that would result if we told all those people to go home because we've had a murder here."

"A lot of them probably wouldn't go anyway," I said. "They'd hang around and complicate things. We'd have the dickens of a time keeping them away from the crime scene."

"True." The chief grimaced, as if imagining the resulting chaos.

"Then let me go break the news to the staff and put them all on notice that they're not to say a word about it to anyone," Cordelia said. "I can also organize a few volunteers to help make sure the tourists don't stray over here to interfere with your investigation. And Meg can fill you in on how the annoying Terence spent his last day on Earth, which will give you a rundown on all the people who might have had it in for him."

"Seems reasonable," the chief said.

Just then Horace arrived, guiding the local medical examiner. She was a tall, angular redheaded woman of forty or so, with a reassuring no-nonsense manner. She and Dad had worked together before. He greeted her arrival with glad cries of welcome, and to my relief she seemed equally pleased to see him again. She made the official death pronouncement, which freed Horace to turn his forensic attentions to Terence's body—with Dad and the M.E. hovering over his shoulder. The three of them were soon cheerfully debating the various factors that might have hurried or retarded the onset of rigor mortis.

I glanced at Chief Heedles and wondered if my facial expression mirrored hers. Not quite squeamish, but definitely not as thrilled with the discussion as the three of them.

"At moments like these I'm reminded how glad I am that I didn't let Dad talk me into going to medical school," I said.

"Takes all kinds, doesn't it?" She shook her head and chuckled. "Let's stay within earshot, in case any of them make any fascinating discoveries that they insist on sharing immediately. But I think we can make ourselves a little more comfortable."

Chapter 17

The chief's idea of comfort seemed to be putting more distance between us and Terence's body. I approved. She went to the far edge of the little clearing and, after carefully inspecting a leaf-covered patch of ground that seemed completely undisturbed, sat down cross-legged there. I followed suit.

"So I remember some of what Cordelia told me yesterday afternoon," she said. "But pretend I don't and tell me who you think my prime suspects should be."

"You're going to have to start with me," I said. "And Michael and Cordelia. Because he's been a thorn in our sides all summer."

"I gather that puts you in the majority," she said. "And—all summer? I thought the Faire had only been running for four weeks."

"Sometimes feels like four decades," I said. "With Terence around."

"I gather." She smiled. "Just tell me what you know."

So I filled her in on Terence's stay at Biscuit Mountain and the countless annoying and disruptive things he'd done. How we'd had to make it clear to him the first weekend that he'd have to rein in his bawdy conception of how a sixteenth-century character would act to avoid a twenty-first-century sexual harassment charge.

"And he's behaved since then?" she asked. "In the limited sense of avoiding sexual harassment, that is."

"As far as I know," I said. "In public, at least, he's kept it to a lot of leering and double entendres, but I can't vouch for what he's done in private. Although I hope anyone he harassed would have let one of us know—me or Michael or Cordelia."

I continued with the list. A representative selection of the pranks he'd played on nearly everyone, most of them innocent, but a few destructive or humiliating. And then, this weekend. His attempt to maneuver the Game so Dianne was forced to interact with him more than she would have wanted. His attempt to undermine Nigel's sobriety.

"And I have no idea what you'd call what he did to Tad," I said. "Obviously it's not illegal, and as Terence pointed out, Tad was lying to his boss, but it's not as if Tad wasn't putting in the hours or getting the work done, and Tad was only deceiving his boss about where he was because his boss was a total control freak and Tad was worried about Faulk."

"Sounds to me as if Mr. Cox wanted to lash out at someone after your grandmother put him on notice," the chief observed. "And Mr. Jackson was unlucky enough to be the nearest someone."

I nodded.

"Anyway, that's all I can think of," I said. "At least right now. It's still way too early for me to be coherent."

"I'll be around if you remember anything else. Can you set me up with a room for interviewing people?"

"Cordelia's office would probably work well," I said. "I'll let her know so she can get you a key. And I bet you'll want to talk to a bunch of people."

"Starting with all of the ones you mentioned as having had the more memorable recent conflicts with the deceased."

"Nigel Howe, Dianne Willowdale, Jacquelynn Morris, Tad Jackson, Greg Dorance, and Faulkner Cates. And George Sims, of course—he wasn't exactly in much conflict with Terence but they'd worked together before, so he might be able to shed more light on his character than the rest of us. More than I can, anyway. He actually seemed to like Terence and find his pranks funny, which might make him a refreshing change. And Michael and Cordelia. And—"

"See which of those first seven you can find for starters," she said. "I'll stay and keep an eye on the crime scene. Got a few more officers coming, and a few volunteers I can deputize to help keep the site secure, but they're still en route."

"I'll make sure the gate knows to admit them," I said.

"Thanks—although I think most of them will come round the back way."

"Back way?"

"Yes—a dirt road that circles around just outside Cordelia's property. Passes by about a hundred yards in that direction." She pointed in what I was pretty sure was the opposite direction from the main house. "That's how I got here—good call, setting up the lantern—that made finding you a breeze."

"Dad's doing," I said. "So that's what Cordelia meant by taking the logging road."

"Yes. Anyway, I gave directions for most of the officers to come up that way."

"Cool," I said. "I wonder if the presence of the road has anything to do with finding Terence's body here. I mean, was he killed here or dumped here?"

She frowned slightly and turned toward where Dad, Horace, and the local M.E. were at work. Their discussion seemed to have moved on from rigor mortis to livor mortis.

"Have you been able to determine if he was killed here or merely left here?" the chief called out.

"We can't be absolutely sure until we have him on the autopsy table," the M.E. said.

"That's right," Dad said. "Although the livor mortis does seem to suggest that he was probably killed here. But that's only a preliminary finding."

"I haven't seen anything so far to suggest he was killed elsewhere," Horace said. "There's a fair amount of blood here—although not as much as we'd see if the dagger hadn't acted as a sort of stopper."

"We should absolutely wait till the autopsy to remove it," the M.E remarked.

"And so far the pattern seems entirely consistent with him being stabbed." Horace stood up and walked over to another tree about six feet away. "The way I see it, after being stabbed he staggered a bit, then fell back against the tree—" Horace reeled back against the new tree, demonstrating his theory.

"Yes," Dad said. "Fell back or was pushed."

"Then he slumped to the ground, and bled out in place." Horace demonstrated, remaining sitting in in place with his eyes staring and his tongue sticking out.

Both Dad and the M.E. were nodding their agreement.

"But it's early times yet." Horace scrambled to his feet and brushed the leaf debris off the back of his pants. "So we'll keep our eyes open for any sign that he was killed elsewhere."

"In short, we're probably not looking at a body dump," the chief said, turning back to me. "Proximity to the road could be accidental."

"Or maybe he was meeting someone here—someone who arrived via that road."

"Someone who wasn't staying here at Biscuit Mountain, in that case, since I gather most of the folks from out of town weren't familiar with the road."

"Yes." I nodded. "At least, I wasn't, and I suspect most people here at camp weren't, but this close, anyone could have stumbled on it if they took a fancy to wandering around the woods."

"Stumbling on it's one thing," she said. "Knowing where it leads and using it to set up an assignation . . . seems possible, but less likely, given that most of the people staying at Biscuit Mountain aren't local."

"True," I said. "I have to say, I rather like the theory that the killer came from outside. But I could be biased."

"It's a point to keep in mind," She scribbled a little more in her notebook.

"I'll go see if I can round up any suspects." I stood up.

"And I'll head down to Cordelia's office as soon as one of my officers gets here."

I headed for Camp Anachronism, where I suspected the majority of the chief's suspects—no, make that witnesses—would be still hanging about this early.

But all I found there were empty tents and a few stragglers hurrying off to breakfast, none of them on my witness list. Then again, it wasn't all that early anymore. A lot of time had passed while we'd been waiting for the police to arrive, and then while I was briefing Chief Heedles. It was past eight. Most of the camp's inhabitants would already have gone up to the main house for breakfast. Many of them would already be putting on their costumes or readying their shops for the opening bell.

I turned my steps toward the main house.

In the Great Hall Michael, already mostly in costume, appeared to be holding court, with a milling crowd of staff and performers gathered around him. When I drew closer I realized he was answering their questions about what was happening and spreading Cordelia's orders for the day.

"So remember," he was saying as I drew near, "don't answer questions like that—not even if it's from someone you know or at least know isn't a reporter. You don't have to be a reporter these days to spread a story around the world."

"And if someone won't take 'no comment' for an answer?" one of the jugglers asked.

"Send them to the press office. Yes, as of this morning,

we have a press office—located in the office by the front gate and staffed by Meg, Cordelia, and me. If someone says they're a reporter—or acts like one—send them to the press office and notify the three of us, and one of us will handle it."

"But why are we trying to cover up the murder?" asked a tavern barmaid.

"We're not trying to cover it up," Michael said. "We're following Chief Heedles's orders to help protect the crime scene until her officers can process it. She has a very small department—I think only about a dozen officers—and they're going to be stretched to the limit handling this on top of their regular duties. I expect she's reaching out to the state police and neighboring counties for help, but it will take time for that help to get here. If word got out that there was a crime scene in the woods behind the Faire, do you think we have enough people to keep the tourists from stampeding over there to take pictures?"

"Selfies with the corpse," someone said with a shudder. "Horrible."

"And if anyone has any information that might be relevant to the murder, please speak up," Michael added. "If you don't see any police officers, tell me or Meg or Cordelia."

He sounded tired—not surprising, given how early we'd been awakened. And tired of the words he was saying—I suspected he'd been repeating much the same points for quite a while now, starting with the first campers to stumble over to the main house for their caffeine fix, and now including not only the campers but also commuters—locals from Riverton and the few craftspeople and performers who'd opted to stay at nearby bed-and-breakfast establishments but still liked to start their day with a trip through the Biscuit Mountain's legendary breakfast buffet.

"And now I'm going to have *my* breakfast," he said, staring pointedly at one of the jousters, who was eating a heavily buttered blueberry muffin while standing so close he was occasionally shedding crumbs on Michael's black-and-red doublet.

The jouster backed away with an apologetic gesture. Michael stood and put an arm around my waist and we strolled toward the buffet line.

"Any interesting scoops?" he murmured into my ear.

"The murder weapon was probably one of those cheap knockoff knives the Bonny Blade sells."

"Seriously? I wouldn't have thought you could cut butter with one of those."

"That's what I told the chief."

We then clammed up while we went through the buffet line. The servers were staff, and thus in theory sworn to secrecy—or at least discretion. Still, no sense adding to their temptation by making them privy to inside information.

When we sat down—uncharacteristically at a table in the far corner of the room, away from prying ears—Michael's mind was still on the murder weapon.

"Hard to believe anyone would be stupid enough to attempt murder with a piece of junk from the Bonny Blade," he mused. "And what a bad break for Terence that they actually succeeded. Although it should narrow down the chief's suspect list quite a bit. It would take considerable strength to stab someone with a blade that dull."

"Unless the killer sharpened it first," I pointed out. "We won't know about that until they take it out."

"I'd have thought they'd have done that by now."

"According to Horace, it's acting as a stopper." I could tell Michael didn't like the image that conjured up any more than I had. "I assume removing would spill more blood on what is probably already a pretty complicated crime scene, so they're waiting for the autopsy. And if you want any more details on that part of the case, let's wait till after breakfast."

"Agreed. Who are you looking for?"

He'd noticed me eyeing the crowd.

"People the chief wants to interview."

"Suspects?"

"I think she'd prefer to stick to 'persons of interest' for the time being."

"George, Jacks, Dianne, Nigel, and I are supposed to rendezvous outside the Dragon's Claw at the opening bell to kick off today's episode of the Game," he said. "I expect they're all on her list, so any of them you don't catch beforehand . . ."

"I'll let her know. And she'll probably want to talk to you and Cordelia, of course. She's going to use Cordelia's office as her interview room—do you have time to set her up in there while I see who I can hunt down?"

"Can do."

Chapter 18

Michael and I both bolted our breakfasts with a speed that did no justice to the quality of the food. Michael disappeared down the corridor that led to Cordelia's office. I made the rounds of the various places where the persons of interest on my list might be lurking—the kitchen, the back terrace, the Great Hall, the costume shops.

The only one I found was Greg, the falconer. He wasn't all that high on my personal suspect list, but he'd definitely had a loud public altercation with Terence the previous weekend. And perhaps more usefully, at least in my book, Greg was seriously worried that Terence would try to repeat whatever prank he'd played on the falcon. Whenever Terence got anywhere near Falconer's Grove, you could be sure that Greg's eye was on him. As a result, Greg might have noticed something useful. He took the news that the chief wanted to speak with him rather calmly.

"Ooh," he said. "I get to help the police with their inquiries."

"A lot of us will be doing that," I said. "Starting with anyone known to have had a disagreement with him. Cordelia forgot to fill me in—just what was it Terence did last weekend that led to the quarrel?"

"I found him hanging around the mews after hours." Greg's expression darkened at the memory. "He had a fishing pole, and he was casting bits of meat tied to the line through the slats and then reeling them back out again. Not only was it driving the birds crazy, but if one of them had actually caught the bait and swallowed it, they could have been seriously injured."

"What a jerk. You didn't tell Grandfather about that, did you?"

"It never came up." He frowned. "Wait—surely you don't suspect your grandfather of killing him?"

"No, but if he knew Terence had done that, he'd be furious that the actual killer got to him first. Or at least got to him before Grandfather could deliver a tongue-lashing of epic proportions."

"If it comes up, tell him I did my best." Greg was grinning again. "In the tongue-lashing department, that is. I draw the line at homicide. Say, Terence wasn't found with talon and beak marks all over his face, was he?"

"Like Tippi Hedren in *The Birds*? Not that I know of. So Harry and Gracie are off the hook."

"Well, I never suspected Harry." Greg shook his head with the bemused look he had whenever he talked about his junior bird. "He wouldn't hold a grudge. But Gracie did. After Terence pulled that stunt with the fishing pole, I kept warning him to stay away from the Grove, and he paid no attention, until one time he was stupid enough to cruise by when she was off the tether, and she flew at him. He's lucky he has good reflexes. They probably saved his eyesight." His face fell. "Had good reflexes. Anyway. I'd be happy to talk to the police. Where should I go and when?"

"How about dropping by Cordelia's office when you finish eating, and you can get it over with."

"Can do." He went back to devouring a large blueberry muffin and I left the dining room to continue my search outdoors.

I decided to make my way methodically through the Faire, up one winding lane and down the next—which was pretty much what the last hour before opening usually found me doing. Cordelia thought it was important for one of us to inspect everything, to see for ourselves that all the booths and tents and stands were making satisfactory progress toward being ready to open at ten, and most mornings I was the one who could find the time. But before the first weekend was out I'd realized that seeing was less important than being seen. If people had problems, questions, or suggestions, my morning rounds, as I called this pre-opening inspection, were the time they'd approach me with them—before they got caught up in the day's activities, and before the tourists were around to eavesdrop. Even if I hadn't needed to hunt down people for the chief to talk to, it was probably a good thing to be seen doing exactly what I'd normally be doing at this time of day—inspecting the Faire and scribbling notes in my leather-covered notebook.

My rounds also gave me the chance to assess the mood of the Faire. On the whole, pretty close to normal so far today—maybe even a little more upbeat than usual.

Not surprising. At this time of day, the weather had more than anything else to do with everyone's mood, and the morning was bright, sunny, and not yet all that hot. Clouds were supposed roll later in the day, but if the weather apps were correct, they'd help keep temperatures down in the eighties, which was something to be thankful for during a Virginia summer, even here in the foothills of the Blue Ridge. And no rain in the forecast till after closing time. Good—nothing damped the participants' cheer like the prospect of rain. After much debate, umbrellas had been declared an anachronism, which meant that everyone had to depend on cloaks, capes, and hats for protection against precipitation, and by the end of a rainy day the entire Faire smelled like a wet sheep.

Yes, the mood was upbeat, and everywhere things looked reassuringly normal. A couple of people approached me with questions about Terence's murder. More people had questions about perfectly ordinary things. Had I made the

arrangements for more frequent garbage pickups in the
food service areas during peak eating hours? Had anyone told me about the leaky faucet in the women's shower
shed? Could we rearrange the food booths so people
waiting in line for vegan salads and pilafs didn't have to
breathe the smoke from the frying Italian sausages? Was
there any word about the tourist who'd been bitten yesterday by that pair of so-called emotional support Chihua-
huas?

Okay, some of the questions were only normal at an
event like the Faire. But at least they had nothing to do
with Terence's murder. A few people looked more solemn
than usual—probably the ones who shared John Donne's
view that "any man's death diminishes me." Or maybe
just the ones who realized what an immediate hassle to
them and potential long-term threat to the Faire's well-
being the murder could be. But most people looked, if
anything, pleasurably excited. It was very sad, of course,
but the Muddy Beggar pegged it.

"It would be different if anyone thought the killer had
picked a random victim and they could be the next target," he said. "But even the people who didn't really know
Terence knew *of* him. They see a certain sense of . . . well,
not quite justice . . ."

He frowned as he groped for the right word, pausing
in the middle of pouring another bucket of water onto
the spot where he planned to situate his main puddle for
the day.

"Logic," I suggested. "Or cause and effect."

"Yeah," he said. "Either of those would cover it. 'How can
anyone possibly kill another human being?'" he exclaimed,
in a manner slyly reminiscent of Rose Noire. "'The horror!
The tragedy! The—oh, the victim was Terence? Well, I suppose that makes sense.'"

"Yeah, that works," I said. "Carry on!"

"I need another bucket or two," he said with a sigh. "If

this dry spell persists, I might have to change into the Dusty Beggar."

"Thunderstorms predicted tonight," I said, which seemed to cheer him up.

I strolled on. Passing the green-and-yellow tent that held the Bonny Blade shop, I made sure to wish them a good morning in the same cheerful tone I used with everyone else, and tried not to stare at their glass-topped case full of daggers and stilettos. The chief hadn't yet re-leased any information about the murder weapon, much less its source.

Make that possible source. After all, I didn't know for sure that the murder weapon had come from the Bonny Blade. Just about every Renaissance Faire or science fic-tion/fantasy convention had at least one vendor of cheap blade weapons, to say nothing of the dozens of online sites that sold them. Even if the Bonny Blade had sold the weapon, it wasn't their fault the purchaser used it for ne-farious purposes.

But if the Bonny Blade had sold the weapon, maybe there was a way we could help the chief. I had no idea if they kept good records on their purchasers. Faulk and I did, and used the information to let past custom-ers know when we were doing upcoming events in their area. I didn't think the owners of the Bonny Blade were that organized, but you never knew. But even if they had no records at all, we could still give the chief some use-ful data. When someone bought a weapon, whether it was a cheap ankle dagger from the Bonny Blade or one of Faulk's massive Crusader swords in damascene steel, they didn't get to take it with them—we tried to discourage weapons on the grounds except in the hands of Cordelia and the few actors who were stage combat experts. We'd walk with our purchasers to the gate and force them to at-tach the very anachronistic bright-orange peace-bonding strips if we couldn't talk them into depositing the weapon for safekeeping in the ticket office, where its owner could claim it on his or her way out. And just to avoid problems, every weapon was methodically entered into a log book, and signed for by the purchaser when claimed. We even insisted on getting the purchasers' names, addresses, and emails or phone numbers, since we quickly realized that some people—under the influence of too much mead, perhaps—forgot about their newly purchased toys until they arrived at home without them.

I was about to call the chief to tell her about the weapon log when someone behind me called out my name.

"Meg?"

I turned to see Lenny, the other half of the palace guard. For that matter, probably the whole of the palace guard until Horace finished his forensic work. He was tall and lanky, with an open, honest-looking freckled face and hair so short and blond that you could easily see the matching freckles on his scalp.

"What's up?" I asked him.

"I'm helping the chief—have you seen Tad and Faulk?"

"Not since yesterday afternoon," I said. "No idea about Tad, but by now Faulk should be in the smithy."

"I'll check there again." He turned to go.

"Again? You already checked?"

"Yeah, but that was a while ago." He furtively pulled a wristwatch out of his tunic and stole a quick glance at it. "Half an hour ago. You're probably right. He should be there by now."

Lenny had no ability to hide what he was thinking. Probably something he'd have to work on if he wanted to go far in his law enforcement career, but useful to me at the moment. Most of the time his expression reflected his generally cheerful nature, but right now he looked worried.

"Did you check his tent?" I asked aloud.

"Yes." Lenny looked more worried. "He wasn't there.

Neither was Tad. And their van wasn't in the staff parking lot when I looked there."

Not good. Of course, it didn't necessarily have anything to do with the murder. Maybe they'd had to run up to D.C. for something connected with Tad's firing.

"I'll keep my eyes open," I said aloud.

"And I'll check their tent again." He turned to leave.

"Let me know if you find one of them," I said. "And I'll do the same, of course. Any idea why the chief is looking for them?"

"She wants to use that big room across the way from Ms. Cordelia's office as a sort of common room for the officers involved in the investigation, but there's all this stuff there that someone told her belongs to Tad. She wants to see if he can pack it up before the officers move in."

"If I find him, I'll tell him," I said. "And if he's disappeared off the face of the planet I'll arrange for someone to clear the room. Or just do it myself."

"Thanks, ma'am."

Even if Tad hadn't disappeared off the face of the planet, I doubted he'd have any problem with me arranging to pack up his electronics gear. He wasn't likely to be doing another round of green-screen broadcasting anytime soon.

As I strolled toward the main house, I pulled out my cell phone and dialed Tad's number. It went to voicemail.

"Hey, Tad," I said when the beep had given me the go-ahead. "Cordelia needs to use the room where your green-screen equipment is—I'm going to get it all safely packed and move it into the storage room for safekeeping. It's nine thirty. If you get this before, say ten thirty, come up to the main house and help. If you don't, don't worry about it. Talk to you later."

So why wasn't Tad here? Or Faulk? Didn't they realize how suspicious this looked when—?

I had to laugh at myself, which startled two craftspeople

who happened to be passing. I felt a pang of guilt when I realized they were both scanning their costumes for something that could have inspired my mirth. I wanted to run after them and apologize. Explain that I was laughing at my own short sightedness.

Because no, Tad and Faulk probably didn't realize how suspicious it looked, being AWOL from where they were expected to be this morning. If they'd had to go someplace last night, for whatever reason, they probably didn't even know about the murder yet.

Lenny was checking Tad and Faulk's tent. It wouldn't be that far out of my way to drop by the forge.

The forge was still dark as I approached, and its shutters were locked up tight. But then as I approached one swung open.

I quickened my pace. It wasn't necessarily Faulk. The boys had been spending more and more time helping out at the forge.

But as I drew near, relief washed over me. It was Faulk, now sitting on a stool in the small side room that served as our shop. But relief turned to concern when I reached the doorway to the shop.

He was just sitting there with his eyes closed. And he looked terrible. His face was ashen and drawn. I'd met his father once, not long before the old man died—not a happy memory, since the many things the elder Mr. Cates disapproved of included anything and anyone connected with what he called Faulk's "feckless vagabond blue-collar existence." Back then I'd had a hard time seeing any resemblance between Faulk and his father. Today I could see it all too well.

Something was definitely wrong with Faulk.

Chapter 19

Faulk looked up, noticed me, and tried to rearrange his features into a less bleak expression.

"What's wrong?"

We'd said it almost simultaneously. Faulk laughed and looked a little more like himself—but only a little.

"I'd claim that I asked first," he said. "Pretty sure it was a dead heat, though. How about 'I got here first'?"

"Have you heard about Terence?" I asked.

"Not him again." Faulk grimaced. "What's he done now?"

"Got himself murdered," I said.

Faulk blinked a couple of times, as if he was having trouble deciphering what I'd said. Then his mouth fell open and he seemed to be groping for something to say.

"You're not kidding, are you?" he said finally.

"'Fraid not."

"Damn." He shook his head slowly. "I won't pretend I'm going to miss him. But I'm sorry for him. I'm a big fan of people getting to live to a ripe old age and die painlessly in their sleep. Even monumentally annoying people. Do they know who did it?"

I shook my head.

"I presume the police will be swarming all over the Faire today, then." He smiled, a little wanly. "So spill. Where and when and how?"

"Out in the woods behind the fairgrounds early this morning," I said. "Or possibly late last night. I think the police are checking on everyone's alibis between midnight and dawn."

"Oh, great." He grimaced and blew out a long breath.

Not the utterly unconcerned reaction I'd been hoping for. But not panic, either.

"After that stunt Terence pulled on Tad yesterday—"

"The police will want to know our whereabouts." He nodded. "I guess we're better off than most people."

"You can alibi each other."

"And the whole ER staff can alibi the two of us."

"ER staff? What happened?" I didn't see any bandages. Bandages might be preferable to some of the dire possibilities that flitted through my mind. Then again, maybe Tad was sporting the bandages and Faulk was merely exhausted from being up all night.

"Long story."

I pushed down the panicky thought that it was a longer story than he had the energy to tell.

"We've got some time before opening," I said. "So—ER in which hospital?"

"Whatever the nearest one is." He chuckled. "At least I assume Tad found the nearest. Me, I'd have been panicking and waking up people to ask for directions, but he just typed 'hospital' into his phone and off we went."

Presumably the hospital in the next county. I knew Riverton itself had no hospital—they'd only recently acquired an urgent care center.

"I deduce you were the patient, then," I said aloud.

He nodded again.

"And you're not going to tell me what happened?"

"Just a little cardiac false alarm."

Damn.

"You want Dad to check you out? Not that I want to cast doubts on the abilities of the doctors at whatever hospital—"

"I'll be fine," he said. "And your dad's probably busy with the murder anyway—is he getting on the local medical examiner's nerves yet?"

"No, they seem to be buddies. He'll be hurt if he finds out you went to the ER and didn't even tell him afterward." For that matter, I was curious why they hadn't checked with Dad before dashing off to the hospital.

"I'll check in with him later." He smiled. "Don't worry— I'm never one to turn down free medical care. I might have awakened him before dashing off to the ER. Tad was hell-bent on getting me back to civilization, as he called it."

"Maybe we should cut back on our scheduled demonstrations," I said. "After getting up when it was still dark to take Grandfather owling, I'm already so beat that I was hoping to finagle you into doing my first demo today, so I could take a nap. But you look as if you need the rest more than I do."

"Probably wise." Faulk sounded reluctant. And a little wistful, as if in saying so he'd surrendered something cherished. "I'm supposed to be resting, and given what's happened, I'm sure you'll be busier than ever."

"Look," I began—and I was intending to keep pressing until he told me exactly why he'd ended up in the ER overnight. But my phone dinged to signal an arriving message. I pulled it out to look.

"The chief wants me," I said. "Probably because she wants me to clear out the room in which Tad was using all his green-screen equipment. She plans to use it for her investigation. I left a message for him about that, but he probably hasn't had time to listen yet, so if you see him anytime soon, ask him to come up to the main house to help."

"Will do." He seemed more comfortable now that the conversation wasn't about his health.

"And I'll make sure the boys are here by opening time, and you can let them do the lion's share of the work."

"I won't say no. Now run along and help the police with their investigation."

"They'll want to interview you, too."

"I figured as much. If I'm not here, I'll be in my tent."

He stood up and began erasing the chalkboard on which we kept our schedule of demonstrations. I paused long enough to text Lenny that Faulk was in the forge, then hurried off toward the main house.

The energy level had picked up, as it usually did in the last hour before the opening bell. Cooks at some of the food venues were firing up their grills. Down by the jousting field several of the knights, still dressed in jeans and t-shirts, were riding their horses around the ring, in what I assumed was a warm-up. Madame Destiny and her mother sat in front of the fortune-telling tent, studying a tarot layout with intense concentration. Craftspeople were arranging the wares on the front counters of their booths. The glassblower had started his furnace. A perfectly normal start to the Faire.

Up at the main house, nothing was normal. A dirty white panel truck was parked right in front of the building, with two Riverton deputies watching over it. The chief was standing in the doorway, looking mildly annoyed. Which was about as agitated as you ever saw her, so I figured things must be going very badly.

"There's Meg now." Her face cleared. "Do you know where we can find a wheelbarrow or something? When Horace is finished searching Mr. Cox's tent, we want to bring it and the contents up here to secure them."

"I'm sure we have a wheelbarrow on the grounds somewhere," I said. "Finding it's going to be the problem. How about if we haul the stuff up here in the horse-drawn cart we use for kiddie rides?"

"That would work." The chief's expression showed that she found my suggestion acceptable, if odd. I texted the driver of the cart to ask her to bring it up to the main house ASAP. "I have an interviewee waiting for me. A Ms."—she checked her notebook—"Willowdale? Could that possibly be correct?"

"I suspect it's a stage name," I said. "But legal now—it's what we have on her payroll forms."

"Willowdale it is, then. Incidentally, I've been told you can deal with the equipment that's currently in the studio opposite—"

"Tad's equipment, yes." I set off toward the craft wing. "That's what I came up here for, to deal with it. I already left Tad a message that we needed to move his stuff, but—"

"He and Mr. Cates still appear to be absent." She had fallen into step beside me, her face impassive.

"They're back," I said. "I just talked to Faulk down at the forge. Tad had to take him down to the ER."

"In Jessop?" The chief's tone suggested she found this interesting.

"If that's the nearest ER."

"Not much of an ER. Hope there was nothing serious wrong." The chief's dismissive tone reminded me that there was a long-standing tension between Riverton and the surrounding county—of which Jessop was, presumably, the county seat.

"A cardiac false alarm, according to Faulk."

"He should get it checked out someplace that actually knows what they're doing," the chief said. "Most people go down to Richmond if they have anything that's beyond the urgent care clinic. Or up to Fairfax or Loudoun. I'll suggest that when I talk to them."

We had reached the lower floor of the studio wing, and passed between the racks of yesterday's costumes to reach our destination. Someone had placed a couple of dining room chairs in the corridor outside Cordelia's office. Dianne, already dressed in the lace-trimmed pink-and-blue gown she wore on Saturdays, was sitting in one, busily texting on her phone. She glanced up when we arrived, and I could tell she was working hard on maintaining the solemn expression she seemed to feel was appropriate for the occasion.

"Ms. Willowdale." The chief's face didn't show the slightest hint of how implausible she'd found the name only a few minutes ago. She ushered Dianne into Cordelia's office and shut the door.

I pulled out my phone and glanced at it. Still half an hour till the opening bell. And I had nothing mission-critical to do in the first few minutes of the Faire. I could at least make a start at clearing out Tad's stuff.

It was easier than I expected. He'd obviously come back sometime and begun to pack. The green screens and the light aluminum frame that had held them up had been taken down, and presumably packed in several large black cases that were conveniently equipped with wheels. Another open case had a foam insert with dents that were exactly the right size and shape to cradle the large, flat monitor. I gathered up the various cords, cables, clamps, and other miscellaneous bits of electronic flotsam and stuffed them into an empty black nylon duffle bag. If that wasn't where they belonged, Tad could sort them out later. Then I dragged the cases down the hall to the storage room and locked them up there. My eye fell on Terence's battered cardboard boxes. I should tell the chief about them.

Just then the opening bell rang and I had to fight a quick stab of guilt that for the first time I wasn't there watching as the gates opened. Maybe that was why I didn't feel the surge of joy and excitement that the opening bell usually inspired.

I was writing out a note to Tad, telling him what I'd done with his stuff, when Dianne emerged from Cordelia's office and hurried off toward the stairs that led up to the main floor.

The chief followed more slowly and frowned when she saw that the two chairs outside her door were empty.

"I've packed up Tad's things and moved them into storage," I said. "And now I'm going to head out and find you some more witnesses to talk to."

"Good." She glanced at her notebook and then up at me. "Ms. Willowdale seems to be under the impression that Mr. Cox was about to be fired. I thought he was on probation—not quite the same thing."

"Cordelia had a long talk with him last night," I said. "And made it very clear that he'd used up all his chances. One more offense and he was gone. But she knew she might be inviting legal hassles if she didn't give him at least one chance to shape up. Dianne, on the other hand, was a fellow employee, so there'd be nothing to keep her from expressing her opinion on how likely he was to suc- ceed in that shaping-up thing."

The chief nodded.

"One more thing—" she began.

My phone vibrated. I pulled it out and glanced down to see who was calling.

Chapter 20

"I should probably take this if it's okay with you," I said after I'd checked my phone. "It's the front gate, and they don't generally call unless they have a problem."

The chief waved her consent and I caught the call before it went to voicemail.

"What's up?" I asked.

"Could you come and help us with something?" the voice said. "There's someone here who claims he's Terence's guest."

"Terence's guest?" I echoed. The chief looked up with an interested expression, and I put the phone on speaker so she could hear.

"Yes—he says Terence was going to leave a ticket for him with us, but he didn't and the guy's asking us to call Terence and I don't know what to say and . . ."

"I'll be right there." I hung up.

"And I'll go with you," the chief said.

We set out at a brisk pace. The chief wasn't quite as tall as I was, but she had probably gotten a full night's sleep and was a lot more awake and alert, so we were well matched.

"Does the front gate know what happened?" she asked.

"I'm sure they do by now, but Cordelia would have ordered them not to tell anyone, and to say no comment if anyone asks them about it. Which is why they called me instead of just telling the guest what happened."

She nodded her approval.

As we passed through the Faire, I tried to assess the

crowds. They were at least as big as yesterday's, weren't they? Of course, as far as we knew, the news about Terence hadn't gotten out yet, so it was too soon to tell what effect the murder would have on attendance.

And was it shallow of me to worry about attendance? I hoped not. After all, if Terence's murder ruined the Faire, it might cause serious financial problems for Cordelia.

And if the murder drew hordes of gawkers who'd try to invade the crime scene, the chief wouldn't be very happy.

As we drew near the gate, I was pretty sure I'd spotted the man who was causing the ticket sellers such stress. He was standing just outside the gate—rather a large man was my first impression. And then I began second-guessing that impression. He couldn't have been more than an inch or two taller than me, so barely six feet if that. And beefy, but not fat—though you could tell he was starting to fight the effects of middle age on his waistline. He just seemed to take up more space than the people around him. An actor's trick. He was dressed entirely in black, which seemed to be a popular wardrobe strategy for theater folk. And he looked vaguely familiar. Probably an actor. Someone Michael had invited to replace Terence, maybe? But no. A replacement would have asked for Michael. He was claiming to be a friend of Terence.

The gate staffers wore looks of relief, and I didn't need their discreet gestures toward the man to tell that I'd guessed right.

"May I help you?" I asked the beefy man. His face was still handsome, though starting to go a little soft in the jowls. I wondered if the stubbly three-or four-days' growth of beard festooning his jaw was intended as camouflage.

"There seems to be some mix-up." His tone and expression were designed to convey that while the mix-up was entirely due to our stupidity, he was deliberately exercising a positively supernatural degree of patience.

"Let's see if we can straighten it out, then. Will you come into the office?"

I led the way into the large shed we grandly called the office, although its main purpose was to have a secure place to lock up stuff, like the lost-and-found collection, or anything bulky that we didn't want to haul all the way up to the house at the end of the day. And to check the weapons people had bought here at the Faire, although this early it probably didn't contain many of those. I made a mental note to ask the chief if she wanted to see the notebook in which we logged the weapons.

At present the office also served as an overflow bunk-house for a couple of the rank-and-file staff members whose tent had developed a leak, and I was relieved to see that they had followed procedure and hidden away their stuff before going on duty.

Chief Heedles followed me into the office and closed the door behind us.

"Maybe I should speak to the boss-lady," our visitor said. "Ms. Cordelia Lee."

"I'm Meg Langslow, her second-in-command," I said. "Maybe I can help you."

"Neil O'Malley."

No wonder he looked familiar. But what was the way-ward director doing down here, instead of up at Arena Stage auditioning actors for his *Hamlet* production?

He shook my hand with what he probably meant as a crushing grip. Or was he actually oblivious to how over-the-top his handshake was? No. The look of surprise when I didn't wince or even react told me the overkill was delib-erate. But he'd have to find another way to intimidate a blacksmith.

Curiously, he didn't ask who Chief Heedles was. Did he assume the senior management of a Ren Faire normally traveled with a police escort? Or was the chief deploying her superpower of unobtrusiveness to avoid his notice?

"And you're a friend of Terence Cox," I said.

"We've worked together on a number of productions. I'm a director—"

"Yes, I know. And Terence said he'd leave you a ticket?"

"He did. I came up here especially to see him. I'm casting him in a show I'm directing—*Hamlet,* at the Arena Stage in Washington. He's going to be my Polonius."

Casting Terence as Polonius? Well, that was interesting. Another reason to be grateful that Michael had declined to audition for Laertes. If he'd won the part, he'd be spending time with O'Malley *and* Terence. Then again, maybe O'Malley would have given the part to someone else, and even Michael might be a little hurt at being rejected by someone who'd rejected him and cast Terence.

O'Malley was looking expectant, and maybe a little peeved, as if he thought it was long past time for one or both of us to exclaim "Oh my goodness! Are you Neil O'Malley the *director*?" Clearly he didn't get out in the real world much.

"If I may," the chief said. It wasn't exactly a request—more a polite order. I didn't mind—in fact, I was already happy to turn over dealing with O'Malley to someone else.

"Be my guest," I said aloud.

"Mr. O'Malley." At her words, he jumped as if only just noticing her. "I'm Chief Heedles of the Riverton Police Department. I'm sorry to be the bearer of bad news, but Mr. Terence Cox is dead."

"Dead? Dead? Oh, my God!" He covered his mouth with both hands in what struck me as a rather stagy gesture of shock.

Or maybe I was allowing my initial negative impression of him to influence me. No—that first "dead" sounded more like happy surprise than shock or grief. He'd fixed that quickly, and by "oh, my God!" his grief had sounded as genuine as you could wish, but still—that first reaction.

From her expression, I deduced that the chief had noticed the same thing.

"What happened?" O'Malley went on. "I didn't even know he was ill. He looked fine the last time I saw him."

"And when was that?" The chief had her notebook in hand.

"Let me think." O'Malley frowned in visible effort. "Tuesday? Or possibly Wednesday? I'd have to ask my assistant to be sure. He came up to do a second audition."

"Came up where?"

"To the Arena."

"Arena? What arena?"

"The Arena Stage." O'Malley didn't hide his look of astonishment that she had to ask. "It's a theater," he added. "In Washington. D.C."

"And it was at that meeting at the theater that he promised you a ticket to the Renaissance Faire?" the chief asked.

"No, that was . . . Thursday, I think. When I called to confirm that he had the part. He told me he was currently working down here and asked when the *Hamlet* rehearsals started, so he could give notice if he wasn't going to be able to finish out the summer here, and I said I didn't think we'd start quite that soon, and he should definitely keep working here. You see I gathered a lot of what he was doing here was some kind of improv, and we're definitely going to do a lot of that in my production, so it was a good thing, keeping his improv instincts alive. And then he suggested I should come down—I could join in the improv if I liked, and I said it sounded fabulous, and he said he'd leave a ticket for me at the box office."

I kept my face neutral. Which was more annoying—that Terence had auditioned for and accepted another part and hadn't even told Michael so we could start to work on replacing him? Or that he'd invited this consummate jackass to join the Game, again without telling Michael?

And improv in a production of *Hamlet?* I could imagine how Michael would react to that.

The chief merely nodded.

"Are you going to tell me what happened to Terence?" O'Malley asked. "Because I'm thinking if he'd merely dropped dead of a heart attack or something I wouldn't be standing here telling a police officer when the last time I talked to him was. Was there an accident?"

"Mr. Cox was murdered," the chief said.

O'Malley's face took on an exaggerated expression of shock and concern. Or maybe he really was shocked and concerned and just had an annoyingly melodramatic way of expressing it.

"Sometime this morning or late last night," the chief went on. "We're waiting for official word from the medical examiner on time of death. So we're taking an interest in anything he did over the last few days."

"Naturally." O'Malley nodded absently and pulled out his phone. "Damn! He'd have made a great Polonius. I should call my assistant. Have her remind me who else we liked for the role. And I could ask her to check on exactly when Terence was up at the Arena, if that's of any use."

"Before you do, I'd like to ask you a few more questions about Mr. Cox," the chief said. "Meg, do you mind if I use this office for now?"

"No problem," I said. "And in the meantime, I'll round up a few more of the people you want to interview." I picked up the weapons log and looked around for something to use as a temporary substitute.

The chief nodded.

"And Mr. O'Malley," I added, "if you still feel like checking out the Faire, I'll leave a pass for you at the ticket office."

"Yes, of course." He was still frowning down at his phone.

I lettered TEMPORARY WEAPONS LOG at the top of a sheet of paper torn from a yellow legal pad, put it in the center of the desk, then went out and closed the door firmly behind myself. The gate staffers were all busy, either selling tickets or collecting them and passing out programs, but they all glanced over, obviously curious.

"The chief's using the office for the time being," I told the head ticket seller. "So keep everyone out. And if Mr. O'Malley, the guy she's talking to, still wants a free ticket, give him one and log it to the PR account."

The ticket seller nodded and went back to explaining the difference between children's and student tickets to a harried-looking parent with, by my guess, two students and five children in tow.

I dodged into the costume shop and commandeered a basic women's costume—white blouse, brown skirt, red vest. Who knew when I'd get back to our room in the main building to change? Then, once I was properly in uniform, so to speak, I found a quiet corner where I could call Michael—who didn't answer until the fourth ring.

"Hope I'm not interrupting anything," I said.

"I'm due at the Dragon's Claw any second to trade insults with George," he said. "But I can always show up a bit late if you need anything. Or better yet, if you have news."

"News, of a sort, but first a question—did you find anyone to replace Terence?"

"Not for today, alas," he said. "For tomorrow I've got a former student who's driving up from Atlanta, but he won't be here until late. We'll just have to work around it. What's the news?"

"Neil O'Malley just showed up."

Chapter 21

"O'Malley? Seriously?" He whistled, and I wondered briefly if whistling was an anachronism. "That's weird. Any idea why? I know better than to assume he's asking for me."

"No, he's asking for the free ticket Terence was supposed to be leaving for him at the gate."

"Weirder still. Wonder how they know each other."

"According to O'Malley, Terence was going to play Polonius in his production of *Hamlet*."

"Polonius? Are you sure? Because— Got to run. Meet me at the Dragon's Claw; there's much to discuss. Bye!"

Much to discuss? Now my curiosity was piqued. So, since he hadn't specified when I should meet him at the Dragon's Claw, I decided to head over there now, so I could find out what needed discussing as soon as there was a break in the Game.

A thought hit me, so I crossed the lane to the men's costume shop and sought out the head of the crew.

"Did you see that guy who was making a fuss at the gate?"

"Demanding a free ticket? Yeah. What about him?"

"Actor. Friend of Terence."

"Oooh—suspect?"

"No idea yet. If the chief turns him loose and he wanders in here looking for a costume, comp him one of the fancier nobleman outfits on my tab."

"Can do."

I set out for the Dragon's Claw. Judging from the

occasional gales of laughter coming from the general direction of the inn, whatever theme they'd chosen for today was starting out well.

There were five of them in action. Michael and George were standing at opposite sides of the ring of spectators, occasionally casting scornful glances at each other, but mostly looking on while Jacks and Nigel argued over who should succeed Queen Cordelia. Dianne just stood nearby, looking elegant, beautiful, and very, very cheerful.

Jacks was arguing persuasively that Michael was the most qualified, while making it clear that Nigel was mainly interested in marrying his daughter to the new king and running the kingdom from behind the throne. Nigel didn't have a whole lot to fight back with, apart from implying, in a distinctly oily manner, that Michael kept such unsuitable company that it disqualified him from the throne. I found myself wondering if we couldn't draft Nigel to be the official troublemaker in Terence's place. It wouldn't be typecasting, as it had been with Terence, but judging from how well he was doing now, Nigel could manage it.

"Why can't Duke Michael marry the Lady Dianne?" someone in the audience eventually called out.

"I have already given my heart elsewhere," he said, in such a simple and straightforward manner that I suspect it instantly undid most of Nigel's efforts to blacken his name.

"To a baseborn wench who cannot possibly become queen." If Nigel had mustaches, he would have been twirling them.

"To a maid of humble station," Michael countered. "But as honest as your daughter, and as fair."

I was relieved that he didn't single me out in the crowd, and hoped the other players would take their cue from him.

"Your Majesty!" Lady Dianne interrupted the debate by announcing Cordelia's arrival and sinking into a deep curtsey. All of the other players and quite a few of the audience bowed or curtseyed.

"Rise, good people." I could tell Cordelia was stressed, but I doubted the audience could. "No ceremony today, as we celebrate the summer in this festive grove."

"Welcome, Majesty." Nigel took a brown leather tankard from a nearby table and offered it. "Will you share a cup of cheer with us?"

"At a later time, good Sir Nigel. At present, we have other pressing matters in hand. Lady Jacquelynn, will you have the goodness to walk with us? We have need of your counsel."

I suspected it was actually Chief Heedles who wanted to speak with Jacks—who looked anxious for a moment, then regained most of her composure.

"Of course, Your Majesty." She curtseyed deeply.

Cordelia took Jacks's arm as if she needed the support to steady herself, though from Jacks's strained expression I suspected she was the one more likely to need support. We all bowed and curtseyed again as the two sailed away.

Michael and George tossed a few more witty insults at each other, then bowed and agreed to meet again at noon to watch the archery contest.

As the actors were all wishing each other good morrow, Michael said a quick word to Nigel, who fell in step with him. They headed my way.

"Let's use the inn's private room," Michael said.

We made our way inside the Dragon's Claw, collected mugs of fake ale from the bar, and then climbed a flight of stairs to the so-called private room. It wasn't actually all that private—it was a sort of balcony on top of the bar, so anyone who sat there was completely visible to almost every customer in the room. But even if there weren't any musicians playing on the postage-stamp stage across the room and all of the patrons were drinking in morose silence, a would-be eavesdropper would have a hard time hearing conversations in the private room. Anyone who truly needed a break from talking to tourists could retire to the room to regroup while still being a visible part of the Game, and it was one of the best places for participants to have a private conversation.

I noticed that Nigel took a careful sniff at his tankard before sipping it.

Michael wasted no time once we were seated.

"Tell Meg what you told me," he said.

Nigel winced and closed his eyes. Then he opened them again and turned to me.

"I told Michael I was afraid the police are going to suspect me," he said.

"Because of Terence trying to trap you into drinking?" I asked.

"Well, that too."

That too? There was something else? I made sure I had my pleasant, nonjudgmental listening face on.

"Remember last weekend when I missed most of the day?"

"I remember," I said. "You told us you were down for the count with a migraine."

"That wasn't exactly true." He took a long pull on his diluted tea with an intensity that made it all too easy to visualize him back in the bad old days, when he might have wanted a drink to steady himself. "I did have something of a headache by the end of the day. All the stress of sneaking around and lying to people who have been so good to me."

"You could have asked for the day off," Michael said. "Not that I mean to give you a hard time, but if it comes up again—"

"Yeah, I know that now. I should have known it then. But I was on edge—you know how it is when you're getting ready for a big audition. I just thought, I'll keep it under my hat, and if nothing comes of it, no one will ever know."

"I'm still in the dark, remember?" I said. "No one will ever know about what?"

"I went up to D.C. for an audition," he said. "A callback. I know Michael wasn't keen, but he has a great career now, teaching. It could mean all the difference to me. Get my career started again. But I didn't want to seem ungrateful for the chance you'd given me, and I didn't really want people to know anyway, in case it didn't work out, so . . ."

He took another deep gulp of tea.

"I think I get the picture," I said. "You snuck off to audition for Neil O'Malley's production of *Hamlet*."

He nodded and swallowed hard.

"For what part?"

"Polonius. And I got it." He smiled, and I realized I hadn't seen that broad a smile on his face in the several weeks we'd been here at the center. My heart sank a little.

"Polonius? You're sure?"

"Reasonably sure, yes." He struck a deliberately theatrical pose and intoned "'Give thy thoughts no tongue, nor any unproportioned thought his act. Be thou familiar, but by no means vulgar. Those friends thou hast, and their adoption tried, grapple them unto thy soul with hoops of steel.'" His face fell a little. "Guess I didn't do such a great job of that last part, did I? I should have told you guys. Before the callback. Better still, before the first audition. But for sure afterward, once I had the part."

"And how solid was it, getting that part?" I asked. "Did you have anything in writing? Like a contract?"

"Well, not exactly." Nigel frowned slightly. "Not a contract. But he told me after my reading I was in, and that evening he sent me an email thanking me for coming up for the second reading, saying I'd nailed it, and that his assistant would be mailing out the paperwork soon. Paperwork as in contracts, I'm sure."

"Interesting," I murmured.

Michael, who knew very well that "interesting" was rarely a compliment in my family, stifled a grin.

"Look, I can tell him I need to finish out my contract here," Nigel said. "I'm sure he'll understand. Especially if I point out that thanks to Terence's murder you're already shorthanded. And I'm sorry about missing Saturday, but I skipped my breaks on Sunday and I was scheduled to have Wednesday off from the costume shop during this week and I worked it anyway and—"

"Relax," Michael said. "I get it. A part like that could restart your career. If you'd asked, I'd have given you the day off, and I'm not going to give you a hard time now that you've landed it."

"If you feel guilty about missing last Saturday, just help us pull off today's Game without Terence and we'll call it quits," I said.

"Thanks," he said. "But I still have to worry about what the cops will think, don't I?"

"But why?" Okay, maybe not a fair question, since I already knew what O'Malley had said, but I wanted to see what else I could learn before disclosing that bit of information. "Why would they care that you snuck away to do an audition last weekend?"

"Because Terence was blackmailing me about it."

Chapter 22

"Blackmailing you?" Michael echoed. I could tell from his tone that it didn't sound all that plausible to him. "About sneaking off to audition?"

"Yes." Nigel nodded, then hurried on. "You see, I was so excited when I got the call to go up for the second reading that I had to tell someone, and unfortunately Terence was the only person nearby. And as soon as I told him he started warning me that I'd better keep it a secret. That maybe you'd understand—or maybe not—but that Cordelia would go ballistic if I asked for the whole day off. And he offered to help me—to cover for me. He was the one who suggested the migraine idea. I felt a bit guilty, but I really wanted to make that callback, so I took him up on it. Maybe I should have been suspicious about how nice he was about it."

"Not exactly in character, yeah," I said. "But it was a smart idea, the migraine cover story. Just about everyone would understand. And be especially sympathetic, since coping with a migraine—or even an ordinary headache—is bad enough when you're home in your familiar surroundings, with whatever usually helps."

"That was the idea," Nigel said. "Terence even suggested that if anyone went looking for me and found my tent empty, he'd figure out some way to cover for me— like saying that he'd helped me find a quiet place in the woods where I could get away from the noise." He turned to Michael. "I remember Saturday evening, when I told my migraine lie, you said you wished I'd told you I was sick, because you could have found someplace quiet, dark, and air-conditioned for me in the house." He shook his head. "Can you imagine how guilty I felt? And then Terence started . . . well, I guess blackmailing's the right term for it. He wasn't asking for money—at least he hadn't yet. But maybe he'd have worked up to that. Maybe he was testing the waters by seeing if he could get me to do whatever he wanted to do in the Game. Like agreeing to the betrothal with Dianne."

"That did seem a little out of character," I said. "Since you'd probably figured out even sooner than the rest of us what a bad idea it would be to take the Game in a direction that gave him more reasons to hang around with Dianne."

"Yeah." Nigel nodded. "He hit me with it yesterday morning, and hinted that if I helped him out, he wouldn't have any reason to spill the beans on my going AWOL. I gave in, but it bothered me. I started thinking that if I let him get away with that, the sky was the limit. He'd hold it over me forever.

"Well, after this summer it wouldn't matter that much, would it?"

"True, but I wasn't thinking clearly. And I'd overheard him—at the time, I just figured he was having an argument with someone over the phone. But later I realized he was probably talking to someone he was blackmailing."

Michael and I exchanged a worried glance.

"Just what did you hear?" I asked. "And when?"

"One night this week I went out on the terrace after dinner, and he was on his phone. And as soon as he saw me he waved me off, looking a little annoyed, as if I should have known he'd gone out there for the privacy, so I went all the way to the far end and only overheard those first few words. Something like 'I don't care, I want it. Remember, I have the goods on you!' At the time, I didn't think much of it. But then when he started pressuring me to go along with his storyline for the Game, it came to me that maybe I'd overheard him blackmailing someone. No idea who."

"Do you remember exactly what night it was?" I asked.

"What night?" Nigel's expression showed that he thought it a peculiar and irrelevant question.

"The police can probably trace whoever he was taking to anyway," I pointed out. "But they can do it all the more easily if they know when it was. And if he really was black-mailing someone else, maybe about something a lot more serious than being AWOL from the Game—wouldn't the blackmailer be a good murder suspect?"

"I hadn't thought of that." He frowned. "I think it was Wednesday. I went outside to see if I could catch a breeze—it was that really hot day when the air-conditioning at the main house went out, and they had it fixed by the end of the day, but the house was still stuffy when we went in for dinner."

"Yeah, definitely Wednesday." I'd spent most of the day dealing with the air-conditioning repair service.

"Anyway, when I saw all the trouble the thing with Di-anne caused, I decided maybe I should face the music. Tell one of you or Cordelia about it. But by the time I got up my nerve last night, you'd all three vanished."

"We went to bed early," Michael explained. "So we could get up before dawn to take Meg's grandfather owling."

"Yeah, I realize that now. No idea what Terence was doing, but I couldn't find him, either. I even went out to his tent—the new solitary one across the camp—to tell him the deal was off, but no luck."

"When did you go?" Michael asked.

"No idea." Nigel shrugged. "Couple times over the course of the evening. The last time was just before I went to bed. Eleven-thirty, or maybe midnight."

"Make sure to tell the police that," I said. "It will look

better than if you fail to mention it and someone else saw you and reports you."

"Because I'm a suspect." Nigel tightened his jaw. "I know."

"Join the multitude," I said. "Anyone who didn't have a reason to dislike Terence wasn't paying attention."

"You see why what you said surprised me," Michael said, turning to me.

"Should we tell Nigel?" I asked.

Michael nodded.

"Tell me what?" Nigel looked anxious. I wished we could go back, just for a moment, to that broad smile he'd showed when he'd told us he'd gotten the part of Polonius."

"Neil O'Malley showed up here just now, asking for Terence," I said. "He mentioned that he'd just given Terence a part in his *Hamlet*."

"Oh, great," Nigel said.

"The part of Polonius."

"Wait—he what? No!" Nigel's face cycled through shock and disbelief and ended up in anger. "No—that can't be. That's my part. O'Malley told me I'd nailed it. He can't have gone behind my back and given it to someone else. And of all people, to Terence."

"O'Malley's always been pretty . . . feckless," Michael said.

"I'll sue." Nigel's face was beet red and his jaw was set. "Breach of contract. Or . . . something"

"Hang on and see what happens," Michael advised. "After all, O'Malley will need another Polonius, won't he, now that Terence isn't around to play the part."

"A good thing Terence isn't still around or I might try to kill him myself," Nigel said. "If he went behind my back somehow and snaked the part away—"

"Regardless of how Terence got the part, or whether he ever had it at all, he can't play it now, can he?" Michael said. "At best, he might be qualified to play the ghost of Hamlet's father, but only if he can figure out how to haunt Arena Stage instead of Cordelia's Kingdom of Albion."

"True." Nigel laughed a little hollowly. "I might still have it, if I can stay out of jail. And I'm sure I just made myself the number one suspect, but I don't really care. He was a horrible man. I'm not sorry he's dead."

"You know," Michael said. "There's just a chance that O'Malley wasn't telling the truth about giving Polonius to Terence."

"Why would he lie about a thing like that?" Nigel's face wore a puzzled expression. I'm sure mine did, too.

"To make himself more important," Michael said. "The victim isn't just one of the multitude of actors he's auditioned over the years—he's the actor to whom he was about to entrust a major role in his much-anticipated new stage production. Not only a cruel loss to the theater, but a profound personal loss to Neil O'Malley."

"You think he'd do that?" Nigel sounded dubious.

"Odds are he's already trying to figure out who to flatter so he can become a pallbearer," Michael said.

"I think he mentioned giving the part to Terence before he heard the news about his death," I said. "Otherwise I'd agree completely. I bet I know what Dad will say when he meets him: narcissistic personality disorder."

"No argument from me," Michael said. He turned back to Nigel. "We may never know for sure—but I think the odds are you had the part all along. Don't let it get to you."

"I know you're only saying that to cheer me up," Nigel said. "But I appreciate the effort."

He glanced down and started, as he'd forgotten that the raised platform we were sitting on was visible to the seventy or eighty tourists currently eating and drinking in the Dragon's Claw. For that matter, I'd forgotten it myself, and had to remind myself that all the upturned faces below might have seen our whole discussion, including Nigel's sudden burst of anger, but they couldn't have heard a word.

"Look at them." Nigel gestured with a slight nod of his head. "All busily watching. They probably think we're hatching up the next twist in the Game. I wonder what they'll think when word of the murder gets out."

"For Game purposes, I suppose we should figure out what we were just discussing with such heat." Michael's expression suggested that he wasn't really feeling inventive at the moment.

"Nigel offered to support your bid to succeed Cordelia if you married his daughter and made her queen," I suggested. "And didn't take rejection well."

"Sounds reasonable," Michael said.

"As good as anything I can think of," Nigel agreed. "Let's work that into the performance when next we meet." He reached into the well-concealed—because arguably anachronistic—pocket in the side of his doublet and pulled out a modern wristwatch, which he shielded with his hands from the view of the tourists below. "When should that be?"

"Why don't you let Michael know when you're finished talking to Chief Heedles," I said. "Because if I were you, I'd go up to the house and get that over with as soon as possible."

"Good idea." He nodded, tucked the watch safely back in his pocket, and stood up. "Once more unto the breach!"

Nigel led the way down the wooden stairs to the main floor of the tavern. Outside, we all bowed and curtseyed and loudly wished each other a good morrow in approved Renaissance fashion. Michael and I watched as Nigel strode off toward the main house.

"I should be off," I said.

"Where to?"

"Back to the forge to check on things." I set off, and Michael fell into step beside me.

"Can't Faulk handle things there for today?"

"I wish." I explained about Tad and Faulk's trip to the ER as we made our way slowly down the lane, bowing and replying in kind to any tourists who wished us a good morrow.

"Damn," Michael said when I'd finished relaying the news. "A good thing the boys are here to help out. Maybe one of us should have a word with them. Clue them in to go easy on Faulk."

"I had the same thought, and I'll do it now, assuming they're at the forge. Also, I want to corner Tad and find out exactly what happened. I'm not sure I'm buying this 'cardiac false alarm' thing. Faulk has never been very good at asking for help or admitting any kind of weakness."

"It's a guy thing," Michael said. "Well, at least Tad and Faulk probably have an alibi for last night. And also—"

"Michael, old boy! Where have you been all these centuries?"

Chapter 23

Michael winced, and we turned to see Neil O'Malley looming into our field of vision, filling most of it. He was wearing a spectacularly ornate costume made of cloth of gold and brown velvet that Mother had designed, based on Hans Holbein's famous portrait of Henry VIII. I happened to know this painting was the source because I'd seen the copy of it hanging in the costume shop while Mother and the seamstresses sketched and played with their fabric scraps.

We'd intended for Terence to use the outfit—either to play a Falstaff-like character in some future edition of the Game, or maybe even to play Henry VIII if we took a break from Albion one day and did straight English history, with Jacks as Catherine of Aragon and Dianne as Anne Boleyn. I'd told the costume crew to comp O'Malley one of the fancier nobleman's outfits, not crown him king. He'd have had to wheedle this costume out of Mother, and I couldn't imagine how such an annoying man could have managed that. And what was he planning to do while wearing the Henry outfit?

I suspected from Michael's expression that he was having similar thoughts.

"Hello, Neil." His tone was surprisingly neutral. "Long time no see."

Maybe it was only because I knew him so well that I heard the subtext: "Not long enough."

"I heard you were short one player, so I got your costume folks to kit me out so I could pitch in to help."

He twirled so we could admire the costume. If I were O'Malley, stocky to begin with and in the early stages of battling middle-aged spread, I'd have chosen a different costume—one not intended to pad out a normal-sized person to resemble the enormous bulk of the mature Henry VIII. But maybe he assumed everyone would think it was the costume that made him look stout.

Or maybe Mother, like me, had taken an immediate dislike to him, and had deliberately talked him into donning the unflattering costume.

"Very thoughtful of you," Michael said. "Did—"

"And may I say this is a fabulous idea!" O'Malley thundered. "Simply fabulous! You know how I love improv. This is going to be a blast!"

Michael's smile might have fooled O'Malley, but not me.

"Did anyone brief you on the Game's overall storyline?" he asked.

"I gather we all dance attendance on the queen," O'Malley said. "Scary old bat! Puts me in mind of working with Maggie Smith. So what's my part?"

"If you want to take over from Terence—" Michael began.

"Of course! Of course! Damn, but that's a shame, isn't it? Did you know I'd cast him as Polonius in my *Hamlet*? Terrible loss to the theater. No idea how I'm going to replace him. So am I one of the contenders to inherit when She of the Steely Gaze pops off?"

"George and I are the leading contenders," Michael said. "George Sims—do you know him?"

"Of course! Fabulous performer!" O'Malley exclaimed, though I thought his face had worn, just for a moment, the sort of puzzled expression that would suggest he didn't know George in the slightest, but wouldn't admit it, in case George turned out to be Somebody after all.

"And you . . ." Michael paused for just a moment, doubtless wishing he didn't have to say what he was about to say.

"You are the troublemaker. The trickster. The Iago of the piece. It's your job to sow discord."

"Between you and George?"

"Between any two characters you like," Michael said. "As long as it amuses the crowd. And remember, we're a family-friendly event, so keep everything G-rated."

"Oh, come on now," O'Malley exclaimed. "The Renaissance was a time of bawdiness! Of riotous living! Of excess and magnificence!"

"Unfortunately we're living in a time of political correctness," I said. "Since you're a volunteer performer, the Faire's liability insurance won't cover you, so if anyone lodges a sexual harassment complaint it'll be on your dime. And, of course, a public figure like you is so much more a target for that kind of thing."

"Really!" O'Malley actually recoiled. "I never would have—"

"How remiss of me." Michael was fighting back a grin. "I didn't introduce you two. Meg, this is Neil O'Malley. I'm sure I've told you about the times we've worked together. Neil, my wife, Meg Langslow. She's au courant with practical things like the Faire's insurance, since she helps her grandmother run the thing."

"Her grandmother?" O'Malley echoed.

"She of the Steely Gaze," I said. "The only really unbreakable rule of the Game is that Queen Cordelia always has the last word. If she tells you to jump, you don't ask how high—you should already know. I should be getting back to the forge."

I winked at Michael—with the eye facing away from O'Malley—and set off again.

As I approached the forge I was so focused on trying to spot Faulk or the boys that I started when I heard my name called.

"Meg!" I turned to see Rose Noire heading my way. "You need to Do Something!"

She was bearing down on me, wearing an expression that suggested that she had a mission. And how had she managed to perfect such a flawless imitation of Mother's imperious voice of command?

"I'm sure I ought to be doing a great many things," I said, in the mild tones I normally used to calm Mother. "Both to keep the Faire running and to help Chief Heedles with her investigation. What would you like me to add to the list?"

"How can we kick someone out of the Faire?" Her voice trembled with—was it rage?

"Kick someone out?" What could anyone have done to get Rose Noire this worked up? "If they've done anything that warrants kicking out—well, Horace and Lenny are kind of occupied, which leaves us without any palace guard, but I could probably recruit someone to put on the gear and do the job. Or I could do the kicking myself if need be. If they've actually broken any laws, we have no shortage of police on-site. Whom do you want to kick out, and what have they done?"

"That man over there." She pointed to a rather gawky thirtyish man standing across the clearing.

"The Mad Monk?" I'd seen him wandering around before. In fact, last weekend, so he was a repeat customer. He was dressed in a badly fitting knee-length burlap tunic tied with a rope belt, wearing muddy braided-straw sandals on his equally muddy feet, revealing the entirety of his singularly unprepossessing shins. An odd sight. Most men of his rather scrawny shape opted for the camouflage of ankle-length robes. And for that matter, most people who bothered to put together their own costumes opted for something with a little more pizzazz, appearing as well-dressed merchant class if they couldn't manage nobility. Well, it took all kinds.

"What's he done?"

"Nothing yet." She was staring at him with narrowed eyes.

"If you're having a premonition, I'm sorry," I said. "We can't throw him out on a premonition. You'll have to wait until he actually breaks the rules."

"Not a premonition—a deduction. Remember the problem Linnet and I reported last week? When someone stuck 'wool is murder' stickers all over the labels on her skeins of wool?"

"I remember." Linnet, one of the Faire's weavers, had been quite upset over the vandalism. I'd had a tough job calming her down, and then I'd helped with the tedious and time-consuming cleanup. I was pleasantly surprised that she'd agreed to come back this weekend. "It took us hours to get all those stickers off, and half the labels were in such bad shape that she had to print up new ones. Did he do that?"

"I don't know for sure," she said. "But he was lurking outside my booth just now, looking at the wool I'm selling and muttering about cruelty to animals. As if I'd ever be cruel to an animal! I tried to explain to him I'd not only spun every hank of yarn I was selling but sheared them, too, under the most humane and life-affirming conditions."

"A pity he didn't stop to listen, then." She could have called me as a witness—I'd watched her shear the sheep belonging to Seth Early, our across-the-street neighbor. I wasn't sure the sheep cared one way or another about the soft New Age music and lavender aromatherapy incense that accompanied the shearing, but they definitely appreciated the full body massage that preceded and followed it. The newly naked sheep kept circling back begging to be sheared again, so the only way to keep traffic moving was for Seth to bribe them with apple slices and drag them back to their pasture.

"And of course they're free range." She continued to frown at her suspect.

"I can testify to that." Seth's sheep were the most freely ranging creatures I'd ever met. They regularly turned up in our backyard. Or in our house, for that matter—they seemed to like drinking from the toilets and found our basement a refreshingly cool place to nap. "But I doubt if the Mad Monk will listen. So keep an eye on him. We can't kick him out just because he looks suspicious. But if he harasses you or Linnet or your customers—"

"If he does that, you might have to rescue him from us!" With that she walked off, chin held high.

I smothered a laugh. Rose Noire was militantly nonviolent. I wondered what she and Linnet, the almost-as-mild-mannered weaver, could possibly do that would require us to rescue the Mad Monk. I could think of nothing—with the possible exception of forcing him to drink one of her notoriously bad-tasting herbal teas.

Still. The man was a menace. I should do something.

I strolled over to the nearest craft stall—Seamus, the leatherworker.

"Mind if I use your back room for an anachronism?"

"Aye, lass." His Irish accent was both charming and authentic. "Any time ye please."

I ducked into the back room, pulled out my well-concealed cell phone, and called Horace.

"What happeneth?"

I winced. Well, at least he was working on period dialogue. "I know you're not doing the palace guard thing while the chief needs you for forensics, and this isn't anywhere near as important as the murder, but—"

"If something's wrong, let me know. Plenty of cops around—I'm sure the chief could spare one to deal with a malefactor. Might cheer her up to have something that she can actually take care of quickly."

"Remember the vandalism we had last weekend at the weaver's shop? Rose Noire thinks she's found the culprit. Have you seen the Mad Monk?"

"The guy who looks like Friar Tuck's evil twin? Yeah. Been keeping my eye on him."

"You have? What's he done?"

"Nothing—yet. But he totally sets off my spidey sense. Although I guess I should call it my cop intuition."

"Rose Noire thinks he's the one who stickered Linnet's yarn with the 'wool is murder' stickers. Not sure if that's illegal."

"Destruction of property. But only if you've got proof."

"We'll keep a weather eye out," I said. "Especially if we spot him near Rose Noire's booth or Linnet's."

"Or any of the other booths that would set off a militant animal rights activist," Horace said. "The leatherworkers, the food concessions that serve meat, the animal acts."

"Good thinking. And I'll spread the word to the rest of the palace guard."

"There was only me and Lenny, you know," he said. "And we're both unavailable for the immediate future."

"I'm going to recruit a couple of temporary guards," I said. "And if we actually catch the Mad Monk doing anything nefarious, we'll pretend there are legions of guards, all foaming at the mouth to apprehend him."

"I hope I'm back to join in by that time," he said. "Well, actually I hope nothing happens—Rose Noire was really upset about what happened to Linnet, and it would definitely stress her out if it happens to her. So if anything does happen, I want to be there to help. If you order him to leave and he refuses, you'd have every right to ask the police to remove him. And I'm deputized in Riverton, remember—so call me."

"I'll keep that in mind."

We signed off. I checked to see if the chief had tried to reach me. No voicemails, emails, or texts. And I'd already sent her several suspects—no, make that witnesses—to interview. I could take a little more time to deal with the Mad Monk.

Chapter 24

I returned to the public part of the booth, gestured to Seamus the leatherworker, and drew him aside.

"We're keeping an eye open for someone Rose Noire thinks might have vandalized Linnet's booth last weekend." I described the Mad Monk.

"I'll keep a weather eye open." Seamus clasped the hilt of the dagger hanging from his belt—a gesture that would have been a lot more menacing if I hadn't known perfectly well that it was only a hilt, with no actual blade in the ornate leather sheath. "Could be the rapscallion who threw red paint on a bunch of my hides last weekend."

"I didn't hear about that." I tried not to sound accusing.

"I didn't notice the damage till after the show closed, so whoever did it was long gone. I was going to tell you about it yesterday, but there's been rather a lot going on. We'll be keeping a closer eye on the goods this weekend. So now you know why my booth is suddenly all abloom with red-dyed leather."

I looked around and had to laugh. Yes, last weekend Seamus's stock of belts, pouches, vests, hats, sheathes, and tankards had been almost entirely done in shades of black, brown, and tan. Now many of the goods—maybe a third—were either brilliant red or deep burgundy.

"And the wretch may have accidentally done me a kindness," Seamus said, with a laugh. "Took me the devil of a lot of work to get those hides completely re-dyed in a shade that looked historically accurate. I ended up throwing more red paint on them all to even the color out before dying them with the usual natural dyes—mostly madder root. But I think they turned out okay, and they're selling like wildfire."

"Okay?" I glanced around at the new items. "More like awesome. You are now officially the king of making lemonade when life hands you the ingredients."

"But seriously—just because I turned it around doesn't mean I approve of what that smug son-of-a-cocker-spaniel did." Seamus scowled. "And if he's back and sees how I've recovered from the paint damage, what's to stop him from going after my goods with a sharp knife?"

"Nothing," I said. "So if you see him acting suspicious, haul out your mobile anachronism and call me. And if he causes any trouble, we'll ban him from the Faire."

"Aye, I'll keep me eyes on him."

As I left the booth, he was grimly scanning the crowd outside. A good thing his wife was there to charm the customers until he cheered up.

I strolled back to where the Muddy Beggar was sitting in his puddle, exchanging jibes with Jacks. Evidently the Beggar had just gotten off an excellent sally, since he was preening, Jacks was pretending to glower, and the crowd was roaring with laughter.

"Away with ye, ye horse-faced poxy rogue!" Jacks exclaimed when she could make herself heard. "Hanging's too good for you and—"

She was interrupted by trumpets, as Cordelia's heralds— three members of the brass section of the Riverton High School Band in black-and-gold doublets—played a fanfare.

"I'm off to the archery contest!" She and the Muddy Beggar glared theatrically at each other for a few moments, then she swept away—taking most of the tourists with her. I sidled over to where the Beggar was sitting.

"Can I recruit you for something?" I asked him.

He raised an inquiring eyebrow.

"Horace and Lenny have gotten sucked into the murder investigation. We need palace guards."

"You do remember why I'm sitting in this puddle instead of joining more actively in the Game, don't you?" He looked glum. "I'm counting the days till my knee replacement, and I can't do that much walking."

"You won't need to walk," I said. "I'll get you the Renaissance equivalent of a patrol car."

He looked puzzled.

"The little donkey cart Cordelia uses when she gets tired," I explained. "It's only for the short term, and we're not talking about you doing any physical enforcement—I want someone with sharp eyes and common sense to keep an eye out for problems. And with the wit to defuse them if it's possible. If anything really dicey happens, you'll have the whole Riverton police force as backup."

"Ooh—both of them?" He chuckled at his own joke, then nodded. "I'll do it, then. If you send the cart over to Camp Anachronism, I'll get cleaned up and into uniform. Assuming I get a uniform, that is."

"Lenny's should fit you," I said. "I'll arrange to get it to you."

He rose–though rather unsteadily—before I could give him a hand, retrieved a stout wooden cane from under some muddy rags, and limped off at a dignified pace.

I headed toward the forge.

I was hoping to find Tad there, but he was nowhere to be seen. Faulk was there, sitting on his stool, watching as Josh and Jamie explained something to a brace of tourists.

Faulk looked a little better. But only a little. An idea struck me.

"How goes the . . . day?" he asked. I suspected he'd been about to say "investigation" before remembering the need for discretion when tourists were around.

"Let's go inside and I'll fill you in."

I led the way into the back room. Thank goodness we had a back room—most days we only used it to make phone calls, but it came in handy now. Spike hurried to the chicken wire barrier and stared balefully at us.

"Back to your guard work," Faulk said. The command would have done no good, except that he accompanied the words by tossing a bit of bacon into the far end of Spike's pen. The Small Evil One dashed off to retrieve it. "So what's up?"

"Level with me." I scowled at him.

"What makes you think I'm not?"

"Look," I said. "I was up at the house just now—Tad left all his green-screen equipment in a room the chief wants to use to store all her evidence. I was helping pack up the stuff—"

To my relief, he interrupted me, since I was running out of ways to avoid admitting that I hadn't yet talked to Tad yet.

"I don't know what Tad told you," he said. "But he's a worrywart. Overprotective."

"Fine," I said. "Pretend I haven't even talked to Tad. Tell me your way. But none of this 'cardiac false alarm' crap."

He closed his eyes for a few seconds, and the anger drained out of his face, leaving only a bleak, tired look.

"It wasn't entirely a lie," he said. "I do have a heart problem. A potentially serious one."

"A heart problem? You?" My jaw dropped. "But you've always been the healthiest person I know. Even before most of us figured out we needed to take better care of ourselves you were always the one eating the right diet, and exercising and—well, doing everything the way we're all supposed to. If you've come down with a heart problem, what hope is there for the rest of us?"

"More than you think." He gave a slight smile. "Most people aren't in any danger of coming down with what

I've got. I guess I never let on that there was a reason I was doing all those disgustingly healthy things—because I knew there was a good chance I'd inherited this thing. Runs in my family. Blue bloods with weak hearts—that's the Cates family for you. You want the intricate medical details?"

"Save them for Dad. Just tell me the prognosis." I braced myself. Given the look on his face, I wasn't sure I wanted to hear the answer.

"I need surgery. If the surgery goes well—and the chances of success are pretty good—then my odds of living out the biblical three score and ten and then some are pretty good. Assuming I continue to take care of myself, and see my cardiologists on a regular basis, and take whatever meds they want me to take."

"That sounds optimistic," I said. "You don't look very optimistic."

"Did I mention that it's really expensive surgery?" Faulk said. "And the medicines aren't cheap. And cardiologists have this peculiar fondness for being paid."

Light dawned.

"And thanks to Terence, Tad's beastly boss just fired him," I said. "Which means that after spending far too long battling to get his health insurance to take care of your heart, now you're completely without health insurance."

Faulk nodded. Then he closed his eyes and took a deep breath, as if trying to steady himself.

I tried to think of something encouraging to say. But all I could think of was how tired he looked. Tired. Depressed. Sick. Old, even, when I knew he was only a few years older than me.

Defeated.

I stopped myself from saying the first thing that came to mind: "Are you a quitter?" I wasn't sure Faulk would remember how many times he'd said that to me, in those long ago days when he'd started teaching me blacksmithing. Or even if he remembered, would he realize I recalled those words with nostalgia, rather than resentment?

I heard the ringing sound of one of the boys striking the anvil with the hammer, and somehow it transported me back a couple of decades, to the ramshackle barn where Faulk had set up his first forge. Where I'd learned to work iron. That first winter, snow drifted down from all the holes in the barn's roof, my breath made puffs of smoke in the frigid air, my fingers were nearly numb, but I kept hammering, slowly but steadily, because I'd be damned if I'd stop and hear him ask me again if I was a quitter. Some days, those words were the only thing that kept me from throwing the hammer at his head and storming out—well, that and the chorus of "I told you so" I knew I'd hear from nearly everyone else in the world.

I'd taken up blacksmithing as a kind of rebellion from what I'd seen as the useless, abstract and all-too-theoretical world of my college classes. And then persevered at the classes anyway, because for a long time I'd been afraid I'd never amount to much as a blacksmith. Never make my arm strong enough or steady enough; never develop the patience to work the iron at its own pace instead of rushing and ruining it. By the time working with numb fingers in the cold of a Charlottesville winter had given way to sweating over the forge in humid, ninety-degree summer weather, Faulk had stopped asking me if I was a quitter. He didn't have to. I'd mutter it to myself when the thought of lifting the hammer one more time suddenly seemed impossible.

"Tad will get another job," I said aloud. In fact, I already had some ideas on that score. Had both of them forgotten that my brother, Rob, ran a rather well-regarded computer game company? A company that could probably use a programmer as expert as Tad? But I'd wait to mention that until I'd talked to Rob. He'd be down tomorrow with his Morris dancing friends. Or maybe I should call him tonight.

"Tad's already sending out résumés," Faulk said. "But at his level, it takes a while. Especially given that these days so many companies prefer hiring contractors to putting people on payroll."

It's not fair, I wanted to say. But Faulk already knew that.

"So I just need to hang in there," he went on. "Stay as healthy as I can and hope for the best."

"And here I was worried enough when I just thought you were depressed."

"I probably am depressed." He sounded almost bemused. "Depressed seems a reasonable response to the situation."

"Is there any chance Tad's boss will change his mind?" I asked. "Read him the riot act and reinstate him?"

"Somehow I doubt it." Faulk shook his head slightly. "I gather it's a real hot button with him, having his employees on-site. And Tad knew that. I kept telling him I'd be fine, just put in the face time with his boss and stop worrying so much about me. But he was worried something would happen to me with him a couple of hours away."

"I wish you'd told us," I said. "Not the whole world, but a few of your friends. Me and Michael, for example. If you'd told us, maybe we could have convinced Tad that we could watch over you so he could stay at the office and keep his boss happy. Hell, you could have had Dad watching over you, and he's pretty good at keeping his patients alive."

"I hope not to need your dad's services, but I certainly won't object to having him watch over me." Faulk smiled faintly. "Or you and Michael. Because you're right—we should have let a few more people in on the situation."

"But now we know—so Tad can go on job interviews without worrying quite so much," I said.

Faulk nodded.

I decided to tackle the remaining elephant in the room.

Chapter 25

"You know," I said. "If Terence hadn't decided it would be fun to blow the whistle on the green-screen setup, maybe Tad would still have his job. Now I have to worry about whether the two of you have an alibi for Terence's murder. I assume you were down at the ER in Jessop for quite a long time."

"Yeah." He shook his head as if the memory wasn't pleasant. "From not quite one a.m. until six or so. No such thing as express service there."

"Full story." I said.

"I woke up around midnight feeling wretched, and Tad insisted on dragging me down there to wherever it was. Total waste of time. We filled out about two miles of forms, then sat around for a couple of centuries, waiting for them to get around to looking at us. And of course there wasn't anything they could do for me, and even if there had been, I think I'd have insisted on going somewhere else to have it done. Down to VCU in Richmond. Better yet, Charlottesville for the UVA system. Guess that makes me a health care snob."

"Makes you a person with a well-developed sense of self-preservation, from what I've heard. Chief Heedles shares your low opinion of the Jessop ER. But at least they can probably give you an alibi."

"There is that. Assuming their record-keeping is adequate, which isn't necessarily a given by the look of the place. I kept wanting to ask the doctor to wash his hands—it was that bad. Should I go tell the chief of police my alibi?"

"I already told her. But you should go talk to her. Get it over with."

I stood up to go. Then I thought of something.

"This expensive operation you need—is it just a question of not kicking the bucket until you can get the surgery? Or is putting off the surgery another problem?"

"The longer I wait, the greater the chance that I'll rack up damage that's harder to fix. Or unfixable. Waiting's not optimal."

"Maybe we should start one of those online funding things for you," I said.

"Not sure I know enough people to pay for this," he said. "Especially since so many of my friends are self-employed craftspeople like us."

"You never know." I decided to leave it there for the time being. Our friends in the crafts community might be self-employed, but they weren't all broke, and there were a lot of them. If we spread the word in the crafts community . . .

Better yet, I could sic Mother on it. If we got her fired up to rescue Faulk, she could tap her side of the family—the entire far-flung Hollingsworth clan, most of whom—unlike our friends in the crafts community—were sufficiently well off to participate regularly in the various charities and projects Mother came up with.

I'd work on talking Tad and Faulk into it later.

My phone vibrated, and I pulled it out to check the screen.

"Speak of the devil," I said. "Tad."

"Tell him I'm behaving myself," Faulk said.

I nodded and pushed the button to take the call.

"Meg, where are you?"

"At the forge. Have you been up to the main house yet?"

"Yes." His voice sounded hurried. That unnerved me slightly. Surely he wasn't going on the lam or anything melodramatic like that. "Look, thanks for packing my stuff, and I got your message, and I'm about to go in to talk to the cops. But I wanted to ask you something—can you figure out a way to keep Faulk from doing any demos today? Long story why—"

"And Faulk already told me," I said. "Don't worry. I won't let him get his hands on a hammer for the time being."

"Thanks," he said. "And good luck. I couldn't get him to lay off. Not even when I reminded him that the cardiologist wanted him to lay off blacksmithing entirely for the time being. And after an episode like last night—does he want to kill himself?"

"Don't worry," I said.

"Fat chance."

"By the way—can I recruit you to help out with something? Just for today?"

"If I can."

"Can you put on Horace's palace guard uniform and march around keeping an eye on things? So it at least looks as if we have some kind of security here?"

"Do I get to carry that enormous cleaver?" Tad asked. "The one that looks like what the Wicked Witch of the West's guards carry when they march around the castle chanting 'O-Ee-Yah! Eoh-Ah!'?"

"Yes, you can carry the bardiche, and you can even chant 'O-Ee-Yah! Eoh-Ah!' if it makes you feel better. And you can look in on Faulk as often as you like."

"Awesome. You're on. I've already sent out résumés to every place I can think of. I need something to distract me while I wait to hear back about them."

With that Tad hung up.

"Don't worry," Faulk said. "I can handle a few demonstrations."

"Not according to Tad," I said.

"Tad's just a worrywart."

"And not according your cardiologist," I shot back.

"He's just a worrywart, too? Because according to Tad, your doctor isn't too happy that you're continuing to do blacksmithing at all, and he made it very clear that you need to rest after an episode like you had last night."

"So you're going to do all the demonstrations yourself?" he asked. "And leave your grandmother to cope with the murder investigation?"

I thought of pointing out that it was Chief Heedles who'd be coping with the murder investigation. But yeah, he had a point. Someone had to run interference, to make sure the murder investigation didn't interfere with the Faire. And for that matter, that the Faire didn't interfere too badly with the chief's investigation.

Because the sooner Chief Heedles caught the killer, the better. The Faire was a hot attraction right now, and in the short run we might even see increased attendance by people eager to visit a murder scene. Not an uncommon interest, and in the case of notorious murders—especially serial killers—this appetite for the sensational often gave rise to cottage industries. I could, after a fashion, understand the plethora of Jack the Ripper tours in London. But the Helter Skelter Tour in Los Angeles, the Zodiac Killer Tour in San Francisco, tours devoted to the crimes of Jeffrey Dahmer, H. H. Holmes, the Boston Strangler, Ted Bundy, and who knows how many others—not my cup of tea.

And a Renaissance Faire was aimed at a more wholesome, family-friendly market. People came to eat turkey legs and drink mead, to watch jugglers and jousters, to have their kids' faces painted, and to have their picture taken with Good Queen Cordelia or the Muddy Beggar—not to visit the site of an unsolved murder, and maybe even rub elbows with a still-at-large killer.

Even a long investigation could hurt the Faire. Maybe even kill it. And Cordelia had invested a non-trivial sum of money in the project—of that I was sure. Money she could lose if the Faire got a reputation as a dangerous place infested with murderers and thieves. And while I doubted she'd have invested more than she could afford to lose, I knew she'd also put her heart into the project.

"Maybe we could find another blacksmith to help out," I said.

Faulk smiled briefly, but didn't otherwise acknowledge my tacit admission that he had a point.

"It's July," he said. "Do you really think there are a lot of competent blacksmiths out there who are willing to do events like this but aren't already booked for this weekend?"

Again, he had a point.

"Um . . . can I make a suggestion?"

Faulk and I turned to see Josh leaning against the door frame, with Jamie looking over his shoulder.

"You don't have to find a new blacksmith," Josh went on. "Faulk could just supervise *us.*"

"We know enough to give a basic demonstration," Jamie said. "And if Faulk corrected us and guided us, that would be educational for the audience as well, wouldn't it?"

"And Faulk wouldn't have to lift a finger," Josh added. "He could just sit on the stool and boss us around."

"He could also talk about how the apprentice system worked in the olden days," Jamie suggested.

They both had their eyes fixed on me, and although they'd kept their tone casual, I could detect the eagerness underneath. I glanced over at Faulk. I knew he was a good teacher—had been a good teacher for me two decades earlier. But did he feel up to coping with two beginners? I lifted one eyebrow. Spike appeared at the chicken wire barrier and uttered a short, sharp bark. I knew he was only demanding more bacon, but it did rather sound as if he were adding his two cents to our efforts to persuade Faulk.

"Why not?" He shrugged. "We can give it a try. Although

I intend to hold them to that not lifting a finger part." He turned to the boys. "For your first assignment as apprentices, I want a tall, cold mug of lemonade and a shepherd's pie. Have the innkeeper put it on my tab. And get something for yourselves if you're getting peckish."

The boys looked at me.

"Did you overhear what Faulk and I were talking about just now?" I asked.

They quickly glanced at each other and then both nodded.

"We didn't mean to eavesdrop," Jamie began.

"I did," Josh said. "And I'm glad I did so I can help take care of Faulk."

"It's private and personal," I said. "So keep it to yourself. Unless you run into your granddad," I added, frowning at Faulk. "You can tell him. Now go fetch that shepherd's pie."

They raced off. Faulk and I left the back room so we could watch over the forge and the shop until they returned. Fortunately, traffic was light—I could hear cheering coming from the jousting field, where Cordelia was presiding over the archery tournament.

"If you're sure you're okay supervising the boys . . ." I began.

"It's the perfect solution," he said. "Tad can relax, knowing that not only am I not exerting myself, I'm also being watched every minute by two guardians who won't hesitate to call their grandfather over to minister to me if I so much as sneeze. And you can go around doing whatever you need to do, secure in the knowledge that even if someone's roaming the Faire looking for another victim, both boys are under the watchful eye of someone who may have a dodgy heart but can probably manage to fend off the killer if need be. We've even got Spike as backup."

I wouldn't have called it a perfect solution. Perfect would require Faulk to be healthy and the boys not even in the same county as whoever had killed Terence. But it would do for now.

"And thanks for thinking of something to distract Tad," Faulk said. "He's going to love marching around carrying the bardiche. Of course, I'm not sure I see him as the law enforcement type."

"Neither do I, but he's not otherwise occupied at the moment, and I think he'll fit the uniform." I winced at how that sounded. "Not that I'd put it quite that way if I were talking to him."

"Of course not," Faulk said. "You chose him for his quick wits and his people skills."

"Actually, yes," I said. "If we can't have actual cops, like Horace and Lenny, then I want people who can defuse a situation with wit and charm."

"You've got the right guy, then," Faulk said.

I nodded. I was texting Horace and Lenny, arranging for them to get their uniforms to Tad and the Muddy Beggar.

"By the way," I asked Faulk. "Do you remember the Muddy Beggar's real name? I'm blanking."

"No." Faulk shook his head. "Not sure I've ever heard it. If I have to call him anything, I generally go with 'Mr. Beggar'—in a suitably ironic tone, of course."

"That's better than 'Mud,'" I said. "But we can't very well call him the Muddy Beggar while he's in the palace guard. Maybe Michael knows."

I texted Michael, being careful to begin my message with "NO RUSH." He'd be occupied with the archery tournament.

A lot of people would be occupied with the archery tournament. Maybe this would be a good time to go up to the main house. The personnel files were in Cordelia's office, and surely the Muddy Beggar's real name would be in them.

And maybe I could get a clue from the chief on how the investigation was going.

Chapter 26

I headed for the main house. But as soon as I was out of sight of the forge, I tucked into a sheltered spot, pulled out my cell phone, and called Dad.

"What's up?" he asked. "I've been busy most of the day with patients—nothing serious, a senior with heat exhaustion and a very pregnant woman having Braxton-Hicks contractions, but I'm completely out of touch with the investigation. Has—"

"I'll fill you in later," I said. "Right now I have another patient for you." I gave him a quick rundown on what little I knew about Faulk's condition. "Of course, he didn't volunteer any details," I added. "All I know is some kind of serious heart thing—"

"Don't worry," Dad said. "I'll dash right over and examine him. Goodness—the Jessop ER? I'm not even sure that place is accredited anymore. Talk to you later."

I peered around the corner of the ring toss booth in time to see Dad, medical bag in hand, bustle across the short distance that separated his medical tent from the forge. Then I set out for the main house with a lighter heart.

I found Mother in the costume shop, frowning at a perfectly innocent length of lace.

"What's wrong?" I asked.

"Feeling guilty," she said. "About all the uncharitable things I've said about Terence, and now the poor man's dead."

I thought of pointing out that being dead hadn't suddenly turned Terence into a saint. But I decided to let

Mother enjoy feeling guilty for a little while longer—it would distract her from her still-painful foot.

I found the chief sitting at Cordelia's desk, frowning at her notebook while gnawing on a roasted turkey leg.

"Be my guest," she said, when I asked if I could check something in the files. "And by the way, thank you—any number of people I want to talk to that my officers can't seem to track down have been showing up here under their own steam, saying you told them to come."

"My pleasure," I said. "By the way, has the murder hit the news?"

"After a fashion. We sent out a statement." She picked up and handed me a sheet of paper—a press release on official Town of Riverton letterhead.

"'The body of a middle-aged white male was found in the woods on Biscuit Mountain early Saturday morning,'" I read aloud. "Do you have any idea how much Terence would have hated being called middle-aged? 'Identity of the deceased is being withheld pending notification of next of kin. The Riverton Police Department is continuing to investigate the cause of death.' Well, that's boring enough to put any sane editor to sleep."

"I hope so," she said.

"Who is Terence's next of kin, anyway?"

"I was hoping you'd know." She sighed.

"Maybe Michael does."

"I already asked," she said. "He doesn't. And we checked his personnel file to see who he put down to be notified in case of emergency. Apparently he listed his ex-girlfriend."

"He might have filled it out before they broke up," I suggested. "Doesn't she know how to reach his family?"

"According to her, he called his mother from time to time, mostly when he needed money. But they never met, and she doesn't have any contact information. At least it gives us a reason to keep a lid on things a little longer. He could have family, and we won't want them to learn about his death from the news." She returned to flipping through the pages of her notebook.

It occurred to me to sic my tech-savvy nephew Kevin on the search for Terence's next of kin. I'd usually found that if Kevin couldn't find a piece of information, it probably didn't exist. Not online, anyway. But while I was trying to think how to phrase the suggestion without insulting the chief's data-finding capabilities, she spoke up again.

"As long as you're here, may I ask you a couple of questions?"

"Ask away. I already found what I wanted." In fact, I'd already taken a picture of the Muddy Beggar's employment form, rather than take the time to write down "Stanislaus Węgrzynkiewicz."

"I'm told your grandfather made unspecified threats against the deceased," she said.

"Unspecified threats?" I repeated. "Grandfather's threats are usually pretty specific."

"I'm sure," the chief said. "But my interviewee didn't remember them."

"Then he or she wasn't trying very hard," I said. "Grandfather threatened to turn Terence into a toad."

The chief frowned and blinked.

"Several times, if memory serves," I added. "He was thinking of either a cane toad or a golden poison arrow frog. I can't remember their Latin names, but I'm sure Grandfather can provide them if you think it's apt to be relevant."

"I can't imagine how it would be." The chief blew out her breath in a gesture of annoyance. "I assume this was in the context of the Game, as these actors like to call it."

"Yes," I said. "Grandfather's eccentric, but rarely delusional. For some reason he's really gotten into the Game."

"He probably thought it would annoy your grandmother," the chief suggested.

"Probably." It occurred to me that I hadn't seen much

of Grandfather this morning. Maybe all the excitement had tired him out and he'd gone off to take a long nap. That would certainly make Cordelia's day more pleasant. Still—I made a mental note to check on him. And then I focused back on the chief's question. "I do hope you plan to tell Grandfather that you suspected him. He'll get such a kick out of it."

"Out of being suspected of murder?"

"Of a murder that, if I'm interpreting the evidence correctly, probably took considerable strength and dexterity. I know Dad would be delighted, and they can be very alike sometimes."

"You're probably right, so I won't do any such thing." She chuckled softly. "And if you tell him, I'll deny that I ever suspected him. I was actually thinking more about the possibility that someone else might have acted on a threat he made."

"You mean someone younger," I suggested. "Someone more capable of sneaking out into the woods in the middle of the night and surprising or overpowering Terence?"

"Someone more unbalanced was my idea."

I thought about it for a few moments, then shook my head.

"Seems farfetched," I said. "I mean, yeah, if Grandfather had made a fiery public denunciation, calling Terence a climate change denier or an abuser of animals, maybe one of his more militant and fanatical followers might have gotten a crazy idea from it. But he hasn't done any such thing, and even if he had, I can't imagine anyone that militant showing up at something as frivolous as a Renaissance Faire. He wasn't accusing Terence of environmental crimes. Just warning him to leave Dianne alone."

The chief nodded and scribbled briefly in her notebook.

"I hope I didn't just derail a promising theory," I said.

"No, just helped me identify another probable red herring. Getting a few too many of those."

"I don't suppose you'd be willing to tell me who reported that Grandfather was making threats."

"Not sure I should." She studied my expression.

"Because you're afraid I'll retaliate against someone who tried to cause problems for Grandfather." I nodded. "I get it."

"Actually, I don't think the person in question was trying to cause problems. They seemed genuinely worried that I might have heard about the so-called threats from someone else and taken them too seriously. They assured me repeatedly that your Grandfather was completely harmless and wouldn't hurt a fly."

"Not someone who knows him that well, then." I thought over the various people she would have been interviewing. "Probably George Sims."

"Any particular reason?" Her face was neutral, but there was a note of curiosity in her voice.

"Because it's exactly the sort of silly thing he'd worry about," I said. "Any kind of conflict or disagreement upsets him, and he's always trying to explain away things that don't need explaining—or can't be explained away and are best left alone. Or calm people down about things they weren't upset over in the first place."

"He seems upset by Mr. Cox's death," the chief observed. "Genuinely so."

"And uniquely so," I added.

"Apparently. And I think it will come as quite a shock to him if we arrest anyone he knows for the crime," she went on. "He went on at considerable length about how the Faire staff—particularly the performers—may have their little squabbles from time to time, but are all warm, wonderful people who are basically like a big happy family."

Did George really think that? Or was his aversion to conflict so profound that he'd try to banish even the thought that someone he knew might not be all that warm and wonderful?

"Of course, at the moment I feel as if I was a fly on the wall during every minor disagreement that's taken place over the last four weeks," the chief said. "I wonder if he realizes how very much information he's revealed about his warm, wonderful colleagues."

"Maybe he does," I said. "Maybe being the eternal optimist wears thin at times, and he gives in to the temptation to being just a little passive-aggressive."

"Very likely," she said. "No one's that nice all the time. But then again—maybe he actually does suspect someone and doesn't want to admit it to anyone—not even himself. Maybe that's why he had to pour out all that detail about how people squabbled and made up, or played pranks on each other and were forgiven. Maybe he had to tell me about everybody so he could bring himself to tell me about *somebody*. But I have no idea who."

She was staring at the opposite wall—at first, I thought she was staring at something and followed her gaze to see if I could figure out what so held her interest. But then I realized she was just staring into the distance while thinking.

"You know what's odd about this case?" she said finally.

"A lot," I said. "What in particular strikes you?"

"I actually met him yesterday. Mr. Cox. Less than twelve hours before he was murdered. Only briefly, but still—I met him."

"Isn't that kind of normal in a small town?" I asked. "Haven't you met most of your murder victims?"

"You say that as if we get a lot of murders here in Riverton." She chuckled. "Murder is very definitely not normal here—but when it does happen, I haven't just met the victims. I've known them since grade school, and maybe even their parents and grandparents before them. And the same for whoever killed them. And if I don't know right off the top of my head who's the most likely one to have done it, it'd only be because the deceased was more cantankerous than usual and had more than one person gunning for him. No, what I meant was that I'd met him—but just for a few minutes, and not under the best of circumstances. Not entirely sure I like that."

"Why not?" Not, I assumed, a conflict of interest.

She thought for a moment.

"Curiously, my initial reaction was to think 'well, at least the victim is someone I know.' And that's not the case at all, is it? I know a few of the things he did yesterday—sexually harassing a colleague, trying to undermine another colleague's sobriety, and . . . well, I'm still not sure I understand how to describe whatever he did to get your friend Mr. Jackson fired, but I know it wasn't a particularly kind thing to do. Not the way I'd like to spend my last day on Earth, but then I don't suppose he was expecting to die today."

"No," I said. "He definitely wasn't. He was expecting to leave Biscuit Mountain in a blaze of glory, having captured one of the leading roles in a well-publicized production at one of the country's leading theaters. Maybe that was why he was so over-the-top yesterday. He was prone to mood swings. Getting the part probably sent him into orbit, and for some reason he wasn't ready to share the news, so instead of bragging and gloating, he celebrated by being perfectly beastly to everyone around him."

"Yes." She nodded, still looking thoughtful. "Sounds in character. I know some of the things he did—more than I did at first, thanks to Mr. Sims—but I don't really know him at all. I feel like I'm playing catch-up. Why those particular toads?"

"What?" The apparent non sequitur caught me off guard. "Oh, you mean Grandfather's threat? No idea."

"Are they both venomous? In which case his choosing

those two could have been a subconscious judgment of Mr. Cox's character."

"Actually I don't think either is venomous," I said. "But I'm pretty sure they're both poisonous."

She blinked.

"There's a difference?" She sounded puzzled.

"To a biologist like Grandfather, a big difference," I explained. "Both produce a toxic substance, but a venomous creature actively injects it into you, while a poisonous one won't harm you unless you're misguided enough to bite into it."

"So rattlesnakes and black widow spiders are venomous and mushrooms poisonous." She seemed to be savoring the distinction. "Active versus passive. Fascinating."

"Though not necessarily useful on your case," I suggested.

"You never know," she said. "Though it does rather torpedo my idea that your grandfather was making some kind of character assessment of Mr. Cox. Not that I like to speak ill of the dead, but I'd say he was venomous rather than poisonous."

"I'd agree," I said.

"And it does raise an interesting question about the crime," she said. "Was the killer venomous or poisonous? Was it someone who actively sought out the opportunity to rid the world of Mr. Cox? Or someone who would never have done anything if Mr. Cox had not provoked them?"

"You're thinking self-defense?" My voice probably telegraphed my skepticism.

"With a stab in the back?" She snorted. "Not hardly. No, more of a worm turning kind of thing. Mr. Cox pushes someone to the limit of his or her endurance, then turns his back, thinking himself perfectly safe with someone who isn't very threatening to begin with, especially since they're armed only with what amounts to a toy weapon. I notice Cordelia's costume includes a wrist dagger that's as elegant as it is lethal—not, I expect, a cheap import."

"My work," I said. "And thanks for the compliment."

"Can you think of anyone whose costume generally includes a weapon? Someone who's opted for the budget version?"

I thought for a moment and shook my head.

"Not offhand," I said. "Not any of the main players in the Game, certainly—if they showed up with anything in their costume that was that . . . um . . ."

"Tacky?" the chief suggested.

"Well, I was thinking more of a word like 'inauthentic,'" I said. "But you get the idea. If Dianne or George or Terence himself had wanted to wear a dagger as part of their costume and couldn't afford a real piece, Faulk or I could have lent them one. But there are dozens of other people in costume. We don't encourage them to wear weapons, but any of them could, as long as they're peace-bonded. We could check the photos."

"What photos?" The chief sounded very interested. "May I look at them?"

"The best of them are online, where the whole world can look at them," I said. "On the Faire's website. Cordelia has an arrangement with a couple of avid local teenage photographers that they get free admission if they let her display some of their work on the website. Plus we have a contest after every weekend for the best photos submitted by visitors. The winners get prizes, we showcase the honorable mentions—dozens of them—on the website, and we have God knows how many also-rans on file."

"On file where? May I see them, too?"

"Let me ask my nephew Kevin." I pulled out my phone.

"That's the tech-savvy one?"

"Calling Kevin tech savvy is like calling the ocean damp." I was typing out a message to Kevin as I spoke. "He runs the Faire's website, and I'm telling him you want to see all the photos. Let me know if he doesn't get back to you fairly soon with a link or a file or whatever. Sometimes when he's working on a big project he goes incommunicado—in the tech world they call it going dark. But I can always send someone over to bother him in real life if it's urgent."

"Thanks," she said. "I don't suppose Kevin has any programs that could sort through all those thousands of programs and flag any that happen to include cheap daggers?"

"I have no idea if such a thing exists, but if it does and Kevin doesn't own it, he can track it down. We can but ask." And while I was at it, I'd see if he had any idea how to find Terence's next of kin. I typed a few more lines to Kevin, then turned back to the chief. "By the way, did I mention to you that we have Terence's things?"

Chapter 27

"Things?" she repeated. "What things? If you mean his tent and its contents, I have them now. They're locked in that room you were so obliging as to clear out. I plan to haul them down to the station house after closing time."

"I mean the rest of his things. Remember my saying that just before he came up here his girlfriend kicked him out, so we didn't really have a permanent address for him?"

She nodded.

"Well, since he had nowhere else to leave them, he brought all his worldly goods with him. He's got twelve boxes stashed in Cordelia's storage room. No idea what's in them, much less whether any of it has anything to do with his murder. For all I know it could be nothing but scripts and programs from every play he's ever been in plus a few hundred copies of his latest head shots. And I have no idea whether he's ever asked for a key to the room so he could get at any of it, so it might be stuff he hasn't touched in weeks."

"But I should take a look." The chief sighed. "It would be the equivalent of searching his house or apartment, if he had one."

I rummaged in the key cabinet and entrusted the chief with a key to the storage room.

"Want me to show you which boxes are his?"

"First let me lock up this stuff in our temporary evidence locker. Any chance you could grab one box?"

I glanced at the boxes.

"Ooh," I said. "Did you confiscate the Bonny Blade's entire stock of daggers?"

"Pretty much." She cocked her head to one side. "I gather you dislike the owners of the Bonny Blade. But why? And do you actually find them suspicious?"

"I don't dislike them," I protested.

"Could have fooled me. Somehow, whenever you talk about them, the word 'cheap' seems to come up. And that it's clearly no compliment."

"If they were here," I said, "I'd be careful to say 'inexpensive.' And—" I stopped and did a bit of self-examination. How did I really feel about the two guys who ran the Bonny Blade?

"I don't dislike *them*," I said slowly. "What I dislike is the way so many people compare their prices with mine or Faulk's and walk away thinking that we're greedy price gougers. Or worse, come and tell us to our faces that we're greedy price gougers. And that's not the Bonny Blade's fault. We no longer live in a society where most people walk around armed with swords and knives—and know that their safety and survival depends on the quality of those weapons. If we did, then people would figure out the reason for the difference in price. At least the ones who survive would."

"Handmade versus machine-made." The chief nodded as if that pegged it.

"No—good quality versus bad quality," I countered. "There's nothing inherently bad about machine-made and good about handmade. Some machine-made weapons are every bit as strong and resilient and well-balanced as the ones Faulk and I make—hell, maybe better. But they come with a roughly similar price tag. And there could be handmade weapons out there that aren't even as good as the ones the Bonny Blade sells—because their makers are still learning the finer points of sword smithing. Or their makers don't even want to bother with the finer points, because they're satisfied with turning out in-expensive goods for the tourist trade. You could make the argument that paying for higher quality than you need is stupid anyway. Most of the people buying stuff from the Bonny Blade just want to take their new treasure home and hang it on the wall. Or maybe wear it as part of their costume to a Halloween party. The Bonny Blade's stuff is fine for that."

The chief seemed interested. I wasn't sure what this had to do with the murder. Maybe nothing. Maybe she needed a mental break.

"So no, I don't dislike the guys from the Bonny Blade," I went on. "They're filling a niche. Serving a useful pur-pose—if they weren't at the Faire, we'd probably have to find another vendor who sells the same kind of stuff, because if Faulk and I were the only place you could buy weapons, the tourists in search of cheap knives and swords would drive us crazy. I do find it kind of annoying when the Bonny Blade guys do a sales pitch about how smart one of their customers is for shopping around to find the best bargains, with a couple of snide comments about swordsmiths who set their prices so high only kings and nobles can afford their blades. They don't need to do that. But they're not really doing any harm—anyone who falls for it isn't going to buy from Faulk or me anyway."

"I see." The chief nodded, staring into space for a few moments. Then she locked her eyes back on mine. "So one thing we do know about our killer is that he isn't very knowledgeable about swords and knives. Because if he were, he wouldn't have chosen such a cheap blade as his murder weapon—I gather he was lucky it didn't break off when he stabbed Mr. Cox."

"I'd have said unlucky," I replied. "Because that would be the best outcome, wouldn't it? Whoever has it in for Terence tries to stab him with a knife so cheap the blade breaks off without doing much harm, leaving Terence free to run shrieking out of the woods and file attempted murder charges."

"Yes, that would have been a better outcome." The chief seemed to find my suggestion amusing.

"But yeah, you could have a point there. No one knowledgeable would rely on one of those blades, either for attack or self-defense. On the other hand . . ." I let my voice trail off as I thought through how to phrase what I wanted to say.

"Why do I suspect you're about to make my case more complicated?" the chief asked.

"Because you know me," I said. "As I was about to say, on the other hand, if I were planning to kill Terence, I certainly wouldn't take one of my own knives. I'd be one of a dangerously small number of people with easy access to them. And the same would go for Faulk's knives. Unlike the cheap mass-produced ones the Bonny Blade sells, our knives are pretty distinctive."

"So you might take along one of the Bonny Blade's cheap knives after all?"

"Only if I were stubbornly determined to kill Terence with a knife and couldn't manage to pocket a good sturdy kitchen knife," I said. "And I think it's a mistake to assume the use of a cheap knife means the killer was ignorant about weapons. He was smart enough to use a stiletto, wasn't he?"

"Was he?" The chief frowned. "They haven't removed the knife blade yet—they won't be doing that until the autopsy. How do you know it's a stiletto?"

"I don't know for sure," I admitted. "But I'm betting that's what it will turn out to be. Two reasons—one's the shape of the hilt." I pulled out my phone and opened up Dad's picture of the murder weapon. You could see a piece of metal twisted into a spiral, with a bejeweled knob at the top. "I'm no expert on medieval weaponry, but I do know a few things. When I see a round hilt like this I tend to think it's for a stabbing weapon, like a stiletto or a rondel dagger. A knife that's used primarily for cutting I'd expect to have a hilt that's more like a steak knife handle. But I could be wrong—as I said, I'm no weapons expert. You could always ask Faulk."

"He's an expert?"

"He knows more than I do—he's made a hundred times more knives and swords than I have. And more to the point, if for some reason you need detailed information about the weapon, he could put you in touch with real experts. People who write textbooks on this kind of thing."

"I'll keep it in mind, though I doubt I'll need experts." She smiled. "For the time being, I can live with your comment that you expect a stiletto based on the shape of the handle. But I think you said you had two reasons for assuming a stiletto—what was the other?"

"The fact that the killer succeeded," I said. "Even a cheap stiletto would have the right shape to be good for stabbing. It's pointier—basically a glorified ice pick. If I had to choose a cheap blade for stabbing with, that's the kind I'd choose. Stabbing people's exactly what stilettos were designed for."

"Yes, you did mention that." She sighed. "You're not making my life any easier. Do you at least agree that it would take a fair amount of strength to stab with it?"

"A fair amount, yes," I said. "But not a superhuman amount, I should think. Dad would be a better judge of that."

"I'll ask him." She was writing in her notebook.

"Just remember that if you're thinking of knocking us frail and dainty ladies off your suspect list—bad idea. I could do it in a heartbeat. There's nothing like blacksmithing to develop wrist and arm strength. Though tennis doesn't do a shabby job—Jacks plays a mean game. Not sure about Dianne." I paused to ponder.

"She's petite," the chief observed.

"Yes," I said. "That's useful for gymnastics—which she did all through college. I bet that gives you reasonable wrist and arm strength. Plus, knowing how she feels about Terence . . . don't underestimate how much strength fear and anger can give a person. I can't imagine any reason why she'd go out into the woods in the middle of the night, either by herself or with Terence—but I can well imagine that if somehow she found herself in that situation, she might panic."

"And her panic would give her enough strength to compensate for the shortcomings of the weapon and her physique." The chief nodded. "No, I know better than to take any of you off my suspect list. Well, with the possible exception of your mother—she went down to Cordelia's house at the end of the day. No way she could drive with that broken right foot, much less hike out into the woods. And I can't see her stabbing anyone."

"Actually, I can," I said. "But not with a rhinestone-studded knife. She has standards."

"Excellent ones." The chief chuckled. "So for now, let me take advantage of that strength of yours and get those boxes moved."

We stowed the boxes in the jewelry studio. Then I led the chief into the storage room and showed her which boxes were Terence's. She studied them for a few moments.

"Those are some big boxes," she said. "And rather a lot of them to drag with you for a stay of, what—three months?"

"I don't think he'd have brought all that with him if he'd had anyplace else to leave it," I said. "So from that point of view—not a lot of boxes to contain the sum total of anyone's earthly possessions."

The chief nodded and looked glum. Then she brightened.

"At least the odds are he'll have something in here that

will give me a clue to who needs to be notified about his death."

She squared her shoulders and strode over to the boxes. I left her to it.

Upstairs, when I stepped out of the craft wing into the Great Hall, I ran into a group of players: Jacks, Dianne, George, two of the jugglers, a dozen or so costumed workers—and O'Malley.

"I think it's worth taking the time to recharge," O'Malley was saying. "This kind of work can really drain your creative juices. So let's take your lunch break and I'll lead you through a few quick exercises."

Jacks spotted me and almost managed to hide her look of intense relief.

"I'm supposed to be seeing Meg about something," she said. "I'll just go do that and join you in progress, shall I?"

"Of course, of course." O'Malley cast an annoyed glance in my direction before turning his attention back to the rest of his flock. "Now someone go get me a dozen napkins."

Jacks came over, took my arm, and steered me back into the craft wing. We headed down the hallway, dodging the tourists, toward the relative peace and quiet of the far end, where there was a small open area in front of the locked door to the stairs.

"Thank goodness you came along," she said quietly as we walked. "O'Malley's going to lead everyone in a series of creative exercises."

"Everyone?" I echoed.

"Everyone he can dragoon into playing with him," she said. "You'll notice he didn't have Michael in tow. Or Nigel. Some of us manage to keep our creative juices charged up by doing the job we're paid to do. Hell, a lot of us really enjoy the Game."

"But O'Malley doesn't get to give orders in the Game," I said.

"You've got him pegged." She chuckled. "Last I heard, he planned to blindfold us all and let us wander around communicating with each other by making nonverbal noises. So give me something to do, too, so I can beg off if someone comes and tries to drag me back to do O'Malley's exercises."

"Especially if the someone is O'Malley," I said. "I expect he's pretty hard to argue with."

"Somehow I doubt if O'Malley will come hunting me down," she said. "You'll notice he didn't argue much when I bowed out. I actually think he'll be happier without me in his session. Just as he's happier when Michael and Nigel aren't around. He feels vaguely threatened when there's anyone around who he suspects knows a bit more about acting or directing than he does."

"What about George?" I asked.

"He'll be happier without me, too."

"Actually, I meant wouldn't O'Malley be threatened by having George around," I said. "But it was a stupid question. George would turn himself inside out to be agreeable to anyone—especially someone who might be holding auditions sometime soon. Why would George be happier without you? That's the more interesting question."

"He just came over and apologized to me for spilling the beans," Jacks said.

"Beans?"

"He seems to have revealed—by accident, to hear him tell it—that I'd once had an affair with Terence."

Chapter 28

"An affair with Terence? " Surely I'd misunderstood her.

"I'm probably going to have to tell the chief about it, right?"

"He was he telling the truth?"

"About his revelation being accidental?" She shook her head. "I doubt it. But about the affair? Technically, yes."

I waited to hear more. She stood there, eyes closed, taking the sort of deep breaths I usually take when I'm counting to ten and trying to recapture my temper. Sometimes waiting people out doesn't work nearly as well as a direct question.

"You could have told us you'd had an affair with Terence," I said finally. "Back when we were recruiting you for the Faire."

"Would you still have hired me?"

"Of course," I said. "But maybe we wouldn't have hired *him*. I mean, if we'd known having him around was awkward for you—"

"Good lord, it wasn't." She laughed. "Not for me, at least. No idea if he found it awkward, having someone around who knew all his tricks, but somehow I doubt it. And just for the record, I'd hardly call it an affair. More of a stupid fling."

"Still. At least it might have been smarter to tell the chief about it."

"Smarter? Maybe. Yes, I get that telling her myself might make me less suspicious than if she'd had to ferret it out herself. But I'm not sure she ever would have ferreted it out without George's help. I certainly haven't told more than one or two close friends about it, and they knew how mortified I'd be if it ever got out. Heaven knows how George got wind of it."

"Terence wasn't exactly a model of discretion," I pointed out.

"No, but he was pretty protective of his public image. And I made sure he knew exactly what unflattering truths I'd make public if he ever told anyone about our fling. Pretty sure he'd have sworn George or anyone else he told to secrecy."

"But you can't expect George—or anyone else—to keep to that after his death. His murder."

"Good point. Anyway, it's water under the bridge now— the fling, and George spilling the beans to the chief. Maybe it's even a good thing—the more she knows about Terence, and the way he used people, the better equipped she'll be to find his killer. And while I understand why someone might long to be rid of him, I don't approve of actually doing anything as drastic as murder—especially since they chose a time that puts me and a whole lot of my friends under suspicion."

"How long ago was this fling?"

"Let me think . . . fourteen years ago. Almost fifteen."

"That makes you less suspicious, don't you think?" I asked. "I mean, if it had been only a few months, maybe she'd think you were still emotional about it. But after a decade and a half . . ."

"Yeah—seems a lifetime ago. It was right after my first husband and I filed for divorce." She sounded curiously nostalgic. "And I really wanted to get away from it all. Away from him—my ex, that is . . . his friends . . . hell, away from *our* friends, and the whole D.C. theater scene. So I took this part at a dinner theater in Wisconsin. In *Two for the Seesaw*, which is a play with literally only two char- acters on stage, so it was just me and Terence marooned together in the middle of the most godforsaken wilderness imaginable."

"The dinner theater was in a wilderness?"

"Okay, it was in a town," she said. "Maybe you'd even call it a small city. Felt like the back of beyond to me at the time. And it was winter. I'd never seen so much snow. I think that was what drew us together."

"The snow?"

"The feeling of being the only two sane people in the world." She snorted with laughter. "There's snowdrifts a foot taller than your head, you go outside for ten minutes and you start getting frostbite on your nose, and all the natives are chirping about what a mild winter we're having and trying to teach you cross-country skiing. It was like being exiled to the Ice Age."

"So you clung together, two orphans in the storm."

"Something like that. It was a mistake, but far from the biggest I've made in my not-quite-half century on this planet—not by a long shot. And over and done with long ago. If either of my ex-husbands ever gets offed, you might want to check out my alibi. But Terence? Pffft."

Maybe the chief would see it differently, but Jacks hadn't just jumped to the top of my own suspect list.

"She has to check all of us out," I said aloud. "I'm probably lucky I have an alibi for the early morning, even if it's only Michael, who's kind of obligated to alibi me whether I deserve it or not."

"I think it's in the wedding vows." Jacks chuckled. "Right after the 'in sickness and in health' bit. Wish I had an alibi like Michael."

Then she frowned, and seemed to be hesitating about something.

Actors. In theory, they should be better liars than the rest of humanity, and quite often they were. Whenever Michael and I needed to beg off anything we didn't want to do—whether it was a tedious social engagement or a request for our volunteer services—I always tried to get Michael to do it. He sounded so much more convincing.

But when they weren't trying to deceive, actors' expressive faces could make it easy to follow what they were thinking.

"Spit it out," I said. "Whatever you're not sure you ought to be telling me."

She took a deep breath and let it out slowly.

"I was already thinking maybe I should talk to the chief again."

"About what?"

"Dianne wasn't in her tent last night. For part of the night, anyway."

Damn.

"Which part?"

"Well, it's not as if I lay in wait for her all night. Her tent's next to mine, and I happened to notice that she wasn't there when I'd have expected her to be."

"Understood. When did you notice her absence?"

"We were both in a group that walked back to Camp Anachronism around eleven, and I think we all went to bed shortly afterward. Then my bladder woke me up around midnight—I should lay off the mead; that stuff always makes me pee all night long. I had to go past her tent to get to the privies. And the moon was full or nearly, and when I glanced over at her tent, I could see through the front mesh window that she wasn't there."

Midnight was toward the early end of Dad's preliminary estimate of when Terence died.

"Did you notice when she came back?" I asked.

"No." Jacks shook her head rather hesitantly, as if still not sure she should be telling me this. "I hit the privies again at three-ish, and again at a little before five—seriously, if you see me drinking mead again, take the mug away. She wasn't there either time. I didn't see her until I went over to shower at maybe seven-thirty or eight.

She was in there getting ready. But the fact that she wasn't in her tent doesn't mean she was off killing Terence—for all I know, she's started seeing someone. Or maybe she felt safer doubling up with one of the other women."

I nodded. But we both knew that of the other women participants, she was closest to Jacks. That Jacks had actually offered to share her larger tent, and that Dianne had thanked her and said it was more than enough protection having Jacks next door.

"I haven't told the chief yet," Jacks said. "Because I wanted to ask Dianne what was going on. I just haven't had a chance yet."

"Do it soon," I said. "And talk her into telling the chief."

I didn't have to say that if she didn't tell the chief, I would. She knew that. And it occurred to me that maybe she'd confided in me as a way of forcing herself to go to the chief.

"Maybe I should just tell the chief," Jacks said. "About my affair, and Dianne being AWOL. And ask her not to tell Dianne who blew the whistle."

"I happen to know where the chief is right now," I said. "And I suspect she wouldn't mind being interrupted. Let's go find her."

Jacks grimaced, then followed me down to the lower level. I saw her safely to the storage room, and made sure it was locked up after the chief led Jacks into Cordelia's office. Then I headed back upstairs.

I glanced around the Great Room, which was largely empty. Was O'Malley's creative exercise over, then? I hoped so. After all, this was our busiest day. We didn't need O'Malley distracting the staff and making them overstay their meal breaks. And what if some of the tourists wandered in on it? The Faire staff, especially those playing the Game, were supposed to stay reasonably in character whenever the tourists were around, and I doubted if people during the Renaissance spent much time doing mime or sense memory exercises.

I glanced through one of the French doors leading out onto the terrace. Damn. O'Malley had taken his crew out there, and the creative exercise was in full swing.

Although the party had shrunk to only seven participants, all blindfolded with dinner napkins. Most of them were humming. One or two of them were cooing or singing wordlessly. One was making remarkably loud clicking noises with his tongue. Some held their arms outstretched before them like cartoon sleepwalkers. Others flailed around like non-swimmers who'd been flung into the water and had begun to panic. The flailers occasionally whacked other participants, eliciting yelps from the victims and sometimes mutters of "Sorry!" or at least "Sor—!" from the whackers.

"No words! No words!" O'Malley shouted after one such apology.

The participants would have been less apt to collide if they'd spread out a bit—the terrace ran the full length of the main building—but they were all shuffling around in a tight-knit cluster near the center of the space. And close to the wall of the building. I'm sure most of them had marveled at least once at the terrace's breathtaking view down the steep, wooded side of Biscuit Mountain. And as a result now they had all-too-vivid memories of the two-story drop waiting for them if they crashed through or flipped over the white wooden rail.

"You're all too timid!" O'Malley shouted. "Bolder! More joyful!"

He wasn't doing the exercise, of course. He was seated on one of the white wooden end tables, tapping his shins with a riding crop. I didn't remember that as part of the original Henry VIII outfit. If memory served, bluff King Hal carried a glove in one hand and a dagger in the other in the Holbein portrait. O'Malley wasn't wearing a dagger.

I wondered if he'd attempted to add one to the outfit and been thwarted. That would account for his current rather petulant expression. Although the rather lukewarm way in which everyone was carrying out his creativity exercise could also account for it. And he did have the riding crop to play with.

The Bonny Blade carried a riding crop just like that— and sold a decent number of them every weekend. Mostly to men who carried them around the rest of the day, tucking them under their arms like an officer's swagger stick, and tapping their boots. The Bonny Blade's whips were cheaply made and looked as if they'd fall apart if you did much more than that with them. We hadn't put whips on the prohibited weapons list, on the theory that you'd need a reasonable amount of skill to inflict more than minor damage with one. Maybe we should rethink that policy.

"This brings back memories."

I started, since I hadn't noticed Michael coming up behind me.

"Not, I gather, pleasant ones."

"You gather right." He put his arm around my waist and we watched the show outside for a few moments. Then I pulled out my phone and glanced at it.

"They've been doing that for at least twenty minutes," I said. "Hasn't it occurred to O'Malley that those people have work to do? I should break this up."

"Don't worry," Michael said. "I already did. Sent all our people back to their jobs. Well, except for Dianne, who seems to be angling for an audition, and after yesterday she deserves a break. The rest are all tourists I recruited to take their places. O'Malley will never know the difference."

"I feel sorry for the tourists," I said. "But if it keeps O'Malley out of our hair . . ."

"The tourists are happy," Michael said. "I gave them all free passes for next weekend."

A smart move. Cordelia was generous with the free

passes because she calculated that the food, drink, and souvenirs people bought more than covered the cost.

"Let's change up the exercise," O'Malley called out. "Everyone lie down. On your bellies. You're snakes. No, don't take off the napkins. You're blind snakes. Hiss! Writhe! Slither!"

Soon things were going better. People were hissing, writhing, and slithering with a great deal more enthusiasm. They didn't seem to be enjoying themselves, but at least they didn't have to worry as much about falling off the terrace. And now that I knew O'Malley wasn't distracting our staff from their busy day, I could actually laugh at his antics.

Michael sighed and shook his head.

"So, question about O'Malley," I said.

"Shoot." Michael's expression grew, if anything, more glum.

"Do you think there's the slightest chance that he actually ever worked with Maggie Smith?"

Michael guffawed, and his expression lightened.

"Not a chance in hell," he said. "Remember, he didn't say it reminded him of when *he* worked with her."

"So, name-dropping poseur." I nodded. "Check. And I gather you're not a fan of his acting exercises."

By way of an answer he rolled his eyes and shuddered.

"Enlighten me," I said. "Because, no offense, what they're doing out there doesn't seem a whole lot different from some of the things I've seen you do with your classes."

"Some of it's exactly what I do with my classes," he said. "Mainly my Acting 101 classes. They're exercises to help beginners develop their confidence. Get over their inhibitions. But none of my troupe here are beginners. They're seasoned professionals. If they need to warm up before they go on, they know what physical and vocal exercises work for them, and can be relied on to do them before we start. They don't need that kind of exercise, and I'm not going to make attending whatever else O'Malley has planned obligatory because I doubt any of them has the slightest interest in going."

"He suggested that?"

"Yes." Michael nodded. "And I vetoed it. Everyone seems to think I'm a fool for passing up the chance to audition for O'Malley's *Hamlet* production, but even if I desperately needed a job, I'd have passed on working with him again. I bet he's going to torture his cast all winter, putting them through every off-the-wall acting exercise he's ever heard of, with a side of New Age mysticism thrown in for good measure. Like that. The whole thing comes very close to my personal definition of hell on Earth."

"Could be worse," I said. "If someone hadn't bumped off Terence we'd be putting up with both of them."

We both laughed more than my joke deserved.

"Of the two, I think I'd rather have Terence underfoot," Michael said when we'd stopped chuckling.

"Knowing we could fire him if he went too far tended to keep him in line," I said.

"And how are we going to get rid of O'Malley if he gets completely out of line?" Michael's tone was gloomy again. "What if he decides he likes it here at the Ren Faire? And enjoys the Game a little too much? What if he decides Biscuit Mountain is the perfect venue for the first phase of his rehearsals and tries to enlist the entire troupe as his repertory company for *Hamlet*? He did that once to another director I know—showed up to watch a rehearsal and took over. Before my friend knew it, O'Malley had lured away two thirds of his cast and pretty much wrecked the first Equity show he got to direct. If O'Malley tries that here . . ."

"If you want him gone, say the word," I said. "Cordelia and I will take care of it. And if things get busy and we need any help, we'll enlist Mother."

Michael looked at me, blinked, and burst into laughter.

Chapter 29

"Yes," Michael said when he'd finally stopped laughing. "I rather think you could handle O'Malley. Any one of you, and the three of you together? Suddenly the idea of having him linger doesn't sound so bad. Seeing the three of you cut him down to size might turn out to be fun." His face grew serious again. "What puzzles me is why Arena's having anything to do with him. I'd have thought that meltdown he had last year at the Oscars would have done it for him."

"Meltdown at the Oscars? Was he nominated for anything?"

"Good heavens, no." Michael chuckled. "No, he just showed up for the ceremony with what turned out to be a counterfeit ticket and pitched a major fit when they turned him away. Then went back to his hotel, shot out all windows in his suite, and started throwing furniture off the balcony. I'm amazed a place as legit as the Arena would have anything to do with him after that."

"Ah, but it was last year," I said. "And I bet he went through the whole rehab and public apology ritual."

"Probably."

Out on the terrace O'Malley's followers were still pretending to be snakes, although with less enthusiasm than at the start. Apparently they'd figured out that if they slithered with the kind of wild abandon O'Malley was calling for, they were prone to picking up rather nasty splinters from the weathered wooden floor. Most of them had given up slithering and were trying to writhe and hiss in place.

"So I assume you won't be too upset that the chief has O'Malley on her suspect list," Michael went on.

"Really? She never mentioned it. Did he come down from Washington that early this morning?"

"He came down last night." Michael sounded a good bit more cheerful. "The chief was asking if we were expecting him or had seen him around, and I told her exactly how astonished we were to see him. Apparently he stayed in a bed-and-breakfast in town. Den Lille Hytta, as a matter of fact—you remember the place, just off Main Street."

"The one with all the gnomes in the yard?"

"Yes. Looks like the witch's cottage out of Hansel and Gretel. I suppose Den Lille Hytta is Norwegian for 'Castle of the Gnomes' or something."

"Actually, it's Norwegian for 'The Little Cottage,'" I said. "Mrs. Larsen—the owner—is actually a very nice old lady. Pushing ninety and stone deaf, though."

"So not much of an alibi."

"She just gives her guests a key and tells them don't worry about waking her up, a cannon couldn't do it."

"Strange place for O'Malley to pick," Michael said. "I mean, if it's the place I'm thinking of, it's a little kitschy, isn't it?"

"A little kitschy?" I chuckled at the idea. "It's completely gonzo kitschy. And if you think the outside's bad, you should see inside. A couple of weeks ago Mrs. Larsen was getting over a cold and Cordelia had me take her some chicken soup. She's a lovely lady, but she never met a china ornament she didn't like, and she has enough crocheted doilies to carpet a football field. But if you happened to be looking for a place in Riverton where you can come and go without being seen, Den Lille Hytta is the place."

"Ah—but how would O'Malley know that?" Michael looked triumphant.

"It's all over the Yelp reviews," I said. "After I saw what it was like inside, I looked to see what her guests thought.

Between people complaining about the deaf old lady who can't hear them knock when they lost the key, and the people praising how wonderfully quiet and private the place is, it would be easy to figure out about Mrs. Larsen. There aren't that many places to stay in Riverton, so it wouldn't take O'Malley much work to figure out that Den Lille Hytta is the best bet if you're up to something furtive."

"Maybe the chief already has him fitted up nicely for the murder, then," Michael said. "If it were anyone other than O'Malley, I'd be feeling sorry for him by now."

"Of course, it would be nice if we could think of a single reason why O'Malley would want to kill Terence," I said.

"Maybe he's feeling guilty about taking the part away from Nigel and giving it to Terence." Michael's face showed he realized how unconvincing this sounded. "No, that won't fly. He could fire Terence without turning a hair."

"Maybe he did try to fire Terence, and Terence pulled a cheap dagger on him, and he took it away and . . . no, there's the whole stabbing in the back thing. Would Terence turn his back on O'Malley under those circumstances?"

"Not really an obstacle," Michael said. "If Terence thought it was what his character would do . . . that the scene called for it . . . I can see him doing it."

"Except it wasn't a scene," I said. "It was real life."

"Terence was always a little confused about the difference."

Outside O'Malley clapped his hands, and everyone stopped hissing and slithering, with expressions of relief.

"Okay, let's do something different. Go into *savasana*."

Two of the participants immediately flopped down on their backs. The rest watched for a minute and then imitated them—well, except for one guy who decided to make a break for it and sprinted for the door.

"What's O'Malley after?" I said. "That's what I want to know."

"He's a strange bird," Michael said. ""Maybe he's just slumming. Enjoying the novelty. Maybe he'll get tired by the end of the day and go home. If you ask me, he's already tired of not being able to run everything."

"Maybe," I said. "But I think he's after something."

"I should go," he said. "The Game is afoot."

I nodded. I was getting impatient to get back to the real business of the day myself.

"Do you have any idea where Grandfather is?" I asked.

"He napped all morning, and now he's hanging out with the falcons." Michael chuckled. "He seems to think it annoys your grandmother."

"What could have given him that idea?"

"I did," he said. "And I worked very hard yesterday to convince him of it. Cordelia drops by periodically and grouses a bit, just to reinforce the idea. I think she likes knowing exactly where he is. Laters."

He gave me a quick kiss and strode across the Great Room.

I was torn between following his example and keeping an eye on O'Malley. I didn't much like the idea of someone with a history of trashing hotel rooms running around loose at the Faire.

As I watched, O'Malley reached in his pocket, took out his cell phone, and tapped on it. He sat for a few moments, running his eyes over the supine yoga participants. Then he tapped his phone again and put it back in his pocket.

I was wondering what that was all about when Nigel strolled over to stand beside me and peered out the window.

"Look at them," he muttered. "Sucking up to the great man."

Should I tell him O'Malley's current victims were all tourists? Maybe not.

"I thought you were a fan," I said aloud.

He grimaced and continued staring out.

"My eyes have been opened," he said finally. "You know, he really did tell me I had the part. Everyone thinks I imagined it. Took a few meaningless words of encouragement too seriously. I didn't. 'You're my Polonius.' He said that. I didn't imagine it."

I nodded. I wasn't sure Nigel saw, but I didn't want to interrupt him and risk shutting him down.

"Now he's dodging me," he went on. "I asked him point blank if I still had the part and he pretended to be distracted by something. I just want a straight answer—do I have the part or not?"

I wasn't sure what to say. I could remind him of what Michael had said about how he never wanted to work with O'Malley again. But Michael didn't need a job. He already had a job. A job—and a life—he loved. Michael wasn't still trying to climb the slippery ladder to fame, or even earn his living as an actor.

"It's Terence's fault," Nigel said. "If he were still around, he'd probably say 'tough luck, old bean—I did the better audition.' I'm not buying that. He poisoned the well. Slandered me. Told O'Malley about my drinking problem and convinced him that I couldn't be trusted. Terence did it."

I was startled at the sheer venom in his tone.

"So no, in case you were about to ask, I'm not going to go out there and abase myself. He can play his idiotic games. He's overrated anyway."

"Sounds as if you're giving up," I said.

"Facing reality," Nigel said. "Terence ruined it. Even now that he's gone, O'Malley won't come back to me for the part. Maybe he'll give it to George. He's better at sucking up than I ever was. I'm over it."

He turned and strode away.

I watched him go, uneasy. I hoped he wasn't talking like that in front of anyone else. Especially not the chief. She'd move him to the top of her suspect list.

And would she be wrong? Was I hearing only the anger

and resentment of an actor who'd won and then lost a part? Or of an actor so desperate to hang on to a part that he'd taken a human life—and was now finding out it had all been in vain?

"Not Nigel," I murmured. "I can't see it being him."

I hoped I was right.

Jacks and the chief appeared from the studio wing. Jacks glanced quickly at me and then hurried toward the front door. The chief came over to stand beside me and gaze out the window.

"Is that Ms. Willowbrook out there?" she asked.

"Willowdale," I corrected. "Yes."

She continued to gaze out for a few more moments.

"I hate to interrupt," the chief said. "But do you have any idea when the yoga class is supposed to end?"

"Not a clue," I said. "It's not a scheduled yoga class— just O'Malley doing his freelance acting exercise thing. Could go on for hours. Days. Feel free to interrupt them."

"It might be less disruptive if you could ask her to come inside," the chief said. "If you don't mind."

"No problem." Actually, the idea of doing something to annoy O'Malley appealed to me.

I opened the French door closest to where Dianne was lying and stepped out onto the deck. O'Malley saw me immediately. He scowled and gestured at me to go away.

I ignored him. I walked quietly over to where Dianne was lying, squatted down, and tapped her on the shoulder.

Her eyes flew open and she gasped slightly. She relaxed when she realized it was me—but why was she so on edge? And in a yoga class. Clearly O'Malley was a flop as a yogi.

"May I talk to you inside for a sec?" I whispered.

She nodded, got up, and headed for the open French door. I glanced over at O'Malley again. He'd grown red in the face and his scowl had given way to a sort of twitching grimace, as if his rage were so great he could barely keep from bellowing at me.

I waved and smiled at him, then followed Dianne inside. Almost ran into her, actually. She'd stopped just inside the door and was staring fixedly at Chief Heedles.

"Ms. Willowdale," the chief was saying. "I hope you don't mind if I interrupt your yoga class. I have a few more questions."

Dianne glanced back at me with a betrayed expression.

"Just tell the chief where you were last night," I said. "Then you can go back to the class." Maybe I should have just left her to the chief, who frowned slightly at my interruption.

Dianne burst into tears.

Chapter 30

The chief and I exchanged a puzzled look, then focused back on Dianne. I snagged a box of tissues from a nearby table and handed it to Dianne, who made generous use of them.

"I was so afraid," she wailed finally. "And Jacks told me more than once that I could always stay in her tent, but I didn't want to look like a complete idiot. I know she thinks I'm a total wimp. So I found someplace else to stay."

"Where?" the chief asked.

"There's this little room by the kitchen," she said. "A closet really, though there's never anything in it but a few boxes of canned goods. There's no window, and it's kind of damp, and smells musty, and there was only just barely enough room for my sleeping bag, and I had no idea there would be so many bugs in it. Horrible jumping bugs. Like brown grasshoppers, and they can jump a mile. I had to get rid of them before I could stay there, so I found some bug spray in the kitchen and sprayed them, and then swept out all the dead ones. Then I piled up the boxes of canned goods in front of the doorway, so no one could sneak up on me, and I got the first good night's sleep I've had in days."

"Why were you so afraid?" The chief's voice was gentle. "Did Mr. Cox do something . . ."

"It wasn't Terence," she said. "Well, not *just* Terence. Yes, he creeped me out, always whispering at me and insinuating things. But I could have taken that if it wasn't for the whole outdoors thing."

"Outdoors thing?" the chief echoed.

"Being in the woods makes me nervous," Dianne said. "And sleeping there, even inside the tent, just frayed my nerves to the limit. I'd lie awake every night hearing all these weird noises and terrified that something was creeping up on me. Bears—there are bears around here; don't try to tell me I'm imagining things. Meg's grandfather says it's true. And foxes. And snakes. I wasn't getting very much sleep to begin with, but then yesterday I complained to Terence about it, and that was a mistake. When he found out how I felt he started teasing me about it, and I was afraid he'd do something. Like throw a snake in my tent. Or find a bear costume and run around the camp in it. That was the last straw. I just couldn't take it any longer. So I went up to the main house and found a place to hide."

The chief looked at her with an odd expression. I couldn't tell if she felt sorry for Dianne or was annoyed by her. Probably a combo, actually. Sorry for her but annoyed that her confession didn't provide even a partial alibi.

"I don't suppose anyone saw you there," she said finally.

Dianne shook her head.

The chief suppressed a sigh.

"I didn't realize I was going to need an alibi," Dianne said. "I just wanted to get a good night's sleep for a change."

"I understand," the chief said. "Keep this to yourself for the time being."

"Okay." Dianne frowned slightly. "But why?"

"Because if you're not the actual killer, we don't want to give him or her any information that would make it easier to cast suspicion on you."

Dianne nodded, with a rather dubious expression on her face.

"Thank you," the chief said.

Dianne was turning to go.

"Wait a sec," I said.

Dianne tensed and turned back.

"Why didn't you tell us how much you hated sleeping in the tent?" I asked. "Me or Cordelia or Michael?"

"I don't like people knowing what a scaredy-cat I am," she said. "And besides—I was getting a free place to stay. Complaining about it would have felt . . . I don't know. Rude and ungrateful."

"We can't all be sturdy pioneer women," I said. "Do you see me sleeping in a tent?"

She smiled wanly and shook her head.

"If that closet by the kitchen is really so much of an improvement over a tent, I'll ask Cordelia if you can have it officially," I said. "We can probably squeeze a twin bed in there. And install a lock on the door so the rest of the world can't barge in."

Her face lit up.

"Do you think she'd let me?"

Instead of answering, I took out my cell phone and called Cordelia.

"Something wrong?" Cordelia answered.

"You know that closet we were going to make Terence sleep in so we could get him out of everyone's hair? Mind if we let Dianne sleep there? She hates tents to begin with, and the murder's made her hate them even more."

"Fine with me. Was that it?"

"Pretty much. I'll have to get the handyman to install a lock on the door."

"Needs one anyway," Cordelia said. "Make it so."

We hung up. Dianne was beaming.

"Thank you!" She glanced back at the chief. "Do you have any more questions?"

The chief shook her head. Dianne turned and headed for the front door.

"Not rejoining O'Malley's exercise?" I called out.

"Oh!" She stopped and looked stressed again. "It's not that I wasn't enjoying it or anything like that."

Liar, I thought.

"But I really feel I ought to get back to the job I'm being paid for." She raised her chin as if boldly taking a stand on a controversial issue.

"For the record, I'm ordering you to do just that," I said. "Carry on."

"Thanks." Her face lightened again.

"Actually," the chief called out. "I do have one small question. The bugs didn't bother you?"

Dianne looked blank.

"In the closet?" the chief added.

"Oh, them." She shrugged. "They're just bugs. And I managed to get rid of them before I went to sleep."

The chief nodded. Dianne turned and almost skipped out the front door.

"Takes all kinds," the chief said. "Me, I'd much rather sleep in a tent, even if I knew there were bears around. The very idea of having camel crickets hopping all over me in the middle of the night gives me the heebie-jeebies."

I nodded. I was texting the head of our maintenance crew, delegating the job of getting Dianne's new room ready.

"Have you seen any signs of this before?" the chief asked. "Ms. Willowdale's phobia, I mean."

"Aha," I said. "You're wondering whether to believe her." I thought for a few moments. "She hasn't mentioned it before. And she hasn't ever freaked out or anything. But now that I think about it, she is always very careful to find someone to walk with her when she goes down to Camp Anachronism in the evening,"

"Making sure Mr. Cox didn't have an opportunity to make a nuisance of himself?"

"Just being sensible, I'd have said—not that different

from avoiding dark alleys if you can help it. I'm more capable of self-defense than most women—probably a lot more than Dianne—but I wouldn't go wandering around in the woods by myself."

"Still, curious that her fear happened to overcome her on the very night when Mr. Cox was killed."

"She'd had a particularly difficult day, thanks to Terence," I said. "And even if she is exaggerating a healthy wariness of the woods into a phobia, I still have a hard time imagining her creeping out into the woods in the wee small hours to kill him."

"You could have a point." She nodded slightly.

Her phone buzzed. She pulled it out and glanced at the screen.

"Finally." As she lifted the phone to her ear her face took on an expression of exaggerated patience and cheerfulness—the sort of look mothers cultivate for times when their little darlings have begun working on their last unfrayed nerve. Odd—she just seemed to be answering a regular call, not a video one.

"Chief Heedles speaking . . . why hello, Your Honor. Thank you so much for getting back to me."

She sounded surprised. She'd looked at the number—hadn't she known a judge was calling?

"Yes, Your Honor. What—" Then she stopped and appeared to be listening with growing impatience. She even rolled her eyes once.

"I understand, Your Honor." Her voice had suddenly taken on a much more noticeable mountain accent. "I've already asked Ms. Cordelia, and in theory she's perfectly fine with the idea of my searching, but she doesn't want to give permission unless I've got those warrants. She's that worried about one of them trying to sue her—a lot of the suspects aren't from around here, you know . . . Yes, Your Honor, but you never know how some court down in Richmond is going to rule on a thing like that." She said

"Richmond" the same derisive tone she'd used before for "Jessop," but I suspected that was for the judge's benefit, not her true feelings. "Yes, Your Honor—normally I wouldn't waste your time, but in this case, I figure better safe than sorry. I'm sure Ms. Cordelia would be happy to give you a call to discuss it if . . . Yes, Your Honor. I'd appreciate it. I'll send an officer right over."

She ended the call and shook her head and shoulders as if trying to clear something that had entangled her.

"Judge Brown," she said. "Who wouldn't experience the slightest bit of culture shock if you could banish him back to the fifties. In fact, he'd be more at home then."

"Would that be the nineteen fifties or the eighteen fifties?" I asked.

"Either one." She gave a rueful chuckle. "I want to search some of our suspects' tents out in the camping ground. Ms. Cordelia's perfectly fine with it, but I don't want to go in without a warrant—we could have any evidence we find tossed if an appeals court finds that the tents' occupants had a reasonable expectation of privacy. Town attorney backs me on that. But I've been going back and forth all day with Judge Brown."

"The hint that a big-city appeals court might overturn him finally sunk in?"

"No, I finally escalated to threatening to sic Ms. Cordelia on him. Even he's got enough sense to be scared of that. Of course, by now anyone who had anything compromising stashed in their tent has probably had plenty of time to hide it somewhere else, but you never know. I'll send an officer over to pick up the warrant, because it would be just like Judge Brown to decide to do it after his nap and then forget all about it. And maybe sometime before nightfall we can do that search. For the time being I'll go back to searching Mr. Cox's belongings." She didn't look thrilled at the prospect. "I found an address book, but the number listed in it for 'Mom' has been disconnected."

"It's probably a decade old, that address book," I said. "A lot of people don't even bother with them these days— they just keep the information in their computers or their phones."

"Very true." She headed back for the studio wing.

I was puzzled. Did she not have Terence's phone? Evidently not, or she wouldn't be worrying about the address book. And I knew he had a phone—Terence was king of the selfie. But of course, it would probably be password protected. So she'd either be waiting for some kind of tech specialist to unlock the phone, or for the phone company to send her the records of his calls and texts.

And with any luck, one or the other would help solve the case. Maybe she would find that Terence had texted someone at three in the morning to say "meet me in the woods between the camp and the old logging road."

Well, I could hope.

And meanwhile, I had things to do. Probably time I checked in at the forge to see how Faulk and the boys were doing. And at the first aid tent, to see what Dad had learned about Faulk. And I'd feel a lot better if I knew what Grandfather was up to—I should check to see if he was still lurking in Falconer's Grove, and while I was at it, take him to task for frightening Dianne with the prospect of bears.

Back to the Game!

Chapter 31

The crowds had grown. Saturday was always our biggest day of the weekend, and I suspected when I checked with the box office I'd find that this was our biggest day of the summer so far. And they all seemed to be having a lovely time, despite the slightly diminished ranks of Game players.

Michael, Nigel, and Jacks were spinning out a scene near the Dragon's Claw. From what I overheard in passing, they were arguing about who Nigel should choose to marry Dianne. Michael and Jacks kept suggesting the names of fictitious noblemen, while Nigel shot down their suggestions and insinuated that he really wanted his daughter to be queen of Albion in due course, so maybe he should marry her off to George. I could see that they were laying the groundwork for the eventual dramatic duel between Michael and George, and meanwhile, the tourists were relishing the Game.

Over at the forge, things appeared less cheerful. Jamie was in the forge, getting everything ready for the next demo. Josh was in the shop, ringing up a big sale—a set of andirons and fireplace tools, and one of my huge overhead kitchen pot racks.

Faulk was nowhere to be seen.

I caught Jamie's eye and lifted an inquiring eyebrow. He nodded his head in the direction of the back room.

I hurried through the forge and into the back room. Faulk was there. And Tad. With both of them in there, the back room didn't have a whole lot of room left for me, but

I squeezed in anyway. They both looked—scared? Angry? A little of both.

"What's wrong?" I asked.

"What makes you think something's wrong?" Tad asked.

"I've got eyes," I said. "Spill."

"Looks as if Tad and I are suspects after all." Faulk tried to sound nonchalant, but failed utterly.

"Why?" I asked. "Have Dad and the medical examiner changed their minds on time of death?"

"No," Tad said. "But those yokels down at the Jessop ER are lying through their teeth."

"They're just trying to cover themselves." Faulk sounded weary.

"You're damned right they're trying to cover themselves," Tad bellowed. "And they don't care if they're framing one or both of us for murder in the process."

Spike, lurking just outside the chicken-wire barrier, growled menacingly, as he often did when humans raised their voices.

"Stop shouting," I said. "You're stressing Faulk out."

"Not as much as those lying liars in the Jessop ER," Tad said—but at normal volume.

"We can't do anything about the stress they're causing," I said. "Don't you add the straw that breaks the camel's back. Tell me what happened."

Tad and Faulk exchanged a look.

"Let me tell it," Faulk said.

"Yeah, you can keep your temper about it," Tad said, looking a little sheepish. "Sorry."

"I don't know what time I started feeling bad," Faulk said. "At first I just figured it was just fatigue. It was after midnight when I realized it was more than that."

"It was after midnight when I finally *made* you realize it," Tad said.

"We took off for the nearest ER," Faulk went on. "I don't know precisely what time we got there. I didn't really notice the time until I started to get impatient about how long we'd been waiting."

"It was twelve forty-four when I finished filling out the inch-high stack of admission forms," Tad said. "There was a space on the form for time of arrival, so I'm sure of that."

"And we just sat there in the waiting room," Faulk said. "Every so often a nurse would come out and take my vitals or ask a question about something on my form, and then she'd disappear back into the bowels of the hospital, leaving us all alone."

"Except for the receptionist," Tad said. "Who couldn't be bothered to look up from her book. Robin Cook's *Coma*, in case you're curious, and I think she was reading it for inspiration on how she could make our stay in their miserable chamber of torture even worse."

"A little before four a.m. Tad pitched a major fit about how long we'd been waiting, and they finally took us in and put us in a cubicle," Faulk went on. "And eventually a doctor ambled in and examined me."

"What did he say?"

"Not much," Faulk said. "At least not much that I remember—I was half asleep on top of feeling rotten, and he left before Tad got back."

"Before Tad got back?" My stomach clenched. "Where had Tad gone?"

"Two blocks down the street to get us some coffee," Tad said. "The ER had a broken coffee-vending machine and an empty soda machine, no water fountain, and I didn't like the look of the tap water in the bathroom. So once they took us back and I got Faulk settled in the cubicle, I got directions to an all-night doughnut shop nearby and headed down to get coffee for both of us. Based on their past performance, I figured it would take them at least half an hour to get the doctor in, but he came and went in the fifteen minutes it took me to make the coffee run."

"I think by this time they were eager to get us out of

there," Faulk said, with a hint of a grin. "Tad had left them in no doubt about what he thought of their performance. I think the words 'incompetence' and 'malpractice' might have been uttered."

"Which is probably why they're claiming we didn't even get there until nearly four, and were seen almost immediately," Tad says. "They're lying. Lying to cover themselves."

"They're also a bit vague on when Tad was with me," Faulk said. "Which was pretty much every minute except for the fifteen or twenty minutes it took him to fetch the coffee."

"I should have known better," Tad said. "I should have taken you somewhere else—Fairfax or Richmond or Charlottesville. We'd probably still be there because they'd have insisted on admitting you and sticking a bunch of monitors on you, but at least they wouldn't lie about what happened."

"So the odds are that we just soared to the top of Chief Heedles's suspect list," Faulk said.

"You probably haven't," I said. "Worst case, she's probably a little testy right now because checking you out is going to be a whole lot more work. But she's definitely not going to take their word against yours without checking."

"Why not?" Faulk asked, sounding puzzled.

"Because in case you hadn't noticed, Riverton and Jessop are like the Hatfields and McCoys," I explained. "When I told her you'd been to the Jessop ER, she said she hoped there wasn't anything serious wrong and suggested getting a second opinion from someplace competent. If your story doesn't match theirs, she's not going to take their word for it without checking."

"But what can she check?" Faulk looked a little less gloomy.

"Did either of you use your cell phones while you were there?"

"I have no idea if I even brought mine." Faulk shrugged. "And what difference would it make?"

"Why didn't I think of that?" Tad exclaimed. He pulled out his phone, touched the screen a couple of times, and peered down at it. "Yes. I checked my messages at one twenty-one. And at two fifteen I called up to get my bank balance, in case we had to pay cash for anything if they ever got around to seeing us. And at four-twelve, when I was on my way back from the doughnut shop, I got a call, and I answered it because it had a local area code and I thought it might be the hospital. Junk call."

"And this helps us because . . . ?" Faulk asked.

"The call would bounce off of the nearest cell phone tower," I explained. "Which will be in Jessop, not Riverton. And speaking of the doughnut shop—did you pay cash?"

"No!" Tad beamed. "I used my bank card. And I bet the cops will remember me."

"Cops?" Faulk asked.

"The place where I got the coffee was an all-night joint—definitely a cop hangout. The only other people there were a couple of cops. And boy, were they giving me the once-over—not only an unfamiliar face, but a black one. And okay, one of them was a local cop, so maybe the hospital can co-opt him, but the other one was a state trooper."

Normally the notion of being subjected to extra scrutiny because of his race would have infuriated Tad—but now the idea had him grinning with relief.

"And hey—look at this!" He held up his phone.

I peered at the tiny screen. I couldn't exactly read what was on it—a document of some sort. No, make that a form.

"Did you photograph the entire admission form?" I asked.

"Just the top part with Faulk's social security number on it, so I didn't have to make him take out his wallet if they asked for it again. But it's got the time I finished filling out the form."

"Excellent," I said.

The sound of a hammer tapping a couple of times on an anvil brought us back to the moment.

"I'd better go out and make sure the boys aren't bashing each other's fingers." Faulk smiled at us and slipped out into the main part of the forge.

"Thank you," Tad said. "We're supposed to be keeping him stress free. Not going so well this weekend. But it should be a little better now that you've talked us off the ledge. I should have thought of the cell phone thing."

"You don't have an insatiable mystery reader in your family," I said. "I know all sorts of normally useless things thanks to Dad."

"Of course there's no guarantee," Tad said. "The cell phone tower information could be inconclusive. They could claim I lied on the form. The cops could pretend not to remember me so no one accuses them of profiling. But Faulk doesn't need to know any of that."

"Agreed," I said. "I'll see you later—I'm going to check on Grandfather."

"And I have to get back to my patrol." He straightened his shoulders, assumed an expression of almost comical gravity, and strode out.

I followed him outside and watched the beginning of the blacksmithing demonstration. The boys were good—amazingly good for their age. I wouldn't complain if one of them followed in my footsteps and took up the trade. Nor would I be disappointed if one or both emulated Michael and went into acting. They were talented at that as well.

And then I reminded myself that it was a little early to be planning careers for them. And that I still hadn't checked on what Grandfather was up to.

I waved at Faulk and the boys and slipped into Falconer's Grove.

Chapter 32

I found Grandfather and Greg giving a demonstration to a small crowd.

Make that trying to give a demonstration. The Mad Monk was standing at the rail, shouting at them and shaking his fist. I could see others in the already small audience edging away and putting some distance between them and the seedy-looking monk.

Greg looked as if he was working to keep his mouth shut—no doubt he was remembering Cordelia's oft-repeated instructions: "The customer may not always be right, but you don't need to tell him how wrong he is." Grandfather, who had never been known to shrink from a battle or argument, was in what my old martial arts teacher would have called a state of relaxed but conscious readiness.

"And you should be ashamed of yourself." The Mad Monk turned to Grandfather. "I guess your image as a big environmentalist is all fake."

"Actually, falconry and environmental consciousness are perfectly compatible." Grandfather sounded completely unruffled. "Back in the 1960s, the peregrine falcon was in serious decline. And do you know why?"

The Mad Monk stood with his arms folded, stubbornly refusing to engage. I decided to help.

"Let me guess: habitat destruction?" I asked. I knew from hearing any number of Grandfather's talks on endangered species that this was always a safe guess.

"Well, that was a factor," he said. "But back in the sixties, the more acute threat was DDT. It was still actively in use, and among other negative effects, it makes a bird's eggshells so thin that they break before they hatch. And thanks to biomagnification—the tendency for nasty stuff like DDT to become more concentrated as it moves up the food chain—raptors like the peregrine falcon started feeling the effects a lot sooner than their prey. Falconers helped sound the alarm on the problem, and then worked hand-in-hand with ornithologists to publicize the danger and bring about the Endangered Species Act in 1973. And not a bit too soon—by that time, the peregrine falcon was effectively extirpated here in the U.S."

"Extirpated," I echoed. "Is that another way of saying extinct?"

"Locally extinct," Grandfather corrected. "Given how popular peregrines are for falconry, there were a fair number of them in captivity, and there are at least nineteen subspecies around the world that were closely related to the one we'd lost, so we were able to breed them in captivity and reintroduce them to the wild here on the East Coast. Not quite the original subspecies, alas, but still, much better than having no peregrines at all. Ecosystems need their predators. And our success with the peregrines paved the way for dozens of similar projects with other raptors all over the world."

Grandfather beamed with such obvious pride that I deduced he'd been actively involved in saving the peregrines—though probably not by doing anything labor-intensive like hand-rearing orphaned chicks. More likely he'd helped finance the rescue—he had an almost uncanny ability to raise funds for any environmental cause he championed. And I could only imagine the effect he'd have on a bevy of bureaucrats or legislators he considered insufficiently supportive of endangered species—it would be rather like turning Gracie loose on a flock of fluffy little chicks.

"And there's another small contribution that falconry makes to biodiversity," Grandfather said. "Falconers don't necessarily keep their birds indefinitely. Many if not most of them take their birds from the wild—but they can't take just any bird. Most jurisdictions only allow you to take a bird that's out of the nest but not yet of breeding age. That's a population whose odds of survival aren't all that great. They're still learning to hunt, so starvation's a very real threat, and when they're that young they're also more vulnerable to being eaten by bigger, more experienced predators. Somewhere between seventy and ninety percent of them don't make it to adulthood."

"Nature red in tooth and claw," I quoted. Grandfather beamed at hearing one of his favorite quotations.

"But the birds falconers take and train tend to survive." Grandfather nodded approvingly at Harry and Gracie. "They get a warm, safe place to live, even in the winter. They get fed, even in a bad year when game is nonexistent. They get medical care that helps them stay healthy—in the wild a lot of birds suffer from parasites, everything from mites and lice to coccidia and tapeworms—you name it. They get plenty of time to grow up, become strong, and learn to be expert hunters. And after a year or two, the falconer releases them back into the wild—and the gene pool. Everybody wins."

"But meanwhile they're living in captivity," the Mad Monk said. "They don't choose to live in a filthy cage."

"Actually, they do choose to stay with their humans," Greg said. "Oh, not at first, but these guys?" He gestured toward Gracie and Harry. "By now they stay around because they want to. In case you hadn't noticed, the only way we can hunt with them is to let them fly free. Any time they want to, they can just fly away. They're complete pragmatists—if they think they can do better on their own, they're not going to stick around."

"And I'd hardly call the mews a cage, much less a filthy one," Grandfather added. "Maybe it looks like a cage to you, but to Harry and Gracie, it looks like a really comfortable place to hang out when they're not hunting. A place where they can sleep soundly without worrying that something bigger than they are, like a great horned owl, might pounce on them. It's scientifically designed to meet their needs, physical and emotional."

"And you can lose that 'filthy' bit," Greg added. "The mews—and for that matter the weathering yard and every tiny bit of equipment we use—all of it's highly regulated and subject to inspection at any time. You find a mews that's not clean and well maintained and I guarantee you the Virginia Department of Game and Inland Fisheries is going to shut it down pronto. That mews is cleaner than most people's kitchens."

"There's just no way of getting some people to see the right." The Mad Monk lifted his chin in scorn and walked away.

"No, there isn't, is there?" I muttered.

"What a moron." Grandfather's voice probably carried well enough for the Mad Monk to hear him.

"How'd he get back in, anyway?" Greg muttered. "I thought Queen Cordelia was going to ban him—he's almost certainly the jerk who tried to set the birds free last weekend."

"Set them free?" Grandfather asked. "What happened?"

"It was right before closing time and almost all of the tourists were gone. I went to take a load of stuff to the car, leaving Vinnie to watch the birds. Someone lured him away with a fake emergency, and when he got back, Gracie was riled up about something, and Harry's leash had been cut."

"Only Harry's?" I asked.

"Pretty sure he tried to cut Gracie's, too, but she didn't let him get close enough. Did you see those nasty half-healed scratches on his neck? Looks like Gracie's handiwork to me."

"Good for Gracie!" Grandfather exclaimed.

"A good thing Harry didn't escape." And now that Greg mentioned it, I was pretty sure Cordelia had put him on the banned list. So how had he gotten in?

"Fat chance of Harry going anywhere." Greg sighed. "To tell you the truth, I'd figured out by a week or two after I caught him that Harry was never going to be the keen hunter Gracie is. But I figured I'd give it a try. He's a handsome bird, with an unusually good disposition—I figured he'd be good for demonstrations at Ren fairs. But he's driving me bonkers. If I go out in one of our favorite hunting grounds with Gracie, the second I pull off her hood her eyes are darting around looking for prey. She's ready! I take Harry and I unhood him and he's like 'Gee, thanks, Greg. Nice scenery. I'm ready for a little nap in the sun. You did bring the snacks, right? Because I'm getting a little peckish.'" He shook his head and looked at Harry with a curious mix of disappointment and affection.

"Have you had him checked out?" Grandfather was frowning as he studied Harry. "That's very odd behavior—it could indicate some sort of medical problem. Clarence Rutledge, the vet we use for the zoo—"

"Has seen Harry so many times by now that he gives us a frequent flyer discount." Greg shook his head. "Harry's not sick. Just mellow. One really laid-back raptor."

"The hawk equivalent of Ferdinand the Bull," I suggested.

"Yeah." Greg nodded.

"That doesn't make him a lot of fun to hunt with, does it?" Grandfather continued to study Harry with an increasingly disapproving look. "And it's not exactly a trait conducive to survival in the wild. Could be genetic, in which case taking him out of the gene pool wouldn't be a bad thing."

"I'm worried that he's already taken himself out of the gene pool. I tried to hack him out this spring and the whole thing flopped."

"Flopped how?" Grandfather asked.

"And what is hacking out?" I added. "Doesn't sound like fun."

"Hacking out is what we call a soft release," Greg

explained. "You give the bird the freedom to go and let him choose when he wants to leave."

"We do it all the time with birds raised in captivity and then released into the wild to rebuild the population," Grandfather said. "You provide food and a predator-resistant shelter, you let the bird come and go, and they choose to leave when they're ready."

"Harry never left." Greg sounded wistful. "I thought of trying to chase him off—shout at him and bang things. Make him scared of humans."

"Sometimes necessary." Grandfather nodded. "Trusting humans isn't a survival trait for wild creatures."

"But he's a pretty lousy hunter," Greg said. "I worry that he'd starve if I chased him off. So I plan to keep giving him plenty of chances to leave, but I'm kind of resigned to the fact that he could be around for the long term."

"How long is the long term?" I asked.

"The record for a red-tailed hawk in captivity is almost thirty years." Greg sighed and shook his head. "He's only about two. I know it's a little selfish of me, but he's filling up one of my three slots."

"Three slots?" I echoed.

"Falconers start as apprentices," Grandfather explained. "Who are only allowed to possess a single raptor. After two years they can become a General Falconer and possess three. And if they keep at it, after another five years they can become a Master Falconer and own any number they like. But right now Greg's limited to three."

"It's not an unreasonable law," Greg said. "There's a limit to how many birds one falconer can properly care for. But the problem is, right now I've got Gracie, and Harry, and Delilah, an elderly red-tailed hawk with only one wing. She can't fly, so it's not as if I can turn her loose. I rescued her when I found her losing a fight with a Great Horned Owl and nursed her back to health, which wasn't easy."

"Good man." Grandfather said. "You might be able to

find a raptor sanctuary that would take her. In fact I know an excellent one not far from here."

"She's used to me." Greg shook his head. "I don't want to disrupt her life—not at her age. And if I keep at it, I should make Master Falconer in a little over two years."

"But right now, you've only got one falcon willing and able to hunt." Grandfather looked thoughtful. "I wonder if we could develop some kind of training program to spark Harry's interest in hunting."

"You think it's possible?" Greg looked hopeful.

"I have no idea," Grandfather said. "First time I've ever heard of a hawk too lazy to hunt. But there's no harm trying, is there?"

Greg looked more cheerful. And Grandfather was studying Harry with the satisfied expression he always wore when he'd just found an interesting new project.

"Well, I should get back to work," I said.

They both nodded absently, and I left them there, staring thoughtfully at Harry.

But as I left, I noticed that the Mad Monk hadn't gone far. He'd merely crossed the clearing, gone a few feet into the woods, and sat down cross-legged. Had he tried to go farther in, encountered the nearly invisible black net deer fencing and settled for his present position? I think I'd have noticed that happening. Would-be trespassers usually got caught up in the net and often needed help extricating themselves. At the very least, they'd usually utter a few unflattering words about the ancestry of whoever had strung up the netting. The Monk had made a beeline to the spot and settled himself quietly—make that stealthily—with the trunk of a large tree between him and the mews. I was willing to bet it wasn't the first time he'd occupied that spot—a spot where Greg and Grandfather probably couldn't see him.

And now that he was sitting down, I noticed something else. His monk costume included a scabbard, hanging from his rope belt.

Chapter 33

I shifted a little so I could get a better view of the Monk. I was relieved to see that the scabbard was empty.

And dagger-sized. I wouldn't have seen it if not for the fact that when he sat, his robes shifted slightly and the scabbard poked out.

I retraced my steps to the fence around the mews, right beside where Greg and Grandfather were sitting. I was right—you couldn't see the Monk from there.

"Just so you know, the Mad Monk hasn't gone far," I said. "He's hiding behind a big tree across the clearing."

"The oak?" Greg asked.

"White oak," Grandfather clarified.

"My tree identification is sadly lacking," I said. "The tree with the biggest trunk—the one that has the weird bulge on the right side that sort of looks as if something was trying to burst out of the trunk, like the creature in *Alien*."

Grandfather and Greg both looked at me for a moment with an odd expression.

"Okay," Greg said. "The white oak."

"Was he hanging about here yesterday?" I asked.

"Didn't see him," Greg said. "It was last weekend that he tried his *Free Willy* nonsense on the birds. And like I said, I thought he'd been banned."

"Did he have anything in his scabbard last weekend?"

"His scabbard?"

"It's hard to see when he's standing, because of the baggy, shapeless costume, but he's got an empty scabbard hanging from that rope belt—a short scabbard. About the right size for a small dagger. Was it empty last weekend?"

"No idea," Greg said. "I didn't even notice it this weekend. Is it important?"

I was about to explain that from what I could see, the Monk's scabbard was the very sort of cheap, machine-made scabbard that the Bonny Blade sold. Since I'd never bought anything there—had never even spent more than a few polite moments browsing their wares—I had no idea if the Bonny Blade sold their daggers and scabbards as a set or merely made sure to stock a selection of scabbards that fit their various blades. But they definitely sold them—had great rows of them hanging from racks outside their booth, waving gently in the breeze, no doubt provoking Seamus, the leatherworker, to the same feelings of annoyance that I felt when I saw their ill-made swords and daggers.

But last I heard the chief hadn't released any information about how Terence had been killed.

"It just makes me . . . nervous," I said aloud. "An empty scabbard's weird, and I really don't like the idea that a loon like that might have a weapon stashed somewhere."

"Point taken." Greg nodded.

"We'll keep an eye on him," Grandfather assured me. He fixed his eyes on the white oak tree with the unblinking intensity of one of his beloved owls.

"And I'm going to ask Cordelia if we shouldn't kick him out." I was already texting her to that effect.

I returned to the forge. Faulk was sitting on his stool, watching as the boys entertained the crowd. They weren't doing any actual blacksmithing at the moment, but allowing interested tourists to heft the various tools to see how heavy they were.

I felt the buzz that signaled a text coming in. Cordelia, confirming that she'd banned the Mad Monk last weekend.

I ducked into the back room and called the chief.

"This may be nothing," I said.

"But you're going to tell me about it anyway because I get to decide what's nothing and what's a vital clue."

"Right. There's a guy we call the Mad Monk. Wears a filthy robe with a rope belt."

"I think I've seen him," she said. "Smelled him, too— not overly fond of bathing, I'd say. But that isn't even a misdemeanor, more's the pity. Do you have some reason to suspect him?"

I explained about the vandalism at the weaver's and leatherworker's stalls the previous weekends, his attempt to free the falcons, and the curious fact that he was wearing an empty scabbard of the kind the Bonny Blade sold.

"Again, the Bonny Blade." Her tone was light, but I could tell she thought I had a bee in my bonnet over my so-called competitors.

"It's not so much that it's one of their scabbards," I said. "It may not even have come from there—although it's the kind of scabbard you'd buy for your dagger if the Bonny Blade was where you did your weapon shopping. But it was empty. Why is he running around with an empty scabbard? Most people would either rig up a fake hilt or just leave the scabbard at home with the dagger."

"You think he left it in Mr. Cox."

"Could be."

"And his motive?"

"The same as Greg Dorance's: Terence was trying to harm the falcons. Of course, the Mad Monk thinks Greg is a moral leper for keeping falcons in the first place, so Greg was probably his original target. But if he happened to witness Terence endangering the birds, maybe he'd put dealing with Greg on hold till he'd dealt with Terence."

"It's a possibility," she said. "Where can I find this Mad Monk?"

"In Falconer's Grove, hiding behind a big white oak.

And if you're like me and wouldn't recognize a white oak if it fell on you, just look for the tree at which Grandfather is staring fixedly."

"Roger. I'll send one of my officers over to escort him up here."

"And after you've finished with him, can you have them escort him out?" I said. "Cordelia put him on the no-fly list last weekend. Not sure how he got past the ticket crew, but even if he's not a murder suspect, he's a trespasser.

"Can do."

I tucked my phone away and opened the door so I could keep an eye on the shop. And then I pulled out my notebook and scribbled in a new task. We needed a way to ensure that tourists in costume followed the same rules as everyone else. Everyone, including the palace guards, tended to assume that anyone in a reasonably good costume was part of the Game, and let them get away with some pretty crazy stuff. I'd talk over the problem with Cordelia and Michael after closing. And—

"Excuse me—did you buy that here?"

I glanced up to see a young woman in a fairy costume peering through the door into the back room. She was staring at my notebook with covetous eyes.

"The book." She pointed to my notebook-that-tells-me-when-to-breathe. "Did you buy it here?"

"Yes, from Seamus, the leatherworker." I held my notebook out so she could take a closer look. "His booth's right by the Dragon's Claw. But it's a special order, and not cheap."

"Ooh . . . if it's a special order, maybe he could make one even more like what I want. Not that yours isn't just about perfect."

"It's perfect for me." I held the book out so she could see the detail. "But if your budget's healthy, nothing Seamus would like better than coming up with one that's just as perfect for you."

"Thank you!" She stroked one of the embossed drag-ons lightly, then dashed off in the direction of Seamus's booth.

I studied the intricate leather for a few more moments. Maybe I wouldn't go back to the more utilitarian binder I'd been using for the notebook. See if Seamus was right that his work would last a lifetime.

Then I tucked it away and left the back room. Jamie was hammering on an iron rod under Faulk's close supervi-sion while Josh explained to the crowd what his brother was doing.

As I watched, Faulk made a correction to Jamie's tech-nique with a few quiet words and a swift gesture. Yes, that awkward way Jamie had been holding his wrist made my own ache, as if it imagined how tired and sore he'd be if he kept that up. Much better now. I found myself nodding in satisfaction at the improvement, and smiled when I re-alized that Faulk and I were nodding in unison.

"Don't force the hammer down." Was Faulk telling Ja-mie the same thing he'd told me so many times in those early days? "You'll tire yourself out before the rod's half cold. Let gravity and the weight of the hammer work for you, not against you."

He was a better teacher than I was. More patient. Bet-ter at explaining things. Better at demonstrating things. I'd lost track of the number of times when I'd been trying to teach the boys something and found myself thinking, "How did Faulk manage to teach me this part?"

And some of the best times in the forge these days were when one or both of the boys were working with me, as I'd worked with Faulk. The clang of two or even three ham-mers, falling into the same rhythm even if we were work-ing on separate projects. Having another pair of hands to work the bellows for me—or taking a break from my work and working the bellows for someone else. Sharing that moment when you shove the piece you're working on into the water to cool it down so you can touch with an assessing finger what your hammer's been making.

Maybe I should persuade Faulk and Tad to come to Caerphilly when the summer was over. We had plenty of room in the house for a few more people. I'd expanded the forge when the boys had started taking an interest. It was big enough for three—it would probably serve for four. I could introduce Faulk to Ragnar, my best customer—a retired heavy-metal drummer who'd bought a local mansion and was redecorating it with vast supplies of black velvet and wrought iron. Ragnar always had more projects than I could possibly handle, and so far he'd rejected all the other blacksmiths I'd tried to introduce him to. But if I introduced him to Faulk, my own teacher? It gave me a sudden flash of pleasure, imagining what a din four hammers could make in our old barn.

Jamie finished what he'd been doing—turning a small, straight, metal rod into an S-hook—and held it up to show the audience. Faulk beamed with pride and reminded him, quite tactfully, to cool it off before taking it within reach of the tourists.

The forge was in good hands.

I glanced across the way to the first aid tent. It occurred to me that Dad might be able to shed some light on Dianne's alleged phobia. He'd taken an interest in phobias at one time. The subject had been pushed into the background by any number of other, more recent obsessions—including, at the moment, Scottish tartans, the Tolpuddle martyrs, growing his own tea, and whether the gelada monkeys of Ethiopia were really domesticating wolves or only coexisting peacefully with them. But Dad's intellectual obsessions never completely died out—they could smolder for years, only to be revived by a few chance words.

Unfortunately, I saw that Dad was fussing over a newly arrived patient—a young woman who'd just hopped over to the tent, partially supported by a solicitous friend. Even from across the way I could see that the woman's ankle was swollen to the size of a grapefruit. I'd drop by a little later.

I lurked near the entrance to Falconer's Grove until I saw Lenny stroll in. He was dressed in street clothes, rather than a uniform, and gave the impression that he wasn't in a particular hurry. I liked that. Seeing a uniformed officer dashing anywhere on the grounds would probably pique the tourists' curiosity and draw a crowd. But no one paid any attention to a fairgoer dressed in t-shirt and jeans ambling from one part of the Faire to another.

With the Mad Monk taken care of, I decided to satisfy my curiosity about something else and headed for Camp Anachronism. I'd been there often enough, but since Michael and I had bagged a room in the main building—part of my reward for being Cordelia's second-in-command—I didn't know the layout as well as I would have if I'd been camping there. I wanted to get a better mental map of the camp—and its relationship to the logging road and the murder scene.

And now was a great time to do it—the trumpets were just sounding to announce the start of today's first joust—a big draw for the tourists, and pretty much an all-hands event for most of the ambulatory staff—the minstrels, jugglers, strolling salespeople, and of course anyone playing the Game.

Which meant that Camp Anachronism would be about as empty as it would ever be.

I made my way there in a leisurely fashion—so many of the tourists were heading in the other direction, toward the joust, that I had to step out of the path a couple of times to let the throng pass. Around me I could see shopkeepers and food servers taking deep breaths and beginning to enjoy an interval of relative peace and quiet.

When I got to the gate that separated Camp Anachronism

from the main fairgrounds I stopped and looked around. Tourists respected the STAFF ONLY signs for the most part, but for some reason seeing someone else go through a forbidden gate often inspired them to imitation. When he had time, Cordelia's handyman was going to figure out a way to install a lock with a keypad—camouflaged from the tourists' eyes of course.

Satisfied that no one was watching me, I slipped through the gate. The fenced-in path made a sharp dogleg to the right, to keep passersby from getting a view of the completely unhistorical camp when the gate opened. I paused, as I usually did, to make sure no one came barging in behind me.

While I was doing that, I heard movement to my left. Out in the camp. I sighed with exasperation. Since I wasn't occupying one of the tents here, I'd probably have to explain my presence. And "I just wanted to see how easy it would be for someone like you, who's staying here, to sneak out into the woods and stab Terence" wasn't really an explanation I wanted to make.

Inspecting to make sure the police hadn't messed anything up when they confiscated Terence's tent and its contents. Yeah, that would probably pass muster.

But when I stepped out into the main part of the camp and spotted the person who'd been making the noise I quickly ducked back into the dogleg and peered around the edge of the fence.

What was O'Malley doing here?

He was walking quickly along a path between two rows of tents. As I watched, he stumbled over an object someone had left out in front of their tent, swore under his breath, and continued on his way.

Maybe I wouldn't be quite so suspicious of O'Malley if he'd been walking normally, but his body language was furtive. He'd glance over his shoulder from time to time—although never, luckily, in my direction. He seemed more worried about glancing into all the tents he passed in case someone was hiding there. And he was stepping carefully now, as if to avoid making any noise that might betray his presence. Of course, the distant cheers from the jousting field plus the louder strains of several minstrels bellowing out a mildly bawdy song just outside the gate to the camp would have drowned out any noise he might make, but you had to hand it to him: his stealthy creeping was very amusing to watch.

Actors. It wasn't just their faces that could give them away. If they were stage actors—and I gathered that was where O'Malley had made his bones—they could also convey immense amounts of emotion and information with their bodies. If I were a director and wanted O'Malley to convey that he was trying to sneak around someplace he wasn't supposed to be—using only body language—I'd be on the verge of yelling "Cut! Bravo! Nailed it!"

But at the moment, all his very eloquent body language did was put me on high alert that he was up to something.

I followed him using my own brand of stealth—which I hoped didn't look the least bit like sneaking around. A couple of times, when he whirled around, I took advantage of available cover—it was easy to predict when he was about to turn, because he froze and tensed his body first—it was almost as if he wanted to telegraph what he was about to do. Most of the time I just walked slowly and smoothly through the camp, glancing at the ground often enough to keep from tripping over anything that would make a lot of noise.

He emerged from the rows of tents that formed the main body of the camp and paused briefly, glancing across to the far side of the clearing—where we'd exiled Terence on his last night, with Horace and Lenny to keep watch over him. I ducked behind a tent. Sure enough, O'Malley turned and swept his eyes back and forth, scanning all the tents he'd passed by, before turning to walk briskly across the clearing. His new body language was that of the soldier who had ventured out of the trenches and was hoping not to draw sniper fire.

He kept on past Horace's and Lenny's tents and came to a sudden stop right where Terence's would have been if the chief hadn't confiscated it and hauled it off. He darted glances right and left, as if looking to see which way the tent might have gone. He looked . . agitated.

Sooner or later he'd turn around and notice me, so I decided to use the element of surprise while I still had it.

"Looking for something?" I asked.

Chapter 34

At the sound of my voice O'Malley jumped and uttered a small yelp.

"Do you always sneak up on people like that?" he demanded.

"I didn't realize I was sneaking. Are you looking for anything in particular?"

"Terence's tent. It's gone."

"The police have taken custody of it," I said. "Evidence."

"Ah." He nodded and stared rather gloomily at what I assumed was the spot where Terence's tent had been.

"Was there a reason you were looking for his tent?" I asked. "Maybe I can help."

O'Malley didn't answer. I was pretty sure he heard me just fine but for the moment had chosen to project an aura of dark, brooding melancholy.

"If you think he had something of yours, you can ask the chief," I went on. "And if you're just into the whole true-crime sightseeing thing, you'd probably find the actual scene of the crime more interesting. I can show it to you if you like, but probably not till sometime tomorrow, though—last time I looked it was festooned with yards of crime scene tape and guarded by a very watchful Riverton police officer."

He continued to brood.

It occurred to me that O'Malley thrived on having an audience. And also that I was profoundly not in the mood to be that audience, even if his performance were as fascinating as he imagined it to be. I should head back to the main part of the Faire. Although it was peaceful here, and out of view of the tourists. I shrugged, pulled out my notebook and did a little quick updating—crossing out a couple of things I'd done, adding a few new items. I might not be in O'Malley's league as an actor, but I was pretty sure my body language communicated that I'd lost interest in what was happening here and was on the verge of moving on.

About the time I pulled out my phone and began tapping out a query to Kevin on how he was doing with his research, O'Malley seemed to grow tired of being ignored.

"I seek atmosphere," he intoned, in what probably wasn't intended to be a Vincent Price imitation. "The emotional resonance! A man—a man who was my friend—lived out the last few weeks of his mortal life here. I need to pick up the vibes!"

"I understand," I said, which was a lie. I had no idea what he meant. Maybe I could enlist Rose Noire to translate. She knew a lot more about vibes than I did.

Then again, even I could see that O'Malley was making Terence's death all about him. And I'd picked up the odor of mead on his breath. Had he, perhaps, had a little too much of the stuff?

He was lifting his head and moving it about, eyes closed, nostrils flaring. It rather resembled the way dogs react when someone opens a food container in the next room and releases a faint but enticing scent into the atmosphere.

"If you're having trouble picking up any vibes, it could be because he didn't spend the last few weeks of his life here," I suggested. "Up until last night he was camping over there with everyone else. See where there's a gap in the line of tents? You might want to do your vibe sniffing over there."

If I hadn't been studying his peculiar behavior with an eye to describing it to Michael later, complete with snarky

comments, I'd have missed the expression of exasperation that flitted across his features, just for a second. Then
he recovered his expression of romantic melancholy.

"Alas! A 'name writ in water' indeed!"

Thanks to the many evenings I'd spent making polite
conversation with Michael's faculty colleagues, back before Caerphilly College's Drama Department seceded
from the English Department, I recognized the melancholy words that John Keats had wanted carved on his
tombstone. I'd heard at least half a dozen somewhat-
inebriated English professors quote them while whining
about how underappreciated they were by the department. I wasn't quite sure how applicable the words were
to Terence, but I decided to respond in kind. Nothing apt
from Keats sprang to mind, but I could lob back a little lu-
gubrious Percy Bysshe Shelley. "Ozymandias" would work.

"'Nothing beside remains,'" I recited. "'Round the de-
cay/Of that colossal Wreck, boundless and bare/The lone
and level sands stretch far away.'"

The odd sidelong look O'Malley gave me was rather
reminiscent of a horse preparing to shy. Not, I deduced, a
genuine fan of the English Romantic poets.

"It's hopeless." Was he casting aspersions on my ability
to recite poetry? "And I had such hopes. I wanted to get
a better handle on his character. It would give so much
more . . . depth to my performance."

"Ah," I said, in what I hoped sounded like a sympathetic
tone.

I probably needn't have bothered. He sighed heavily
and began shambling away with his head bowed and his
shoulders hunched. Not toward the gap in the line of
tents at the far left side of the camp, where Terence's tent
had rested for four weeks, but in a more direct line back
toward the gate.

"Curious," I said aloud.

"What's curious?"

I started slightly, and turned to see that Horace had come up behind me and was standing at the entrance to his tent.

"O'Malley." I nodded in the direction where we could still see the actor, making a beeline for the exit.

"I was wondering why you brought him here," Horace said.

"I didn't bring him here," I said. "I followed him. Found him standing here staring at the place where Terence's tent used to be, claiming he wanted to pick up the vibes so he could get a better handle on his character."

"Some of these actors are pretty peculiar that way." Horace wasn't saying anything I hadn't said, more than once. "And meaning no insult to Michael and the rest of the players in the Game, because what they do is not only entertaining, but pretty darned challenging, although the characters aren't exactly deep. How would learning more about where the real Terence Cox was camping help him play Sir Terence of Albion any better?"

"I have no idea," I said. "And here's an even better question: how did O'Malley know where Terence's tent used to be pitched? It was over there in the main part of the camp for the last four weeks—it was only the last twelve hours of his life that the tent was here."

Horace whistled and looked thoughtful.

"Maybe someone told him?" he suggested. "Gave him directions?"

"Damn good directions," I said. "I was watching. He made a beeline here. No hesitation. It's as if he knew the way already."

"Like if he'd been here before," Horace said. "Tell Chief Heedles."

I was already pulling out my phone. Horace grabbed something from his tent—a Blake Foundation tote bag full of something or other—and headed back toward the gate. I followed more slowly as I talked to the chief.

The chief found O'Malley's pilgrimage to the site of Terence's tent as interesting as I had.

"Did you confront him about what he was doing?" she asked.

"I asked if I could help him find whatever he was looking for," I said. "But I didn't push it. I thought maybe you'd rather I left any heavy confrontation to you. And maybe I'm being overly imaginative, but what if he was looking for Terence's tent because he wanted to search it for some reason?"

"To retrieve something incriminating, for example."

I nodded and then, realizing the chief couldn't see it, said aloud, "Yes. Exactly. Or plant something incriminating."

"Keep this to yourself," she said.

"One more thing," I said, in case she was about to hang up. "You have all of Terence's stuff locked up, right?"

"In that studio you cleared out for us."

"We're reasonably careful with the studio keys," I said. "Because we usually have a lot of valuable craft works and supplies in the studios—especially that one, since it's the jewelry-making studio. And I'm sure you remember that summer we had all the sabotage here at the center."

"Vividly."

"We're careful—but not paranoid, because we don't usually have anything in them anywhere near as important as critical evidence in a murder case. And unless you have some prime suspects I've never met, I bet most if not all of your suspects have been around the center long enough to figure out how to get the key to that studio if they really wanted it."

"You think we should move our evidence?"

"Or put a guard on it."

"Probably a good idea. By the way, are you still anywhere near the falcon place?"

"Not that far away—why?"

"Could you drop by to see me? I'm with your grand-father and Mr. Dorance."

"On my way."

What now? As I passed by the forge, I waved at Faulk and pointed in the direction of the entrance to the grove. He nodded and went back to supervising as the boys demonstrated to the tourists how the bellows worked.

In the grove I found Greg, Grandfather, and the chief gathered by the falcon enclosure, staring at what I now knew was a large white oak. Perhaps I should remedy my woeful incompetence at tree identification by studying it and then seeing if I could identify other nearby white oaks.

Maybe later. After I figured out what the chief needed.

"Thought you said the Mad Monk was behind that tree." Greg pointed to the oak.

"He was."

"He isn't now," the chief said. "Lenny couldn't find him. I went and looked behind it myself. Behind several other oaks, too."

"And he didn't leave the grove," Grandfather said. "I was keeping my eye out for him."

I glanced around. The Mad Monk wasn't visible anywhere else in the grove.

"Well, he can't have vanished into thin air," I said.

I left them and strode over to where I'd seen the Monk. They were right—he wasn't behind the tree. I glanced back. They were watching me. Greg and Grandfather had "I told you so" written all over their faces. The chief's face was neutral, but then it usually was.

I looked around to see if the Monk had moved on to another tree, or perhaps taken refuge behind some bit of shrubbery.

I took a step or two deeper into the woods—but only a step, because I didn't want to get tangled up in the mesh deer fencing.

I glanced over at the mesh, just to be sure I wasn't about to run into it and spotted something: a break in the net. I drew closer. Not a break—a cut.

I gestured to the chief. She strolled over. Grandfather tagged along. Greg didn't leave the falcons, but he was paying more attention to us than to the birds.

"He went thataway," I said, pointing to the slit in the fence.

The chief frowned and stepped closer to examine it. From a few feet away you couldn't easily see the mesh, much less the cut.

"I'd forgotten you had the place fenced in," she said. "The stuff's invisible from a foot away. Looks like a relatively new cut."

"It can't be more than a few days old," I said. "We inspect the fence about once a week to make sure it's more or less intact."

"Only more or less?" The chief smiled slightly. "Isn't that a rather cavalier attitude toward security?"

"We don't expect the fence to stop a determined trespasser," I said. "We just want it to slow down the clueless tourists who don't realize that beyond the fence in that direction there's thousands of acres of park and timberland and not much else. Most of the time the only problem we find is places where trees have fallen on the fence and dragged it down. Never seen anything like this before."

The three of us stared at the hole in the fence in silence for a few moments.

"So," the chief said finally. "Is it your theory that this Mad Monk of yours killed Mr. Cox? And fled when he noticed you were watching him? I'm open to considering the idea, but what's his motive?"

She was looking at me, but Grandfather spoke up before I could.

"He killed someone he'd seen trying to abuse the falcons, of course," Grandfather said.

"And after doing so," the chief went on, "Instead of making good his escape, he hung around—"

"In the hope of taking out others he considered to be animal abusers." Grandfather nodded as if he'd been expecting something of this sort.

"But upon seeing that Meg had spotted him, he was so unnerved that he sliced a hole in the mesh fence so he could make his escape the long way round, by hiking through the woods."

"Maybe he didn't cut the hole to make his escape," I pointed out. "Maybe he cut it this morning to sneak in after the front gate turned him away."

"And was leaving by the same route he used to enter," the chief said. "Could be."

"Doesn't that logging road run somewhere by here?" I asked.

The chief nodded and took out her phone. Grandfather and I listened while she gave orders to her officers, sending one to search up and down the logging road for either a parked car or a hiker fitting the Monk's description, another to stake out the place where the logging road met the main road, and a third—evidently the lone officer still patrolling the rest of the town—to establish a roadblock at an intersection I recognized as the first place a fugitive leaving Biscuit Mountain could possibly take a turn instead of heading straight on to Riverton.

"That was quick work." Grandfather nodded with approval. "Catching the killer in less than twenty-four hours."

"We haven't caught him yet," the chief said. "And we don't know yet that he's the killer."

"Then why would he flee?" Grandfather asked. "Guilt! That's why."

"But maybe he wasn't guilty of killing Terence," I said. "Maybe all he did was sneak in without paying. We could ask the ticket sellers—I bet they'd remember him. And when he saw us staring at him, it unnerved him and he fled."

"If that's all he did, the chief won't have any reason to hold him," Grandfather argued.

"Trespassing," the chief said, nodding to the hole in the fence. "Vandalism. And in a murder investigation I have considerable latitude to detain persons of interest who flee when I try to question them. Even if he's not the killer, he could be a material witness."

Just then Horace appeared. He carried his forensic kit and the tote bag he'd fetched from his tent.

"Ready whenever," he said.

"First let's see if you can tell me anything about this." She gestured to the slit in the netting.

First? If the netting wasn't what Horace had come over to do forensics on, what was it?

The chief noticed me watching.

"Thank you," she said.

I could take a hint.

"Could you let me know if you find the Mad Monk?" I asked. "I'm probably not the only one who's a little wound up about having him lurking around."

"Will do."

As I strolled toward the opening in the trees that marked the entrance to the grove, I began noticing crowd sounds—cheering and laughter and occasionally the sort of "ooooh!" that usually accompanied those moments when a tightrope walker pretends to lose her balance.

And when I drew near the forge, I found the crowd was gathered around it. What the—

Chapter 35

As I drew closer to the forge I heard someone bellowing loud enough to be heard over the crowd.

"'Before my body I throw my warlike shield!'"

O'Malley's voice. And not his everyday speaking voice, either—this was the sort of exaggeratedly dramatic voice that I'd expect to hear when Michael's first-year acting students did their auditions. Could the man get any more annoying?

"'Lay on, Macduff!'" O'Malley declaimed. "'And damned be him that first cries, "Hold, enough!"'"

Macbeth, I noted. And then, even though I hadn't said it aloud, I corrected myself, in deference to theater superstition: The Scottish Play.

Still, I was curious, so I pushed my way through the growing crowd until I could see what O'Malley was up to. He was standing in front of the fence surrounding the forge with a huge leather tankard in his left hand and an unsheathed longsword in his right. He let the point of the sword droop toward the ground as he lifted the mug to take two deep gulps. I could see his Adam's apple bobbing beneath the stubble. He swayed slightly as he lowered the mug.

The tourists were gathered around in a rough semicircle. A reasonably large semicircle, but not large enough for my taste. A few stumbling steps was all it would take for O'Malley to be at their throats. How clueless could they be?

Of course, I couldn't think of any reason he'd have to skewer the tourists. But this was O'Malley. Quite possibly an inebriated O'Malley. Reason didn't enter into it.

He set the tankard down and scanned the audience around him with a surly expression.

"Get on with it!" someone called.

"Yeah, let's see some action!" another tourist shouted.

As if he needed encouragement.

"I order you to hold your tongues!" O'Malley began to turn slowly in a circle, pointing his sword toward the tourists and waving it slightly. "I dare the floor collectively to utter another sound! I challenge you, one and all! I will take down your names."

People backed away a little. Not nearly enough.

I glanced over at the forge. Faulk was standing in front of the door to the back room. Behind him I could see that the door was partly open, and Josh and Jamie were peering out. Josh, Jamie, and Spike.

"'Step forward, budding heroes! Let all who wish to die hold up their hands! Not a name? Not a hand? Very good. Then I proceed.'"

Not Shakespeare, I thought absently. But familiar sounding. *Cyrano de Bergerac,* perhaps? I shoved the question aside to ask Michael later and began pushing my way through the crowd again, aiming for the side of the forge. If I was careful, maybe I could slip inside the fenced enclosure. I didn't want to leave Josh and Jamie—or Faulk—to deal with O'Malley by themselves.

"'If we are mark'd to die, we are enow,'" O'Malley was declaiming. "'To do our country loss; and if to live, the fewer men, the greater share of honour.'"

Back to Shakespeare. Probably *Henry V.* If the wretched man wanted to do a Shakespearean monologue, why didn't he just ask us for a slot on one of the stages? And where the devil had he gotten his hands on a sword?

I had reached the far side of the forge. I hopped the fence and went over to join Faulk—staying toward the back of the enclosure.

"'We would not die in that man's company,'" O'Malley

shouted, "'that fears his fellowship to die with us.'" He was waving the sword more wildly than ever, and I was relieved to see that the crowd was now giving him plenty of room. But they hadn't yet realized that this wasn't a scheduled part of the entertainment. Some of them were laughing—maybe a little nervously—some were looking uncomfortable and uncertain what to think, and a few were looking at their watches with an expression that clearly said "if this doesn't get a lot more interesting pretty soon, I'm moving on."

"'Once more unto the breach, my friends!'" O'Malley roared.

"What the hell happened?" I asked Faulk in a low voice.

"We heard Spike going crazy during the demo, but we figured it was just another squirrel teasing him." He was breathing heavily—not a good sign. "I sent Jamie back to check on him, and he found O'Malley rummaging through the back room, with Spike firmly attached to his ankle. Jamie pried Spike loose and I frog-marched O'Malley out. He didn't put up much resistance, but once I came back into our enclosure, he pulled out his sword and started doing that."

"Have you called for help?"

"Not sure the Beggar's up to dealing with him," Faulk said. "And Tad would overreact."

"I didn't mean the palace guard." I pulled out my phone and called the chief.

"Is something wrong?" she asked. "I can hear the crowds—"

"We have a violent drunk right outside the forge who's waving a sword and shouting insults," I said. "Normally I'd sic Horace and Lenny on him but—"

"Officers on the way," she said.

I hung up and tucked my phone back in my pocket.

Emboldened by my arrival, Josh came out of the back room.

"Don't get any closer to the fence," I said. "In fact, go out the back way and fetch your grandfather. Faulk might need him."

"Okay." He glanced over at where O'Malley was taking another long pull at his mug.

"And tell Jamie to be ready to let the police and your grandfather in the back door when they get here. And don't let Spike bite any of them."

"Roger." He disappeared into the back room again.

"'Ring the alarum-bell!'" O'Malley bellowed. "'Blow, wind! Come, wrack! At least we'll die with harness on our back.'"

As he said the last lines, he pointed his sword in front of him and began lumbering toward the forge.

"Protect Jamie," I said, shoving Faulk through the door to the back room.

"The fence will slow him down," Faulk said, but he didn't fight me.

"Yeah, right." I slammed the door and leaped aside. O'Malley vaulted the fence with surprising agility and was striding forward, pointing his sword at the back room door. Then he paused and looked at me.

"Vile harlot!" he exclaimed.

I heard nervous titters from the crowd, and a low muttering of comments.

"That's going a little far," someone said.

O'Malley seemed torn between continuing on to the door and turning on me. Then he narrowed his eyes and took a step in my direction.

Maybe fleeing would be the smartest thing to do. But if I fled, he'd probably turn his attention back to the back room. Start trying to batter down the door. And Jamie was there. And Faulk.

I grabbed the nearest weapon—a huge crusader's sword the boys were fond of letting the tourists try to lift—and held it in front of me in what I hoped was a good defensive stance.

"Get out of here," I told him. "Now."

O'Malley smiled as if in triumph, and I was suddenly quite sure that he was only pretending to be drunk. He took a few steps toward me, raised the sword, and then lurched forward as he brought it down in a fierce, downward cut.

I slashed upward. Our two swords met with a loud clang. His shattered into several pieces, and he staggered and fell to one knee. I staggered a bit myself, but managed to stay on my feet and turn, ready to defend myself again.

"Freeze, varlet!" A bardiche slashed down so that the shaft pinned O'Malley's right arm to the ground, with enough force that the unsharpened blade cut several inches into the packed dirt.

I glanced up to see Tad at the other end of the bardiche, glaring at O'Malley with frightening intensity.

The tourists burst into applause.

Chapter 36

While the tourists continued to clap and cheer, two uniformed Riverton police officers burst out of the crowd and vaulted the fence.

"Break it up here," one said.

I nodded, and dropped the sword. The officer, correctly deducing that I was not the problem, went over to where Tad was still guarding O'Malley. I heard them exchange a few words in a low tone. Then the officer took her handcuffs off her belt and began putting them on O'Malley.

"Show's over." The chief pushed through the crowd to stand just outside the fence. "Move along now. Nothing more to see."

"You heard the chief," the second officer said.

The tourists grumbled. Some of them left. The rest just shuffled back a little at a time until the second policeman seemed satisfied, and continued to watch us.

Josh stuck his head out of the door to the back room.

"Grandpa's here if anyone needs him." He scanned us and, seeing no apparent bloodshed, pulled the door shut again.

"What happened?" the chief asked me.

"She completely overreacted," O'Malley whined. "I was—"

"Quiet!" The chief turned to glare at him. "You'll have your turn."

O'Malley, wisely, fell silent. The chief turned back to me.

"O'Malley was drunk—or pretending to be." I picked up the leather tankard he'd dropped and sniffed it. No alcohol smell—only the faint lemon scent of the iced tea we used to fake alcohol. I handed it to the chief, who sniffed it in her turn and nodded.

"He drew his sword and was waving it around, endangering the tourists. And then he charged into the forge and I thought he was going to go after the boys. Or me. So I disarmed him."

The chief took a few steps over and picked up the three main pieces of O'Malley's broken sword.

"Not your work, I gather."

I shook my head.

"From the Bonny Blade?"

"Or someplace like it," I said. "If it's from the Bonny Blade, they shouldn't have let him walk off with it. He's not cleared to draw a weapon, or even carry one unsecured."

The chief turned to O'Malley.

"Where did you get this?" She held up the sword fragments.

"From the other sword shop," he said. "I explained to them that I needed one for my costume, and they let me borrow this one. They're going to be seriously pissed that she broke it. And—"

"Mr. O'Malley." Cordelia had appeared. She hadn't raised her voice, but O'Malley shut up in a hurry.

I probably wasn't the only one who had to suppress the instinct to make my deepest curtsey.

Cordelia turned to Chief Heedles.

"This man is no longer welcome at the Faire," she said. "I know you're busy with the murder investigation, but could you spare an officer for long enough to supervise him as he returns that costume, and then escort him off my property?"

"Absolutely," the chief said.

"You can't do that!" O'Malley protested.

"Yes, I can." Cordelia fixed her stare on O'Malley, and he actually cringed. "My Faire. My rules. And I have a zero tolerance policy for people who put my guests and my family in danger."

"She started it." O'Malley indicated me—with his chin, since he was now securely handcuffed.

"Quit while you're ahead," the chief advised. "Lenny!"

"Yes, Chief." The tall young officer, now back in his uniform, stepped forward.

"You heard Ms. Cordelia."

Lenny helped O'Malley to his feet and led him off. O'Malley was visibly unhappy, but at least he had the good sense to shut up until he was out of earshot.

Make that almost out of earshot.

"It's not fair!" we could hear him whining in the distance.

"I will be giving the proprietors of the Bonny Blade a refresher course on the Faire's weapons policy." Cordelia's brittle tone suggested that the discussion would not be a pleasant one for the offenders. I hoped I could manage to be within earshot. "And if they really did let Mr. O'Malley walk off with one of their swords—well, getting reimbursed for it will be their problem."

The chief turned to me.

"Are you interested in charging Mr. O'Malley with assault?" she asked.

"Do I have to decide now?" I asked. "If he leaves quietly and doesn't try to come back, I'd rather just let it drop. Avoid any publicity."

"But he might behave better if he knows there's something bigger than trespassing hanging over his head if he ignores Ms. Cordelia's instructions." She nodded, and from her expression I deduced that she liked my decision. "I'll make that clear to him before he goes. I need to talk to him anyway. Warn him not to leave town without my permission."

Had O'Malley just risen much higher on the chief's suspect list? Not unreasonable. So far he was the only person we knew of who'd tried to attack someone with a cheap, flimsy reproduction blade weapon.

"Looks as if I'll be rather busy for the rest of the afternoon." The chief paused, frowning slightly. "I don't suppose you could clue me in on how it turns out," she said at last.

"How what turns out?" Was she being sarcastic—hinting that I was withholding some vital clue?

"The Game. Who wins. Who inherits the kingdom, and who gets to marry the rich heiress, and all that. Or do we not find out until the end of the summer?"

"Not even then." I had to chuckle at the thought. "At least we hadn't planned to announce a winner. Near the end of every day, usually during the final joust and closing ceremonies, we try to set up a confrontation between Michael and George—one that ends in a sword fight. And as the fight goes back and forth, Cordelia checks out the audience response—how many people are rooting for Michael and how many for George, and she gives a signal, and whoever the audience is rooting for wins."

"What if she can't tell who's ahead?"

"Then I guess she'd flip a coin or something—so far it's never been a problem." I frowned, because this was something I'd been worrying about. "In fact, so far Michael's always won—ten out of ten times."

"Isn't that a little . . . difficult for Mr. Sims?"

"You'd think so," I said. "He seems to take it in stride, although I've been meaning to suggest to Michael that we mix it up a little."

"Let Mr. Sims win every so often?"

"Yeah." I nodded. "Two problems with that—one is that Terence has—well, had—an amazing talent for making George look bad."

"Which won't be a problem in the future," the chief pointed out.

"Yeah. But the other problem is that poor George

is a past master of making himself look bad. Like when they're sparring verbally he'll make snarky comments to Michael, and the audience will laugh, but they don't really like him for it. I suspect he's overly conscious that Michael's the boss and thinks that means letting him win. He never seems to realize that Michael's not the kind of actor who insists on keeping all the good lines and big scenes to himself."

"Yes." She nodded thoughtfully. "But then, he's also the director, isn't he? Which I assume means having the whole production succeed is at least as important as shining in his own role."

"Exactly." A strange thought struck me. "You know, next to Michael, I think Terence was the one who really got it. That the play's the thing, as Hamlet would say. Terence never cared whether the crowd was cheering him or booing him, as long as he was getting a reaction."

"That might be the nicest thing anyone's said about Mr. Cox all day. I assumed it was a case of 'since I cannot prove a lover, I am determined to prove a villain.'"

"*Richard the Third*," I said automatically—Name That Quote was a perennial family game. "Yes, he certainly was good at laying plots and 'inductions dangerous.'"

"The next time you replace Mr. Cox—at least I assume you'll need a replacement, and Mr. O'Malley's just made himself persona non grata—maybe you should choose someone who can give Michael a run for his money in winning over the audience. I'm sure Mr. Sims is a talented actor, but he's a character actor, not a leading man."

"Probably a good idea," I said. "Michael would be the first to admit that when he did the casting, he was thinking more about which of his actor friends could really use the work than anything else. Of course, I don't think it would be a good idea for whoever we recruit to replace Terence to simply swap roles with George. He'd make a

pretty sniveling villain. Maybe we could make him Dianne's father and have Nigel play the villain. Anyway, to
answer your original question—we didn't plan for anyone to completely win the game. At the end of each day
someone—usually Michael—has got the upper hand, but
the next day it starts all over again. But maybe we should
plan a grand finale for the last day—have Cordelia actually name her successor. It wouldn't prevent us from doing
much the same thing next year if she decides the Faire's
worth continuing."

"And if you did the right kind of publicity, that final day
would be a big draw," the chief said. "In fact—"

"Chief?" We all turned to see Horace standing just outside the smithy's fence. He was holding a brown paper
bag—probably an evidence bag. The chief walked over
to the fence and conferred with him. Her demeanor was
suddenly all business again.

As if seeing her move away were their cue, Josh and Jamie popped out of the back room.

"Mom! That was awesome!" Jamie exclaimed.

"Not bad, Mom," Josh allowed.

"How's Faulk?" I asked.

"He looks bad," Jamie said.

"Grandpa said it's probably just anxiety," Josh added.

"But he's going to keep an eye on him," Jamie said.

I went to the door of the back room. Faulk, Dad, and
Tad were all in there, so I was reduced to standing in the
doorway peering in.

"Not really up to a long car ride right now," Faulk was
saying. "Let me just go to bed and see how I feel in the
morning."

Tad was shaking his head.

"Not a bad idea," Dad said.

"I don't want him sleeping in a tent tonight," Tad said.
"It's bad enough in good weather, but it's going to rain tonight and turn colder."

"My sleeping bag's a subzero model," Faulk said. "I'll be fine."

"Maybe we can find him a bed up at the house," Dad said.

"He can have our room," I said. "I'm sure Michael won't mind."

"That will be great," Dad said. "And I'll set up a cot nearby so I'll be handy if he needs me."

I was taking out my phone to call Michael when he appeared right behind me.

"Are you all right?" He grabbed me in a bear hug.

"I'm fine," I said, "At least I will be when I can breathe again. By the way, the Game will have to get along without O'Malley. Cordelia kicked him out. And Faulk needs to sleep indoors in a bed, so we're trading places for tonight. I'll move our stuff down to their tent."

"O'Malley was less a help than a hindrance anyway," Michael said. "And while I'm sure Faulk and Tad have a lovely tent, I'd rather be indoors. Let's take our bedrolls into one of the craft studios. After all, it still counts as camping if we're in sleeping bags, right?"

"I'd call it camping lite," I said. "But good idea. Let's make it the jewelry studio—it's should be empty now, and quiet."

"And I should run," he said. "Closing ceremonies in a few minutes."

"I'll put in a token appearance, then go up to move our stuff."

"Before you both go"—the chief had finished her conversation with Horace, apparently—"I have a couple of questions. Meg, you said that Mr. O'Malley wasn't cleared to draw a weapon. What did you mean by that?"

"Only a small number of Game participants are allowed to draw their swords," I said. "And then only to perform stage combat routines that have been previously rehearsed. Exhaustively rehearsed. Of course, I don't know if anyone explained that to O'Malley."

"I did," Michael said. "At the beginning of the day. And I gave him a refresher course when I saw him running around with that cheap sword, and put the peace-bonding on it myself. So if he tries to claim he had no idea he was breaking the rules, he's lying. He'd been warned twice, and he had to have cut off the peace bond to draw that thing."

"Thank you." The chief nodded and strode over to where Horace was waiting for her. The two began talking again in low tones. The chief didn't look happy.

"Skip the closing ceremonies," Michael said to me. "You've had a long day."

"As have you," I said.

"And I plan to take a nap as soon as the closing ceremonies are over," he said. "If you skip the ceremonies and take our stuff down to the jewelry studio, we can both nap as soon as closing's over—without worrying about inconveniencing Faulk."

"You're on," I said.

He gave me a quick kiss and ran off toward the jousting field, with the boys on his heels. I watched, a little anxiously, as the chief and Horace trailed after them. Were they also heading for the jousting field? Well, why not? If the chief wanted to talk to anyone, Horace would know that almost everyone would show up there at this time of day.

But not me. I turned my steps toward the main house. Why did I suddenly feel so tired, now that I knew rest was in sight?

All around me the Faire was winding down. Most of the tourists were either at the jousting field or headed that way, and any wandering food vendors who hadn't already emptied their trays or carts were heading in the same direction. The ring toss, the crossbow shoot, and the other game booths were nearly empty, their costumed staff leaning with

weary contentedness on the counters and scarcely bothering to harangue the passing tourists. The craft shops were
discreetly beginning to pack up their wares—they might
make a few more sales from tourists who stayed to the very
end and were still in the mood for shopping on their way
out of the Faire, but all of vendors wanted to be packed up
as soon as possible after closing, to be ready for the traditional Saturday night all-hands feast.

Up at the main house, delicious smells wafted from the
kitchen. If it looked as if the rain would hold off for a few
more hours, we'd have the feast around the fire pit on the
front lawn, as usual. I could smell chickens roasting, pork
being barbecued, and beans baking. Fresh loaves of bread
and several kinds of pie would be cooling on racks in the
kitchen, and the kitchen helpers would be shucking corn
for roasting and chopping fresh vegetables for enormous
vats of tossed salad.

And there would be singing and dancing, telling horror
stories about things the tourists had done, and eventually
real ghost stories. Normally I loved the Saturday night party.

Right now I wasn't in the mood. And I was afraid it
would take more than a nap to fix that.

When I entered the Great Room I spotted O'Malley sitting on the sofa nearest the front door, with Lenny hovering nearby to keep an eye on him. O'Malley was dressed
in his own clothes again, except for the shoes. He had the
right shoe on and was taking so long to tie his laces that I
wondered if he needed remedial work on the technique.
Or maybe he was having understandable second thoughts
about wearing the thing. Its mate lay on its side on the rug
in front of him, looking rather like a traditional oxford
shoe's awkwardly chunkier cousin, and made out of what I
hoped was not real alligator hide. The sort of shoe that had
to be fashionable, because no one would buy it for its looks.

"Reminds me of how my kid brother used to dawdle
when he had to get ready for school," Lenny said to me in

a low tone. "But don't worry—we should have him out of here in a few minutes. And maybe it's a good thing most of the tourists will be gone by the time I kick him out."

"Thanks," I said.

"It's going to take two of us, of course," Lenny said, favoring O'Malley with a look of annoyance. "He's too drunk to drive. Horace is going to run his car down, and I'm taking O'Malley in my cruiser and bringing Horace back."

"Strange," I said. "I could have sworn the mug he dropped at the forge was only tea."

"Maybe the servers realized he was drunk and cut him off."

Or maybe he was pretending to be too drunk to drive to give himself an excuse for hanging around. If that was his plan, it wasn't going to work.

"You're sure he's not faking it?" I asked aloud.

"He blew a point one six on the Breathalyzer," Lenny said. "So no, he's well and truly soused."

"Meg, dear." I turned to see Mother making her grand exit, seated in the wheelchair with a fringed paisley shawl draped over her lap. One of the costume crew was pushing the chair, and several others trailed along behind carrying various bags and parcels.

Mother gestured imperiously, and the cavalcade stopped in front of me

"Something for the lost-and-found." She handed me a cell phone and reached up toward me. I bent down so she could give me a kiss on the cheek. "Sleep well, dear."

The procession sailed out the front door, and several men who happened to be lounging in the Great Room leaped up and raced out to help Mother into whatever car was taking her down to Cordelia's house.

Chapter 37

It wasn't until after we'd all waved good-bye that I glanced down at the phone in my hand and wondered if Mother had some particular reason for handing it to me.

It was an iPhone, not too different from the one in my pocket. I pressed the button that would bring it to life—always a chance that the owner would have a startup screen that gave me a clue to their identity. But it was completely out of power. I'd drop it off in the lost-and-found when I went down there.

Meanwhile I put it into my pocket and trudged up to the room Michael and I had been sharing. It didn't take long to pack what we'd need for the night—I grabbed an empty carry-on bag and swept my toiletries and his into it. A change of clothes for tonight, another for tomorrow, nightclothes, and the books we'd been reading. If Faulk and Tad ended up staying longer than the one night, we could relocate the rest tomorrow. Our sleeping bags and air mattresses were in the closet—we'd used them before, when we'd given up our room to elderly relatives staying for a night or two. I managed to take everything we'd need for the night down in one trip.

I dropped the gear in the jewelry studio and then went into Cordelia's office to deposit the cell phone in the lost-and-found cabinet. Then it occurred to me that Cordelia had an iPhone, too, and there was a charger cable already plugged in with the business end sitting on her desk. I attached the unknown phone. Should I wait until it got enough of a charge to come to life? Not in the mood. I scribbled a note to Cordelia, in case she came back while it was still there—*Someone misplaced this. Easier to find the owner if it's got power*—and tucked it under the phone.

I was heading back to the studio to set up the sleeping bags when my own phone rang. Michael.

"You want the good news or the bad news?" he said when I'd answered.

"Your call," I said.

"Okay—good news: the police found that Mad Monk guy. Cordelia confirmed that she had banned him, and the front gate staff say they didn't let him in in spite his pitching a major fit. So apparently he snuck in by cutting open the fence. He's probably only guilty of trespassing and being a first-class jerk, but just in case, he's on his way down to Riverton for questioning."

"Awesome."

"Bad news: so is Nigel. On his way down to Riverton for questioning, I mean."

"Why?"

"They found something suspicious when they searched his tent."

"Suspicious as in connected with Terence's murder?"

"A note from Terence, asking Nigel to meet him in the woods at midnight."

"Yikes. But wait—they found it in his tent? Pretty easy to plant something in there."

"I think it was in his footlocker," Michael said. "At least I saw one of the Riverton police officers carrying the foot-locker out of Camp Anachronism—not sure anyone else has one like it."

"That battered old drab green army surplus thing?"

"Yeah. He keeps a padlock on it, so it wouldn't be so easy to plant something there."

"Sounds fishy to me," I said. "Why would Terence want Nigel to meet him in the woods? What could he possibly have to say that he couldn't say at some less inconvenient time?"

"Agreed," Michael said. "Besides, even if Terence wanted a meeting, why would Nigel go? Although probably not an idea to push that thought too much. A prosecutor might say he jumped at the chance to do Terence in. Nigel's been pretty vocal about how much he hated Terence. Not quite saying 'good riddance to bad rubbish' but damned close."

"Damn," I said. "Is that ex-student of yours still coming? The Game's getting a little short on players."

"He should be there sometime this evening," Michael said. "I told him if he gets there late and no one's up to help him settle in, he should just crash on one of the sofas in the Great Room."

"So will he be replacing Terence or Nigel?"

"Good question. Depends on whether or not Nigel's in jail."

"Maybe we need to switch it up even more," I suggested. "Let George replace Terence or Nigel, and have the new guy be your rival—if he's right for it."

"Someone who can give me a run for the money with the audience, you mean," Michael said. "Yeah, the new guy will be the right type for that—too pretty to be the villain, and not much older than Dianne, so I already let George know I might be asking him to change roles. Probably as troublemaker. Not sure who can fill in if Nigel's in jail."

"Stan the beggar," I suggested. "He could spend most of the time sitting in state at one of the outdoor tables at the Dragon's Claw, and everyone could bring the Game to him. We could make it work. But before we switch George out of being your rival—could we maybe let him win the sword fight? Just once?"

Michael's initial reaction was a heavy sigh.

"Yeah," he said. "I'm starting to feel guilty about always coming off the winner. And I thought we could wangle it today, but somehow it never came off. Maybe Nigel did too good a job of filling in Terence's shoes. And George was at his whiniest today—probably the stress from the murder investigation. It has everyone on edge. But yeah—let's figure out a way to give him a win."

"We can worry about it tomorrow."

"Yes. Right now, I'm going to follow Nigel down to the police station. See about getting him a lawyer and arranging bail."

"You've still got all the family lawyers in your phone?"

"Of course," he said.

Mother's vast extended family had a disproportionately high number of lawyers. Including a reasonable number of capable criminal defense attorneys whose contact information Michael and I had long ago learned to keep handy, since our circle of friends contained rather a lot of people with a penchant for getting themselves in trouble.

"Keep me posted," I said.

"Will do."

I hung up and looked around. The studio looked uninviting—a great bare space with only a small heap of our belongings in the middle of it. Maybe I'd feel differently if the rain had started already.

Then again, maybe it wasn't the studio that was bringing me down. Nigel, whom I'd always considered one of the good guys, was under suspicion for murder—or was he under arrest by now? Or would the Mad Monk turn out to be the killer? And what about O'Malley? At least the chief has told him not to leave town—but was she trying to find out why he'd been looking for Terence's tent? Maybe it had something to do with the murder. Or maybe O'Malley had some other nefarious scheme in mind.

I needed distraction. And I needed dinner.

I left the studio, locking it behind me, and headed for the stairs. And was slightly spooked when I heard footsteps somewhere nearby. The only things down here were

Cordelia's office, the storage room, the jewelry studio, and the laundry, none of them usually occupied at this time of day. Why—

"Oh! I didn't know anyone else was here!" A young woman had stepped out of the laundry, startling me as much as I'd startled her.

"Don't tell me you're still on duty?" I asked. "The feast is starting."

"And I intend to head up there in a few minutes," she said. "But anything I can do now is something none of us have to face in the morning. And your mother's always so delighted when the place is in perfect shape when she comes in. I thought I'd load all the machines before I go."

In the interest of making Mother happy, I pitched in to help. We spent the next quarter of an hour grabbing armloads of costumes and setting the dozen big commercial washers going.

"I hear you kicked out that O'Malley creep," she said, as we were pondering the right amount of stain remover stuff to add to a load of unusually muddy tights. "Good riddance."

"I agree," I said. "But how did you manage to run into him? Aren't you usually backstage?"

"Mostly," she said. "But he was always snooping around the costume shop."

"Why?" I asked. "I mean—was he harassing people or doing a Peeping Tom number or anything gross like that?"

"Goodness, no," she exclaimed. "We'd have straightened him out right away if he'd tried that, and sicced your mother on him if he didn't listen to us. No, it was more like he was obsessed with the costumes."

"The costumes?" I echoed.

"Yeah. The fancy ones, not the rank-and-file peasant ones. He was always touching them and asking who they belonged to, and exclaiming over the workmanship. And then when he thought we weren't looking he'd rummage through the pockets."

"Did he take anything?"

"Not that anyone saw," she said. "But then, who leaves anything in the pocket of a costume after they take if off for the day? Apart from the occasional used tissue."

"Ick." I made a mental note to always check the pockets of my costume before turning it in.

"So the only people who aren't glad he's gone are a few of us who were looking forward to figuring out if he was a perv or a klepto," she said. "Does he get his jollies caressing crushed velvet? Or was he looking for stuff to steal? There was a rumor that someone saw him rummaging in the pockets of the civvies—you know, the modern clothes a lot of people leave on the rack when they get into costume. But once we heard he'd been booted, we were trying to figure out who saw that, and all everyone admits to seeing is him molesting the costumes, so maybe that was just one of those rumors that gets started about someone nobody likes."

"Still, interesting," I said. "Mind if I tell the chief about that?"

"No problem," she said.

"Good. In fact, let's give her a head's up now." I pulled out my phone, opened up a text to the chief, and typed "one of our costume crew has some information about O'Malley." Then I handed it to the woman. "Text her your name and cell phone number," I said. "I doubt if she'll get back to you before tomorrow, but this way neither of us will have to remember to tell her then."

"Can do." She typed with enviable speed, and then handed me back my phone. "And now I'm off to dinner."

"If I have any energy, I'll see you there," I said. "And we've done a good job here."

We gave each other a high five, and then she trotted off toward the stairs. I followed more slowly.

What if O'Malley had been searching for the phone Mother had given me? Cell phones were one of the few things people actually carried around in the pockets of their costumes. But if he'd lost his cell phone, the logical thing to do was to report it missing. Borrow someone else's phone to call it—or better yet, use the Find My iPhone app, if he'd bothered to set it up. Curious. If it was anyone else, I'd have gone back upstairs to ask if he'd lost his phone. But O'Malley? He could go through channels.

Upstairs in the Great Room, I found Cordelia. She was in modern dress again, and carrying her purse and a small tote.

"Good," she said. "I was about to call you. This has been a difficult day, so I'm going to get away for a bit."

"Get away where?" I asked.

"I'm going down to my house in town."

Probably a good idea—she had also been up before dawn. But—

"You're not going by yourself, are you?" I asked aloud. "The chief may have two potential murder suspects in custody, but there could be other thugs roaming the countryside."

"Your mother's there," she said. "And Jacks and Dianne are coming with me. Some wimps canceled, so I've got a room to offer them."

"Canceled why?" I asked, suddenly anxious. "Because of the murder?"

"No," she said. "That's still being billed as a body found in the woods near the Biscuit Mountain State Park. And consequently getting almost no coverage. No, these wimps canceled because the weather forecast calls for rain tonight, and possibly a little more tomorrow. Which is why I wanted to see you before I left—can you go around and check the doors and windows before bedtime?"

"Of course."

"And your Dad's going to bunk in my room," she said.

"He wants to be nearby in case Faulk needs him. The boys can keep an eye on your grandfather. I think I see Jacks's car now." She gave me a peck on the cheek and strode out, looking remarkably energetic. I trailed out onto the front porch in her wake and waved good-bye as the car set out.

And as I was about to go back inside, I spotted Dad struggling to carry his medical bag, his duffel bag, a backpack, and a couple of tote bags filled with who knows what.

"Let me carry some of that," I said. He didn't protest—in fact, he let me take the lion's share of his load, and we headed upstairs for Cordelia's room.

"I feel bad about deserting the investigation," he said. "But I think Tad will feel much better if I'm around to help with Faulk. So will I, in fact."

"Is there really that much to worry about?" I asked. "I mean, I see you're bringing your portable defibrillator." I'd peeked into one of the totes I was carrying and recognized the defibrillator's bright-yellow case.

"I doubt if we'll need it," he said. "But having it around seems to raise a cardiac patient's morale. And they don't really need me that much for this stage of the murder investigation—Riverton's lucky to have such a highly qualified M.E."

Clearly Dad, though determined to do his duty, was a little wistful at missing out on what could be the grand finale of the investigation.

Maybe I should try to distract him.

Chapter 38

"By the way, Dad," I said. "I have a question for you."

"A medical question?"

"Well, a psychological question. And one that could relate to the investigation."

As we unpacked his stuff and found places to stow all of it in Cordelia's bedroom—which, though not large, was uncluttered enough to feel spacious—I told him about Dianne sleeping in the maid's closet Friday night.

"This is fascinating," Dad said. "From what you describe, it sounds as if Dianne could have a genuine phobia. It would be interesting to find out which one."

"Not a big mystery," I said. "She's afraid of sleeping in the woods."

"Which would mean that she probably has nyctohylophobia." Dad nodded. "Fear of being in forests or dark wooded areas at night. But if she's also afraid of them in the daytime, then it would be just plain hylophobia. Probably not dendrophobia, which is fear of trees. I've always considered that a lot less rational, as fears go."

"And phobias have to be rational?"

"Well, there's usually a reason for them if you dig back enough," Dad said. "But no, phobias aren't rational."

"She also seems pretty nervous about the possibility that bears will invade the camp. Is there a name for that?"

"Arkoudaphobia," Dad said readily. "Of course, it's only a phobia if it amounts to an irrational fear of them. Nothing wrong with a healthy respect for a wild animal as powerful as a bear. Respect and maybe even a little perfectly reasonable fear. Being fearless around bears can get you killed."

"So fear of spiders in general might be a phobia—"

"Arachnophobia," Dad said.

"But being afraid of the brown recluse that just landed on your arm is merely a rational response to the situation."

"Precisely."

"So how do we find out if Dianne really does have nycto-whatsit-phobia or if she's only pretending to have it to account for being absent from her tent at around the time Terence was being stabbed?"

"That's a tough question." Dad frowned, but it was the slight frown of concentration you usually saw on his face when you'd just given him a difficult but interesting project. "Let me work on that. Are you coming down to the feast?"

"I'm beat," I said. "If there's anything left in the kitchen, I may just grab a plate there and curl up in my sleeping bag."

"If the cupboard's bare and you want me to bring you a plate, just let me know," Dad said as we headed down the stairs again.

"Will do."

I ventured into the kitchen and found, to my relief, that someone had thought to arrange a small makeshift buffet for those too tired to make it down to the feast—a dozen bowls and platters containing most if not all of the delicacies that would be served around the fire pit. I filled a plate with my favorites. Then I made another with the items Michael would like, wrapped it up, and put it in the fridge with his name on it.

I trudged back to the jewelry studio and nibbled at my dinner while getting our camping-lite site ready. I inflated our air mattresses and arranged the sleeping bags on them, just inside the entrance door. And then I realized that if we slept there, every time we got out of our sleeping bags we'd step on the incredibly loud squeaking floorboard, so I moved them over by the windows. More privacy there anyway. I dragged the table Tad had been using close to the sleeping bags, so it could serve as a combination dresser, desk, and dining table. I arranged our few belongings on it. I texted the boys to let them know where I was, and where their dad was. Then I sat down on one of the folding chairs to finish my meal.

"As good as it's going to get." I don't talk aloud to myself that often, but there was something a little creepy about the empty, echoing studio. "And considerably better than being in a tent if the weather forecasters are right about the coming thunderstorm."

I glanced over at the enormous floor-to-ceiling windows. In the daytime they'd have shown the beautiful view down the steep, wooded slope. Now all I could see was my reflection in the glass.

Peaceful now, but it would rain before morning. I made sure the windows were closed. And then, remembering how much light those acres of glass let in during the daylight hours, I lowered the window shades. No getting up early for me. If Grandfather or anyone else wanted to go owling in the rain, they could do it without me. I planned to sleep in. And no doubt Michael would as well.

I thought of calling him, and decided to save it as a treat. A reward for finishing whatever useful things I could accomplish by bedtime. If nothing else, I had to make Cordelia's rounds. I finished my meal, except for the brownie I'd save for a delayed dessert. Then I set out.

I trudged to the other end of the building and began by checking that all the windows were closed in the Great Hall, the dining room, the library—all the public areas. I made sure that all the burners, ovens, faucets, lights, and appliances were off in the kitchen. That all the trash had been taken out, and cinder blocks placed on the lids of the cans to discourage the raccoons. That the back door was locked. And the side doors.

We didn't worry so much about locking the French doors out to the terrace, on the theory that any burglar determined enough to climb up the side of the building like a human gecko would just break a pane to get inside if he found the doors locked. But I made sure they were closed, after checking that no one had left anything out on the terrace that could be ruined by the rain.

From the terrace, I could hear strains of music from the other side of the house. Nearly everyone was down by the campfire, toasting marshmallows, making s'mores, drinking mead and mulled wine and cider. Maybe I should go back and join them. See if the camaraderie lifted my mood.

Maybe later. I still had the craft studios to check.

Maybe I should be doing this every night for Cordelia. She was no spring chicken.

But if I offered, she'd say nonsense—the exercise kept her fit.

I was relieved when I finally reached the last part of my rounds and was back where I had started, in the lower floor of the studio wing. Forget going out to the campfire. When I finished, I was going to crawl into my sleeping bag and call it a day.

The storage room door was locked. When I rattled the door of Cordelia's office to make sure it was also locked, I remembered the phone. It should be charged enough to turn on by now. It would almost certainly be password protected, but with luck the user would have something on their home screen to give me a clue to their identity. And if not, I could email my nephew Kevin to ask if he had any suggestions on finding the owner.

The screen came on, revealing a picture of the comedy and tragedy masks.

"Okay, so you belong to an actor," I said to the phone. "That doesn't help me much. We have quite a few of those around."

Although it occurred to me that the contact list in my phone probably contained cell phone numbers for most of the actors in the Game. I could call them all in turn, and if the phone rang I could return it to its owner. I took out my own phone and started scrolling through my contact list.

And the first actor's name I came across was Terence Cox.

"It couldn't be," I said aloud. Wouldn't the chief have mentioned if Terence had been found phoneless? Unless she was trying to keep that detail quiet for some reason.

Yeah, like making sure the killer didn't find the phone before she did.

I clicked Terence's number to dial it.

The phone on the desk began to ring.

I quickly ended the call and sat for a moment staring at the phone.

Terence's phone.

Chapter 39

I checked the time and decided that it was still early enough to call Mother.

"Hello, dear," she said. "I do hope you're enjoying the party."

"Getting up to go owling this morning has done me in." Well, that plus everything else that had happened today. "I'm back at the house, vegging. I have a question—was there a particular reason you gave me that phone just now?"

"Because we found it in the pocket of one of the costumes," she said. "So I figured it belonged to someone on staff."

"Any idea which costume?"

"That moss-green and gold robe with the slashed sleeves and the fake ermine collar," she said. "The one with that lovely subtle pattern of pineapples in the gold jacquard."

Okay, obviously a correct answer, and a detailed one to boot, but not one that helped me out all that much. It sounded familiar, but I'd long since learned to leave costuming to the costumers.

"Any idea who was wearing it?" I asked.

"Nigel, of course." She sounded as if surprised that I had to ask. "It's one of his two regular outfits—the one he wore today."

"Ah," I said. "I can see it now." And yeah, I could. "Thanks."

"But I asked him and he had his phone and didn't remember picking one up," she said. "So I figured maybe it fell down from someone else's costume and whoever picked it up put it in Nigel's costume by mistake. I do hope you can find the owner—these days people find it so stressful to be without their phones."

Should I tell her it belonged to Terence, who wasn't in any shape to miss it? No. She sounded relaxed and cheerful. Why remind her of the murder?

"Don't worry," I said. "I'll take care of it. How's the foot?"

A heavy sigh.

"Your father keeps saying it should heal fine," she said. "But what if he's just trying to make me feel better?"

Oops. Maybe I should have stuck with talking about the murder.

"I wouldn't worry," I said aloud. "You know how he loves to fret about rare conditions and dire complications—but look how blasé he's been about your foot. I'm sure that means it's healing in a boringly normal way. If it was anyone but you he'd probably have lost all interest in it."

"I hope you're right, dear." She sounded a little more cheerful.

"I'm sure of it," I said in my heartiest tones. "Goodnight—and say goodnight to Cordelia."

I hung up and stared again at Terence's phone. Damn. Michael had gone down to see about getting Nigel out on bail and finding him a lawyer. If I told the chief about this, it wouldn't help Nigel.

But I couldn't not tell her.

Maybe there was a reason the chief hadn't mentioned that Terence's phone was missing. Maybe she already suspected that one of the actors was the killer. And maybe she knew that if the phone were found under circumstances that implicated one of our tight-knit little band, the finder's first impulse would be to protect their friend. As mine was now.

Or maybe she hadn't mentioned the missing phone

because she'd been so busy. She might not even realize that she hadn't mentioned it.

And really, if Nigel had been in possession of the phone, surely he could have found a better place to stash it than in the pocket of his own costume. This looked less like incriminating evidence than planted evidence.

Would the chief see it that way?

No telling. But I couldn't not tell her about the phone.

I picked up my phone, took a deep breath, and called.

"Meg? What's up?"

"So am I correct in thinking that you might be looking for Terence's phone?"

"We are. Of course, I'm hoping he was smart enough to back up everything on it to the cloud, which would mean that eventually we can get his carrier to cough up all the data on it. But it might save time if we could find the phone itself. Dare I hope that's why you're calling?"

"We had one turned in to the lost-and-found." I explained about having to charge the phone before I could figure out whose it was, and then having it answer to Terence's number.

"Who found it?"

"One of the costume crew. She found it in the pocket of one of the costumes and gave it to Mother, who gave it to me."

"Any idea who was wearing that particular costume today?"

I took another deep breath.

"Nigel," I said.

She didn't say anything.

"Of course, pretty much anyone around here would know that it's Nigel's costume," I pointed out. "And would have access to it."

"Access to it how?" I could almost see the slight frown that no doubt accompanied her realization that I was about to introduce a complication.

"We all turn our costumes in at the end of the day for laundering," I explained. "That's the reason for those big rolling racks in the hallway outside Cordelia's office. Plus the muted washing and drying noises you could probably still hear even with her door closed."

"I'd assumed those were for the costumes you rent to the tourists," she said.

"That's probably the biggest part of the laundry workload," I said. "That and the costumes for all the rank-and-file participants—the food vendors and servers, the staff who run the games, the ticket sellers—all the people who just need a basic period costume. But there's a special rack for the Game players—a lot of those costumes need hand-washing or dry cleaning. And anyone who knew the system could figure out that Nigel's costume would be there shortly after closing time."

A brief silence.

"Well, at least that does narrow things down a bit," she said. "Either the phone was in Mr. Howe's possession, or it was planted in his pocket by someone with after-hours access to the craft center."

"Or someone who had a chance to slip the phone in his pocket while he wasn't paying attention."

"Either way it narrows down the field."

I nodded, then realized she couldn't hear that.

"Agreed," I said. "Of course, it only narrows the field down to about two hundred people. Do you want me to bring you the phone? Or maybe arrange for someone else to bring it—I'm pretty beat."

"Lock it up in Cordelia's office for tonight," she said. "The state police have a cell phone forensics specialist, and I've had her on call in case we found Terence's phone, but I doubt if she can get here tonight. I'll email her to let her know we found it. And I still have a key to the office, so in the unlikely event that the forensic specialist is so gung ho that she decides to drive up here from Richmond this late, I can send someone out to fetch it for her."

"Will do," I said.

"Thanks."

We hung up, and I reached for Terence's phone, ready to lock it in the drawer. But then I remembered how many times I'd seen Terence pull it out and rapidly enter the passcode. I had a vivid mental picture of him doing it—the quick, efficient way he'd tap the face of the phone. Most people used a single finger, but curiously he used three: index finger, middle finger, ring finger, all in a row, and then back to the index finger. And their motion was all sideways, not up and down.

I pushed the power button and looked at the screen. If I was remembering the motion correctly, the password was most likely 1231, 4564, or 7897. Always possible that the fourth number went to the row below or above the first three. But even if that were the case, it would still give a very limited number of possible passcodes. If I was calculating it right, only seven. Could I type six wrong numbers into the iPhone without messing things up for the forensic phone tech?

"I shouldn't even try," I said aloud. "I should just lock this thing up."

I remembered what my cyber-savvy nephew Kevin was fond of saying: if you were trying to figure out someone's password, the first thing was to search their desk, to see if they'd written it down someplace. Not possible with Terence. But the second thing was to figure out if they'd used a number that held some personal significance.

The last four digits of his phone number? Even Terence probably wouldn't be that clueless. His birthdate? A lot of people used that.

I opened the drawer that contained the Faire's personnel records and pulled out Terence's file. And there it was on the first page—his birthday. December 31. 1231.

I tapped the phone again to wake it up, and typed in 1231.

The phone unlocked.

I should have just turned it off, locked it up, and texted the chief the passcode. But the idea of snooping was so tempting.

And I've never been good at resisting temptation.

I started with his email inbox. Not a whole lot in it— maybe he was uncharacteristically efficient and deleted emails when he was through with them. Or maybe he just didn't get that many. It was interesting to see that he was already angling to get an audition with O'Malley when Nigel had gone up to do his callback. And apparently O'Malley hadn't been lying about giving him the part.

It was in the outgoing mail that I struck pay dirt. I found an email he'd sent to O'Malley a few days ago that said "Thought you might like to see this. Let's get together and I'll show you the rest."

I opened the attachment and nearly dropped the phone. It was a picture of O'Malley and a woman. She was tall and shapely, dressed in a skin-tight black leather dominatrix outfit, and judging by the expression in her eyes— the only part of her face visible through her mask—she found their photo shoot supremely boring and possibly even slightly distasteful. O'Malley was stark naked, which allowed me to notice that he seemed to be a great deal more enthusiastic about what was going on.

"Holy cow," I muttered. Holy cow didn't even begin to cover the situation, but I was pleased that even this rather startling situation hadn't tricked me into reverting to words I didn't want the boys to learn from me.

I didn't see any other emails with attachments. But when I switched over to Terence's photo collection I found several dozen more shots that seemed to have been taken on the same occasion. A second dominatrix appeared, slightly shorter and bustier than the first, but equally bored with what was going on. And—holy cow again—Zack Glass, in the same state of undress as O'Malley. Middle age had definitely not been kind to the former teen heartthrob.

I scrolled through the pictures. O'Malley and Glass posing with one or the other of the dominatrixes—or should that be dominatrices? I'd look it up later. The two women never appeared in the same photo, which suggested they'd taken turns as photographer and no fifth wheel had been present. And raised the question of how Terence had gotten hold of the photos.

"I think I'm going to wish I could unsee these," I muttered. O'Malley's nude body draped languorously on the glass top of a large desk, in much the same pose as Ingres's *La Grande Odalisque*—but viewed, alas, from the front. O'Malley and Glass snorting lines of white powder on the same glass desktop. I could see two-thirds of a brass-and-wood nameplate at one side of the picture, and I suspected if I typed those letters into a search engine I'd come up with the name of somebody on the Arena Stage staff—and not a particularly low-ranking somebody, if the size and elegance of the office was anything to go by.

And to top it all off, a series of shots showing O'Malley and Glass, with or without one of the sullen leather-clad women, striking rude poses in the middle of what even I recognized as a stage set—and not just any set, but the strikingly beautiful and much-photographed set of one of Arena's recent productions—the set that had recently won a well-deserved Helen Hayes Award—D.C.'s equivalent of the Tonys. Knowing theater people, I rather suspected the Arena's management would find the pictures taken in someone's office a venial sin compared with the mortal sin of desecrating that remarkably distinctive set.

I snooped through the rest of his pictures. Nothing much but selfies of himself, with or without other people, including a couple with people I recognized—a well-known actress and a celebrity chef, both of them wearing expressions that shouted "Who the hell is this jackass taking a selfie with me?" Nothing else incriminating.

For the grand finale, I checked the calls, outgoing and incoming. No voicemails. Not a whole lot of phone calls made or received in the couple of days leading up to his death.

But thirty-two missed calls today, all from the same phone number. Not, alas, a familiar phone number—though it was one that had called Terence three times in the week before he was killed. I could have called it to see who answered, but I decided maybe I'd taken my illicit snooping far enough.

I picked up my own phone and took a picture of a screen that showed the number of Terence's persistent posthumous caller. Maybe I'd figure out later who it belonged to. Then I texted the chief.

"I realized I knew Terence's password," I said. "Sending you something I found on his phone."

Then I grabbed Terence's phone again and forwarded her the email with the picture attached. Then I texted her some of the more offensive pictures. Six of them. That should be enough.

I sat and stared at the phone. At both of the phones, mine and Terence's. In a few minutes, the chief texted back to my phone. No rebuke, thank goodness.

"Who is that with O'Malley?" it read. "He looks familiar. One of your troupe?"

"Zachary Glass, the movie star," I texted back. "He has the lead role in O'Malley's *Hamlet*."

"Lock up that phone. Sending someone to collect it tonight."

"Roger."

I realized that my hands were sweating. I wiped the sweat off of Terence's phone, tucked it into the top drawer of Cordelia's desk, and locked it up. Went out and locked the office door behind me.

Then I hurried down the hall to the small bathroom and washed my hands. Twice. With a sinfully excessive amount of Cordelia's rosewater soap.

As I dried my hands I peered into the mirror. I looked tired. Haggard. Lately I'd noticed that being even slightly short on sleep brought out the dark circles under my eyes, and I was certainly running on empty by now. Maybe I could arrange for someone else to meet whoever was coming to pick up Terence's phone, so I could go to bed.

And maybe tomorrow I'd go across the way to Rose Noire's booth and see if any of her herbal remedies would help my poor face. Maybe she'd brought a supply of her organic cucumber eye cream, or her herb-and-mineral mud masque.

And why was I trying so hard not to think about what I'd found in Terence's phone?

I remembered Nigel telling Michael and me about overhearing what he thought was Terence blackmailing someone. What was it Nigel had reported Terence saying? "I want it. Remember, I have the goods on you." Had I told the chief about that? I couldn't remember. Odds were Nigel had by now.

It all made sense, suddenly. Terence was using the embarrassing photos to blackmail O'Malley—not for money, but for something he wanted more than money—the part of Polonius in O'Malley's upcoming production of *Hamlet*. And O'Malley was smart enough to realize that as long as those photos existed, he'd never be free. Every time he directed a play or movie, Terence could hit him up for a part. Terence might start asking for money. Or, if Terence decided O'Malley had nothing else of value, he could try to sell the photos. The tabloids might pay handsomely for them. Blackmail always ends badly for someone.

So O'Malley had come up to see Terence. Maybe he'd just planned to talk to him. Reason with him. Or maybe he'd come intending to kill him. Either way, they'd met out in the woods, and O'Malley had killed Terence. But for whatever reason, Terence didn't have his phone with him—I was sure if he had, O'Malley would have taken it and left. So O'Malley had stayed around to insinuate himself into the group of actors at the Faire. That was why he'd been snooping around Camp Anachronism and rummaging through pockets in the costume shop. And I'd bet anything it was O'Malley who had called Terence thirty-two times over the course of the day. He'd been calling in the hope that the ringing would help him locate Terence's phone. Bad luck for him that Terence, always careless about practical things, hadn't bothered to charge his phone all that recently, so that it had run out of power completely by the time O'Malley had started calling it.

Of course, there was still the mystery of how the phone had landed in the pocket of Nigel's costume. The chief would find out once O'Malley was arrested. I hoped having one of her guests hauled away in handcuffs wouldn't upset poor Mrs. Larsen. Maybe Cordelia and I should plan to drop by Den Lille Hytta tomorrow to check on her and—

Just then I heard a noise. The squeaky floorboard in the jewelry studio. I froze and listened. I didn't hear it again. And I also didn't hear anyone calling out to me. Wouldn't that be the normal thing to do if you were expecting to find me in the studio and didn't see me?

Chapter 40

I reached into my pocket, intending to pull out my phone. Maybe I was overreacting, but I decided I'd rather text someone and make sure there was a friendly face out in the hall when I stepped out of the bathroom and went to see who was sneaking around in the jewelry studio. Heck, maybe I could even text 911.

My phone. It wasn't in my pocket. My key ring was, but fat lot of good that did me. Damn! I'd probably left my phone on Cordelia's desk. I could go and unlock the door and fetch it . . . but not without making noise.

Well, someone would be coming by eventually. A police officer to pick up the phone. Michael arriving home after arranging Nigel's bail. If I could stay here long enough . . .

But if whoever had arrived so silently had evil intentions, he wouldn't let me skulk in the bathroom forever. He might come looking for me. I looked around for something I could use to defend myself.

The available options weren't encouraging. A spray bottle of cleaning solution. But it was an environmentally sensitive cleaner, widely advertised as all-natural, non-toxic, biodegradable, and free from ingredients that might irritate the eyes. Nice that Cordelia was doing her bit for the ecosystem, but I'd have given a lot right now for a spray bottle full of toxic eye-irritating chemicals.

About the only possible weapons I could find were an old-fashioned red rubber plunger and a dilapidated toilet brush, both clearly well used. I had a brief vision of trying to wield one or the other against a killer armed with one of the impressive weapons slasher movies always seemed to feature—a Texas chainsaw, the machete from *Friday the 13th,* and Freddy Krueger's glove with knives on all the fingers. Then I made a mental vow to work harder at discouraging the boys' budding fascination with scary movies and reminded myself that the unseen intruder probably wasn't armed with any of those. If I was lucky, he'd have picked up another cheap, flimsy dagger from the Bonny Blade, and I'd have the advantage of superior weaponry. If I was unlucky, he'd have a gun, and neither of my weapons would be much use.

Unless I could leverage the ick factor. That might prove useful.

Not now, though. I'd stall for time. Every minute that passed increased the chances that reinforcements would arrive.

But what if the reinforcements were less prepared to tackle O'Malley than I was? The boys, for example. Dad. Even a Riverton police officer might be vulnerable if he thought he was just completing a tame—if important—errand to secure evidence.

At least I knew there was someone there. And had a good idea who it was.

I'd creep out, armed with my weapons of mass disgust-ingness, and surprise the intruder.

Or at least bring to an end this miserable crouching and waiting in a bathroom that seemed to be growing smaller by the second.

"Seize the moment," I told myself—mentally, of course. "Time and tide wait for no one. She who hesitates is lost."

But then I paused and looked around for a place to hide something. The toilet tank. Moving swiftly and silently I relocated the toilet paper rolls, still-wrapped bars of soap, and other bathroom clutter that lived on top of it. Ever so carefully I slid off the tank lid. I pulled the key ring out of my pocket and gently eased it to the bottom of the tank.

Then I put the lid back and restored its load of toilet paper and soap. The phone was still locked in Cordelia's office. No sense making the office-door key easy for him to take.

I shoved the bathroom door open with the business end of the plunger, strode briskly down the hallway, and burst into the jewelry studio, shouting "Hai!" with a volume and fierceness that would have pleased my old martial arts teacher.

O'Malley was so startled that he almost dropped the gun he was holding.

"What the hell are you supposed to be?" he snapped.

Okay, the gun was a bad break. But maybe I could talk my way out of this. Or at least stall until the cavalry arrived.

"Good heavens." I pretended to be relieved at the sight of him. "I thought you were a burglar. You might want to leave now. The chief will be arriving any minute, and she won't be pleased to find you ignoring Cordelia's orders to stay away."

O'Malley smiled.

"Nice try," he said. "Now how about giving me Cox's cell phone?"

"And then you'll just go away quietly and never darken our doorstep again," I said. "Yeah, right."

"I know you've got it in your pocket."

"No, I don't," I said. "It's locked up in the lost-and-found."

"Then unlock it."

"I don't have the key."

"Then where is it?" The "is" was halfway to "ish." He was probably still under the influence. Was that something I could use, or did it make my situation worse?

"The chief has it." Not exactly a lie—she did have a key to the office—and I was pleased to see him flinch slightly. "And she also has the photos. The ones of you and Zach Glass and your . . . friends. Just how did Terence get his hands on those, anyway?"

He looked stricken for a moment, then put on an unconvincing air of nonchalance.

"I don't know what photos you— Okay. Yeah. I want the photos. I told Terence I didn't want him to take any photos of our rehearsal. My *Hamlet*'s going to be a bold, new interpretation. Very modern—visually in your face. I didn't want any hint of what I'm doing to leak out. But I guess he ignored me. I just want the photos, If Terence were alive, I'd be able to make him see reason. But since some lunatic decided to knock him off—well, I've been trying to find his phone so I could delete them before they get out and ruin the surprise."

"Interesting," I said. "I must reread *Hamlet*. It's been a while. I don't remember the coke-sniffing scene. Or the dominatrix subplot."

"Just give me the damned phone!" O'Malley took a couple of steps toward me. I thrust the plunger and toilet brush in front of me, and he scrambled to get beyond their reach.

He took a few steps to the left in what I suspected he thought was a subtle, nonchalant manner. I took a few steps to my left, keeping the distance between us the same. We repeated this maneuver a couple of times. I suspected he was angling to get between me and the door. He was welcome to try. I was angling myself to get closer to where I'd dragged the table. If I got close enough, maybe I could leap behind it. The top was good, thick oak. If it didn't stop a bullet, at least it would slow one down. And then—

I needed to keep him distracted.

"We have a stalemate," I said aloud. "You can shoot me. But then you'll never get your hands on the phone. I suppose there's no use pointing out that Virginia's still a death penalty state, since you're already on the hook for killing Terence—"

"I didn't kill Terence!" Suddenly he sounded terrified. "I never saw him down here."

"You came down Friday night," I pointed out.

"I was going to tackle him today," he said. "I didn't come

up here until this morning, I didn't know he was dead until that horrible policewoman told me, and I didn't kill him!"

"Then who did?"

"How should I know?" He sounded exasperated. And sincere. And almost believable. He wasn't that good an actor, was he?

"Well, let's think about it," I said aloud. "Because if we can't figure it out, the chief's probably going to arrest you. Who else had a reason to dislike Terence?"

"Who didn't?" O'Malley said. "I'll tell you one thing: Whoever killed him did me a favor. The thought of having to use that talentless hack in my *Hamlet* was driving me crazy."

"But you didn't kill him yourself."

"No, I—"

Suddenly, from behind O'Malley, an electric iron flashed into sight and struck the top of his head. He groaned, his eyes rolled up, and he would have fallen to the floor if the person who had just coshed him hadn't caught him with one arm and eased him to the floor—while deftly removing the gun from his limp hand. I heard the iron clatter onto the hard boards.

"What an annoying man." George Sims stepped farther into the room, giving O'Malley's crumpled body a wide berth.

I'd have been babbling with gratitude if I hadn't noticed a curious thing: the gun, now in George's hand, was still pointing in my direction.

Maybe I should pretend not to have noticed. Brazen it out.

"Very annoying," I said. "But Chief Heedles will be annoyed if he dies before she can arrest him for Terence's murder. How about if you guard him while I go to fetch Dad?"

I took a couple of steps forward, as if to do so.

"I don't think so."

Why did that bland, self-effacing smile of his suddenly look so sinister? I retreated, and revived my notion of diving behind the table.

"He was telling the truth, you know," George said. "He didn't kill Terence. I suppose he might have tried if I hadn't gotten to the bastard first. And O'Malley would have messed it up, of course. But you knew that."

"No," I said. "I really didn't. And I'm not sure I believe it now. You're just trying to be dramatic. What possible reason could you have had for killing Terence?"

"No one notices." He nodded as if I had just confirmed some sad suspicion he'd held for years. "The man abuses me. Makes fun of me. Plays humiliating and destructive pranks on me. Bad-mouths me to directors so no one ever casts me. And no one notices. He leers once or twice at Dianne and everyone falls all over themselves to make her feel better. He targets me for constant humiliation and torment and everybody says 'Oh, never mind. It's just George. It doesn't really matter.'"

"Are you kidding?" I was having a hard time keeping my temper. "How many times did I offer to speak to Terence? How many times did I ask you if you wanted me to do anything? And I know Michael and Cordelia did the same."

"If you'd really cared about how he treated me, you'd have done something anyway."

"We *were* doing something anyway," I said. "When Cordelia realized he was a problem, she started giving him warning memos—at least for those times when anyone could bring themselves to tell us what happened. Not just for things he'd done to Dianne—we had at least as many on things we could prove he'd done to you. And we were going to fire him. Today would probably have been his last day."

"Really?" George blinked and looked unsure of himself. Then he recovered. "Doesn't matter. Too little too late. And if he thought I'd had a hand in getting him fired, he'd never have let it go. He'd have blackened my name with everyone."

"Only the people stupid enough to believe him," I said.

"But people did." He glanced down at O'Malley. "He wouldn't even give me an audition, the swine." He kicked

O'Malley's shoulder by way of emphasis. "Pretty sure Terence poisoned the well. And he's been ruining things here. Do you think I took this job because I like living in a tent and clowning around for a bunch of stupid tourists? Why would anyone take on a gig like this unless his career was dead in the water? But stupid me—I thought someone would see my work here and want to cast me in a real show. Fat chance of that after the way Terence kept making me look bad, week after week."

At least he was focusing on Terence—not blaming anyone else. Like Michael. Or Cordelia. Or me.

"We all know he was treating you badly," I said. "But we can find a way out of this. Put down the gun. Let us help you. If—"

Just then I heard a rattling out in the corridor. George started and looked over his shoulder.

"Take cover, Meg!" a voice called. Grandfather?

I jumped to side as one of the giant clothes racks, heavily loaded with multicolored costumes, careened into the room and slammed into George. I could see Grandfather riding on the back of it.

"Stay outside!" I shouted. "And go get help! He's got a gun!"

George had fallen, but he was trying to scramble to his feet, and he'd managed to hold on to the gun.

"Scurvy knave!" Grandfather leaped off the clothes rack and strode forward, waving his raven cane wildly. "Drop that infernal fire stick and put your hands up!"

"Do what he says!" Dad would never manage to be one-tenth as menacing as Grandfather, but the ten-foot bardiche he was carrying seemed to get George's attention, just for a second or two.

I took the opportunity to vault over the table and grab George's gun hand. I didn't manage to wrest the gun away from him before he pulled the trigger, but my grip was more than strong enough to keep it pointed steadily away from everyone until he'd fired all its rounds into my poor sleeping bag. Then I stomped on his instep and wrenched the empty gun out of his hand.

"Ow," he said. "I think you broke my wrist. And I've got splinters! Splinters from that nasty floor."

Dad had pulled out his phone.

"Can you bring my medical kit down to the jewelry studio?" he was saying to someone.

That seemed to please George—until he noticed that Dad was focused on O'Malley—who was still unconscious.

"I'm injured too," George wailed.

"Help me tie him up," I told Grandfather.

"On your belly, worm!" Grandfather snapped.

While Grandfather kept George pinned down with his raven staff, I ran to the bathroom, retrieved my keys, and fetched a roll of electrical tape from Cordelia's office.

Just as we finished trussing up George—

"What is going on here?"

We all looked up to see Chief Heedles standing in the doorway. Lenny, Horace, and a third officer were peering over her shoulders.

"Meg caught your killer," Dad exclaimed, pointing to George.

"We helped," Grandfather added.

"He's the killer?" the chief sounded puzzled. "After seeing those photos—"

"O'Malley's a creep, but George is the killer," I said. "It's a long story."

"And one that will have to wait," Dad said. "We need to get O'Malley to a hospital. How soon can we get an ambulance here?"

"At this time of night? Let's take him in the patrol van. Horace! Lenny! Find something we can use as a stretcher. Carlton—take charge of Mr. . . . um . . ."

"Sims," I reminded her.

"Take charge of Mr. Sims. And Meg I'd like you to come along. You can start telling me that long story."

Chapter 41

"Why didn't you tell us you were planning a murder?" my brother, Rob, demanded. At least that's what I think he said. His words were partially drowned out by the incessant jingling of the Morris-dancing bells he was wearing.

"Nobody plans a murder." I was leaning wearily against the fence surrounding the jousting field. "Except murderers, of course, but they don't usually give out advance notice. And once it happened we were trying to keep it quiet to avoid too much negative publicity for the Faire."

"Are you implying that I can't be trusted to keep my mouth shut?" At first I thought he was shouting at me, but then I realized he was only raising his voice so he could be heard above the blasted bells.

"No, I'll come right out and say it," I replied. "If we wanted the whole world to know about something, we would definitely enlist you. You're great at getting the word out. But keeping a secret? No. Discretion is not your forte."

"You're probably right."

"And could you please take those bloody bells off!"

"But we're doing our first performance any minute now!" he protested.

"In thirty-nine minutes to be precise." I was so annoyed that instead of discreetly checking the time on my highly anachronistic iPhone I brandished it in his face. "At eleven o'clock I will come to your performance and applaud heartily. But I will not listen to thirty-nine minutes of random preliminary jingling. I didn't get enough sleep and my head is starting to ache."

"Sorry. Maybe if I sit down." He did so, hopping up on the top of the fence.

"If you can keep from twitching," I said.

"I don't twitch," he protested.

"You do," I said. "You can't help it. It's an ADHD thing. See, you're doing it now."

He was bouncing both legs up and down in a fashion that was perfect for setting off the bells, although from the surprised expression on his face it was obvious that he hadn't realized he was doing it.

"Oh, all right." He hopped down, bent over, and un-strapped the bell pads attached to his shins. I breathed a sigh of relief when the second one landed on the ground. And then winced again when he used his foot to shove them aside.

"Hey, Meg!" Greg Dorance strolled up. "Did you hear the good news?"

"I guess you don't mean the good news that Meg captured the killer last night," Rob said. "Because yeah, she knows about that."

"And if I didn't already say it, congratulations," Greg said. "I meant the good news about Harry and Delilah. Your grandfather might be taking one or both off my hands."

"That is good news," I said.

"Not sure whether they'll end up at the Caerphilly Zoo or at a wildlife sanctuary run by a friend of his."

"The Willner Wildlife Sanctuary?" I asked.

Greg nodded.

"They'll be in good hands in either place," I said. "Caroline Willner loves predators almost as much as Grandfather."

"Yeah—we're going to go down tomorrow to meet her, and see how the birds take to the place," Greg said. "And whether they're at the zoo or the sanctuary, I can visit them. Unless your grandfather succeeds in teaching Harry how to hunt like a proper hawk, in which case I'd be happy to see him go back to the wild. And this means I'll have a slot to take on a new, young hawk." He beamed with delight.

"Great news, then," I said.

"Gotta go." He turned in the direction of Falconer's Grove. "Or your Grandfather will start the next demonstration without me."

He ran off, nearly colliding with Mother. Who was walking. Slowly, leaning heavily on Grandfather's raven-headed cane. But walking. And looking more cheerful than I'd seen her in weeks. She spotted us, waved regally, and continued on her way.

"I guess Dad told her she's ready to start a little light exercise," Rob said. "So I hear Grandfather's been down here all weekend. He and Cordelia must be getting along better."

"Not so you'd notice," I said. "But he's been making himself useful and staying out of her way. Plus he helped save me from the killer last night, so she's giving him more slack than usual. And—"

"Uncle Rob!" Josh and Jamie were running down the path to give their uncle big hugs.

"I hear you guys had some excitement," Rob said.

"Mom caught a killer," Josh exclaimed.

"Grandpa helped," Jamie added. "And Grand. But only a little. Mom had almost rescued herself by the time they got there anyway."

"It was a family effort," I said.

"Then why didn't you call us?" Josh was still annoyed at being left out of the rescue.

"She didn't need us," Jamie said.

"She almost didn't need *us*." Chief Heedles strolled up, looking more cheerful than I'd seen her lately.

"How are the two patients?" I asked.

"Mr. Sims does have a broken wrist," the chief said.

"Go, Mom!" Jamie exclaimed.

"But he was well enough to be discharged, and is now

back in my jail, awaiting the arrival of his defense attorney. Mr. O'Malley has a concussion, but he's expected to recover. The doctors at VCU Medical Center were quite complimentary about your father's first aid efforts."

"Not surprising," Rob said.

"Are you going to be able to charge him with anything?" I asked. "O'Malley, I mean. Although come to think of it, do you have any evidence against George, other than his confession?"

"Well, with any luck the confession should be enough," the chief said. "Considering that he persisted in confessing repeatedly all the way down to Richmond. If you recall, I could hardly get him to shut up long enough to read him the Miranda warning. He seems to feel that he was very badly treated and has grounds to support a plea of justifiable homicide."

"I'm sure he was badly treated by Terence." I probably sounded a little cross. I was. "And we'd have done something about that if he'd let us. Instead of always saying 'Oh, no. It's okay. I don't mind. It's just Terence's way. Isn't he a card?'"

"Pretty good imitation, Mom," Jamie said. "You sound just like Sir George."

"B minus," Josh said. "Not nearly whiny enough."

"As it happens, Horace was also developing some evidence that would eventually have pointed our investigation toward Mr. Sims," the chief said. "The knife wound didn't bleed very much, but we have every expectation that a minute amount of blood found on Mr. Sims's wristwatch will turn out to be a DNA match for Mr. Cox. Ms. Willow . . . er, Dianne has identified the note found in Mr. Howe's footlocker as one she received from Mr. Cox two weeks ago. And we expect to be able to prove that Mr. Sims had ready access to Mr. Howe's keys, since they were in adjoining tents. So even if his defense attorney—"

"Chief Heedles! Chief Heedles!" Dad was running toward us, waving something. "I've got it! I've got it!"

"Got what, I wonder," the chief said. But she turned to welcome Dad with an expression of pleasant expectation.

"My cameras," he said. "It's been so crazy that I didn't even remember that I set them out."

"Motion sensitive night-vision nature cameras," I elaborated. "He's been planning to set them up along all the promising wildlife trails in the nearby woods."

"I've only done two so far," he said. "But one of them was near where I'd been hearing a lot of owl vocalizations, so it occurred to me to check the website—the cameras upload their videos to a website that my grandson Kevin set up—"

"Did you catch anything on these cameras?" the chief asked.

By way of an answer, Dad thrust his phone into her hand. And then, when it became obvious that she had no idea what he wanted her to do with it, he showed her how to access the uploaded video. We all clustered around to watch the little screen over her shoulder. First a pair of deer walked down the path with almost liquid grace. The video came to an abrupt stop when the deer left the camera's field of vision. A clock in the lower left-hand part of the screen showed the time as 11:33:01.

"Very interesting," the chief said.

"I rewound it a little too far," Dad said. "Here it comes."

The time jumped to 12:59:04. A stealthy figure crept past the camera. He paused for a moment to look over his shoulder, and the camera caught his face, for just a few frames. George. Then he continued off camera. Another time jump. 1:05:59. Terence sauntered past the camera and disappeared. 1:39:15. George again, going in the opposite direction.

"That's it," Dad said. "No more sign of Terence."

"As I was saying, even if Mr. Sims's defense attorney tries to have some of his confessions ruled inadmissible, I think we'll have sufficient evidence to make the case. Dr. Langslow—since you showed me this on your phone, I gather the camera itself is still in place."

"Of course."

"Let's find Horace and go with him to collect it as evidence."

"Good idea."

"And here I thought I'd be the one bringing you the key evidence," I said.

"Well, I may not be using the evidence from Mr. Cox's phone," the chief said, with a smile. "But my colleagues over in the Washington MPD are very appreciative. As is the management of Arena Stage. It looks as if Mr. O'Malley will not be directing any shows for them in the foreseeable future."

With that she and Dad hurried off to find Horace.

"We don't have a demo until noon," Jamie said. "Can we go watch Grandpa and Chief Heedles retrieve Grandpa's camera?"

"As long as you don't get in the way."

They dashed off.

"I hope they come back in time to put the bells on," Rob said.

"You haven't figured out how to put them on yourself?" I asked.

"Not my bells—the ones for Spike. He's going to be the world's first Morris-dancing dog. If they don't come back, do you suppose you could—"

"No," I said. "If you want to bell Spike, you're on your own."

"Spoilsport." He sulked for a moment, then cheered up. "Sounds as if you had a wild time yesterday. Dad said even Tad and Faulk were suspects for a while."

"Not very viable suspects, if you ask me," I said. "They spent six or seven hours in the ER at the county hospital, so there was no way either of them could possibly have killed Terence. But initially the ER people lied about when they got there, to cover up the fact that for nearly four hours they pretty much neglected a man who might have been having a heart attack. The chief got to the bottom of it pretty quickly, but it was a little stressful until she did."

"Yikes." Rob shook his head. "Remind me not to get sick while I'm here."

"Or if you do, just call Dad," I said. "If he can't fix you, he'll get you to a place that's competent."

"But what was supposed to be their motive?" Rob asked. "Or did Chief Heedles suspect them just because they disappeared at the wrong time?"

"Terence got Tad fired," I explained. "Long story how— get Tad to tell you—but the heart thing they went down to the ER about needs expensive surgery to fix, so without health insurance—"

"Back up a sec—Tad got fired? Does this mean he's in the job market?"

"He is," I said. "And—"

"Where is he? I need to find him before someone else snaps him up."

"He's not looking for contract work, you know," I pointed out. "He wants a full-time job with good benefits. Especially good health insurance. Faulk has been waiting far too long for his surgery already."

"Don't ask me the details, but I'm pretty sure we have great health insurance," Rob said. "My HR department is under orders to see to that. And not only because I'm stuck with whatever we offer. Skimping on benefits for the staff is a false economy. I need to have salaries and benefits that are good enough to drag the best people away from the big city to Caerphilly County—and good enough so they can focus on their work instead of worrying about whether they can afford to pay the doctor."

He sounded so indignant that I had to laugh.

"Okay, go find Tad and see if you can recruit him," I said. "And on your head be it if the Mutant Wizards health insurance plan doesn't do right by Faulk."

"If it doesn't, we'll take care of Faulk and make some changes in the plan."

"Check the forge," I said. "Tad's probably hovering there, making sure Faulk doesn't overdo it."

"Thanks!" He started to leave, then thought of something else. "I guess it's pretty obvious none of you guys know much about how corporate health plans work. Even if Tad was fired, he should be able to keep on with his health plan through COBRA."

"Through what?"

"COBRA." Rob looked smug at knowing something I didn't. "Federal program that lets you keep your health insurance for up to eighteen months after you're fired. You have to pay the full cost of the premiums, but it's still a good deal. I'll have my benefits guy explain it all to Tad. Make sure they don't have any gap in coverage." With that he turned and ran off.

"Thank you," I muttered to his departing back. I made a mental note to go a little easier on Rob the next time he did something careless or annoying.

"He forgot his bells." I looked up to see Nigel strolling toward me.

"Quick, maybe we can hide them before he comes back."

He laughed and leaned against the fence beside me.

"You look pretty good for someone who spent the night in the clink," I said.

"Only half the night," he said. "Could have been different without you and Michael. I appreciate it."

"We're just glad you're still with us," I said. "Sorry about *Hamlet,* though."

"Sorry?" Nigel looked puzzled. "Why?"

"Word is Arena's firing O'Malley," I told him. "So who knows if they're still going to do *Hamlet* anymore. And even if they do it, they'll almost certainly have another director, which means you'll have to go through the whole audition process all over again."

For some reason Nigel seemed to find this amusing.

"I guess you haven't heard yet." He was wearing the grin of a cat who has eaten a whole cage of canaries. "Oh, look—here comes Michael."

He scurried away, giggling.

"There you are." Michael strode up, looking curiously excited. "I just got the most peculiar phone call."

"Who from?"

"Arena Stage. They're wasting no time looking for someone to replace O'Malley. As in me."

"Seriously?"

He nodded.

"Apparently a couple of my former students are working there and have been talking me up to management."

I wasn't at all sure how I felt about this. On the one hand, it would be nice to see Michael get more recognition for his talents as a director.

But Arena Stage was in Washington, D.C., a couple of hours away from Caerphilly. How could he possibly juggle that and his career at the college? And did he really want to direct *Hamlet* if he'd be stuck with a temperamental former teen heartthrob in the lead?

"I told them I couldn't take the job unless I had control over casting, and they said fine. Apparently O'Malley hadn't gotten around to giving out contracts to anyone."

"Including Zach Glass?"

"Exactly what I asked. And yes, especially Zach Glass, who only had a handshake deal with O'Malley. A deal Arena feels no obligation to honor—the people I talked to made that clear and sounded remarkably cheerful about it. I suspect they'd figured out that Glass's box-office draw wasn't going to make up for the ridicule factor."

"Imagine that."

"So then I pointed out that I had commitments in Caerphilly during the academic year that would probably interfere with the rehearsal schedule. And they said maybe we could work out a way to do the rehearsals down in Caerphilly and move the show to Arena a week or so before opening—which they could probably arrange to happen during the college's spring break."

It sounded as if they were very keen on having Michael direct. And also as if they'd worked the whole thing out.

"Did you tell them you'd do it?" I asked.

"I told them I would talk to my wife and give them a decision as soon as possible, but that it definitely wouldn't be anytime today, because my wife had just captured a murderer and we were going to take some time off to celebrate."

"Good answer."

"Seriously," he said. "I have very mixed feelings about this. It's a great honor, and could be a lot of fun. But if it disrupts our life—"

"If you really want to do it, let's do some serious thinking about how to make it happen without disrupting our life."

"Okay." He looked more cheerful.

"Starting tomorrow."

"Absolutely!" He glanced down. "Are those Rob's bells? He's been going crazy looking for them."

"I suppose we should take them over to the stage."

"If you wrap them up in something they don't make all that much noise," Michael advised. He had taken off his cloak and was wrapping it around them.

My attention had wandered. I was staring at the sky, where Gracie—pretty sure it was Gracie—was soaring high above the woods.

"So beautiful," I sighed.

"The bells?" Michael sounded puzzled. "I thought you found them annoying."

"The falcons."

Michael glanced up, but Gracie had landed again.

"I missed them," he said.

"You'll get another chance," I said. "They always wing twice."

Acknowledgments

Thanks once again to the wonderful team at St. Martin's / Minotaur, including (but not limited to) Joe Brosnan, Lily Cronig, Hector DeJean, Paul Hochman, Andrew Martin, Sarah Melnyk, and especially my editor, Pete Wolverton. And thanks to David Rotstein and the art department for yet another beautiful cover. You've all got me spoiled.

More thanks to my agent, Ellen Geiger, Matt McGowan, and the staff at the Frances Goldin Literary Agency for their expert handling of the business side of writing and their ongoing moral support.

Many thanks to the friends—-writers and readers alike—-who brainstorm and critique with me, give me good ideas, or help keep me sane while I'm writing: Stuart, Aidan, and Liam Andrews, Chris Cowan, Ellen Crosby, Kathy Deligianis, Margery Flax, Suzanne Frisbee, John Gilstrap, Barb Goffman, Joni Langevoort, David Niemi, Alan Orloff, Art Taylor, Robin Templeton, and Dina Willner. Thanks for all kinds of moral support and practical help to my blog sisters and brother at the Femmes Fatales: Alexia Gordon, Aimee Hix, Dean James, Toni L.P. Kelner, Catriona McPherson, Kris Neri, Joanna Campbell Slan, Marcia Talley, Elaine Viets, and LynDee Walker. And thanks to all the TeaBuds for two decades of friendship.

Special thanks this time to Doug Minnerly and Kathryn O'Sullivan, who answered my questions about matters theatrical—if anything about the Renaissance Faire players is inauthentic, chalk it up to my not asking quite enough questions.

And above all, thanks to the readers who continue to enjoy Meg's adventures!

Read on for an excerpt from

MURDER MOST FOWL —

the next Meg Langslow mystery,
coming soon in hardcover from Minotaur Books!

Chapter 1

"Mom?"

I kept my eyes firmly closed and focused on breathing in and out in the slow, deliberate way that was supposed to make you feel better when you were stressed. One . . . two . . .

"Mom," Jamie repeated. "I know when you're doing your yoga breathing we're not supposed to interrupt you unless there's actual bleeding involved."

"Or open flames," his twin brother, Josh, added.

"But I kind of think this might qualify," Jamie went on.

My eyes flew open.

All I could see for a second were the muddy shins and baggy knees of the woolen hose they were wearing as part of their medieval costumes. I craned my neck to see upward, past the well-worn leather doublets to their faces. Josh was leaning on his longbow as if it were a staff. Jamie had his slung over his left shoulder. Neither appeared to be injured. But they both looked . . . anxious. And that wasn't a look I saw very often on the faces of my not-quite-teenage sons.

"What's wrong?" I asked.

They exchanged a glance. Were they deciding what to tell me? Or just sorting out who had to do the telling?

"We think we found a body," Josh said.

"A dead body," Jamie clarified.

I opened my mouth to chide them for interrupting my

yoga breathing with what was obviously a bad practical joke. But I could see by their expressions that it wasn't a joke.

"Where?" I asked. "And who?"

"Out here in the woods," Jamie said.

"And we have no idea who," Josh said. "All we can see is the hands."

"One of the hands," Jamie corrected. "Kind of sticking up out of the ground. And maybe some fingers from the other hand."

"Show me." I sprang to my feet. I'd been sitting cross-legged by the side of a tiny stream in the woods behind our house, trying to relax by focusing on my breath—and the peaceful sounds of the water, the bird calls, and the occasional distant baaing of our neighbor Seth Early's sheep.

Clearly relaxation wasn't in my immediate future. I should check out what they'd found.

They both seemed a little less anxious now that I was taking their report seriously.

"Lead on, Macduff," I said.

"That's 'lay on, Macduff,'" Jamie corrected. "'And damn'd be him that first cries, *Hold, enough!*'"

I should know better than to try quoting lines from *Macbeth* when their father was currently directing a production of it. A production in which they both had small roles.

"'Exeunt, fighting.'" Josh was quoting the stage directions that followed Jamie's lines. "'Alarums.'"

"I'm impressed," I said. "Now show me this body."

The boys set off, and I could barely keep up with them. Not really surprising, since they were now eye to eye with me at five foot ten. And more of their height was leg, so they set a faster pace and were in danger of leaving me behind.

But characteristically, Jamie would glance back occasionally, notice that I was falling behind, and tug at Josh's sleeve to slow him down. And Josh slowed down a lot more readily than usual—that, combined with their expressions, told me that they were putting a brave front on something that had genuinely shaken them.

So I tried my best to keep up the pace. It helped that the last stretch was a slight downhill slope, and we arrived together at the edge of a small clearing.

"Over by that fallen log," Josh whispered.

Jamie merely pointed.

I looked across the clearing and felt the hairs rise on the back of my neck. They weren't pulling some kind of strange prank. There really were two hands poking up out of the half-rotted leaves covering the ground. Only the tips of three fingers of the left hand showed, but all five fingers of the right protruded, and even a little bit of the back of the hand. The fingers were long and slender, but twisted, contorted, as if their owner had died while reaching out to grab something in panic . . . or in agony. And they were deadly pale—the nails were, at least. Almost silvery. The flesh, though, was a little darker. In fact, it had a blueish-gray tint. Decay? Or was it just a trick of the light—the day was quite cloudy, and the branches of the huge oaks and maples at the edges of the clearing met overhead, so not much light made it in.

The boys each inched a little closer, as if having me along made them bolder, and I grabbed one with each hand.

"Keep your distance," I said. "We don't know what she died of."

"She?" Josh echoed. He took a step back.

"Mom's right." Jamie retreated several steps. "Definitely not a man. The fingers are too small."

"Could be a kid," Josh suggested.

Once I was sure they'd stay put I pulled out my phone and called 911.

"What's wrong now, Meg?" Odd. Debbie Ann, the dispatcher, made it sound as if I'd called her at least once already today. Maybe she was just having a bad morning.

"Josh and Jamie found a dead body in the woods behind our house," I said. "I have no idea exactly where we are, but I'll send the boys out to the road. They can lead whoever you send back here. I'll keep watch."

The boys nodded and dashed off. I wasn't exactly thrilled at being left alone with those creepy hands, but it was better than having to leave the boys alone with them.

"Oh, dear," Debbie Ann said. "Do you know who it is?"

Along with her words I could hear the rattle of keys that meant she was sending out a text message to one of the deputies. Or maybe all of the deputies. The more the merrier.

"No idea," I said. "All I can see is a pair of hands, sticking up out of the ground. So it's not just dead but dead and buried, only not very competently."

"Horrible," she said. "Vern's five minutes away, and the chief was already on his way out to Camp Birnam, so he's going to stop by—he might even beat Vern."

"The chief's back from his family camping trip, then?" I felt a surge of relief. And then guilt. I hated the idea that on his first day back in town the chief would have to cope with a dead body—and probably a not-very-recent one at that. Although I was also glad that he'd be here to handle whatever happened.

But wait—

"Why was the chief headed out to Camp Birnam?" I asked. "I mean, if you can tell me. I'm not exactly responsible for the place, but—"

"But you've been trying to keep them in line." She sighed. "I know. Seth Early called up just now, madder than a wet hen. He thinks that the reenactor folks out there have stolen some of his sheep."

I closed my eyes and muttered a few words that I hoped

the boys hadn't picked up from me. For that matter, I made sure Debbie Ann couldn't catch them.

"I hope someone told the chief that wasn't our idea," I said. "Having a bunch of medieval reenactors camping out in the woods. We only let them set up that wretched camp to please the History Department. And if he wants them gone—"

"He's probably already heard about them." Debbie Ann's tone was soothing. "And if he hasn't already heard how hard you've been trying to keep them from causing trouble, I'll tell him myself. FYI, Horace is on his way, too."

"Good." I nodded, even though she couldn't see me. My cousin Horace Hollingsworth was both a deputy and Caerphilly's one trained crime-scene investigator.

"Do you think this body could have something to do with them?" she went on. "The reenactors, that is."

I opened my eyes and studied the hands again.

"I can't imagine it would," I said. "If it turns out that any of the reenactors are responsible, we'll evict the whole lot, but I have a hard time imagining that. And if you're worried about Seth—well, he can be a hothead, especially where his sheep are concerned, but I can't imagine him killing anyone and burying them in the woods. Not even a sheep thief."

"He'd just punch the thief in the nose and then come down to the station to turn himself in," Debbie Ann suggested, with a slight giggle.

"Yes." I thought of adding that the body was obviously not brand-new, and I'd probably have heard about it if any of the reenactors had gone missing for very long, but I wasn't sure that thought would help matters.

I heard the crashing noises of someone approaching through the woods. Possibly several someones, by the sound of it.

"I have visitors," I said.

"Keep them away from the crime scene if it's not Vern or the chief," Debbie Ann warned.

"I will."

But to my relief I spotted Josh approaching. He appeared to be repeatedly running ahead, then backtracking to rejoin another figure. The second figure, sturdy and clad in an impeccably clean khaki uniform, hiked stolidly forward, ignoring Josh's darting back and forth.

"It's the chief," I said to Debbie Ann. "I'll hang up now."

The chief already looked grim. Since the modest town of Caerphilly was not just the largest but the only town in our small, rural Virginia county, he didn't see that many dead bodies. Not nearly as many as when he'd been a homicide detective in Baltimore. But the ones he did see these days hit him harder, since they happened in "his" town. The expression on his round brown face suggested that the boys' find had already undone some of the benefits of his vacation.

"Where is this body?" he said as he drew near.

I stepped aside and pointed across the clearing.

He studied the hands in silence for a few seconds.

"Did any of you go over there?" He didn't take his eyes away from the hands.

"I didn't." I glanced at Josh.

"We didn't, either," he said. "It was pretty creepy. We went to find Mom."

"Good," the chief said. "Let's keep the scene undisturbed. Horace should be here soon. In the meantime—"

He jerked his head around, evidently noticing the same sounds I had. People crashing through the underbrush from two directions.

He sighed.

"With luck, that will be Horace and Vern," he said. "But if it's people coming to gawk—"

"We'll help you head them off. Josh, you go that way." I pointed to our right. "I'll go this way. The chief doesn't want anyone to mess up his crime scene, so don't let anyone go past you into the clearing."

Josh raced away. I circled around until I was roughly a third of the way around the periphery of the clearing. Josh did the same thing in the other direction. He took an arrow out of the quiver on his back and nocked it onto his bow. Then he glared at the woods around him, as if daring anyone to approach. I settled for crossing my arms over my chest and staring fiercely in the direction of the crashing noises nearest me.

To my relief, Jamie appeared, followed by Vern Shiffley, the chief's most senior deputy. Like all of the enormous Shiffley clan, Vern was tall and lanky, with a long, imperturbable face. He appeared to be merely ambling through the woods, but his strides covered ground, and Jamie was half running to keep up with him.

"Why don't you take over guarding this part of the perimeter?" I suggested when Vern drew near. "I'll go help the chief deal with them."

I nodded toward the other group, who were heading for where Chief Burke stood.

"Yeah," Vern said. "That crew's going to get on the chief's nerves in no time flat."

Actually, the two women, dressed in medieval peasant garb, in much the same drab earth tones Josh and Jamie were wearing, would probably behave themselves. But the tall man in the garish plaid kilt was another matter. He was the main reason I'd been out in the woods trying to calm myself with yoga breathing.

"I assume these are some of the people Debbie Ann told me about," the chief said in an undertone when I reached his side. "The ones having their costume party in your parents' woods."

"Not exactly a costume party," I said. "They've set up their idea of what an eleventh-century Scottish military camp would look like."

"Why?" he asked. "I mean, it might make sense in Scotland, but here in rural Virginia?"

"Eleventh-century Scotland is when—and where—the real-life Macbeth lived—the one on whom Shakespeare based his play."

"So this has something to do with the play Michael's directing?"

Before I could answer, the reenactors were upon us. The tall man in the gaudy black-and-yellow tartan stuck out one large and not-very-clean hand.

"Calum MacLeod," he said, in his annoyingly bad fake Scottish accent. "Chieftain of the Caerphilly sept of the Clan MacLeod, and leader of the war-band now encamped in Birnam Wood."

"Henry Burke," the chief said. "Chief of the Caerphilly Police Department and sheriff of Caerphilly County. I'd appreciate it if you'd stand over there and keep clear of my crime scene."

The chief's tone made it clear that, however politely worded, this was an order. Calum's face showed surprise and, just for a moment, a trace of rebellion. But then he did as he was told, gesturing imperiously at the two women to follow him. And it wasn't as if he'd have trouble gawking to his heart's content. The clearing was in a low spot, so that on all sides around it the ground rose like a shallow, tree-filled amphitheater.

"Chief! Chief!"

The chief and I turned to see two more figures racing down the gentle slope toward us. The chief's face brightened—no doubt because he recognized the lead figure as Dad. Since Dad was also the local medical examiner, no doubt his arrival would be timely. But the man following him—

"The guy with Dad is a documentary filmmaker and an avid blogger," I said quietly. "Also a jerk with no concept of privacy or boundaries. So unless you want pictures of your crime scene popping up all over the Web—"

"His name?"

"Damien Goodwin," I said.

The chief strode a few paces toward the approaching figures.

"Mr. Goodwin! Stay where you are!"

Goodwin slowed down but didn't completely stop. Vern, as if anticipating the chief's next order, loped in Goodwin's direction, his long, rangy stride quickly taking him to where he could intercept Goodwin if needed.

"Dr. Langslow," the chief went on. "I could use your assistance."

Dad almost skipped the rest of the way to the chief's side.

"I hear you've got a murder!" he said.

"A body," the chief corrected. "So far we have no cause to suspect homicide." His smile was a little strained. I was never sure whether Dad's obsession with murder was the cause or result of his avid consumption of crime novels, but it was a source of great annoyance to the chief, in spite of how highly he valued Dad's skill as a doctor and a medical examiner. "Over there." The chief gestured toward the clearing, and the three of us turned back toward it.

Behind us, Goodwin was arguing with Vern.

"You have no right to take away my camera!" Goodwin was shouting. "Seizure of private property! Suppression of my First Amendment rights! Freedom of the press!"

"You're not allowed to film here," the chief said over his shoulder.

"I have permission from the owner," Goodwin said. "I'm within my rights—"

"That permission is rescinded until further notice," I said. "Right, Dad?"

"Sorry—what?" Dad was taking his binoculars out of their case. Trust a birder never to venture into the woods unprepared. He probably also had a battered copy of the Peterson Guide in one pocket, to supplement the dozen or so birding apps on his iPhone.

"We don't want this Mr. Goodwin taking unauthorized pictures of our crime scene, now do we?" the chief said. The "our" was definitely a kind of flattery.

"Perish the thought." I shuddered with deliberate drama. "So you're temporarily rescinding Mr. Goodwin's permission to film in this part of the woods, right, Dad?"

"Oh, of course. Of course." He was staring at the hands through his binoculars. "Damien! Go away for now."

Goodwin subsided, grumbling.

"See that he keeps his cell phone in his pocket," I called to Vern. "He's just as dangerous with that as the camera."

I tried to ignore the renewed wrangling between Vern and Goodwin.

"Oh, my goodness," Dad said. "How amazing!"